THE SINNER

ST. CLAIR BROTHERS #1

HEATHER C LEIGH

SHELBYVILLE PUBLISHING, INC.

Print ISBN 978-0-9985209-1-9

❀ Created with Vellum

For those who struggle to overcome their demons.

ACKNOWLEDGMENTS

Cover Photo by Wander Aguilar
Model Andrew Biernat
Cover Art by Mayhem Cover Creations
Editing Robin's Red Pen
Proofreading Charlotte Lynn

1
———

Prologue

Seb

A hem. *Ahem. Acchhh-chhemmm.*
I yanked the pillow further down on top of my head, but nothing could block out the nauseating, God-awful, "this close to punching you in the balls" sound of my roommate's compulsive throat clearing.

Accchhhemmm. Cough. Cough. Acck.

I dug my fingers into the pillowcase and my knuckles actually hurt from squeezing the damn thing so hard.

Ahem. Aaacckkk. Cough.

My left eye began to twitch, the non-stop spasms nearly as maddening as Henri *"Ahem"* Allaire and his mother-fucking phlegmy throat lying in the bed next to mine. Some days, I just wanted to snatch the plunger out of the communal washroom and suction the damn thing over the kid's mouth, then pump that bastard until the permanent, sticky ball of mucus came flying out of Henri's overtaxed lungs.

Ahem. Cough. Cough.

Oh God. A wave of exhaustion slammed into me, hitting so hard my eyeballs literally ached. Speaking of which... *twitch, twitch, twitch.* That damn left eye continued its little dance, the one it did whenever the stress levels got to be too much, which was pretty much all the fucking time in this shithole. The twitching grew exponentially worse whenever Mr. Mucous fell into one of his hacking spells.

Despite not believing in spiritual woo-woo bullshit, I was so desperate for sleep, I even went so far as to attempt a ridiculous relaxation technique one of the dozen inter-changeable counselors showed me. I closed his eyes...*twitch, twitch, twitch.*

Fuck! Concentrate, Seb!

One muscle at a time, I forced my limbs to unclench and began the exercise. Breathe in through the nose, hold for two, then out through the mouth, hold for two. I continued with the stupid breathing, even though every time I inhaled, the sharp scent of antiseptic cleanser and the musty odor of institutional blankets assaulted my nostrils. In...one... two. Out... one... two.

Ack. Ahem. Accchhhemm.

I ground my teeth together, convinced I'd end up with at least two cracked molars by the time I got released. In... one... two. Out... one... two. Two more months. Just two fucking months and I'd be out. I'd already done eight, which, granted was a hell of a lot easier to endure before phlegmy over there ended up assigned to my room. The clueless asshole made an Olympic sport out of ejecting a lung every night. But still, only sixty more days, well, fifty-nine to be exact. I could do that. Then no more Henri

"*Ahem*" Allaire. No more tasteless, colorless, and unrecognizable blobs that were deemed food. No more shapeless, saggy blue scrubs and white, lace-free slippers. No more group therapy. No more of any of that shit.

Cough. Cough. Cough. Accckkk!

I cringed as my left eye spazzed and did the Riverdance. That fucker twitched so hard my cheek muscle jumped right along with it. Apparently, the rhythm was catchy.

Fuck. In... one... two. Out... one... two.

I'd never been more miserable—no, scratch that. I had. Even that miserable place was a dream compared to my life before. So, phlegmy roommate or not, in my mind, every single day spent confined in the bowels of the white-walled government institution was worth it. When I got out I'd finally be able to see my little brother, Rèmy. Then, for the first time in my life, everything would be good. Normal.

No longer would I have to stay alert, tense and watching over my shoulder at all times. I'd be able to relax at Mémère's house, where Rèmy lived with our grandmother, or so I'd been told. Rèmy wasn't allowed to visit, and that was more than fine. In fact, Mémère said she didn't tell Rèmy the truth about where I was or what happened a little over a year ago that ended up sending me away. Mémère told Rèmy that I was spending a year at a boarding school in Nova Scotia. That I had to get away due to undue stress. Keeping my little brother in the dark was fine as far as I was concerned. Since there was no chance I could erase the images in his own head, the least he could do was ensure that sweet, innocent Rèmy never suffered the same, or found out what really went down at our house that night.

Hack. Cough. Ahem.

Fucking Hell. I stared at the ceiling, eye twitching away.

Fifty-nine days. It couldn't come soon enough.

2

The next time we meet on the ice, I'm going to bash that fucker Rocco Calloway's brains out. And why shouldn't I? It's not as though it would be the first time I killed a man.

Seb

"Seb. You gotta stay calm."

I pulled the phone from my ear and stared at it as if it might come to life and take a bite out of my face, which wouldn't be all that surprising. Technology and I are not friends.

"This is calm," I hissed at my younger brother, Rémy.

Dammit.

Everything around me shone with a hazy shade of red, a clear sign I was getting precariously close to throwing a fit. Then, as if I weren't already furious, one wheeze from Rémy and I nearly lost my mind.

"That's it. I don't care what you say, the only way that prick is going to live through the next game I play against him is if you insist that I drop what I'm doing to be with you at the hospital. Management will probably say no, but I can try and persuade them to let me fly to Charlotte, then meet up with the team later in DC. It'd be a tough sell, though."

Gritting my teeth, I snatched a paperweight off an end table and tested its weight in my palm.

A muffled moan floated through the receiver and my left eye did its thing. *Twitch, twitch, twitch...* Near to bursting with barely contained rage, I cracked my neck and paced in front of the windows in the main living area of my Atlanta condo, a slick modern unit on one of the upper floors of the W Hotel. Outside, the roof of the new Mercedes Benz Stadium caught my eye, its odd octagonal shape, all shiny metal and glass, sticking out from the skyline like a billion-dollar sore thumb.

My stupid eye continued to twitch, so I closed my eyes and focused on taking deep breaths. Oh, and not putting the paperweight through the window. Yeah, I put the heavy projectile back down before I actually did it.

"Seb..." Rémy paused for so long I nearly bit my tongue in half in anticipation. Patience isn't one of my virtues. In fact, I don't have any virtues to speak of, and if it weren't so tragically true, I'd laugh. Unless beating the shit out of opponents on the ice counts for something. That's a pretty handy talent considering my line of work, but hardly virtuous.

When my little bro continued, his words were punctuated by ragged, noisy breathing, a result of the cracked ribs, courtesy of Rocco Soon-To-Be-Deceased Calloway.

"I don't... need you to come here... I need you to play... your game and... stay away from... Rocco Calloway."

My grip on the phone tightened and I turned my back on the windows. Honest to god, I feared I might actually go ahead and punch the glass. "I can't do that, Rém, and you know it. He broke your fucking rib!"

"During a game, Seb." Rémy sighed, or tried to anyway. The cracked rib made his breath hitch and the pained grunt that followed made me seethe. "Please, I know you're upset, just... just don't get... kicked out of the league... okay?"

"I won't get kicked out of the league," I snapped. Over the course of the conversation my temper had steadily risen until it hovered somewhere around nuclear meltdown. "But don't expect that bastard to walk away in one piece." I flexed the fingers of my free hand, itching for something to hit. "And I'm not upset, I'm fucking furious. What Calloway did was nothing more than a cheap, illegal hit and you know it."

"And he got fined... for it."

In my head, I plotted the many different ways to incapacitate a man during a professional hockey game. I'm a right wing, and since Rocco Calloway is a defenseman, whenever our teams played the two of us got up close and personal. Made it pretty easy to find an opportunity to, oh I don't know, maim the guy, or at least inflict some serious damage. Considering the previous scuffles we'd gotten into and our antagonistic history, I wouldn't even have to make up an excuse to stuff the business end of my stick up his nose.

We exchanged a few more words, me placating Rémy as usual, not wanting him to worry. Lying sucked, but I went ahead and promised not to do anything that would get me in trouble. It was for Rémy's own good. Promise or not, I had every intention of doing whatever the hell I wanted the next time I set eyes on Rocco Calloway. Also as usual, before I hung up I told Rémy I'd call and check on him in the morning.

The second the line disconnected, I threw myself face

first onto the couch and screamed into the cushion while punching the side of it over and over in an attempt to soothe the boiling fury. After ten minutes, give or take, most of it subsided, but the remaining agitation made my skin crawl and the muscles in my neck were strung tight enough to give me a headache.

My brother, who I vowed to protect, was hurt. Sitting in the hospital with a broken rib. Because of Rocco Calloway.

On instinct, my hand moved to my side as memories of my own broken ribs sent a sharp pain straight into my heart.

Twitch, twitch, twitch.

Ugh! Wonderfuckingful.

To top it all off, my shit-tastic left eye wouldn't stop, which caused the anger to flood back into my body. It slammed into my chest with the force of a SWAT team with a battering ram. Knowing even as I did it, that I would regret my decision, I skimmed through my contacts and pushed Send. It took four agonizing rings before someone answered.

"Can I help you with something?"

Normally, the seductive, raspy voice had me raring to go. Normally, the sound of it made my cock hard and put a wicked smile on my face. Normally, I responded with a few filthy words, describing exactly what I was going to do to Amanda the second I got within reach of her hot little ass.

That night was different. I was a volcano about to erupt, and if I didn't release the growing pressure of the churning, steaming mountain of red-hot lava that pressed against my insides, *and soon*, I'd lose my goddamn mind. Then I'd do something even dumber that hooking up with Amanda.

Again.

After I swore I wouldn't do it.

Again.

The words were out of my mouth before I could stop them.

"I'm coming over. Be ready. I'm not going to be gentle."

No further explanation needed, I hit End, grabbed my keys and wallet, and left the condo, visions of a bloody and broken Rocco Calloway providing an array of entertainment the entire length of the drive.

Kylie

"Who the hell was that just now?"

It was a testament to my ability to stay calm that I held back my instinctive reaction to shriek. Instead, without betraying the fact that Rocco just scared me half to death, I closed the front door behind placed my keyring on the hook. With full knowledge it would drive my brother bat-shit crazy, I toed off my shoes one at a time and slowly let my messenger bag slide off my shoulder to the floor. Only then did I turn to face the immense, fuming man standing in front of me with a thunderous expression and his hands on his hips.

In preparation, I sucked in a breath and did a mental eye roll before I spoke, then made sure to pour every bit of my annoyance into mimicking Rocco's voice.

"Oh, hi little sister. How was your day?"

Rocco snarled, not finding my exaggerated peppy tone amusing in the least. I ignored his attitude, and continued the conversation between fake Rocco and me.

"I had a great day, Rocco. Thanks for asking," I said as myself.

"Oh really? It was that good, huh? Did you get an A on your Mass Media Law exam? I know you studied hard."

"Why yes I did, big brother." I fluttered my lashes and

got a grunt in response. "How sweet of you to be so concerned."

"Wow, Kylie. Great going. I'm so proud of you."

Rocco looked so furious, I honestly thought plumes of smoke might billow from his ears. Immune to my improv skills, Rocco didn't crack a smile. Nope. He crossed his arms over his massive chest and, though I didn't think it possible, those dark, heavy brows of his scrunched up and got, uh, scrunchier, and his grimace became more... grimacey.

"It's not funny, and I'm not joking," he growled, his volume rising with each syllable. "I asked you a question. Who dropped you off?" Rocco threw his arms up in the air. "And on a motorcycle of all things! They're death traps, Kylie. Are you out of your damn mind?"

As Rocco worked himself into a lather, I slid past him into the kitchen. It had been a long day, I *did* get an A on my exam, and I was ravenous.

"Hungry?" I asked, leaning halfway into the fridge so I wouldn't have to see Rocco as he had an apoplectic fit.

I gathered the ingredients to make our mom's chicken marsala. I might have chosen it because it's Rocco's favorite and I knew it would go a long way toward smoothing out his ruffled feathers. It's not that Rocco intimidates me, per se. He doesn't. He does, however, look incredibly scary when he's pissed, but I know without a doubt he would never, ever physically hurt me.

Not to say he *can't* hurt me. Rocco's gift is his ability to inflict excruciating mental anguish. He had it down to a science and guilt trips were his specialty. To the point that when he got started, I pretty much immediately cowed to every last one of his ridiculous demands. It sucks, but it's not entirely Rocco's fault. He can't help himself, being annoyingly bossy all the time. Around a decade ago, our parents died in a car accident. Rocco, only nineteen at the time, stepped up to the plate and became my guardian.

The harping and dictating was all well and good when I was thirteen, but as a twenty-one year-old college student, his overbearing, controlling, and borderline rude helicopter act drove me right off the short end of a pier.

"What if that asshole crashed his bike? Huh? What then? What if I lost you?" Rocco's voice wavered and my resolve cracked right along with it. I closed my eyes as the wave of remorse seeped into every nook and cranny of my soul. With my back to him so I wouldn't have to see the wounded look on his face, I placed the bottle of wine on the countertop.

"No, Rocco. Don't think that way. I'm fine, I swea—*Hey!*"

Two large hands grabbed me by the shoulders and Rocco spun me around. It was so unexpected, if he weren't holding me up I would have wiped out on the kitchen floor. Irritation crawled across my skin and I tried to jerk away but couldn't get out of his gentle, but firm, grip.

It pissed me off. I opened my mouth to shout a few choice words about being manhandled, only I made the mistake of looking up at Rocco glistening, puppy-dog eyes. Any argument I had flew right out the window.

My dear old friend guilt plowed into me with as much force as my six foot six, two hundred-fifty pound brother would hit an opposing player. My nerves sang and my palms grew clammy as the flight or fight response took hold. A burst of adrenaline urged me to run. Not because Rocco would hurt me, but because I always, *always* gave in, and if I didn't have to look at him, I could maybe hold my ground this one time. When I take in his sad, disappointed face, I can't find the strength to tell him off. Dealing with a panicked, overwrought Rocco, exhausted me, and it felt worse and worse every time I let him down.

Despite the cortisol telling my feet to move, I stayed where I was. Not only because Rocco held me in place, but because if I ran, my stubborn brother would follow and continue to argue. Rocco's intense stare penetrated right through my pathetically weak outer shell, right through any attempt at standing up to him. As predictable as the sunrise, I looked away first, unable to withstand the torture of seeing those sad eyes for another single second.

"Ky..."

"W-what do you want me to s-say?" I sniffed back a sob.

In complete contradiction to the anger and guilt he expertly wielded a moment ago, Rocco spoke calmly. He put a gentle finger under my chin and lifted until once again, I found myself staring into his fearful expression. The one that made me want to throw up. The room went blurry behind a sheen of tears and my lungs felt tight.

Why couldn't I ever stand up to him?

"Promise me you won't ever do that again?"

I blinked to clear away the tears. Mistake. When Rocco came into focus, his devastation and distress were as plain as day. My stomach cramped at the sight. I'd take anger any day of the week. Rocco wasn't angry. No, my selfless, generous, well-meaning brother was *hurt*. Because of my thoughtless actions. My possibly, maybe, a little bit deliberate thoughtless actions. It's not that I specifically set out to be reckless, it always just kind of happened.

Except, deep down, hidden in a place no one will ever find, I know I *wanted* Rocco to catch me doing something stupid, if only because subconsciously, I needed to scrape up what little bit of control over my life that I could. And with Rocco around, the only thing I could control was acting *out* of control.

"I won't." The lie rang hollow in my ears. I ducked my head, knowing if I continued to look at my brother and that pitiful, dejected expression, I'd fall to pieces.

"Thank you."

In the span of the next breath, I found myself wrapped in my brother's arms, cheek pressed against his broad chest.

Protected.

Loved.

Smothered.

Caged.

"I love you, Ky."

Throat burning, I wound my arms around Rocco's waist. There would be plenty of time to shatter later. At that moment, all that mattered was making my brother happy and wiping away that heartbroken look.

What did my own happiness matter? It'd been so long since I'd had anything that resembled a life of my own, I didn't even know who I was anymore.

Seb

A blue and yellow streak flashed in my peripheral vision as I flew down the ice, the colors tempered by a familiar, hazy red veil. *Rocco Calloway.* The near murderous fury that built up in the week since Rémy's injury sat like a hard, heavy ball of lead in my gut.

I quickly calculated speed and distance. The big bastard would reach the puck first. Didn't bother me. New plan devised, I grinned around my mouthguard.

Perfect.

Calloway made the mistake of his life the night he illegally board checked my bother. Just like me, Rém plays right wing, only I play for the Atlanta Comets and he plays for the Charlotte Rush. Our identical position on the ice meant we both faced Calloway when either of us played against the DC Kings. Armed with righteous fury and a thirst for revenge, I wouldn't go down as easily as my brother.

I shook it off to concentrate on the present and not the video footage I tortured myself with, watching it over and over—Calloway slamming into Rémy so hard it cracked one of his ribs. To add insult to injury, the prick only got two fucking minutes for that bullshit move, though later the NHL fined him for targeting. Still, not nearly enough in my opinion. That left it up to me to even it up.

We were on my home turf in Atlanta, and as the old saying goes, "payback is a bitch." Calloway was about to get his comeuppance, St. Clair style.

"Sebby, what are you doing?"

I ignored my teammates as I flew past the bench. It's not in me to give a single voluntary shit that technically speaking, I'm not an enforcer. Never stopped me from inflicting a little damage here and there. Head-butting, slashing, throwing a few elbows... I can't help it. I need it like I need air. The violence. The high I get when I lash out and hurt someone. It makes me a head case and I know it, but if I don't have a way to release the snarling knot of pent-up fury that made itself at home inside me, I'd lose my goddamn mind.

The anger would build, its intensity ratcheting higher and higher, growing like a physical presence and burning my insides to ash, until I had to let it out. If I didn't, it would burst free and take matters into its own hands. And that, I couldn't have. Of course I made exceptions and set the fury free on purpose, such as when an overzealous asshat broke my brother's rib.

And when I it loose, all bets were off.

It didn't matter that Rocco Calloway stood roughly the size and shape of Bigfoot. I certainly didn't give a shit that the gargantuan defenseman is not only bigger than me, but that Calloway actually *is* an enforcer, and arguably the most vicious one in the NHL. Fury isn't rational. The second my brother's rib snapped, my course was mapped out, the future unavoidable.

And there we were. The future became the present.

When I got like that, my rage at mushroom cloud proportions, only two things could calm me down, fucking or fighting. Since I was already at the arena, geared up and on the ice, fucking was off the list. That left fighting.

My lizard brain had already downshifted into fight mode. That illegal body-checking piece of shit more than deserved whatever I dished out. Hell, Calloway probably expected a fight. It wouldn't be the first time we dropped gloves, but it was the first time—for me anyway—that my motives went way beyond the game of hockey.

I was enraged.

Sasquatch should have thought twice before injuring my brother in such a bullshit and cowardly manner. Body-checking Rémy at full speed *after* the whistle was hands down, without a doubt, the number one way to land at the top of my shit list. The crack of Rémy's rib flicked a switch that turned me from my usual semi-rational self, to a slave to my emotions, namely, anger.

I pushed off my back blade and skated toward Calloway, no delusions that what I was about to do would catapult the Calloway/St. Clair rivalry over the walls of Hockeyland to land smack dab in the center of Personalville.

Bring. It. On. Sasquatch was about to get schooled.

I watched Calloway reach out with his stick to pull in the puck as it slid along the boards near the crease. Like a raging bull set loose on the streets of Pamplona, I gathered speed and, without slowing, charged directly into my target, hip-checking the ever-living shit out of Rocco Calloway. A deafening crash followed when the impact sent us both into the boards. I hit Calloway so hard my teeth rattled along with the divider. The reverberations rippled outward and shook the high boards halfway to the center line.

The force with which we slammed into the wall, Calloway sandwiched between me and the boards, should have knocked the air out of my lungs, but because according to most people I'm a bit insane, I grinned. Calloway might be strong, but his size made him slow— okay, not slow per se, but slow*er* than me—and because of that, Sasquatch struggled to stay on his feet while he fought to keep the puck on his tape. Idiot didn't realize I wasn't after the puck... yet. He would figure it out soon enough.

I checked him again, this time throwing an elbow into Calloway's throat while I spewed a bunch of crap, in English and French, each taunt specifically chosen to rile the guy up.

"*Ta copine a sucé ma bite.* Fucking pussy. Can't take a little hip action? Such a shame. Your girlfriend loved my hip action last night when she was swallowing my cock." I smirked around my red mouthguard. "Then she screamed my name until she passed out."

To my great amusement, like the silly cartoons Rémy and me watched as kids, you know, the ones where a light bulb flicks on over the character's head when he catches on to something? Calloway grimaced and the gears clicked into place. I could practically see the glowing bulb hovering over his helmet.

Finally with the program, Sasquatch?

It seemed Calloway's pea brain caught up. He knew my vicious attack had zero to do with the small black rubber disc trapped between our skates. I saw the exact moment Calloway put two and two together. Behind his visor, a spark of anger lit up his near-black eyes. Unfortunately for my plan, his reaction was a big fat disappointment. The guy did nothing. No payback, no cursing, no hitting. I was itching for a fight, lay one right at his big fat feet, and he wasn't interested? I scowled. Calloway, the bastard, ignored me and turned his attention back to the game.

I lost track of the puck, too busy pouting over my failed attempt to instigate a fight. Sasquatch had no such issues and took full advantage. He threw his stupidly enormous elbows up and expertly jostled me right out of his space. Calloway had to know I was out for blood because of what he did to Rémy, so *of course* the jerk refused to be manipulated into a brawl.

At least, not easily.

I had my ways.

The swell of rage that began the sequence of events that led up to that very moment wouldn't dissipate on its own. Wouldn't be satisfied until I heard the sweet, sweet sound of one of Calloway's ribs cracking, preferably in half so he'd get benched for the next four to six weeks, just like Rémy. Maybe poke a lung.

Quick as a viper, I struck and jammed my stick between Calloway's legs, only instead of snagging the puck, I yanked back... hard, illegally hooking Calloway's skate and sending Sasquatch and his ugly mug crashing face first onto the ice. As a single unit, the Atlanta crowd leapt to their feet and let out a loud roar. Shouts and cheers echoed throughout the arena, fans chanted my name along with a beautiful chorus of, "Fight, fight, fight…"

Then… chaos.

The leaden ball of rage was set free, and the accompanying release was so satisfying it felt almost orgasmic.

Fuck, I love this game.

The burst of adrenaline. The unleashing of the fury and frustration I kept in check since Rémy's injury. The joy and freedom as I snatched back control of my emotions. The glorious rush of power achieved through savagery and pain. Somewhere amongst the cacophony, I heard the ref's piercing whistle, but what the fuck ever.

My focus was singular. Break Calloway's ribs.

Colors merged as players from both teams surrounded us, the red and black of my team blurring with the blue and yellow of DC. Sasquatch pushed to his skates and—fuck, that bastard is tall—glared down at me. His jaw muscles ticked, his massive chest heaved, and those black, fathomless eyes shone with raw hatred.

I never felt more alive.

I had Calloway on the hook. Now to reel him in. I mouthed my next words so only Calloway saw them. *"Bring it on asshole."*

I don't know why, but that simple sentence worked like a charm. The everyday obscenity somehow crossed whatever line of restraint Calloway had and the guy was ready to blow. The guy was fired up, about to hurtle head first into my waiting hands. He snarled like an animal and chucked his gloves and stick to the ice. I did the same.

Showtime.

Calloway surged forward, but I anticipated his move. In a single smooth motion, I ducked sideways, snagged his blue and yellow sweater in one hand, and yanked the guy's shocked face into the waiting fist of my other. The blow broke the thin skin of Calloway's brow, splitting it open. Blood burst from the gash and trickled into his eyes. Unleashing a ferocious growl of my own, I planted both palms on Calloway's chest and shoved him, satisfied the punch rang his bell hard enough to stun the guy for a few seconds, which would give me the opportunity to pummel his ribcage.

I grinned.

Redemption is mine!

Oh crap.

Maybe not.

Calloway was made of stronger shit than I remembered. The brute was hardly phased by my knuckle-sandwich, which threw a wrench into my plans. Calloway caught me off guard and knew it. A left hook flew out of nowhere and smashed directly into the exposed area near my temple, right above my cheekbone and just below the lip of my helmet. I dropped like a stone, out cold before my back hit the ice.

Fucker.

STUNNED, my eyes fluttered open. *Merde*, my head hurt. I held my breath as the world swam back into focus. For a brief moment, I expected to see the stained acoustical tile ceiling of the institution. Instead, I took in the familiar sight of the steel crossbeams and rows of lights that hung from the roof of the Atlanta Peach Dome.

As I slowly returned to the land of the living, skull buzzing from the blow, I heard the scrape of skates. The sound got closer and closer, unfortunately, my brain was too rattled to react. Though I knew what was coming, I couldn't scrounge up the energy to shield myself as some jerkoff snowed me. Tiny chunks of frozen water shot into my ears, eyes, mouth, and down the neckline of my sweater.

"Hey, Sleeping Beauty. Ready to rise and shine?"

Hajek. *Maudit bâtard.*

With a wince, I struggled into a sitting position and unsnapped the strap of my helmet. I probed my throbbing cheek and eye socket. It hurt, but the bones felt like they were intact. I wiped the ice from my face and glared at my teammate.

"Fuck you and your little snowstorm, Hazey."

Bruno Hajek, our goalie, can never resist adding insult to injury. First, the jerk snows a teammate when he's down. Then has the nerve to poke my neck with the working end of his huge-ass goalie stick. Not that Hazey's actions are in any way surprising. Pretty much every goalie I ever met proved to be more than a few twists short of a slinky. Not that I'm in any position to judge. In no universe can I claim sanity. Hell, I wouldn't even try.

"Get up, lazy. You have date with penalty box now," Hazey said in his heavy Eastern European accent. A chunk of ice slid down my back and melted into my waistband. I winced.

"Shit. Hazey, you asshole. *Vas te faire.*" I almost always cursed in my native Québécois, but I tried to mix in some English so my teammates would know when I insulted them.

I sat on the ice and took in my surroundings. My gaze landed on a bulging-eyed, red-faced ref. He stood at my feet with his arms crossed and gave me a harsh, disapproving look. Whatever. It's not as though I haven't received hundreds of those exact same looks from my father over the years.

Next to the furious ref, who appeared about one heartbeat away from having a massive coronary, Rocco Calloway leaned on his stick. Going by his expression, I'd say he was fuming mad. The dark bruise and open cut on Calloway's brow along with the grisly remnants of a half-assed attempt to wipe away the blood, only added to the menacing look.

After the guy efficiently, and humiliatingly, took me down, I expected Calloway to act all smug.

Course not. The big bastard never gave me the courtesy of doing what I expected him to do. Unpredictable motherfucker. Sasquatch zoomed right past Smug Station, pulled into Enraged Enclave, unpacked his shit, and put his feet up on the coffee table.

Me and Calloway have exactly one thing in common; neither of us are known for our sweet personalities. So it shouldn't have been a surprise that Calloway took my attack personally. It *was* personal. It wasn't the first time we tangled on the ice and it wouldn't be the last, though it was the first time I attacked him on behalf of Rémy. We went head to head every time our teams played, and if nothing else, I'm a master at mouthing off. I had a way of expertly poking and prodding until I worked out a player's weak spot, then I scraped and picked the wound raw until my opponent snapped.

Being a bastard is my specialty, after all. That's how I earned the nickname, The Sinner.

Dizzy from having my brain bounced around my skull like a rubber band ball, it took a minute to climb to my feet. One of my *considerate* teammates—I'm looking at you, Hazey—already gathered my gloves and stick and handed them off. I accepted the gear and skated toward the box to serve my five minutes, which would have been totally worth it if I actually managed to snap one of Calloway's ribs, which I didn't. Instead, I was the one seeing stars while Sasquatch, though a bit bruised and bloodied, remained upright and in the game.

At least the crowd didn't disappoint. They love me and my tendency toward fisticuffs, and cheered as I wobbled across the ice. Like any good hockey player, I ignored the pain and grinned.

Totally worth it.

Waving my stick high, the spectators roared with delight. I had to hand it to them, hockey fans creamed their pants over a good fight, especially in Atlanta. It was why the violent moments in a hockey game were the perfect way to release my anger. Either that or a good, hard fuck.

And if the fans wanted action, who was I to deny them?

"St. Clair! Get your goddamn ass over here." I turned to see Coach V's upper body dangling over the boards opposite the penalty box. A deep frown added extra creases to the man's loose jowls.

I sighed and took a detour from the sin bin across the ice to stop next to the bench. Flustered and with his tie flipped upside down and thinning hair standing on end, Coach Frank Vernon gestured me to come closer. The furious expression on the man's face would have been comical if it weren't directed at me. The shame at being on the receiving end felt worse than usual, especially after such an epic fail at revenge. Coach's cheeks and neck were flushed a shade of red so dark I'd feel confident calling it purple.

Coach clenched his jaw so hard I watched, fascinated, as the tendons in his throat twitched. Unlike the angry ref, who in retrospect I realize was merely pissed, Coach was *literally* one blown gasket away from a massive heart attack.

"Yeah, Coach?"

Coach growled, his struggle to hold back from berating me up one side and down the other obvious, though I had no doubt that would come in due time.

"Get your fucking ass in the locker room, you idiot."

"But I'm fine, Coach. I swear."

"St. Clair," Coach inhaled through his teeth. "Don't. Fucking. Test. Me." He stabbed a thick finger into my chest pads. "That little stunt you pulled ended with you taking a helluva hard wallop up to your even harder head and now you're skating like a goddamn drunk. You're done." Coach shoved his fat thumb over a shoulder toward the tunnel. "Go see the doc for concussion protocol. *Now*."

Pulled from the game? My eye was no happier than me.

Twitch, twitch, twitch...

Defeated, I sagged as my left eye spazzed out. Experience taught me there was no point arguing. Not when Coach used his patented "don't mess with me" voice, a voice aimed at me more often than most of my teammates. Simmering, I stomped off the ice and down the tunnel to the changing room, which would have made a much more menacing picture without the skates and pads that made me waddle like a penguin with a stick up its ass. By the time I stripped off my gear and took an efficient three-minute shower, the doc was ready and waiting by my cubby.

Just great.

My stomach cramped around the lead brick that still sat heavy inside it. A lecture from the team physician followed by an ass reaming from Coach, then a dump truck full of ball busting from my jackhole teammates. And to top it off, Calloway still hasn't paid for injuring Rémy.

The lecturing didn't matter. I couldn't care less about that. The fact that I didn't get my pound of flesh? Yeah, the lack of satisfaction left a bad taste in my mouth. Don't get me wrong, it felt awesome to land a punch on Calloway's face, but it didn't change the fact that I was pissed, which meant I still needed to find an outlet to unleash on. Despite everything that went wrong tonight, even if I could go back I wouldn't change a single thing.

Except maybe hitting hard enough that Calloway ended up being the one to leave the game, while I stayed on the ice to gloat.

Fucking Calloway. What an asshat.

3

Seb

Perched as close to the edge of the bed as possible without falling on the floor, I yanked my shirt over my head and bent to shove my feet into my boots. The rustle of sheets behind me made me tense and I dropped my head into my hands, and propped my elbows on my knees. I knew what came next and for the millionth time wondered why I kept doing this to myself. There were a dozen other women, ready and willing, waiting for my call, yet I ended up at Amanda's. *Again.* I'd made progress. I came around way less often than I used to, but still. Each time I did it I swore it would be the last. Until that damn familiar swell of fury blinded me and the knot of rage tightened in my chest. Then I would blink and discover my car in Amanda's driveway.

Every damn time.

Wasn't there a saying about insanity? Something about doing the same thing over and over or something like that? Except, when my mood plummeted into darkness, when I needed a release as desperately as I did after last week's debacle with Calloway, there was nothing sane about me. When I ended up in a place so black I couldn't see a thing, Amanda was the only one I knew who could withstand—and enjoy—whatever I dished out.

A hand slid under my T-shirt and up my sweaty back. It took an extreme amount of self-restraint to stay still when I wanted to flinch, or worse, spin around, grab her hand, and squeeze. That wouldn't be good as I could quite easily break Amanda's tiny bones. I'm the first one to admit I'm a bastard, and an even bigger one in bed, but I refuse to be a monster. The last thing I'd ever let happen was for the anger overtake me to the point I'd beat up on a woman. I would die before I sank to my father's level. Besides, the incredible pounding I gave Amanda's tight pussy less than five minutes ago satisfied my darker urges.

Until the rage came back. Which it always did.

"Leaving already, baby?"

Baby?

A second hand joined the first and this time, I couldn't help it. My muscles tensed and I jerked away, my back ramrod straight. The hands on my skin stilled, then slender fingers moved higher to grip my shoulders with a little more pressure than necessary.

"Jesus Christ, Seb. Again with this?"

I blew out a long breath and pushed to my feet. In hopes of putting off the inevitable, I cracked my neck and studiously ignored the rude scoffing sound Amanda made by digging my blunt fingernails into my palms.

Twitch, twitch, twitch.

She was skating awful damn close to the no-go zone. The knee-jerk, raw fury I had barely been able to contain over the last few days while on the road with the team might have been gone, temporarily subdued by a couple of hours of highly athletic and savage fucking, but that didn't mean it wouldn't, or couldn't, immediately return.

It ticked me right the fuck off that Amanda was ruining my buzz. And being pissed, in turn, brought on a fresh round of eye spasms. Twitching away, I spun to face the stunning brunette who sat amongst a twisted pile of white sheets. Her green eyes narrowed and chaffed red lips pulled into a deep frown. I dropped my gaze to Amanda's wrists. She subtly massaged one of the raw circles of flesh. Lower, I noted finger-shaped bruises on the pale flesh of her hips.

Visual evidence of just how fucked in the head I am. The sight did nothing to help my current state of mind.

"Don't start with me, Mandy." Frustrated, and furious that I was frustrated instead of relaxed like I was a minute ago, I ran a hand through my messy dark hair, then zipped my fly. "You know how this works. I'm not yours. You're not mine. Were not exclusive in any way." I gestured back and forth between us as I searched for the rest of my things.

"Yeah, I know."

Her morose tone caught my attention and I froze.

When did Mandy get so fucking whiny and clingy?

When you stopped acting like a human being and started treating her like a hole to stick your dick in, idiot.

I really was a bastard, and though I wouldn't excuse my shitty behavior, Mandy knew the deal. We'd been non-exclusive fuck buddies going on two years, and agreed from the get-go that it would never be anything more.

Always on the lookout for new...*outlets* for my fits of anger, when Amanda Brooker came to work for the Comets as a corporate sales manager, all polished and professional and sexy as hell, she caught my eye. The second I spotted her I recognized the darkness we had in common, hidden by her smoking hot exterior and a brilliant mind. Instinctively, I knew I found a partner. One with similar demons. Someone damaged. Ruined. Fucked up in the head, like me. I asked her if she wanted to get a drink and the rest was history.

Until recently.

The changes began subtly. Amanda began to mention she had to get up super early and I might as well stay the night so we could squeeze in one more fuck in the morning. Me arriving for a quick screw only to find dinner laid out on the dining room table. Her acting like she wanted yet another round even when I, a professional athlete in peak physical condition, was so tapped out I could barely walk. *"Please? Just lay down with me a little while and we can go again,"* she'd say.

Merde. It was bullshit.

Everything she said was bullshit to manipulate me.

More recently, she'd dropped all pretenses and would flat out get angry when, like every single other time without fail, I got dressed before the jizz cooled. Nothing changed for me, but clearly something had changed for Amanda.

I started to speak, then hesitated. What if it really was me who changed, and not Amanda?

When we first started screwing, I responded to Amanda's infrequent, but flirty texts. I chatted her up when I walked through the front door instead of immediately silencing her by crushing my mouth on top of hers in order to get straight to the sex. I remember I used to talk to her like she was a person, not an inanimate object or fuck toy. I'd also noticed—while pretending I hadn't—that over the last few months, I wasn't getting the same amount of satisfaction from fucking Amanda.

Not like I used to.

Maybe all of those reasons were why, over time, I'd withdrawn. Pushed her away and started to call some of the other women I had lined up, just so I wouldn't have to deal with her shit. Apparently the writing had been on the wall for a while, and as humiliating as it sounded, I was too chickenshit to cut Amanda loose. Plus, if I did, I'd still see her from time to time at the arena. We'd never have a clean break and I knew it.

So I wouldn't have to deal with the stress of an ex at work, I maintained just enough contact to keep Amanda invested, yet whittled our relationship down to the most basic of activities. No frills. No extras. Insert cock in hole, bust a nut, get dressed, leave. And obviously she had had enough.

I didn't blame her.

"I'm sorry." I stared at my feet. Apologizing for doing nothing wrong made me angry. We had an arrangement. I kept my head down because if I had to look at Amanda's face while apologizing, when she was the one who broke her end of the deal, it would set me off. What infuriated me the most was that I just finished fucking the mountain of issues out of my system, and here she was riling me all up again. It was imperative I remained calm.

"Fuck off, Seb. Just go."

"Mandy —"

"Go!"

Her voice cracked and, though I knew it made me the king of all pricks, I found my jacket, snatched my phone and keys off the nightstand, and left, not once meeting Amanda's eyes or sparing a glance back. I tried to persuade myself not to worry. She was just an outlet, a piece of pussy.

Yeah, I failed spectacularly.

Seated in my truck I began the five mile, traffic riddled, road rage inducing drive across Atlanta to the W.

Fury, fighting, and fucking.

Those were the only three things I took pleasure in, and after dealing with Amanda, I had to admit even those were beginning to lose their shine. Naïve as I had been at the time, I honestly believed the day my father was gone, permanently, would be the day my life became normal. I barked out a humorless laugh. Right. The bastard might be gone but the scars he inflicted remained, and they went bone-fucking deep.

There would never be more to life for me than a hollow empty feeling. One that swung the pendulum between rage and nothing. I was damaged goods.

Damaged. Fucking. Goods.

And always would be.

At least I had something to look forward to. After failing to administer Calloway's well deserved beat down, and breaking things off with Amanda, in less than twenty-four hours, I'd once again come face-to-face with Rocco "Sasquatch" Calloway. A glittering diamond on the pile of dogshit of my life. Tomorrow night I got another chance to break Calloway's ribs.

Despite the inherent glee from the image of busting up Sasquatch, the stress from the sequence of events caused the black cloud to return. The gaping emptiness I screwed out of my system filled back up as the twisted darkness took root and grew.

Twitch, twitch, twitch.

I swatted at my stupid eye while dodging an idiot in an overloaded pickup truck, thoughts of the Beverly Hillbillies popping into my head. Naturally, the constant eye spasms brought back a barrage of negative memories and my mood plummeted further. By the time I pulled into the W Hotel's parking garage, the atmosphere in the cab of my truck was so fucking cold I wouldn't have been surprised to find icicles on the ceiling. The ache in my chest flared and I scratched at it as if I could make it stop. I fucked away my issues with Amanda and already felt like I was going to explode. The cycle was exhausting.

While waiting for the elevator, I thought about my pathetic excuse for a life and realized, if I didn't have Rémy, hockey, and my teammates, I wouldn't have anything.

"YOU REALLY ARE A BASTARD, you know that?"

I slouched further down in my seat on the private jet the Comets used to fly us around the country and kicked Evvy in the shin. I should have kept my damn mouth shut about breaking it off with Amanda, but I guess I needed to tell someone. Being an island only got me so far and Ev was the only one who knew enough about my demons to understand.

"You're supposed to be on my side, Evvy."

Calvin Everette got called up the same year as me. As rookies, they paired us up to room together on road trips. I despised Ev on sight and didn't hesitate to tell him exactly what I thought. Evvy responded by popping me in the mouth, giving me a fat lip. I reciprocated. After wiping off the blood, we exchanged begrudging respect for one another and have been best friends ever since. Maybe it wasn't the normal start of a friendship, but it had lasted seven years and counting. With the exception of my brother, Ev was my longest relationship.

That was pretty fucking sad, and it said a lot about me.

Evvy chuckled and thumped me in the bicep. "If you want someone to suck up to your inflated ego and agree with everything you say, you're barking up the wrong tree." He lowered his voice and shifted closer. "You know you're going to run into Amanda every now and then, dude. I'm just sayin', you could have been nicer going about dumping her."

"I didn't dump her," I hissed. "We were fuck buddies, that's it."

Ev snorted. "Yeah. If you consider the shit you're into to be fucking."

"What's that supposed to mean?" I leaned toward him, offended by his choice of words. Evvy was the only person in the world who knew about me. *Everything* about me. Rémy knew a lot, but there were certain things I never wanted my brother to find out. With Ev, I didn't have to edit things out. He knew my past, my childhood, and my screwed up way of dealing with things. While I knew Evvy didn't judge what I did in bed as long as it was with a consenting adult, it stung to hear what he really thought.

Evvy shrugged. "Don't get all bent out of shape. You know I don't care if you have massive orgies and use your dick to swing from the chandelier, as long as you show up and play hockey. Just..." The drawn out pause made my hackles rise.

"Just *what*?"

"I dunno, man. You gotta wonder about a chick who likes that shit."

My jaw dropped. "Who are you and what have you done with my friend?"

Seriously. Ev isn't a deep thoughts kind of guy. That's why I like him. He's fun, easy to be around, and rolls with the punches. The fact that he put any thought whatsoever into the mindset of my sexual partners was disturbing to say the least. Evvy turned and stared at me, his hazel eyes so somber, my stomach dropped.

"Dude, you can't tell me you've never been curious why the women you screw her into... You know." He made a rolling motion with his hand.

"Into what, Evvy? If you're trying to make a point, have the balls to say it out loud."

Evvy's gaze darted around then he tilted his head closer to me. "Shhh. Lower your voice, Sebby."

I grimaced, but knew he was right. I definitely didn't want any of our teammates eavesdropping on our conversation. A conversation I couldn't believe I was having.

"Women who are into being tied down and hurt during sex, that's what you mean, right?"

Evvy's cheeks reddened. "Well, yeah. What's going on up here for them to want that?" He tapped the side of his head.

I sat back and sighed. "No. To be honest, I've never given any thought. It's difficult enough to find someone who's not only willing and able, but knows how to keep her mouth shut afterward. So no, I don't care why they like it, just that they let me do it." I left unspoken the part where I figured my partners were probably just as screwed up as me. Which said *a lot*.

Evvy laughed. "Back to what I said before. You're a real bastard."

That comment earned him another sharp kick to the shin.

"They don't call me The Sinner for nothing, Evvy."

My tone was joking, but I knew damn well there was nothing funny about any of it. The darkness that lived inside me, the crushing guilt, the cold, detached manner in which I treated Amanda and any other woman who temporarily warmed my sheets. What did it say about me that I didn't know most of their names, and not only that, I didn't give a flying fuck? Ev was right. Why would any sane female put up with my shit?

But like I told Evvy, I had enough of my own problems. I couldn't worry about the baggage someone else carried around. What I had with my sexual partners was always mutual. I got relief from the intense, aching pressure in my chest, and they got their kicks from being held down and hurt a little. End of story. The day I gave it any more thought was the day I jumped off a cliff. The careful juggling of the various aspects of my life would get all disturbed, and then the whole thing would come crashing down on my head.

No. I was better off doing things my way. Besides, without my coping methods, my carefully chosen "outlets," considering the violent way I reacted to stress, I'd end up fighting everyone I met instead of fucking them out with a hot chick. And if I did that, my career would be over. Then I wouldn't be able to watch out for Rémy. I'd been down that road once before and more than ten years later I still struggled with guilt over leaving my brother alone.

Never again.

Mindless fucks it is.

4

Kylie

The Kings scored the first goal of the game and I leapt from my seat to dance and cheer along with the twenty thousand or so other DC area fans. My grin was so big my cheeks were sore.

"Ky, that was awesome."

I laughed and squeezed Nat's arm as we jumped up and down and screamed while clinging to each other, our faces rosy with excitement.

"Right? It really was." I couldn't stop smiling.

Nat and I met a few years ago as freshman at Georgetown University. Nat slogged through the tough physical therapy program, while I studied journalism, my passion ever since I was a little kid and my parents had to shoo me away from the more disturbing news segments I loved to watch. Our career paths couldn't have been more different, but in our first semester we ended up in a few intro classes together. When Nat loudly snorted at something the professor said that he didn't realize sounded like thinly veiled sexual innuendo, I giggled in response and we made eye contact. A match was made and we've been best friends ever since. Nat was my plus one whenever I went to Rocco's hockey games, and I never missed one at home. Not even if I had a test the next day and Rocco insisted I stay home to study.

Speaking of... Rocco skated by and grinned around his garish yellow mouthguard. The women in the seats all around us went absolutely nuts. Nat and I exchanged a knowing look and simultaneously rolled our eyes at the squealing females. Objectively speaking, I know my brother is an attractive guy. It's just... well, none of those women knew him. My brother. The real Rocco Calloway. I would even bet at least half were puck bunnies, women who went from game to game, hanging out where they knew the players would be, with the sole focus of landing a hockey husband, preferably by getting knocked up.

The bunnies had to have some sort of a clue as to what they were getting into when it came to professional athletes. But for the most part, regular everyday women knew less than nothing about athletes, or specifically hockey players, period. Because if they did, they'd bolt for the hills and run far, far away in the opposite direction. Most hockey players are—my loving brother included—by trade, notoriously quick-tempered, hard assed, immature, rough around the edges, uber-masculine alpha dogs who curse a lot. To the extreme. Pain doesn't stop them, words can easily send them into a rage, and from the maniacal behavior I'd witnessed over the years, I honestly believed every single one of them took a few too many hits to the head at one point or another.

Yeah, yeah, there are exceptions and I love my brother more than anything, but he's no different from the majority. Okay, so Rocco is by far one of the most loyal and kind people I know. That loyalty and kindness, however, doesn't extend outside Rocco's seriously minuscule inner circle. Meaning, he doesn't give a rat's patootie about anyone he doesn't know and won't hesitate to use his massive muscles to prove a point.

When our parents died, I was thirteen and Rocco was nineteen. The accident occurred a couple months after Rocco got called up to the Kings from the Canadian Junior Hockey League and landed a contract for some ungodly sum of money. I was glad that at least after everything they sacrificed so he could play hockey, Mom and Dad lived to see Rocco achieve his dream. At the time, with the exception of Rocco's success, the rest of my life sucked. Yet no matter how bad it got, my brother never let me down.

Despite being young, single, and suddenly wealthy, Rocco didn't hesitate to step up and become my guardian when he could easily have pawned me off on a relative. In fact, he refused to entertain the idea of me going anywhere but with him. Rocco dedicated himself to taking care of me; he put a roof over my head, made sure I went to school, got good grades, got into a decent college, and paid for my education. He always, *always* protected me and would likely do so for the rest of his life.

The scrape of skates on ice caught my attention and I watched Rocco stop in front of us. He tapped the boards with his stick, ignoring the squeals of eager fans. Nat and I performed what was now our ritual, and simultaneously spun to flash Rocco the back of our dark blue jerseys, both sporting number seven with Calloway printed across the back in big yellow letters. I glanced over my shoulder just in time to see Rocco give us a thumbs up. At least, I assumed it was a thumbs up. It's hard to see much of anything with those thick, padded hockey gloves. Nat and I laughed and fell back into our seats to watch the game.

It was down to a few minutes left in the third period when a scuffle broke out in front of our seats. Since Rocco's tickets were in the first row near the Kings' bench, we had a prime view of the action. Rocco descended on the puck, ready to flick it out of scoring range for the Comets by sending it to his center. From the left, a blur of white powered toward my brother, who didn't notice. Rocco was busy handling the puck, lining it up for a pass. He located his teammate, only to find an Atlanta player all over the guy. On the fly, Rocco spun and flicked the puck behind the Kings' goal. It skimmed along the curve to DC's right-side defenseman.

The speeding Atlanta player didn't get the message that the puck was gone. Instead of changing course and moving into position in front of the net to wait for DC to make a mistake so he could intercept and score, the jerk slammed full speed into Rocco. The men crashed into the boards, literally a foot from my face. Horror struck, I watched Rocco's helmet slam against the plexi and bounce off the hard surface.

My heart clenched and I cried out, blindly reaching for Nat's hand. Unfortunately, she had no more of a clue what was going on than me. Nat leaned in so I could hear her over the loud boos and shouts of the crowd. "Ky, what the hell is that guy doing?"

"I don't know." I was honestly confused as to what could possibly be going through number nineteen's head.

Wait. Number nineteen.

Ugh!

I knew who that was. Nineteen was Sebastian St. Clair. "That's *The Sinner*," I spat. My lips twisted into a grimace as I patently ignored the flip-floppy, butterfly-flapping feeling in my belly.

Nat gave me a questioning look. "The Sinner?"

With a loud huff, I explained without taking my eyes off the fight, and boy were they going at it—helmets were off and they were grappling and swinging at each other, trying to snag the others' jersey in their gloved hands. It was no holds barred, complete and utter chaos.

"Number nineteen." I pointed at the sexy jerk who wore white and red. "That's the same guy that punched Rocco at the game the other day in Atlanta. The one you were supposed to come over and watch with me but skipped because you had a date." I smirked at Nat then returned my attention to the ice. "He's a total ass. I swear, I think his goal is to maim as many opposing players as possible."

Rocco took a blow to the side of his face and I inhaled sharply through my nose. He didn't look phased by the punch, so I relaxed and continued.

"The irony that his last name starts with Saint, combined with the fact that he's a violent jerk, earned him the nickname 'The Sinner.'" Yes, I made air quotes. "I mean look at him, Nat. The guy is so unhinged he shouldn't even be allowed to play." The men continued to grapple and I sucked my tongue between my teeth. My pulse fluctuated with each punch thrown. "The really sucky part is that he's drop-dead, inhumanly gorgeous." I snorted and rolled my eyes. "Not that it matters. His personality is awful. Sebastien St. Clair is hands down the biggest jackass in the entire NHL."

I can admit he's good looking. I may have poured over pictures of Sebastian St. Clair, and, as an aspiring journalist whose brother plays professional hockey, watched a lot of press conferences, some of which coincidentally included the Atlanta player. It would be highly unlikely to find a single straight woman, including myself, who didn't drool and get all hot and bothered at the sight of Sebastian St. Clair. What's unfortunate, is the second he opens his beautiful, bow-shaped mouth, those stunning good looks dissolve like a mirage. The guy is a hot mess of anger, curses, and total assholeiness, both on and off the ice.

Which, because I'm an idiot, ended up turning me on like nothing else ever had. And *that* made me angry.

I will never forget the first time I laid eyes on Sebastian St. Clair, two, maybe three years earlier. I couldn't forget, and not just because the man turned my crank. Because of the way Rocco—who as upset as he got at times, never, ever raised his voice at me—did just that.

Rocco and I sat on the couch to watch SportsCenter, my brother nice and relaxed since he didn't have a game for two more days. The commentators discussed the day's NHL highlights, showing clips of the best and worst plays, then they ran various snippets of post-game press conferences from across the league. A couple minutes in, Sebastien St. Clair's face, in all it's perfection and glory, filled Rocco's enormous flat screen TV. I must have been unconsciously drawn to him, because without realizing it, I shifted to the edge of the cushion, eyes glued to the eighty-inch image of the most beautiful man I'd ever seen.

"Don't even think about it." I flinched at Rocco's bark and turned to find him doing his grimacey thing. At me. His expression was so harsh, chill bumps popped up on my arms. "That guy," Rocco pointed a finger at the screen, "is a complete horse's ass. I don't want you anywhere near him."

Like always, I began to protest just for the sake of protesting. "But —"

"No buts!" Rocco practically roared. I shrank back into the couch. Rocco never yelled at me. Ever. The only response I could manage was a quick nod. "I mean it, Ky." He leaned in close. "Stay away from him."

Faced with Rocco's serious stare, flared nostrils and burning eyes, I swallowed tightly. Even though the warning only made the temptation to get close to Sebastien St. Clair a thousand times stronger, I said what he wanted to hear.

"Okay."

WHISTLES WENT off and the clock stopped, but Rocco and St. Clair were on another planet. Refs or not, the brawl continued. Their blue (Rocco) and white (St. Clair) jerseys moved so fast, I couldn't lock onto any one single thing, seeing only a mish-mashed blur of colors. Before I could blink, their gloves were off and punches were thrown.

Right. In. Front. Of. Me.

I gaped and my mouth hung open like a largemouth bass. The big jerk with the name St. Clair stamped on his jersey in bold red, hauled back his fist, swung. When it connected with Rocco's nose, I winced.

I managed to choke out an "Oh my god!" and leapt from my seat as if zapped by a cattle prod. My iced tea went flying everywhere, not that I cared. Screaming, I pressed my palms on the divider and banged on it hard enough to rattle the boards. "Hey you!" Despite the deafening noise in the arena, the shouts, the boos, the cheers, and the hiss of skates on ice, by some miracle, Sebastien St. Clair heard me. He must have, because he glanced up, and when our gazes met time stopped.

I swore, right then and there, the man I secretly fantasized about for years, was able to see right through me.

Knew I wanted him. Read me like a book from cover to cover. The moment was short — just long enough to catch a glimpse of his incredible blue eyes, filled with sparks of playfulness that defied the violent actions of their owner. It was long enough. I was mesmerized by him. That one shared look may as well have lasted hours instead of a fraction of a second.

Then it was over and Sebastien St. Clair returned his attention to beating on my brother. What did it say about me, that even when he was exchanging blows with Rocco, who gave back just as good, I still found St. Clair sexy? Maybe it was the lure of the forbidden. Or maybe it was because during that infinitesimally small moment in time, that one teeny exchange we shared, my body had burst into flames, the fire flickering and growing into a frenzy of lust and want and need.

No. I was not attracted to Sebastien St. Clair.

I mean, yes. I was attracted to him, but only physically. The man was a jerk of the highest order, with an ego so large you could probably see it from space.

Again, the men slammed into the boards and my heart leapt into my throat. I held my breath, but not because of the brutal violence that played out a few feet away. My breath was stolen by the intensity of the feelings triggered by those fiery blue eyes. Another sharp whistle and I inhaled, bringing much-needed oxygen to my burning lungs. Palms still on the plexi, I stabbed at it with an index finger.

Okay fine. I can admit Sebastien St. Clair is sexy. Didn't matter. Rocco is my brother and I will *always* support him on the ice.

"Hey you! Yeah, you, St. Clair! Back off, you big jerk!"

The refs futilely pushed their way through the thick

crowd of bulky players who gathered in a tight circle to egg on the fight. Rocco detached from St. Claire's grip and used the back of his hand to swipe at his nose. When it came back bloody for the second time in two straight games against Atlanta, Rocco glared at the red smear. His dark eyes flashed with fury and he stared holes in Sebastien St. Clair's face, while the muscles in his jaw ticked.

Uh oh. I recognized that look. Things were about to go away, way south.

I pounded harder on the partition and screeched at the clearly insane, and regrettably hot, Sebastien St. Clair. "Stop it, you... you *asshole!*"

Amazingly, he heard me again, and those eyes, the bluest I'd ever seen, locked onto mine once more. Startled by the potency of his stare, and its ability to send a flush of prickly heat over my skin, I jerked away from the partition and for a moment forgot where I was and what I was doing. The two of us stared at each other through the handprint-smudged divider.

"Ky," Nat said, shaking my arm. Only I couldn't tear myself away from St. Clair's hypnotizing sapphire eyes. He couldn't move either. Well, not until Rocco's fist flew out of nowhere and connected with the side of his face. I winced as St. Clair's eyes squeezed shut and his head snapped sideways. Then, I started to scream.

"Oh my —"

It was St. Clair's turn to have *his* head slammed against the boards. His chiseled cheekbone crashed into the exact spot where I rested my palms. In a 'blink and you missed it' moment, the infamous Sinner ended up with his face smooshed against the half-inch piece of plexi that separated us. He blinked, glanced down at my Calloway jersey, and gave me a cruel—and *ugh!* too sexy—smirk before turning to retaliate on my brother.

"Oh thank god." I clutched my shirt above my heart and exhaled when the useless refs finally made it into the center of the fray and ended the fight before either idiot threw another punch.

"Geez, that was intense," Nat said under her breath. "Come on, sit." She tugged on my hand and we both slumped down in our seats.

My earlier thoughts were confirmed yet again. Hockey players are quick-tempered, hard assed, rough around the edges, uber-masculine alpha dogs. The smear of blood left on the plexi was proof enough for me.

It didn't stop Sebastien "The Sinner" St. Clair from being the sexiest man alive. The big jerk.

Seb

"I really wish you would stop doing that, Seb. I'm serious. You can't attack every single player that checks me. You know as well as I do that getting hurt is part of the job."

I strode across the room—the hotel's décor indistinguishable from every other one I stayed in when the team traveled—to gaze out the window. Sometimes, having something to look at helped control my temper. Not that night, unfortunately.

I stared, eyes unfocused, too damn distracted to really see anything. With the heel of my hands, I rubbed my eyes until my vision cleared long enough to note the brilliant lights of the nation's capital. Lights illuminated the Washington Monument an eerie yellowish-white, the smooth stones glowing from base to tip. I placed the palm of my hand on the underside of my chin, shoved my head up and to the side, and groaned with pleasure when my neck cracked.

"Rémy, that *ciboire* had it coming." I kept my voice even as my gaze drifted from the United States' national monuments to the pitch-black sky, hundreds of pinprick stars sprinkled across the inky darkness.

"Christ, Seb. I'm a fucking winger in the NHL. Do you have any idea how humiliating it is to have your big brother do your fighting for you?" Unlike me, who tried my best to remain calm, Rémy had no such reservation. His tone pitched higher and the volume went up right along with it.

"Screw that." Calm became impossible. As I grew agitated, my words slid into French. "You'll always be my little brother. It's my goddamn job to protect you."

More than you will ever know.

Tired and beyond disgusted by my failures both the other night in Atlanta and earlier that evening in DC, I turned from the window, flopped on the bed, and kicked off my shoes. I managed to successfully ignore Rémy's calls for three days after the game in Atlanta, too pissed with myself to listen to another one of my brother's lectures about enacting revenge on his behalf. Besides, I had been somewhat indisposed. It took an unusually long amount of time to fuck the anger out of my system after Calloway put me on my back and knocked my head hard enough to have me yanked from the game for concussion protocol. The only reason I answered tonight was because I didn't want Rémy to get stressed out and worry.

"No Seb, it's not. It's not your job." He let out a loud huff. "I get where you're coming from, really, I do." At least Rémy's breathing sounded better, which meant his ribs were almost healed. "You had to act like a parental figure because our dad —"

"This isn't about Dad."

Twitch, twitch, twitch.

Fucking perfect. I slapped a hand over the offending eye and cursed the damn thing.

"Oh, screw you. It's always about Dad. Mémère did the best she could, but we both know it was tough to grow up without parents."

I didn't respond. Mostly because Rémy was one hundred percent *wrong* and had no clue what he was talking about, but hell would have to freeze over before I destroyed the lie I created to protect my brother from reality and all of its horrors. Okay, yeah. I maybe missed our mother, barely. She was drunk more often than not and a shitty parent. But at least she cared. Dad... well, I had zilch to say about the man that didn't include a string of obscenities colorful enough to make a porn star blush. Rémy, oblivious to my inner torment, continued.

"It's not that I don't appreciate what you do for me, bro. Growing up was...difficult." Rémy swallowed and as usual, the guilt from the layers upon layers of lies crushed down on me. "And I know it was ten times worse for you, I mean, you still being a kid and all and having to act like the man of the house." Another pause meant there was plenty of time to toss another suitcase full of guilt on my teetering mountain of baggage. "But, I'm twenty. It's time to let me try and take care of myself. I think I've done a pretty decent job being on my own for the first time in my life. You need to worry less about me and focus on fixing your own shit."

I slid my hand from my twitching eye to massage the back of my skull, where a dull ache throbbed. I heard what Rémy said. I got it, I really did, but he didn't understand, and if I had my way, he never would. I couldn't stop caring or worrying that Rém had everything he needed and was protected from the douchebags of the world anymore than I could choose to make my heart stop beating. It had been my responsibility to watch out for Rémy for so long, I wasn't sure I even knew how to turn it off. It was part of me. Kind of like the ever present rage and self-loathing.

With the final rub to my pulsing head, I let my arm fall and sighed. "I'll try." Rémy barked a sarcastic laugh and I scrambled to reassure him. "No, really. I will. Promise. I just... I can't guarantee I'll be perfect."

Rémy did another one of his dramatic pauses, this one so long I pulled the phone from my ear and checked to make sure the call hadn't disconnected, like I did so often when talking to my brother. It wasn't all that unlikely the thing would actually crap out, as every electronic device I ever laid hands on broke, fell apart, or somehow magically exploded. In fact, if I remember correctly, this was my fourth phone in as many months.

Right as I was about to ask if Rémy was still there, he soothed my thoroughly frayed nerves.

"Thanks, bro. For everything." Rémy's voice hitched and a lump formed in my throat. It caused both my stationary and my stupid, twitchy eye, to burn with unshed tears. "Just," it was Rémy's turn to sigh. "You have to try and let me be my own man now, okay? I really, really need this."

"Yeah." I sounded like I gargled with gravel. "I get it." I changed the subject before I said something monumentally idiotic that messed everything up and made the already tense situation a thousand times worse. "When do the doctors think you'll be back on the ice?"

Rémy didn't—and as far as I was concerned, would never–know the extent to which I had gone, and wouldn't hesitate to go to again, to keep him safe. Could never know. I had literally been protecting my brother for well over a decade. From nightmares, from pain, from the reality of our shittastic childhood... from our father.

Rémy grunted. "I hate riding the bench. Doc says probably next week."

"Just in time for my team to whip your team's ass."

"Yeah, okay." He snorted, amused. "We'll see."

"Catch you later, *mon frère.*"

Rémy chuckled. "Bye, bro."

My head was killing me. I tossed the phone next to me on the too-soft duvet where it sank down a couple inches. The thick material puffed up around the device, nearly obscuring it from view. I put my hands behind my head and stared at the ceiling. The phone beeped, indicating it was low on power, and I groaned. Every damn device I touched somehow ended up malfunctioning. It's like I'm some kind of human EMP. My very presence makes everything electronic spontaneously combust.

I didn't have to look at the screen to know the battery was dying, because the stupid charger fritzed out yesterday. When I plugged it into the hotel's wall socket, sparks literally shot out of the damn thing. Without the stupid cord, my stupid phone would just have to up and stupidly die.

Shit. I dug both hands into my hair and swallow down the urge to scream. Rémy had no idea how much control he was asking me to give up. To go against more than fifteen years of deeply ingrained behavior. A decade and half of throwing myself on the grenade time and time again, in a bid to shelter my brother from the horrors of what used to be our life. Shielding Rém from Mom's drunken binges and general neglect. Going to desperate measures to redirect Dad's explosive anger and increasing violence onto me. I was the one who fed and clothed my brother. Made sure he got to school and took a bath and did his homework. I was the one to try and give Rémy the semblance of a normal childhood.

Okay, fine. We were dealt a shitty and no matter what I did to try and change things, our childhood was never going to be normal, but I hope I gave Rémy the *illusion* of normal. It was the best I could do and a thousand times better than growing up perpetually black and blue, haunted by pain and fear, telling your teachers your injuries were from hockey.

I know because that was me.

Then... I wasn't there for Rémy, and I would never forgive myself for my absence, even though it was the end result of something that needed to be done.

A sharp pain on my scalp brought me back to the present. I dropped my hands from where they were fisting my hair and yanking on it.

Twitch, twitch, twitch.

I got up and must've paced the room a hundred times, jaw clenched, fingers laced on top of my head, but it was pointless. The memories brought back the rage. I was too far gone. Too angry. Too worked up over both Rémy's injury and his request that I basically distance myself from him.

I growled and snatched up the remote. Maybe there was a game on. Or SportsCenter. Something, anything to distract me from the burning hot fury that sat in my stomach like a ball of magma. I smashed the power button.

Nothing.

Why the fuck didn't anything ever work right?

Again and again I jabbed the button with the same result, until I hurled the remote across the room. It ricocheted off the wall and left a pretty serious dent. This time, I couldn't hold back my shout of frustration. Shaking, I sat on the bed and rubbed my twitching eye. I wiggled to get comfortable and felt rather than heard the crack of glass under my left butt cheek. I shifted to one side and pulled out my phone. The second I saw the spiderweb pattern across the screen, it was game over.

There was no calming me. Not if I was stuck in that room. And not when, in less than fifteen minutes, I was supposed to meet some of the guys in the lobby bar to grab something to eat.

Only two things worked to squelch the feverish anger once it built to such explosive levels. Both involved taking control. At that moment, it was strong enough where I could feel it, like this physical... *thing*, a big, dark mass that pressed against my insides and made my skin feel all tight and hot, ready to split open any second and pour out of me in a stream of uncontrolled violence reminiscent of dear old dad. Problem was, even if I used both of my coping methods between now and the next game, I knew damn well the second I stepped on the ice I would snap.

How was I supposed to keep my promise to Rémy and come face to face with Calloway tomorrow night for our final game in DC?

Kylie

"Where the hell have you been?"

I flinched so violently at another of Rocco's sneak attacks, my keys flew out of my hand and clattered to the tile floor. I bent over to retrieve them while I fought to not drop dead from shock. Once my heart stopped trying to beat its way out of my rib cage, I straightened, looked at my brother, and gasped. The aftereffects of Rocco's fight with Sebastian St. Clair earlier in the evening were blatantly evident. Scrapes and bruises littered his skin, and his bottom lip was all puffy and split down the middle.

Fine. Rocco was angry. It's not as if I didn't know he would be. I did kind of leave Rocco hanging by grabbing Nat and ducking out, skipping our traditional after game dinner. Maybe notifying him by text message wasn't the greatest idea, but I knew he wouldn't get it until I was long gone and there was no way he could stop me.

At the time, I felt bad about it... for roughly zero point four seconds, then a flurry of nerves—the rush I crave, the adrenaline from the excitement of the unknown and doing something Rocco would hate—held me in its trance. Sheltered for so long by my well-meaning, hovering, helicopter brother from hell, sometimes I needed to do something dangerous. Something I knew Rocco would disapprove of, if not flat out for bid. *If* he found out, and I went to pretty extreme lengths to make certain he never did.

Unfortunately, even the best laid plans went sideways. Like tonight. I hadn't planned on Rocco discovering certain things about me, such as the reason for my spontaneous moments of reckless abandonment, or maybe, last week when I hopped a ride home from the campus library on the back of my acquaintance slash study partner's motorcycle, somewhere in my subconscious I wanted Rocco to see me pull up on Grant's rumbling crotch rocket. I had been over an hour late getting home and studiously ignored every single one of Rocco's avalanche of texts and calls. Which meant I knew with one hundred percent certainty, my over-protective brother would be staring holes down at the street, waiting for me to arrive.

I can't explain it but there are times when I can't help myself. Can't control my actions. I don't like to think I torment Rocco on purpose, but I'm pretty sure that would be a lie. I want to say it's an unconscious decision, to poke at the beehive the very sharp stick just to see what happens. But it's not. The rare times I rile Rocco up, it's most definitely a calculated move. A personal, if petty, little rebellion that only one of the sides knows is deliberate.

In my defense, I actually knew Grant, unlike some of the other guys I'd gotten rides home from. Grant was in all of my journalism classes and came from old DC money, so even though Rocco didn't like it, I knew Grant wasn't a serial killer or something.

I felt sick and my hands were clammy, because Rocco—being the big jerk that he is—pounced the second I walked to the front door. He towered over me, a full foot taller than my five-six, and crossed his thick arms over pecs as wide as three of me standing side to side, as he glared down. I shifted from foot to foot, uncomfortable with the scrutiny. My face heated in humiliation. Rocco's stare was so intense it was almost as if he somehow knew what I had been up to earlier in the evening. Just the thought of Rocco finding out was humiliating enough, despite the fact I chickened out.

And what if I had gone through with it? I was an adult and could make my own decisions. Maybe I was impulsive at times, intended to act first and think later, it was still well within my rights to make my own mistakes. Even if my actions were usually knee-jerk rebellions to Rocco's well-intentioned smothering.

"You jerk. You have to stop doing that! You scared me half to death." I tried to return Rocco's glare, but nobody threw shade like my brother. With my body still suffering the aftereffects of the sneak attack, I prayed he wouldn't notice how my hands trembled.

"Yeah? Well, you scared me," he snarled. "So I guess we're even." Perma-scowl in place, Rocco's fury made me even more resentful. I was angry at him, but even more so at myself. Since he was perfectly good target, I directed all of my shame and frustration and fury at the tiny wrinkle between Rocco's dark brows.

"I guess we are," I snapped back. No way was I in the mood to deal with Rocco's issues. Not when I had so many of my own crashing down on me. I stepped around him and headed for my room.

"Hey! Don't you dare walk away from me."

Oh no you didn't. I stopped dead in my tracks and tensed so fast my shoulders nearly smacked my ears. He did *not* just speak to me as if I were a five-year-old child.

Furious in a way I'd never been before, I spun on my heel and did something I almost never ever did. I took everything I felt, gathered it into a ball, and heaved it directly at Rocco's head. I marched right up to him, tilted my head *way* back to meet his seething glare, and went off.

"Don't you even start with that." I stabbed a finger into Rocco's sternum. Of course, because he's built like a Mack truck, on the second poke, my index finger bent funny. "Ow! Dang it." I waved my hand around in a ridiculous and futile effort to stop the pain.

Rocco lunged to catch my hand, which I narrowly avoided by spinning away, and almost landed on my ass for the effort.

"Christ, Ky. Lemme take a look. You might have broken it."

Not feeling charitable in any way, when Rocco tried to grab my hand again, I yelped and cradled it to my chest. He did not get to treat me like crap then act all concerned and heroic. He did not get to be the good guy. Not tonight.

"No. Go away."

Rocco rolled his eyes and scoffed. He held out his hand,

palm up, with the clear expectation I would comply. "Stop being so damn stubborn and let me look."

My jaw dropped so fast I might have felt my chin smack the floor. "*Me?* Stubborn?" I let out a very unfeminine snort. "*You're* the one who bulldozes over me to get your way and makes ridiculous demands by treating me like a kid."

Using my uninjured hand, I waved at the den. Rocco followed the motion and his bruised cheeks flushed pink. Every light in the condo blazed bright, the huge television blared loudly, and six empty beer bottles sat like good little soldiers next to my brother's favorite chair... which just so happened to be next the windows that overlooked the front of the building.

"Case in point, Rocco. It's three in the morning and you're the one who decided to wait up for me like I'm a virgin on prom night. I don't need or want a lecture from you, especially one I didn't ask for."

Rocco winced and covered his ears. "Shit, Ky. I don't want to hear about your sex life."

Considering an hour earlier, I almost broke my two-year dry spell, Rocco struck a nerve. I wanted to cry, and that made me angrier. Emotions all jumbled up, every last drop of my mental acuity drained, the dam that held me back finally collapsed. Every feeling I had, came exploding out of me like Mount Vesuvius.

After the cluster-you-know-what of a night—first watching Rocco get into a fight, then the guilt of thinking the guy who punched him was smoking hot, followed by me skipping out on Rocco after the game. Add in my failed attempt at a one night stand, having to call Nat from his place, her listening to me cry and snuffle as she calmed me enough to ask Grant to take me home, and top it off with Rocco giving me a ton of crap—the pressure became too much. And because I always hold back, too worried about hurting Rocco, my emotions decided to take matters into their own hands, and spewed forth in the form of a scathing rant.

"If there are things you don't want to hear, there's an easy solution, Rocco. Butt out of my personal life! God! It's not like I asked you to wait up and lecture me. I'm an adult, A-D-U-L-T."

My words struck their mark. Rocco slumped, but the hardened glint in his eyes didn't budge. Not one bit. When I finished my tirade, my chest heaving from exertion, Rocco replied, eerily calm in response to my rare outburst.

"You know I only worry because I care. If anything were to happen to you —" Rocco closed his eyes and shuddered. When he met my gaze once more, I was, as usual, over-whelmed by the sheer amount of worry and fear radiating from his eyes.

I was so tired of arguing. An enormous wave of exhaus-tion crashed over my head, so immense and all consuming, I could have slept for days. I rubbed my eyes. It was late and I needed to get to bed or else I would collapse. I let out a long sigh and shook my head. Nothing ever changed.

Nothing ever *would* change.

Not if I kept giving in to the guilt. Which in turn, caused my spontaneous recklessness. Which then led to more guilt. And so the cycle continued. I just didn't know how to stop it. It was like being on a roller coaster as it crested the peak of the highest hill. Once you got to that point, there was nothing you could do to stop from going over the edge. But I had to try, didn't I? Otherwise we continue to have this conversation over and over until one of us eventually said something we couldn't take back.

My righteous fury drained. All I wanted was to go to my

room and overthink every last second of my crappy night. Rocco would never back down, so it was up to me. I made sure to hang on to the edge the roller coaster tracks by my fingertips to keep from going over.

"I know you care, Rocco, but you have to understand. I'm twenty-one, not sixteen. I go on dates *(ha-ha, not really)*. I have friends I do things with. Sometimes, I'm studying at the library. My point is, it doesn't matter what I'm doing. You need to get over yourself and stop demanding to know every little thing I'm up to or who I'm with."

I didn't mention how I purposely did things to upset him and that his smothering only made the urge to do those things worse.

Rocco's brows smushed even closer, and that stupid crease grew stupidly deeper, while I watched his stupid chiseled jaw grind back and forth.

"I'm not going to stop caring, Ky. *Ever*. And I'll wait up every single night if I goddamn want to."

If that was how he wanted it...

Imitating my brat of a brother, I stuck out my chin. "Fine."

Rocco blinked and cocked his head. "Fine?"

"Yep." I popped the P. "Go for it. Wait up as long or as often as you like, but make no mistake..." I took a step back, not because I thought Rocco would hurt me, but because he really did look like he was on the verge of losing it. "I'll let you know when I'm going out, but remember, I don't answer to you. Then, when I get home from wherever I was doing whatever the hell I wanted to do, I'm not speaking to you about it or justifying my actions. Not a word. I'll come inside and go straight to my room. Period. You'll get what you want —to see with your own eyes that I'm not dead or injured. That's the full extent of what you deserve to know."

"But –"

Oh, hell no. No more capitulating.

"No, Rocco." I inhaled a deep breath and it felt like every muscle in my body went slack from lack of energy. "I love you and I appreciate everything you've ever done for me, but you're not bullying me into getting your way. Not this time."

Focusing on anything but Rocco, my tumultuous emotions began to settle back into place... for the moment. My psyche might have been taken care of, but my body continued to react. Tiny beads of sweat trickled down my spine and my heart pounded as if I ran a marathon. I felt the ache of every single one of the imaginary twenty-six point two miles down to my bones.

For an almost college graduate, I had the distinct impression that I was terribly naïve. Nat tried to warn me, said I wasn't cut out for one night stands. And she was right. When I bumped into Grant at the bar and he asked if I wanted to leave, my mouth worked faster than my brain and I said yes. Reckless Kylie had been in the driver's seat, eager for an escape, even if temporary, desperate for a moment of freedom from the constant anxiety and guilt. When I got to his place, I freaked out and locked myself in his bathroom. All I got out of my failed one night stand did, was to feel worse. And confused.

Despite how bad an idea going home with Grant was, I think I needed to do it. To attempt to step out of Rocco's suffocating protective bubble. When Nat and I bumped into him at a college bar in Dupont Circle, Grant seemed like the perfect option for my first foray into no strings sex. He's good-looking, and looked completely unlike his usual buttoned-up self. Instead, Grant wore a leather jacket and had a couple days of stubble on his jaw. His eyes shone with just enough danger to pique my interest, much different than he acted in class.

Fine, in retrospect it wasn't my best idea, but Grant really did put off some seriously sexy vibes. Why I freaked out, I don't know. Nat admitted she was glad I didn't go through with it. She said he gave her the creeps.

None of which mattered. Not Grant, not my inability to have meaningless sex, and not Rocco. It was a lose-lose situation. Part of me was angry, afraid, and ashamed at what I did, and worse, an even bigger part of me wished I had gone through with it.

Rocco scowled, still standing over me, waiting for me to give in. I hung my head, and exhaled.

Once again, I would hand over another piece of myself in order to make Rocco happy. Sometimes, I felt like a carcass, picked clean to the bones. Every scrap gone, my remnants hollow and empty. I took a deep breath through my nose and pushed onward. I made sure to keep my voice light to soothe Rocco's worries, if for no other reason than to get him off my case.

"You gave up a lot for me. I know that, and you've been there for me when no one else was." Rocco opened his mouth but I was determined to get it out. If I was going to submit to Rocco's wishes to worm my way out of the situation, I was at the very least, going to cling to a teeny, tiny bit of pride. "But I *need* this, Rocco. I need to do my own thing. Please? How about a compromise?" I bumped him gently with my hip and smiled. "How about when I go out, I promise to call if I'm going to be late getting home so you won't worry?"

Rocco scrubbed his hands over his face. His palms scritched across the quarter-inch of growth on his cheeks. His arms dropped to his sides and, *dammit,* he looked crushed. My big, strong, rock-steady brother was breaking. I swallowed.

I did that.

I put that vulnerable look on Rocco's face, and even though I hated seeing it, I did have needs of my own to take into account. Needs Rocco didn't need to know about. Needs that required fulfilling. Needs my brother wouldn't understand. I was stuck between a rock and a firing squad, either way, I lost.

"I'm sorry." I whispered.

"Me too."

Rocco reached out and wrapped his arms around me. Surrounded the familiar, comforting warmth, and the scent of the body wash he'd used for as long as I could remember, I allowed myself to feel loved. I emptied my mind, used the moment to let go of my problems, all of them—Grant, the look on his face when I told him to bring me home, fighting with Rocco. For that moment, I loosened the binds that connected me to the piles of stress and worry that stuck to me since the day our parents drove to a party and never came home, a tragic result of impossible circumstances. The harsh Minnesota winters combined with a broken streetlight and a perfectly placed patch of black ice.

I laid my cheek on Rocco's wide chest, closed my eyes, and sank into the embrace. As usual, the silence in my head didn't last nearly long enough, and the heavy weight of guilt and doubt crept back in.

How could I be so heartless to my brother? After all he did and sacrifice for me? He took me in. Raised me. Fed me. Hell, he was *still* taking care of me, paying for my undergrad degree and the roof over my head. I felt like an ungrateful, whiny, brat.

Rocco squeezed tighter. "I think your compromise sounds good. Thank you," he murmured into my hair.

Overwhelmed by both Rocco's unwavering love and the truck full of guilt that dumped its load on my shoulders, I stepped back and Rocco dropped his arms. I picked at the hem of my shirt and gave him a watery smile.

"I-I'm pretty tired. I'll see you in the morning?"

"Yeah." Rocco patted my arm and I snuck one last peek at his face. At least he looked more like himself. Gone was the deep wrinkle and furrowed brow, along with the hostility he used to mask his stark fear of something awful happening to the only remaining member of his family. "Oh, one more thing," he said. I froze, worried Rocco might know something, maybe about Grant or even the weird semi-crush I had on Sebastian St. Clair. "No more motorcy-cles, Ky. My heart almost gave out when I saw you on the back one." He squeezed his eyes shut and shook his head. "I nearly shit my pants."

That, I could do.

I exhaled and quickly nodded. "No problem."

I was lucky to have him and I knew it. Rocco was so brave and reliable it was easy to forget that I wasn't the only one who lost my parents. Rocco suffered too, and from that unspeakable day forward, he was absolutely petrified he might lose his sister as well.

After facing way too many hard truths about myself, I was done. While the getting was good, I fled to my room and locked the door right as the first hot tear fell onto my cheek. I flopped onto my bed fully dressed, and wondered why I changed my mind about Grant.

I could have told myself it was fear. Or inexperience. But I knew the truth, something no one else would ever know.

Not even Nat. And if Rocco found out... I shivered. He couldn't.

I could keep it from them, but not from myself. As Grant led me out of the bar, I pictured someone else holding my hand. I imagined what it would be like if Sebastian St. Clair was the one taking me home, not Grant. Fantasized about what Sebastien would do to me, whether he would be gentle or rough, what he smelled like, what he tasted like, what his skin would feel like under my fingertips. And I knew, Grant was a poor substitute. He wasn't who I wanted. It didn't matter that I would never have Sebastian St. Clair, my mind knew the difference and rejected Grant flat out.

Eyelids heavy, I pictured Sebastien's beautiful face. The bright blue eyes, the full lips, and that knowing look he gave me at the game. I closed my eyes and imagined his bedroom, and the hungry, urgent kisses he would rain down on my mouth and throat. I could almost feel the power contained in his muscular body and the way he harnessed it, in a fierce, take no prisoners attitude. I decided he would be aggressive and forceful. In my fantasies anyway. My body tingled as I pictured him throwing me down, pinning me to the mattress, and making me feel deliciously helpless as he kissed me.

I was just getting to the good part when my rational mind kicked and I realized what I was doing. I couldn't fantasize about Sebastian St. Clair. Nothing good would ever come of it, and even though none of it was real, I felt guilty doing it. Like I was betraying Rocco. What kind of sister wanted to get down and dirty with her brother's worst enemy?

And because I'm warped, the idea turned me on that much more.

I had to stop torturing Rocco with my tendencies to

engage in spontaneous and reckless activities. Like the time I hopped in a car with a couple classmates and we drove to New York City for the day and ended up staying the night in some fleabag motel outside Trenton, New Jersey. Oh, and maybe I forgot to call Rocco and tell him where I was. Or the time Nat and I blew off class to go skydiving on a whim. Boy, did Rocco blow his top over that one when I may have, sort of, accidentally, possibly on purpose, posted a video of it to my Instagram account where I knew he would see it.

God, I really am a sucky sister.

The image of Sebastian St. Clair popped back into my head and my cheeks burst into flames. No way. I refused to entertain fantasies of him. At least not while I lived with Rocco. *Wait, what?* No! Not even when I moved out. It was out of the question. The temperamental hockey player was off-limits.

I buried my face in my hands, so stressed I couldn't even enjoy an erotic fantasy about a hot guy. I hated to seem ungrateful. I was beyond blessed to have such a wonderful, caring brother and I knew it, but why did I have to be so messed up in the head? Why couldn't I do the one night stand thing with a regular guy without panicking like a freak?

Why did everything always have to be so freaking complicated?

Sebastian St. Clair's face flashed through my mind again.

Ugh. Like I said, complicated.

Seb

"No man, I'm telling you, she was without a doubt the hottest chick I've seen in my life."

"Who?" Evvy asked as he accepted a new beer from our server.

I took a long swig from my bottle before answering. "The one I saw tonight, you know, when I was throwing down with Sasquatch." Evvy gave me a blank look. "Sasquatch." More blank staring. I rolled my eyes. "Dude, c'mon! Rocco Calloway."

Evvy rolled his eyes back. "Oh. Riiiiight, I think you might have mentioned her a time or twenty. The blonde in the Calloway jersey, the one you won't shut up about. How could I forget?"

I punched Ev in the biceps and scowled. "First of all, it's a *sweater*, Evvy, not a jersey. Second, you didn't see her, you unlucky bastard."

I closed my eyes and conjured up an image of the breathtaking blonde. At the time, she had been all riled up, furious even, but somehow the anger aimed my way did nothing to detract from her stunning good looks. In fact, the slight curl to her upper lip and the blazing fire in her eyes only made her that much hotter.

"Too bad you missed her, because she was smoking. And for the record, Evvy, you're an asshole."

Fucking Everette raining on my parade.

I sucked down the rest of my beer and stared off into space. Thinking about the girl had me half-hard, which served as a reminder to how I left things with Amanda. I winced at the memory.

And I was calling Evvy an asshole? Pot meet kettle.

"You got that part right," Ev said as he slugged down the rest of his drink and belched. "At least I'm proud to be an asshole."

"Whatever, Ev."

Evvy didn't get it and obviously, I was terrible at

explaining exactly what about the girl at the King's game made her different, and why her face decided to imprint directly on my gray matter. Even I didn't fully understand why I couldn't shake her loose. Not that it mattered. Hell, I didn't know why I bothered to tell Evvy about her in the first place. I didn't discuss women—or feelings, or any other girly crap—with anyone. Though the rare times I felt the need to purge something from my system, Ev was my go to guy. Still, I never waxed poetic about women. Especially not one particular woman.

I lounged back in my chair and pretended to check out the bar. No way did I want to look at Evvy after spewing all that embarrassing shit. Apparently, my mouth to brain filter broke. Probably when Calloway dropped me to the ice. There was no other explanation, because I hadn't been able to stop talking. After spotting her, I yammered in Evvy's ear, going on about Hot Blonde from the final buzzer right up to the present, minus the ten minutes I took to duck into my room and call Rémy. In the span of a few hours, the blonde had become an unhealthy obsession.

I picked at the label on my beer and tried to figure out how to get my man card back, but my one-track mind had other plans. When I locked gazes with Hot Blonde, something happened. Not that I'd ever admit that out loud. Christ, I could hardly admit it to myself. It was like we had an instant connection or some other equally ridiculous bullshit. You know, the kind of fantasy nonsense they put in chick flicks to get women all mushy and teary. The kind of crap that's so far-fetched you know damn well it never happened in real life.

Except it did. To me.

The primitive part of my brain didn't seem to care that, unlike most women, Hot Blonde hadn't been flirting or tossing me sultry looks. Quite the opposite. When we locked gazes, Hot Blonde was furious. She repeatedly slammed her hand on the plexi while cursing me out. Worse, despite the fact that she looked like she wished my face would melt off, I *felt* something. *Saw* something. Something in her bright chestnut colored eyes. Fuck me, I sounded like such a pussy. I drained the rest of my beer, snorted at how ridiculousness it was, and patently ignored Evvy's questioning stare.

I was losing my damn mind.

It wasn't my fault. Whatever mysterious woo-woo magic spell Hot Blonde cast on me, it worked. She sank her claws right in and refused to let go.

My cock thickened when I remembered her luscious mouth. Thick, red lips that would look perfect wrapped around my hard length. Hot Blonde was fucking gorgeous. In fact, her only visible negative trait was her downright hideous taste in hockey players. Who in their right mind wore a Calloway sweater? In public?

Evvy's inability to understand, combined with the knowledge that I'd probably never see Hot Blonde again, pissed me off, and I didn't need anyone's help getting angry, thank you very much. Bottle empty, I raised my hand and signaled the server to bring another round.

Evvy tipped back his chair until the front legs lifted off the ground, and did an exaggerated stretch so he could not so subtly scope out the DC hotel bar. His eyes flared and the chair dropped to all fours with a bang, startling me. Naturally, I was taking a sip of my brand new beer and jerked at the sound. The glass rim of the bottle clanked against my front tooth.

"What the fuck, Evvy?" I put a hand to my mouth and pulled back my fingers to check for blood. None.

"Check it out, Sebby." Evvy leaned across the table and

used a tilt of his head to point to his left. "Brunette and blonde, big tits, tight dresses, and two almost empty cocktail glasses."

I followed Evvy's gaze and found the women. Not that it was hard to figure out who he meant. They stood at the corner of the bar and were so out of place, they may as well have been wearing dresses made out of flashing neon lights. Yep, Evvy might not know what those women were, but he could tell they were easy prey. They were attractive, hot actually, *if* you went for the super high maintenance type. The kind that wore loads of makeup and had fake tits and big hair and would let you do whatever you wanted to them, just so they could say they fucked a hockey player.

On a normal day, I might be interested... as long as one of them was agreeable to my preferences. Tonight? Even with anger that simmered just beneath the surface of my skin, desperate for release, there wasn't a single thing about either woman I found appealing. Not in the least. Though it was blatantly obvious they were interested in us. No one with a set of functioning eyeballs could miss the way the women used their mouths to do provocative things to their straws while boldly attempting to make eye contact.

I shook my head and took the easy way out. "Dude, I told you hundred times, I'm done with puck bunnies."

That part was true, but also I wasn't about to explain to Evvy that it wasn't the fact that the women were bunnies, so much as I just wasn't in the mood to fuck. At least not anyone who wasn't Hot Blonde. And wasn't that realization a shocker? The fight with Calloway and subsequent argument with Rémy were the exact types of confrontations that cranked up my stress level, which made having a handy outlet on standby a necessity. In essence, I should have jumped at the chance.

But I didn't.

Evvy continued to drool over the bunnies. He couldn't peel his gaze away. Good for him, I guess. It sucked that I couldn't manage to scrape up even a tiny spark of interest, because puck bunnies are easy lays and perfect for releasing all kinds of tension. I'm a pretty good judge as to whether or not a woman would be interested in my brand of kink, but I wasn't in the mood.

First time for everything.

Besides, they really were bunnies, and yes, I would do any number of depraved things, but I refused to fuck puck bunnies. I wouldn't touch one even if it meant I imploded from sexual frustration.

Evvy glanced at me and checked out the women again. His forehead wrinkled and he grunted. "You positive they're bunnies?"

Puck bunnies are hockey groupies. Women whose solitary goal in life is to fuck hockey players, typically with the aspiration of landing one as a husband. Or trapping one. And I would know.

At the beginning of my rookie year I got the exact same speech as every other newbie. Management warned us about the flocks of women that hung around arenas and scoped out the bars of the hotels the team stayed at. They advised us to keep our distance from the bunnies. Awkward as it was, they even laid down rules and insisted every player follow them when it came to puck bunnies, or any hookup for that matter—keep your cock wrapped, never give out your phone number, and don't bring anyone to your place.

Of course, every rookie idiot nodded and said, "Okay, no problem." Then those same idiots went and screwed their way through the pack of bunnies anyway. What nineteen-year-old man on his own for the first time passed up such easy pickings, especially when it was flung in his face left and right? Not me, and not most others, either.

Clearly, I outgrew the bunny phase faster than Ev, who was practically drooling at the posing women. I quit the scene cold turkey after a particularly terrifying incident involving a puck bunny, a pregnancy, and nine months of sweating it out until the paternity test proved the kid wasn't mine. Seemed Evvy was gonna need a scare of his own before his wayward dick learned its lesson.

"They're definitely bunnies. Not interested." I waved a dismissive hand.

It was surprisingly easy to say no to guaranteed pussy. My mind was still back in the arena with Hot Blonde. Picturing her standing on the other side of a smudged piece of plexiglass, staring at me with loathing... and what I blatantly recognized as desire. Too bad there wasn't a way to find out who she was. I might pass on puck bunnies, but no fucking way would I pass up a night with her. Shit, I'd even be the bigger person and overlook the fact that her taste was so bad she wore a Calloway sweater. I might even be willing to fuck her vanilla, if it was all I could get. She was that hot.

Evvy pushed back his chair, stood, and shot me a wicked grin. "Well, if you're not down for some action, all the more for me." He rubbed his hands together like some kind of movie villain. "Catch you later." He winked and sauntered, yes, motherfucking *sauntered,* over to the puck bunnies. Minutes later, the three left the bar, one of Evvy's arms thrown over each girl's shoulders.

I shook my head and chuckled. *Idiot.* I tossed down some bills to cover the tab and headed up to my room. Alone. Yeah, I was thrumming with electricity, and I was tense and pissed I lost the fight with Sasquatch, and still needed to release the rumbling mass of pent up energy that vibrated inside my body. Screw it. I'd just have to jerk off in the shower like a horny teenager. It wouldn't do much, but it would take the edge off.

Like I told Evvy, Hot Blonde or not, when it came to puck bunnies, lesson learned.

A COUPLE WEEKS after DC and Hot Blonde—and spending countless hours stroking my dick raw to the memory of her face, while imagining what she'd look like naked and tied to my bed, screaming my name—I entered the Comets' locker room. My shoes squeaked as I came to an abrupt halt.

Something felt off. Way off. Confused, I glanced around before I dared to cross the threshold. It didn't take long to figure out what was wrong. The boisterous sounds were missing. The pregame excitement. The hustle and bustle. The teasing, the jokes, the cursing. It was quiet. *Too* quiet. Especially for game day. The guys were always extra hyped and crazy loud before every game. I frowned.

Son of a bitch.

There wasn't a player in the league who didn't know what a silent locker room meant.

Trade.

Since I didn't get a call from management, and I didn't get one from Evvy, I knew neither of us was shipping out. For sure my best friend would have phoned me right away if he were getting sent off to god knows where.

So if not us, then who?

The whole thing sucked. Most days, I enjoyed my job —especially the cheers of the crowd when I knocked a guy down on the ice—but I loathed trades. They were by far the worst part of playing a professional sport. At any given moment, my entire life could be uprooted. Within hours, I could be required to pack my crap and get my ass on a plane to a city I didn't know, with nowhere to live, a bunch of teammates I'd never played with before, and on top of all that–I would still be expected to give my very best performance on the ice. Sometimes that very same night.

Thank god it hadn't happened to me... yet. I reached out and quietly knocked on the wooden panel of the nearest row of wardrobes to prevent a jinx. I left Canada for a reason, and just the thought of getting traded to a team north of the border sent my terrified balls crawling up into my body.

On a deep inhale, I stiffened my spine and, after disrobing and hanging my suit in the first changing area, which consisted of a simple row of upright wardrobes, strode into the second changing area. No one wants their suit to smell like used, sweaty hockey gear, so everything is kept separate. Clad in only my boxer briefs, I padded into the actual locker room and approached my cubby, the one I use to store my gear and uniform and where I dress for practice and games.

Nearby, a small gathering of players huddled around a guy who—since I was staring at the guy's back—I didn't recognize. I didn't, however, miss the fact that whoever it was, was one tall motherfucker and had blond hair. What I did know, was that he wasn't one of my teammates, which meant he was new. From there it wasn't hard to put two and two together and figure out I was looking at the back of Unlucky Traded New Guy's head.

Someone thumped me in the arm and I heard a familiar cackle.

"Ow! Shit, Evvy. What's your problem?" Ev isn't exactly

the gentle type. I grimaced and rubbed my shoulder. Out of the corner of my eye I caught him grinning like a lunatic.

Still smiling, and still creepy as fuck, Ev leaned in to conspiratorially whisper in my ear.

"Lookie who we got." As Evvy said the words he tipped his head in the direction of Unlucky Traded New Guy. "It's your number one favorite person in the whole wide world," he sang. "After me, of course."

I narrowed my gaze and focused on the back of the big, dirty blond head that sat perched atop a super tall, super wide, super stacked body, and wracked my brain to figure out who the hell it could possibly be.

Almost as if Unlucky Traded New Guy felt me staring at him, he slowly twisted his thick neck until I got a good look at my brand new teammate.

"Oh, fucking hell," I murmured, only not nearly as quiet as I thought, because Ev snickered, and at the same time, *Bastard* New Guy's mouth curled into a sneer.

New Guy wasn't the unlucky one. That particular prize went to me.

Because I was staring directly into the Cro-Magnon-like face of Rocco "Sasquatch" Calloway.

He's my new teammate? What the ever-living-fuck? Why would they send that shithead here?

I dropped my chin to my chest and sighed.

Aw, fuck.

Last week, our best defenseman, first line player and one of the coolest guys on the team, Gordon Hatcher, broke his ankle. And yeah, in theory I knew they'd have to replace Gordie at some point, but never in my worst nightmares did I think his replacement would be Rocco Calloway.

The sour look on Calloway's face reflected my exact

thoughts—basically, a summary of every single obscenity in the Urban Dictionary.

"St. Clair," Calloway growled.

Great. Just great. Put a cherry on top of the shit sundae and call it a day.

In an attempt at awkward politeness, instead of walking up and socking the guy in the solar plexus like I was dying to do, I cleared my throat and remained calm-*ish*.

"Uh, hey Calloway. Does this mean you're one of us now?"

Twitch, twitch, twitch.

Dammit. I blinked in a futile effort to stop my spazzing eye. If I was gonna have to play with Sasquatch on a daily basis, I needed to try to make things a little less weird, right?

One thing I learned at an early age is that you don't disrespect your teammates. They're your family. Granted, it looked like we were about to be a big-ass fucking Sasquatch family, but still a family. The trade also meant the two of us wouldn't face each other on the ice anymore, which was kind of irritating. Punching Rocco Calloway was one of my favorite pastimes, plus I wouldn't get another chance to break the guy's ribs.

Rocco Calloway, it appeared, held no such standards in keeping things civil. Likely due to the fact that less than a week after our fight in Atlanta, the one where Calloway knocked me out cold, we had our second epic rumble in DC. The one that went down right in front of Hot Blonde— a.k.a. she of the hideous taste in hockey players. The woman who currently haunted my dreams and left me with a perpetually chaffed dick from the never-ending need to rub one out.

"I'll never be one of *you*, asshole," Calloway spat as he took a step toward me. Naturally, the others caught on to the

suddenly hostile environment, and being a bunch of immature brats, reverted to second graders and called out
"*oooooooh*" as Calloway puffed out his Sasquatch chest and
stalked in my direction. He sported an expression that let
me, and everyone else in the locker room, know he was
itching to turn my face into an unrecognizable smear.

At six-foot-two, two hundred and forty pounds, I packed
pure muscle and was in no way small. During a game, I have
zero reservations extracting a little pain from someone as
big as Calloway. Off the ice, well, that's another thing altogether. Going toe-to-toe, without the benefit of pads and
skates that made me look bigger and taller, Rocco Calloway
made me feel like the Keebler fucking Elf. The dude
towered over me, his blond-haired, behemoth body, big
enough to eclipse the sun.

Calloway came to a stop mere inches away and extended
a thick, rock hard finger to stab me in the chest. I growled
and fought the urge to snatch Sasquatch's fat digit and snap
it in half.

"You stay the hell out of my way and I'll stay out of yours,
St. Clair."

The familiar dark fury awoke from its slumber. Deep
inside, it churned and pulsed as the pressure grew more
intense by the millisecond. I growled again, but before I had
the chance to lash out with one of my patented, highly
insulting, and expertly wielded verbal slap downs, Rocco
spun on his size sixteen heel and stomped off, then—

Everyone in the locker room, including me, sucked in a
loud breath and cringed.

Holy shit! That was close.

Sasquatch had to have been beyond furious to make
such a careless mistake. Idiot didn't look where he was
going and almost stepped directly on the white and red

Comets logo woven into the black carpet in the center of the room. At the last second, Calloway tottered on his tippy toes and took a clumsy leap to the side to narrowly avoid it.

Asshat. He almost broke *the* golden rule of hockey. The near miss of his big fat Sasquatch foot on the logo brought on another round of *"oooooooohs"* from my useless teammates. Not that Calloway didn't deserve it. Everyone, from old-timer to rookie, knew you didn't step on the team logo. *Ever.* That was peewee hockey 101 right there. I wouldn't have minded lending a helping hand in giving the inevitable, and well deserved, beat down, had Calloway actually stepped on it.

I sighed and scratched my chest where I still felt his phantom finger jabbing into me. Too bad that beat down would have to remain a fantasy. Stupid Sasquatch reflexes.

Once Calloway left the locker room, I dropped onto the bench in front of my cubby, scrubbed my hands down my face, and groaned. That was when another of my jerk teammates decided it was the perfect time to kick me when I was down.

"He good addition to team, *da*?"

Next to me on the bench, Evvy silently laughed. Traitorous jerk's shoulders shook and Ev covered his mouth with his hands. I stared up at Hajek and frowned at the goalie's unwanted two cents.

"Yeah, fucking wonderful, Hazey. It's gonna be so awesome to skate with someone whose number one wish in life is for me to drop dead."

Hazey's face lit up. "*Da*, I agree. It shall be quite entertaining to watch."

With that, Hazey, clueless as usual, turned and walked away. I heard him cackling like a hyena and realized Hazey might not be as clueless as I thought. Fucker. Evvy was no better, I suppose, my friend now bent in two, clutching his stomach as he burst into hysterics.

Ha-fucking-ha.

Entertaining for *them,* maybe. I was pretty sure I wasn't going to have anywhere near as much fun with Calloway around as the rest of my team.

Whatever. I suited up in home gear and ignored the ribbing. Eventually they would get bored of the St. Clair-Calloway rivalry and shut the fuck up. As a unit—minus Calloway, whose selfish ass must've already gone on ahead —we trudged through the tunnel to emerge onto the ice. Coach was in rare form, already barking out warm-up drills like Cujo on crack as fans trickled into the arena. When I snuck a glance over at Coach, I half expected to find foam dripping from the man's dangling jowls. A half-hour later, all red-faced and wild eyed, a rabid looking Coach shouted for us to get our sorry asses off the ice.

We gathered in the tunnel and waited for the game to start. I patently avoided the harsh glare aimed in my direction. It wasn't that I feared Calloway, it was that I feared I wouldn't be able to hold back. Once the rage overflowed, there was little that could get me to stop. Beating down my teammate would certainly get me ejected from the game. Or fired. My hands were completely tied, and not in a good way.

It sucked.

Kylie

I double checked my ticket stub and reread the seat number for my very first game in Atlanta. It wasn't as good as Rocco's seats in DC, but I certainly had nothing to complain about. Like DC, it was in the front row. The problem was that it was on the opposite side of the ice from the players' bench. Opposite from where I'd been sitting since I was thirteen years old, doing my homework in the arena while I waited for Rocco's game to begin. Also, the new location meant my seat was directly behind the penalty box.

Just perfect.

Now I'd have to listen to the nonstop, unique and colorful, curse-filled rants the players unleashed when they spent their big-boy version of a timeout in the bin. Not that foul language bothers me. My brother is a hockey player after all and I practically grew up at the rink. I figure I know every single possible swear word in English, a bunch in French, a handful in Russian, and a whole lot more in languages I couldn't even begin to guess at. I've been known to drop a swear or two myself now and then, so I couldn't care less about the cursing. I watched the games for one reason and one reason only, to support Rocco. It was not being seated up against the ice that bothered me. Especially since my brother tended to be prone to fighting.

To say Rocco had been upset when he got the call that he was traded would be the understatement of the twenty-first century. Rocco played for DC since he got drafted seven years ago. The memory of the day we moved from Minnesota and left the only house we'd ever known was as clear as if it happened yesterday. Rocco purchased his Georgetown condo with his signing bonus and we'd lived there ever since. Because I went from a family of four to being raised by my brother in a city thousands of miles away, I didn't have time to grieve for my parents until Minnesota was gone. Moving to DC and leaving everyone I knew behind, made it that much more difficult to adjust. Moving again, this time to Atlanta, felt almost as traumatic.

When word of the trade came down, Rocco went bat-shit

crazy. He was beyond livid. If he wasn't my brother I would have been seriously afraid of him, that's how angry he was. The look in Rocco's eyes could only be described as borderline murderous. The only way I got him to calm down and accept the trade—after he shouted he was going to quit the NHL—was to agree to move to Atlanta with him. Apparently, the thought of leaving his little sister to fend for herself in DC sent my overprotective brother into one of his patented, full-blown, uber-controlling freak outs. This time with a serious injection of flat-out rage over the unexpected trade.

To Rocco, it didn't matter that I was twenty-one and one semester from completing my journalism degree, or that most of my peers already lived on their own. Nope. My insanely uptight and overbearing big brother made it perfectly clear he wouldn't be going *anywhere* without me. After everything he sacrificed for my benefit over the years, I wasn't willing to let Rocco quit the NHL and ruin what he worked so hard to achieve over something as stupid as where I finished school. It didn't take any prodding on his part to get me to agree to the move. Luckily, my journalism advisor said I had enough core courses to get my degree. All I had to do to complete the remaining credits was find an internship in Atlanta.

Which was how I ended up at the Peach Dome, sans Nat, wearing a *Comets* jersey of all things. Just a generic one with no number on it, since they hadn't printed any with Rocco's name yet. How could they? He only got the call thirty-six hours ago and everything else happened in a such whirlwind I could barely remember. I spoke to the University while Rocco arranged to have our stuff packed and shipped as he began to search for a place to live. Temporarily, we were staying in a suite in the enormous hotel connected to the arena via an upscale shopping mall. The move was so sudden, I rushed around like a chicken with its head cut off and still only managed to pack a single suitcase. I was so frazzled, I forgot to bring my beloved hair straightener and my favorite pair of heels.

Resigned to making the best of it in Atlanta, I settled in my seat and tried to get a feel for Rocco's new home arena. The five-year-old Peach Dome was impressive, huge and modern with massive hi-def screens that hung over center ice. The seats were bright red in some sections, black in others, and as much as I missed DC and the familiarity, I had to admit these chairs were a lot more comfortable than the ones in the old TeleBank Arena.

After player introductions—during which I was stuck in the restroom, the line much longer than I thought it would be—then the national anthem, the sides took their positions and the puck dropped. Right from the start I knew the game would be exciting, if nothing else. The instant the tiny black rubber disc hit the ice, the game went from zero to Millennium Falcon hyperspace in two point five seconds. Zipping back and forth, up and down the rink, the players were streaks of color—red for Atlanta and teal for Charlotte.

To my surprise the fans in Atlanta were way more animated and into the games than those in DC. So much for the stereotyped genteel Southerner. If they existed, they weren't at the Peach Dome. It made me miss having Nat at my side. Atlanta fans shouted, clapped, cursed, roared with approval, booed their displeasure, and stayed wholly invested in the game from start to finish. Though it felt like swallowing glass shards and betrayal to Rocco's old team, even if it was only in my head, it might very well have been the most fun I'd had at a hockey game.

Rocco and one of the Charlotte players began to tussle a

bit and my stomach dropped. The men battled hard for the puck, sticks and elbows flying everywhere, bodies crashing into the boards. Because I wasn't seated right up on the ice, I became frustrated. I couldn't get an up-close and personal view of the brawl, like I did for Rocco's last fight.

Just thinking about it made me frown. Rocco's last fight was with that cocky, sexy, jerk, Sebastien St. Clair. *The Sinner*. Even though I didn't have my ringside seat, I was close enough to read the name on the Charlotte player's back without difficulty. It said... I squinted, then my eyes bulged.

Wait... no.

I blinked, knowing it was a mistake. Surely, I misread the name. After blinking a few more times, I waited for the men to spin around so I could read the Charlotte jersey again. When I did, my breath caught.

The guy's name was... *St. Clair?*

Thoroughly confused, I racked my brain and shuffled through my memories, trying to recall the name of the team Rocco played a few weeks ago in DC. The game where St. Clair and Rocco got in that horrific and bloody tussle. The one where Sebastien St. Clair's smug and stupidly handsome face got squished against the boards right in front of me. It couldn't be...

That exact moment, the Charlotte player looked up and I found myself staring into a pair of crystal clear blue eyes. *Familiar* blue eyes. When I realized where I had seen those eyes, goose bumps broke out down my neck and arms. I scrambled to reach under my seat, blindly groping for the program an overeager usher shoved into my hands as I went through the turnstile. Flipping through the pages, I found the one with the Comets' team roster. I quickly scanned the column and stopped on number nineteen. Just as I thought.

Right there was a color picture of a man I vividly remembered. The one who winked at me in DC, all playful and super sexy with his big blue eyes. *The jerk.* After giving the photo a nice, leisurely once over—for research purposes only—and ignoring the way my skin flushed with prickly heat, I read the description.

•**Sebastien St. Clair**, number 19, age 26, 6'2", 240 lbs, right-winger, born in Trois Rivières, Québec, Canada. *Atlanta Comets.*

So if St. Clair is listed on the Comets' roster how could he possibly be fighting Rocco again, this time wearing a Charlotte jersey? Did St. Clair get traded at the same time as Rocco? I glanced back up at the ice. That didn't make sense, because—I looked back down at the program—Yep, Rocco's name was already on the Comets' lineup. If they changed Rocco's trade status, they certainly would have changed Sebastien St. Clair's.

I should've paid more attention to the visiting teams at all those games I attended instead of gossiping with Nat. While I examined the roster over and over, trying to make sense of everything, the fight ended and regular play resumed.

I peeked over the edge of the program. No one sat in the penalty box so it must've been a clean fight. I scanned the ice until I located the Charlotte player with the blue eyes and the number thirteen on his back. Almost as if I expected what I already knew to be fact to have somehow changed, I found myself shocked that it still said St. Clair above his number. Completely dumbfounded, I shook my head.

I don't get it. St. Clair is still with Atlanta yet he's also with Charlotte.

A streak of red flew past my seat and the light behind the Charlotte goalie flashed red. The loud buzzer echoed throughout the arena. As a single unit, the crowd surged to their feet and cheered as the announcer's voice boomed over the PA system.

"Goal, number nineteen, Sebastien St. Clair. Time of goal, seven minutes, thirty-two seconds of the first period. This is St. Clair's thirtieth goal of the season, putting him on track to set a team record for most goals in a single season."

My body moved faster than my brain. Without consciously doing so, I leapt to my feet with the other fans and craned my neck. In the swarm of red and black I located number nineteen. And there it was. "St. Clair" stitched over a one and the nine. He skated in a circle in front of the net, hands and stick over his head as his teammates jumped all over him and slapped their gloves on the top of his helmet.

No way. Two St. Clairs? How did I not know this?

While the rowdy crowd continued to go berserk over the goal, I sat back down and flipped the program to the Charlotte roster. Halfway down the list I found him. *Wow.* The man in the photo next to the player's profile definitely held a resemblance to Sebastien St. Clair, but there were subtle differences. For example, he had dirty blond hair and somehow looked... *kinder* than his brother. It was in the eyes. Even though they're the exact same intense, bright blue shade as his brother's, they appeared less jaded, less hostile. Less *angry*. At some point, something hardened the elder St. Clair. Something that didn't touch the other. I looked past the picture to read the bio.

• **Rèmy St. Clair**, number 13, age 21, 6'1", 230 lbs, right winger, born in Trois Rivières, Québec, Canada. *Charlotte Rush.*

OHMYGOD. Two of them. The brother is young, and probably new to the NHL. But more important, how had I failed to put two and two together? After that gruesome show and infuriating wink he gave me in DC, I should have remembered the game was played against Atlanta, which meant I should have realized the assholey Sebastien St. Clair was one of Rocco's new teammates. For a future journalist, I felt mighty unobservant making such a big gaffe.

Mid-chastise, an ear-piercing whistle stopped the game, and I glanced up from the program. The two refs and the two linesmen huddled at center ice, probably sorting out a penalty. I used the break in action to pull out my phone and quickly Googled the St. Clair brothers. Two seconds into my search, the announcer broke my concentration.

"Penalty, Atlanta. Number nineteen, Sebastien St. Clair. Two minutes, hooking. Ten forty-four of the first period. Power play, Charlotte."

The crowd booed and did so loudly and enthusiastically, protesting the call. *Hmph,* of course it was Sebastien St. Clair. Typical. Except for noting the name of the player, I paid zero attention to whatever else the announcer said. I was too busy holding my breath and scrunching down in my seat in an effort to look as small as possible, because the sexy as sin, penalty-loving jerk in question was skating in my direction.

When St. Clair stepped into the box, it highlighted just

how close he was. The back of the penalty box, and the tall
sheet of plexi that separated it from the crowd, stood less
than two feet from my chair and, *oh crap*, he turned and
stared at me the exact moment I stared at him. St. Clair's
eyes widened comically and his gaze fell to my Comets
jersey. That wicked smirk of his emerged—the provocative
one I remembered all too well—and when he raised a dark
brown in question, I knew he was mocking my shirt. Embarrassed, I crossed my arms over my chest.

Ugh!

The guy was so infuriating! He had an unnerving, and
totally annoying, expression of approval on his stupid handsome face. Despite loathing the man, my stomach did a
somersault and landed at my feet. While St. Clair continued
to smirk like the cocky jerk he was, he threw another of
those irresistible winks my way, then turned around to wait
his two minutes.

Once his eyes were off of me, I was able to exhale. If I
could sink into the floor and disappear, I would. The
tempting and frustrating Sebastien St. Clair was Rocco's
teammate.

Oh. My. God. Kill me now.

During the intermission between the first and second
periods someone tapped my arm, and I flailed at the unexpected contact.

"Excuse me."

Once my heart stopped trying to beat out of my chest,
I glanced up to find an usher standing next to my seat.
The sweaty young man wore a red polo embroidered with
the Atlanta Comets logo. He clutched an envelope in one

hand and balanced a large flat box on the palm of the other.

Annoyed that he startled me, and irritated with myself for being so jumpy, I squinted up at him. When he said nothing, I held back the urge to roll my eyes. The usher literally looked so nervous I thought he might pass out, and there was no way I was doing CPR on him. Okay, fine. I would do CPR, but I didn't have to like it.

It seemed as if we were going to get anywhere, I'd have to speak first. I raised my brows. "Can I help you?"

"I'm, uh, supposed to, uh, give this to you." The usher held the box as far from his body as possible, thereby, shoving it in my face. He sounded so nervous I felt kind of bad for him. Wisps of blondish-red hair stuck to his forehead and his fair cheeks flushed bright red. Even his hands shook. The guy couldn't have been any older than me, maybe not even. In all likelihood, he was new at his job, and it showed.

Baffled, I gave him a blank stare as he squirmed and tried to work out whatever the heck it was he needed to say.

After an eternity, the usher cleared his throat. If the entire situation weren't so weird, I would think the his life depended on him delivering whatever it was he held in his trembling hands.

I scrunched my nose and looked at the box as if it were a live grenade, or maybe a basket of venomous snakes. Who the heck would send me a gift? And why? And during a game of all things?

"Are you sure that's for me? I'm not expecting anything."

"I'm, uh, positive." The usher's head went up and down, over and over, like a deranged bobble head doll.

Okay, now I just wanted to get rid of him. "Fine. I guess."

He exhaled much too loud and his shoulders visibly

slumped. Then the sweaty usher threw the box in my lap and tossed the envelope on top of it. Good thing I have quick reflexes, or the corner of the box would've poked my eye out.If that happened, the top would've flown off and then there would have been snakes everywhere.

Carefully handling the package, I treated it as if it were an IED, one jostle away from blowing up in my face. When I turned to thank the sweaty usher—for what I have no idea, as the kid almost blinded me—he was halfway up the stairs.

Okaaaay...

Whatever. I set the box flat on my thighs and picked up the envelope. Still trying to process the peculiar notion of being sent a gift during a hockey game, I held the white rectangle and ran a fingertip around the edge. The paper was high quality, thick and weighty. Naturally, because nothing in my life is easy, the outside of the envelope was blank and had no distinguishing features or watermark. The hairs on the back of my neck stood on end and I had the oddest feeling that someone was looking at me.

I glanced around the rink as chills rippled down my spine. The whoosh of my pulse thundered in my ears, dulling the noise of the enthusiastic crowd. Was someone watching me right now? The thought released a burst of adrenaline and my anxiety skyrocketed. I gave the envelope a suspicious glare and flipped it over several times, wondering who, and why, until my head hurt.

After several minutes of freaking out, I straightened in my seat and huffed, feeling stupid. I wasn't in a James Bond movie. Besides, I had nowhere near the qualifications to be a secret agent or double-crossing spy worthy of receiving a Mission Impossible-style exploding message. It was a hockey game for god's sake.

Relax, Ky. It's a note.

Before I could torture myself with anymore overthinking, which would only cause more stress, thus, more anxiety, I jammed a finger under the flap and tore open the envelope. Tension broken, I exhaled and only then did I realize I had been holding my breath. Annoyed, I yanked out a neatly folded sheet of the same thick paper as the envelope. Hmm, maybe Rocco sent something? Maybe he couldn't meet for dinner after the game and it was his really, really strange way of apologizing?

No. I shook my head. If that were true, at the end of the game my brother would simply send a text. Even if Rocco did need to cancel dinner, it wouldn't explain the box. Rocco isn't the gift giving type. He prefers to show his love through actions, not material things.

I skimmed the note and the first thing I noticed was the personalization at the very top. *From the desk of Frank Vernon.* Next, my gaze landed on a tiny Comets logo in the corner. Frank Vernon, Frank Vernon... I'd heard that name before, but for the life of me, I couldn't place it. The scrutiny continued as I took in the sum total of the note—a few meager lines of messy scrawled ink. Definitely a man's handwriting, and *not* Rocco's. I read the brief blurb then froze, the paper ready to slip from my fingers.

What the—?

I reread it four more times.

I'M glad to see your taste in teams has improved. I wonder if your taste in players has as well? Meet me after the game in the lobby bar of the hotel attached to the arena and maybe I can persuade you to root for someone else.

MY MOUTH HUNG open and my pulse skipped. Three sentences. A mere handful of words. Words that said so much yet told me nothing. No signature, no indication who it was from. Was it from *him*? Sebastien St. Clair? The Sinner? That was the only thing that made any kind of sense, and that was a stretch.

Nervous and twitchy, I fumbled and almost dropped the note. It had to be from him. And he wanted to meet. For what? My brain downshifted and conjured up a bunch of inappropriate and filthy images. Images of Sebastien St. Clair doing things to me. Things I would only admit I wanted in my darkest fantasies.

Face flaming hot, I glanced up from under my lashes to scan the—

Oh my god.

One thing I learned in journalism school was to trust my instincts. If it felt like you were being watched, you were.

Sometimes, I hated being right.

As if drawn to his presence, my gaze landed on Sebastien St. Clair. He sat on the Atlanta bench, and despite being all the way across the ice, I could clearly make out his bright blue eyes as he studied my face. My *bright red* face. It didn't matter that a little over eighty-five feet separated us, the scorching heat in his intense stare was unmistakable, as was the way his lips pulled into that annoying smirk.

The smirk may as well have been a sensual caress because my insides burst into flames, the desire so potent it left me feeling raw and exposed. The sensation grew and thrummed and made my body respond in ways I didn't want it to. My complete lack of control over my reaction made me angry and I gnashed my teeth.

I hated him. Okay, fine. It's not that I hated *him,* so much as I hated what he did to me. Hated the way my stupid body reacted to him. Was drawn to everything about him. *I* was drawn to him. There was something about Sebastien St. Clair, a buzzing undercurrent of danger that he emanateed, and *that* was what easily seduced my reckless side.

Feeling a little bit humiliated and a lot furious, I broke the connection first and dropped my attention to the box in my lap. Well, if it was from Sebastien St. Clair, it most likely wasn't a box of snakes. I inhaled a shaky breath and closed my eyes. What was he playing at? Besides the obvious, which was a full out assault on my senses with the singular goal of driving me insane with lust.

The Calloway stubborn gene kicked in. I refused to give St. Clair the satisfaction of knowing he got under my skin. I focused on the gift in my lap, steeled my expression, and kept it neutral as I lifted the lid. After peeling back several layers of red tissue paper—and no sign of snakes, thank you Jesus—I almost broke my vow to remain straight-faced. It took a lot of effort to bite back the laugh that threatened to burst free. Sitting amongst the tissue lay perfectly folded Atlanta Comets jersey. An odd choice of gifts since I damn well knew Sebastien St. Clair saw the one I had on. His note confirmed the fact.

No longer caring whether or not he saw me react, I frowned. Honestly, I should have just slammed the lid back on the box and shoved it under my seat. Made the guy sweat it out by refusing to accept his stupid gift and his even stupider suggestion that we meet.

Yeah, no.

I was way too curious to give in, and *that* made me even angrier. The fact that Sebastien had me curious. Infuriated by my lack of self-control, I lifted the present out of the box and held it up. My eyes narrowed.

What a pompous jackass.

On the back of the jersey, embroidered in bold, thirteen-inch numbers, were a one and a nine. Above that, in three-inch lettering, was the name St. Clair, stitched horizontally over the shoulder blades.

"Nice shirt. He's a really good player." The woman in the seat behind me had taken it upon herself to look over my shoulder and comment on my gift. "And he's sexy, too." She chuckled and went back to watching the game.

I grimaced. Like I needed or wanted anyone's opinion on Sebastien St. Clair. Even though I knew he was waiting, *dying* to see me lose my cool, I couldn't help but cram the stupid thing back into the box and force the lid on. So what if he knew I was mad? He's clearly a first-class jerk, so why should I care?

I pressed my lips together in a hard line, knowing what I was about to do. I couldn't help myself. I was weak. With a sigh, I gave in to the urge and glanced over at the Comets' bench to locate Sebastien St. Clair, so I could glower at his arrogant ass. He needed to see just how much of a jerk I thought he was. Only, instead of leveling my best stern glare across the ice, I flinched and let out a humiliating high-pitched squeak.

It was patently obvious my luck was nonexistent when it came to all matters St. Clair. Because the teams swapped sides for each period, the man for whom my glower was intended was standing mere feet from where I sat. His position at right wing meant he was directly in front of my seat, skating in slow, sensual circles while he waited for the ref to set up the puck drop.

Of course, because I'm me, he stopped skating right in time to catch me staring. Those glittering blue eyes locked on to mine and I became helpless. Sebastien was so close, I could see the desire that burned in his heated stare as he unapologetically checked me out, raking his gaze up and down my body without shame.

A current of electricity crackled through the air between us. My body tingled and my blood sang as my breath hitched in my lungs. I was trapped. Frozen. Held in place by Sebastien St. Clair as surely as if he were physically pinning me down with his strong hands, and damn if that thought didn't unleash a jolt of desire that quickly spread low in my abdomen.

Screw what I was *supposed* to do. What I *wanted* to do was worship at his feet. Prostrate at the altar of St. Clair.

I blinked a few times before I shook myself free of his trance, and put a hand to my blisteringly hot cheek. It grew hotter as I wondered if Sebastien St. Clair knew how much I wanted him.

I glanced back up and his lips twitched. *Of course* he knew. Did the man miss nothing? Then, Sebastien did the unexpected. He didn't smirk or laugh or wink. No, the man *smoldered*. The look Sebastien St. Clair aimed my way was so scorching, so intense, so consuming, my entire body went up in a conflagration of invisible flames. The air grew so hot and sticky, sweat beaded along my temples and a single drop trickled between my shoulder blades. My overwhelming response to the man reminded me of something Nat used to say whenever she spotted a hot guy.

"Ky, call 911. My panties are melting."

God, how I used to tease her about it. Told her no one was *that* good-looking. I was wrong. I'd never make fun of Nat again. It seemed I finally found the one man who could actually make my panties melt.

Unfortunately, it just so happened to be the infuriating, frustrating, devastatingly sexy jerk, Sebastien "The Sinner" St. Clair. God, he was such a bad idea. There wasn't even a word for how bad an idea he was, and *that* only kicked Reckless Kylie's interest up another sizzling notch.

Nat, call 911. My heart's about to stop and my brother is going to kill me.

Because I knew, no matter how stupid it was, I was going to meet Sebastien St. Clair at that hotel.

5

Seb

I showered and dressed faster than I thought possible, wanting an advantage over Calloway when I confronted him. Or beat the snot out of him. Whichever. The guy had been a dick throughout the game, even refusing to speak to me about plays, which was unacceptable. The team shouldn't suffer because one guy wants to be a bastard.

Speak of the devil... Sasquatch emerged from the showers, a towel wrapped around the tree trunk he called a waist. Wearing my NHL mandated suit and tie, I at least felt like I had the upper hand as I approached, what with Calloway half naked and all.

The big defenseman's back was facing me when I came to a stop a few feet from Calloway's cubby.

"Calloway."

His heavily muscled shoulders bunched up tight. Oh yeah, Sasquatch knew I stood behind him, yet the rude asshat continued to get dressed, forcing me to wait, which pissed me right the fuck off. *Twitch, twitch, twitch...* The brushoff combined with the infuriating spasms in my left eye sparked an all-too-familiar wrath deep in my gut. My emotions, and actions, were about to spiral out of control if I couldn't get a grip.

I closed my eyes, clenched my hands, and breathed. In through the nose... one... two. Out through the mouth... one... two. I continued breathing as I pictured the invisible demon that rode me for most of my life, and with both hands, pushed back at my infamous temper. In... one...two. Out... one... two. When I was calm enough to open my eyes, I found Calloway in his suit, looming over me, scowl firmly in place.

"What do you want, St. Clair?"

Calloway's tone held the disdain of someone who stepped in a pile of dog shit while wearing a new pair of Pradas. I swallowed back the urge to say fuck it and pummel Bigfoot's face into ground beef. Instead, I shoved my hands into my pockets to make them behave. Punching a teammate in the locker room on his first day was highly frowned upon. I would know. I may or may not have done it once... or twice. Possibly three times, but that one was not my fault.

I exhaled and worked my jaw back and forth, then stepped closer, hating that I had to tip my head back so I wasn't staring at Sasquatch's thick neck. *How tall was he anyway? Seven fucking feet?* I sucked up as much pride as possible and swallowed down the bile that threatened to rise.

"We're teammates now, which means whether we like it or not, we have a duty to protect each other's asses."

Calloway raised a single dark brow, which made me want to slap the condescension right off the motherfucker's face. "So?"

"So..." I growled, already sick of the patronizing attitude. "Just because we're on the same team doesn't mean I'm going to sit back while you intentionally injure my little bro. Don't think for a minute there won't be repercussions if you do." Without realizing it, my hands had curled into fists in my pockets, squeezing so tight my fingernails were going to leave grooves in my palms.

Sasquatch's response to my threat wasn't anger, wasn't aggravation. Wasn't even slight annoyance. No, the fucker grinned.

"Repercussions? Like what?" He scoffed and summarily dismissed me with a casual wave of one of his massive meat paws. "Fuck off, St. Clair."

When the *maudit bâtard* turned around and showed me his backside, I darted out a hand, grabbed Calloway's massive bicep, and squeezed just hard enough to let him know it wasn't an empty threat. I was dead serious. His wide grin faded into a sneer and his black eyes flashed.

"Get your hand off me before I rip it from your body and use it as a puck."

Hmph. Straight to violence. Maybe we're more similar than I thought. And wasn't that as unwelcome as a turd in a punch bowl.

I released Calloway's arm, but didn't back off. "You're going to learn something about me, Sasquatch." I ignored Calloway's low growl. It took most of my concentration not to slip into my native Québécois. I wanted him to know exactly what I was saying. "I might be an asshole with a violent streak a mile long, but I'm *very* protective of my friends and family, and I'm fiercely goddamn loyal." I leaned in closer. "Believe me when I say, you don't want to test exactly how protective or how loyal I can be." I relaxed my features and took a step back. "Now, you can either be a part of the group I protect," I brushed off my lapels, "or the object of my anger. It's your choice."

The world must've stopped spinning because, to my utter shock, Calloway's harsh expression faded. Not much, but hey, I took what I could get, if it meant I wouldn't end up suspended for busting Sasquatch's big fat jaw, or flattened under his size sixteens. He nodded and I thought I might have just landed in the *Twilight Zone*.

"That's the first thing that's ever come out of your mouth I actually respect."

My jaw hit the floor. Honest to god, I hadn't expected him to agree and had no response when he did. For once in my life, I was struck dumb. I scrambled for a reply that didn't involve hitting something or come across as condescending.

I failed spectacularly.

"Uhhh, oh. Well, okay then. So... good talk." I took another step back. "I'm glad we agree." Calloway cocked his head, narrowed his eyes, and gave me a strange look, then turned back to his locker to finish getting dressed.

That was... weird. And unexpected.

I took a moment to mull over our conversation, then decided it was time to leave before Calloway changed his mind and rounded back on me with a donkey punch to the head. Plus, I had somewhere to be, and I couldn't fucking wait. I wasn't ashamed to admit I was a little freaked out by Calloway's seemingly easy capitulation, but I was also vibrating with excitement to see if Hot Blonde accepted my invitation.

"Sebby!" Evvy caught up with me by the door and walked out to the player's lot alongside me. The hotel was attached to the arena, but there was no way I was leaving my car here. Too many questions. "A bunch of us are going out. You in?"

"You know I hate it when you call me Sebby."

Evvy smirked. "Yeah, but St. Clairey or Clairezy doesn't have that snappy sound to it." He gave me a playful shove.

I chuckled and pretended to take a minute to think about his offer. Didn't want Ev to start asking questions. No way was I about to jinx my chance with Hot Blonde by talking about her. Plus, I had no doubt Evvy would have plenty to say about my stalkerish way of reaching out.

"Nah, go on without me." I had to believe she would be at the hotel bar. The alternative was too pathetic to consider. I began to walk away.

"Whoa." Evvy snagged the collar of my suit jacket and jerked us both to a stop. Bastard made me stumble back. I turned to glare at my friend for almost putting me on the ass of my best Tom Ford. "*You* don't want to go out?" Evvy's eyebrows flew to his hairline. "I know you broke up, uh... whatever you had with Amanda, so you're not going to her place." He squinted at me. "Who are you and what have you done with Seb?"

I gave what I hoped was a casual shrug and with a genuine smile, gave Evvy's back a hardy smack. "Guess I'm just not in the mood."

For the millionth time that night, my thoughts drifted back to Hot Blonde. The shock on her face when she opened the box was priceless. And then there was that amazing moment. The one where our gazes met. *Merde.* I shook my head. I had to stop thinking about her. It bordered on creepy and wasn't healthy. Plus, I was in serious danger of popping wood in front of Ev. If that happened, he would pelt me with questions I wouldn't want to answer. Friend or not, better to keep Evvy out of the loop. In fact, I was beginning to regret I mentioned her to him at all.

"*You're* not in the mood," Evvy repeated. "You?"

Amused, I grinned and walked backwards toward my truck. I tossed the keys in the air and caught them as I spun around and called out, "Yep," over my shoulder.

The system beeped when I unlocked the doors and without another word to my dumbstruck teammate, I got in my truck, pulled out of the parking space, and steered toward the exit. As I drove down the block to the hotel parking lot—yes it was walking distance, but it was fucking cold out—I glanced in the rearview to find Evvy standing in the same spot I left him in, catching flies with his gaping maw.

I threw my head back and laughed.

If Hot Blonde never existed and I was still screwing around with Amanda, I knew exactly how my evening would have gone. I'd go out for a few beers with the team, then head over to Amanda's despite knowing it was a shitty idea. Tonight, thank fuck, I had other plans. I sent up a quick prayer that Hot Blonde not only showed up, but was miraculously into bondage, otherwise, the evening could still turn out to be a bust.

You know she probably isn't, idiot. Most women aren't.

Nope. I shut down that train of thought immediately and forced my thoughts to stay positive. But I wasn't stupid. I knew I'd be spending my life alone. The likelihood of finding a woman who not only wanted the kink, but could deal with the rest of my fucked up baggage, didn't want me for my money, had no interest in the status of a hockey wife, and didn't set out to trap me with a baby, was statistically less than zero.

So, was asking for Hot Blonde to align with just one of my measly criteria too much to hope for?

Dear god, if it can only be one, please let it be the bondage.

While idling at the red light at the far corner of the arena parking lot, I glanced out the passenger window. Poor Evvy still hadn't moved. Even with all the crap going through my head, my screwed-up thoughts and near dangerous obsession with Hot Blonde, I found myself in a rare good mood. So good in fact, I couldn't stop laughing at my confused friend.

Evvy would have to get used to me not hanging out after games as much as I used to, because whether or not Hot Blonde showed up tonight, I wasn't going to be around much. I'd either be busy spending all my free time on achieving my new number-one goal: getting the feisty woman in my bed until she squirmed and panted and cried out beneath me, or my new number-one pastime: fucking her senseless.

I brought up an image of her defiant expression when she opened the box—eyes blazing and thick, cock-sucking lips pulled into a frown—and my dick began to swell. She was just so damn hot. I pressed my palm against my crotch and groaned. My entire body ached with need, yet the smile never left my face.

Feisty, gorgeous, *and* a hockey fan? All I needed to do was confirm she had no interest in me beyond getting naked, and a penchant for rough, slightly kinky sex, and I was golden.

Jesus, I really, really hoped so. Only one night so far and already Hot Blonde proved to be fun to chase. I knew she would be even more fun to catch, and breaking her down piece by piece until she screamed my name over and over would be my greatest achievement so far.

If she blew me off, she'd better be equipped to handle what came next, because there was no way in hell I was going to stop pursuing her. Not until I got what I wanted. I pictured Hot Blonde's look of disgust as she held up my gift. Her pissed off scowl. The glare she aimed my way. All of it sent a white-hot streak of desire careening down my spine. Just knowing how irritated I made her, made me happy and pleasure unfurled in my groin.

Did it make me sick that her potentially hating me turned me on? Maybe, but what difference did it make? I was already twenty kinds of twisted and forty kinds of fucked up in the head. There wasn't much that could make it any worse.

Hot Blonde was a challenge. *That's* what got me hard. The challenge. The thrill of the chase and what I would do once I caught her. I reached down, adjusted my cock, and drove, single-mindedly, into the parking garage of the hotel.

Game on, blondie. Game fucking on.

Kylie

This was so stupid. Probably the dumbest thing I'd ever done.

I glanced in the mirror behind the bar to check my makeup. Huge mistake. The woman reflected back at me was a freaking wreck. My cheeks were flushed and bottom lip swollen from where I kept chewing on it, hair all tousled from running nervous hands through the length. I was a hot mess.

"Excuse me. Can I buy you a drink?"

I closed my eyes and counted backwards from three. He was the third man to hit on me since I took a seat at the hotel bar twenty minutes ago. When I opened them, I took one final look at myself. The woman I saw, the one whose stomach twisted and flipped, didn't appear nervous. In fact, she looked like she might feel several different emotions, but definitely not nervous. Excited? Yes. Turned on? Yes. Thrilled at the prospect of coming face to face with Sebastien St. Clair? Definitely.

She looked... hungry for sex.

Maybe that was why men were drawn to me like flies. They sensed my longing. Could read my filthy thoughts. Maybe I projected every single dirty fantasy I ever had about Sebastien St. Clair for the world to see.

"Hi, I'm Ken. What's your name?"

It took a lot of effort to hold back both the epic eye roll and the annoyed huff I so badly wanted to unleash. I had to remember it wasn't Ken's fault. I should be flattered he found me attractive. The irritation was on me, not him. Like the good girl I was pretending to be, I whipped up an insincere smile and let him down gently, just as I did the two men previous.

"Kylie. And no, thank you. I'm waiting for someone."

Ken smiled, and *wow*, he was beautiful. Two perfect rows of gleaming white teeth framed by adorable dimples that gave him a playful look. One that likely got him any woman he wanted. When you took his bright green eyes and dirty blonde hair into consideration, plus the tailored suit that showed off his fit body, Ken was a walking dream. Only, he came across as *nice*. And lucky me, because I'm completely depraved, *nice* turned me off.

"That's too bad. I'm in town for a convention and could use some company."

My mouth fell open and my face heated up. Maybe Ken wasn't all that nice, because that sounded a lot like a proposition. And yes, the only reason I was sitting at this bar was due to a proposition made by Sebastien St. Clair. I was well aware my judgment made me a hypocrite. Ken, who had to be some kind of mind reader, knew what I was thinking, and did damage control by holding up his hands and letting out a deep chuckle, though he looked somewhat horrified.

"Wait! No. I mean, I wasn't looking for... *that*, necessarily." He checked me out again, gaze flicking up and down, and my face burst into flames. "Though I wouldn't say no. But seriously, I'm just looking for company as in someone to talk to."

Okay, so maybe he was nice. Mostly. I opened my mouth to politely decline, but someone beat me to it. Someone not so polite. Someone with a slight French accent that made my insides quiver.

"Hey, asshole, you're sitting in my seat."

Ken and I turned at the same time. When I got a look at the newcomer, I nearly swallowed my tongue. Standing next to me, closer than friends, yet not as close as I would have liked, was Sebastien St. Clair in all his tall, athletic, and muscled glory. His black suit hugged every inch of his impressive frame. Paired with a charcoal gray shirt and black tie, the look came across as sleek and refined. I'd seen the man out of his hockey gear before, talking at press conferences on the television, but *damn*, TV does *not* do him justice. Sebastien St. Clair is stunning. With his dark hair slicked back and the matching dark suit, his light eyes popped. And at the moment, those brilliant blues were laser-focused on Ken, shooting him a withering glare.

If looks could kill, poor Ken would be six feet under.

"It's okay," I said to Sebastien to cut off a confrontation before it started. "We were just —"

"I said, fuck off." Sebastien growled, ignoring me as he continued to glower at a bewildered Ken. Hostility poured off Sebastien in thick, suffocating waves. Ken steeled his jaw and slid off the barstool, ready to exchange words with the boorish interloper, except, when he got to his feet, poor Ken got a good look at how many inches Sebastien towered over him and how much broader he was across the shoulders. Ken gulped and his defiance slid away.

"My mistake," Ken said calmly. He glanced at me to make sure I was okay, and I appreciated the gesture. I gave him an almost imperceptible nod. "Then I was just leaving." The man took off as fast as his feet would take him, and I didn't blame him one bit.

My 'date'—*what a joke. We both knew why we were here and it wasn't for a date*—seated himself on Ken's vacated stool, pleased as punch, as if he hadn't just scared a man shitless. Then, agonizingly slow, he ran his hungry gaze from my head down to my toes, giving me a thorough once-over that was more of an eye-fuck than anything else. Never in my life had I been so ecstatic to have dressed up for a hockey game. With zero idea of what was to come, I put on my best jeans and a cute off-the-shoulder shirt. The only change I made between the arena and that moment was to strip off the generic Comets jersey and stash it in my car.

"Great first impression," I said as I leveled a flat look at an unapologetic Sebastien. "That wasn't very nice."

Sebastien waved off the approaching bartender. While doing so, his piercing gaze never once strayed from my face. "He was trying to take what was mine. That doesn't go over well with me."

Was this guy for real?

"Yours?" I scoffed. "I'm not yours." I didn't know why, but that wasn't exactly true. The thought of being 'his' sent my pulse racing and made every muscle in my body clench tight with anticipation. Yeah, part of me absolutely *loved* the idea belonging to Sebastien St. Clair.

He leaned in close—the scent of his aftershave made me swoon, light and crisp and masculine— and whispered. His voice was all raspy and seductive and went straight between my thighs.

"I promise, after tonight you'll beg to be mine."

The assumption that I was a sure thing offended me, yet I couldn't deny that I came to the hotel knowing exactly what he expected.

"I don't beg."

Another lie. Well, maybe not quite. I would happily beg... For the right man. I just wasn't sure I'd met him yet.

Sebastien shifted even closer and his breath ghosted across my ear. "There's a first time for everything. What's your name, gorgeous?"

I shuddered. Such unrepentant cockiness should be a turnoff. And to most people it would be. So far, Sebastien was rude, arrogant, and to be honest, kind of intimidating. But I'm not most people. I loved every single second of it. Ate up his attitude with a spoon like I was a lonely cat-lady and it was a pint of mint chocolate chip Häagen-Dazs. My mouth watered and my nipples pulled tight. I had no idea what to say.

Yeah, I'd totally beg.

"Kylie."

"I'm Seb." As if I didn't know that. Seb casually produced a room key and held it up between two fingers. "Care to get out of here..." His heated gaze felt like a physical caress and I had to bite my lip to keep from moaning and embarrassing myself. "Kylie?"

I shouldn't. In fact, I should run. Far, far away. But before I set foot inside the bar—heck, before I left the game—I knew wouldn't. I *couldn't*.

Except, sweet, naive, Kylie Calloway doesn't do one night

stands. She doesn't do dangerous men. And she definitely doesn't do cocky jerks. But Reckless Kylie? *Oh god*, she wanted what he offered. More than anything. Was aching for it. And she was sick and tired of sitting on the sidelines, waiting for life to find her.

So yes, I was going to do this.

"Lead the way."

Seb's lips pulled into a knowing smile that somehow managed to convey every sordid fantasy I'd ever had about the man, and at the same time let me know he had no problem with making each and every one come true.

I followed him into the elevator and breathed. This was really happening. My pulse was brisk, but I wasn't frightened. Something about the man at my side kept me calm. Like his very presence soothed my nerves. Seb made it easy to do what felt right, even as my brain shouted at the top of its lungs that it was inherently wrong.

The door beeped as it unlocked and Seb held it open for me to enter first.

"Nice." I glanced around the large room to mask my anxiety. It was the same hotel Rocco and I were living in until we found something more permanent, so I knew what to expect. While Seb didn't have a suite—because, let's be real, why bother for a booty call—the room had the same inviting décor as ours, done in cool shades of blue and grey. My gaze locked onto the king-sized bed, with its fluffy white duvet and piles of thick pillows. I gulped.

"Drink?"

I tore my gaze from the bed to find Seb standing by a small bar in a corner of the room, a decanter of amber liquid in his hand. I knew he wasn't interested in drinking. He was giving me a chance to relax.

I shook my head. No way did I want my senses compromised. Not because I thought he'd take advantage of me, but because I wanted to remember every single second of whatever happened next. Sear the images onto my brain so I could recall them any time I chose.

Seb's mischievous smile returned. It's amazing how the one tiny action sparked every nerve ending in my body. Little electric jolts crackled and snapped, sending a flush of heat from the top of my scalp to the soles of my feet. He took a step toward me and my breath hitched.

Nervous? Yep. But mostly, I was exhilarated. Being on the receiving end of the gorgeous, dangerous man's focused attention was completely addictive and entirely too arousing.

Seb stopped in front of me, eyes searching my face for a brief moment before he lifted his hands to cup my cheeks. His fingers were so long they curved all the way around the back of my head. He leaned in and pressed his lips to mine. When our mouths connected, it felt like a pile of TNT detonated. Instantly, I went up in flames, from passive observer to active participant in the blink of an eye. Suddenly, I couldn't get enough of him. I shoved my greedy hands under his jacket and swept them up his sides, then gasped at the rock-hard muscles that shifted beneath my palms.

That gasp gave Seb the opening he needed, and likely never one to miss an opportunity, he took full advantage. When my lips parted, Seb thrust his hot, slick tongue into my mouth, devouring as much as he could get. He tasted amazing, dark and sinful, and wholly masculine. I couldn't believe it. Sebastien St. Clair, object of most of my fantasies over the last year and a half or so, was kissing me, Kylie Calloway.

At some point Seb's hands wandered, because he was kneading my backside in a sensual massage. He used a firm grip and tugged me forward until our bodies collided. The hard ridge of his erection dug into my hip and Seb groaned into my mouth. The vibrations traveled straight between my thighs. Knowing I was the one who got the infamous Sebastien St. Clair, the "bad boy" of hockey, all worked up and growly and desperate, was so erotic I was shaking.

I clawed at his clothing, trying to push his jacket over his shoulders, but Seb wouldn't let go of my ass long enough for me to succeed. When he tore his mouth away, I whined. *Literally* whined. I should have been humiliated, not just for sounding so pathetic, but because after one—granted, smoking hot—kiss and two minutes of dry humping, Sebastien reduced me to a trembling, needy mess. Good thing in the heat of the moment, I couldn't have cared less what he thought. In the bar less than an hour ago, I said I wouldn't, but honest to god, I was ready to *beg* if that was what it took to get Seb naked.

"Strip."

I blinked at the command. *He wanted me to...?*

"S-strip? You... you want me to, ummm, strip?"

I might have been willing to beg, but putting on a show was a whole different disaster in the making considering I was about as graceful as a baby giraffe on ice skates.

Sebastien's eyes darkened and he licked his swollen lips. "Yes." He let go of me and sat on the edge of the bed, expectant.

Oh my god. I could be persuaded to do a lot of things, but not that.

I opened my mouth to say no and my throat practically closed up. Dress shirt wrinkled, tie loose and tugged haphazardly to the side, hair mussed—Sebastien St. Clair was a sight to behold. His cheeks were flushed and his full lips were all puffy and red from kissing me. He looked like pure sin. And as tempting as he was, it wasn't his physical beauty that did it for me. No, it was the look in his eyes that had me saying, "Yes." The man was so turned on, the black of his pupils eclipsed the bright blue.

The fact that I, Kylie Calloway, a girl who scurried away like a coward when faced with having sex with the lowly Grant Pierce, could affect a man like Sebastien St. Clair, *that* was the rush I was after, and it gave me the confidence to do what he asked.

I ran my fingers along the waistband of my jeans flicked open the button. "Like this?" Sebastien made a strangled sound and I preened at the response. As I lowered the zipper, I pulled my lower lip between my teeth and sucked.

"*Mon dieu, oui.* Just like that," he whispered, his breaths coming fast and hard. Sebastien's glorious chest heaved up and down, causing the buttons of his shirt to strain. "*Tu est parfait.*"

I didn't know French, but he could have made a comment on the weather and I'd have been turned on.

Ignoring my zipper, I reached for the hem of my shirt. Sebastien's eyelids were half-closed, and he licked his lips like he couldn't wait to get a taste. He reclined on the bed, upper body propped on one elbow as he massaged the straining bulge through his pants. I inched my shirt to expose the taut skin of my abdomen a sliver at a time. As I pulled it over my head, I heard a low growl. Large hands grasped my waist and I squealed as I was tossed onto the bed.

I bounced on the mattress and was divested of my shirt before I reacted. I blinked twice to regain my bearings and found Sebastien already kneeling between my splayed legs. His jacket was gone and his shirt halfway undone. Face-to-face with his perfect, rippling six pack, I could only gawk.

Seb chuckled and I glanced up. He froze, mid-unbutton, his eyes burning with need.

"Sorry, I changed my mind about the show."

I had no response. My brain short-circuited. I couldn't think. Not with Seb's shirt hanging open, exposing the most exquisite torso I'd ever laid eyes on. Wide, sculpted pecs that were surprisingly smooth, with only a tiny amount of dark hair sprinkled in the center, topped a set of abs cut with so many grooves and ridges it would take a week to explore them all... preferably with my tongue.

"You going to help me out, or just lie there?" I tore my gaze from his mouthwatering body to look at Seb's face. He smirked and gestured toward my jeans. "Take them off." His fingers continued to work on removing his own clothes. Seb unbuckled his belt and the clang of metal made me flinch. Seb shucked his pants and waited for me to obey the command.

Yes, sir.

I couldn't move fast enough. Unfortunately, skinny jeans cannot be removed quickly. It took a bit of maneuvering, but after the most frustrating fifteen-seconds of my life, I finally kicked them free. I turned back to Seb and bit the inside of my cheek to keep from pouncing on him like an animal. Stripped down to only a pair of charcoal gray boxer briefs and a rosy flush that stained his neck and upper chest, Seb was without a doubt the most stunning human being alive.

Once I was down to a matching lacy black bra and panties —*thank you Jesus for reminding me to do laundry yesterday*— Sebastien lunged. In one swoop, he gathered my wrists in one of his huge hands, maneuvered them over my head, and held them there, using his body to press me into the mattress. He was no lightweight. I was trapped beneath him with no way to escape. And I *loved* it. The walls of my pussy clenched around nothing but empty space and I whined with need. Desperate, I lifted my hips to get some friction.

"Ah, ah, ah. No moving," Seb chastised. I stared into his eyes, and wondered what he saw in mine. Could he see how frantic and horny I was? How much I wanted what he was doing to me? "You like this," he rasped and gave my wrists a squeeze. My belly clenched as a bolt of pleasure shot straight to my pussy. I gasped and squirmed in his tight hold. "You do. You like being held down." The excitement in his voice was unmistakable, almost reverent. Like me, Seb hovered on the edge of losing his composure.

Was it possible he shared my darkest fantasy? The carnal look on Seb's face said yes, so I pushed every ounce of embarrassment aside, and for the first time in my life, confessed my desires to another person.

"Y-yes. I like being held down. I mean, I like having *you* hold me down," I clarified, because, let's be honest, I'd never been held down. Seb's eyes flashed hungrily and another wave lust crashed over me. I had to concentrate not to arch off the bed or rub up against him like a dog in heat.

"Can I tie you up?" Seb thrust his hips down, finally pressing his hard, thick length where I needed it most. Of course, Seb knew what I wanted and ground his hips in teasing little circles, enough to drive me crazy, but not to get me off.

A plaintive wail escaped before I could stop it. *Oh god.* I did want him to tie me up. So much. But... I didn't really know him. Being rendered vulnerable sounded good in the recesses of my fantasies, but to do it for real? The thought was daunting. I chickened out with Grant Pierce, afraid of being helpless. Only, I wasn't afraid of Sebastien St. Clair. For whatever reason, I trusted him.

I gave a sharp nod. "You can tie my hands together. That's it. Not my feet, and not to the headboard."

Baby steps.

Seb grinned. "Couldn't do that even if I wanted to." He winked and once again, ground his cotton-clad erection between my thighs, driving me wild. I thrashed beneath him as pleasure rippled through me. "Which I do. God, I really do. Too bad the headboard is solid and mounted to the wall. There's nothing to tie you to."

Oh.

Without letting go of my wrists, Sebastien groped behind himself with his free hand. He found what he wanted and brought it around where I could see it. My nostrils flared.

His tie.

"Now," he said, his voice so sexy and deep, he may as well have reached down and caressed my wet slit with his fingers. "You're going to be good while I do this." Slowly, building up my excitement until I was practically shaking with desire, Seb wrapped the silky material around my wrists. "I won't make it too tight, that way you'll be able to get free if you need to." The swish of the fabric sliding against itself as he tied the knot added to the erotic atmosphere. "There." Seb tugged on one end and sat back on his haunches to inspect his work. His pupils grew as his gaze flicked up and down. "Fuck, you're even hotter than I ever could have imagined."

By that point, my attention had fixated on Seb's body, taking in every last dip and curve. I was too busy studying the flex and ripple of muscles beneath smooth, tan skin, and the tantalizing trail of dark hair that disappeared under the band of his boxer briefs, to notice the way he was staring at me. Until, that is, I finished my perusal and glanced up. He stole the breath out of my lungs.

No man *ever* looked at me the way Sebastien St. Clair did. Like he wanted to devour me whole. Like he had so many delicious options spread out in front of him, he couldn't decide where to start. The ensuing blush burned all the way to my ears. I squirmed and rubbed my thighs together, horny, wet, and beyond ready.

Seb shuffled back and placed his hands on my ankles. He took his time torturing me, sliding his palms up my legs inch by inch. I couldn't take my eyes off of him and held my body perfectly still as I waited to see what he would do next. When he neared the place I so desperately wanted him to touch, the bastard skipped over it, instead shifting up to caress my ribs. When he reached my shoulders, Seb straddled my hips. The pressure felt good, but wasn't nearly enough. He knew that, of course, and that crooked, handsome smirk came out to play. In an unexpected move, Seb stuck his index fingers in the cups of my bra and yanked them down, hooking the material beneath my exposed breasts.

"Fuck, you're so goddamn gorgeous."

With him sitting on my hips, looking but not touching, I was beyond desperate, ready to beg for something... *anything*, to ease the pressure that throbbed between my thighs. He cupped my breasts and gently kneaded them. The callouses on his hands provided an amazing sensation, rough and abrasive against my delicate skin. Watching my reactions carefully, Seb rolled my nipples between his thumbs and forefingers. I was never much for nipple play, as it didn't really do it for me. But when Seb gave the tender buds a firm twist, my hips flew off the bed and I nearly came.

"Yessss..." I hissed.

"Too hard?"

I stared up at my smoking hot, slightly deviant, sexy as hell bed partner through hooded lids. After licking my parched lips, I shook my head and admitted what I wanted.

"Harder."

Seb's expression transformed from turned on to wicked. He looked like a man who just received the best present of his life. Blue eyes glittered with an almost sadistic glee.

Seb did as requested and pinched my nipples with more force and twisted them. I screamed in ecstasy as my pussy spasmed. The orgasm took both of us by surprise. Seb grinned as I writhed and moaned and wriggled beneath him. By the time the final shudder ran through me, I lay on the bed, sweaty and panting,

"Oh baby, you and I are going to have so much fun."

Seb

I had to be the luckiest bastard in the world. Not only did I have the sexiest woman I'd ever seen in my bed, but she was my perfect complement. Hands above her head, bound together with my tie, breasts exposed and trussed up by her own bra, and only a tiny scrap of black lace between me and her pussy, Kylie was my ultimate wet dream.

Her body was a work of art. But not one of those fussy, snobby paintings. More real. She was meant to be touched, played with, roughed up and used. Not kept on a shelf behind glass. All those sleek muscles and pale skin were the perfect complement to her swollen lips and her raw, red nipples.

I dared to hope Kylie was into the same kind of shit as me, not that it mattered. The woman was so damn hot I would have gladly fucked her even if she said hell no to being tied up. But she didn't say no. She said *yes*. Then she climaxed just from having her nipples abused. That's when I knew I was in trouble. Kylie could easily become an addiction. A complication. One I didn't need.

You have a hot, kinky, half-naked woman in your bed panting for you to fuck her, you idiot. Worry about all that other shit later.

A light sheen of sweat glistened on Kylie's chest and her breaths were hard and fast as she came down from her orgasm.

"Fuuuck. That's so hot," I said as I trailed my fingertips down her arms. She wiggled and goose bumps broke out on her skin.

"That tickles."

I shifted and flexed my abs, pleased when her gaze lasered in on them. "And you don't want to be tickled, do you?" I didn't give her time to answer. "No, you don't. You want something a little harsher." Already flushed from coming, Kylie's cheeks grew even redder. She glanced away, unable to look at me. I grabbed her chin and tugged until she had no other choice. "You do, don't you? You want me to hurt you." I waited, but she said nothing. Impatient, I huffed. "I need you to tell me, Kylie, otherwise I won't do it. I have to be sure you want it."

Lips parted and eyes clouded with lust, Kylie nodded.

"Say it. Out loud."

She squirmed, then closed her eyes and took a deep breath. "I want that. I want you to..." She swallowed. "To hurt me, just a little."

A little. A lot. I didn't care and neither did my neglected cock, which throbbed at her admission. I couldn't take it anymore. I had to get some friction on it or I'd go insane. I shifted until I lay completely on top of her, our bodies pressed together from chest to toes. In what must be a nervous gesture, she licked those thick, cock-sucking lips again. If only she knew how every time she did it, a ripple of lust shot directly to my groin. I crashed my mouth down on hers for a hot, wet kiss, then licked and bit my way down her neck and throat. Her skin tasted salty, yet divine, the scent and flavor utterly feminine and frighteningly addictive. I gave each of her nipples a quick suck followed by a vicious bite. Kylie cried with pleasure and her back bowed off the bed.

I wanted to linger on her breasts. See if I could make her come again by sucking and biting them, but I had a bigger goal in mind, and refused to be sidetracked. Kissing along her abdomen, I paused to lap at her belly button.

Kylie bucked and thrashed, and not in a good way. Her breath caught as she squealed, "Stop it."

I grinned against her skin. "You're ticklish here too?"

Kylie sounded wrecked, her voice pure sex. "Y-yes. And I don't...*ahhhhh*, like it."

I stopped what I was doing and met her gaze. Christ, Kylie had no fucking clue how stunning she looked, especially writhing at the receiving end of my tongue. Her pupils were blown and she had her bottom lip caught between her teeth.

"I didn't think so," I said. "You prefer the bite of pain."

She surprised me by admitting it without hesitating. "Yes."

Fuck, I had to have more. Needed to know everything Kylie liked, everything she craved, fulfill her darkest desires, leave no inch of skin unexplored. Make her scream until she was hoarse then make her beg until she cried for more.

Then, when she was tapped out emotionally and physically, I wanted to start all over again.

I moved lower, my mouth hovering over her lace-clad pussy.

"Pleasure before pain," I said with a smile.

"Oh god," she whispered. Unable to stay still, Kylie wiggled her hips.

"Don't move."

She stilled, but I could tell she struggled to comply. Going by her heavy panting, Kylie really wanted what I was offering, which made me smile. I gripped either side of her hips and pressed them into the mattress, then exhaled over the damp fabric.

"*Ohmygod*. Seb... I need..." I breathed out again and Kylie threw her head back and let out a long, raspy moan that made my dick throb. "*Ahhhh*, I need more."

Fuck, I couldn't wait to taste her. I yanked the scrap of lace to the side, then stuck out my tongue and licked a wide stripe along her slit. *Fuuuck*. My eyes rolled back in my head. Everything else about Kylie was perfect. Why would she taste anything but delicious?

"D-don't stop."

Kylie pushed her bound hands against the back of my head. Without moving my face away from her pussy, because no way was I going to move from my new favorite place, I used one hand to grab her wrists and put them back over her head.

"I'll give you more. Be patient." She groaned, but didn't say another word. I pushed her wrists into the mattress and growled, "Stay."

I smiled and released her arms, pleased when she didn't try to move them. With both hands, I grabbed the thin lace straps on either side of her hips. Taking my directive to stay still to heart, Kylie didn't lift her hips to help as I removed the tiny thong. Her compliance made my dick throb. Again, she was fucking perfect.

Except for the bra trapped under her breasts, I had Kylie completely naked and exposed.

"*Calisse de crisse de tabarnak d'ostie de ciboire de testament.* You are so damn hot. Better than I imagined."

She was a natural blonde, of that I had no doubt. The trimmed strip of hair above her shaved pussy was only a shade or two darker than the golden waves on her head. With a hand on her thighs, I spread her wide. The pink flesh glistened with her arousal. Normally, I prided myself on my control. With Kylie, I wasn't sure I could remember the meaning of the word. She smashed my composure like a sledgehammer. I couldn't wait any longer.

Time for the teasing to end, more for my own sanity than hers. I dove in and ate her out like my life depended on it. Kylie gasped and again, placed her bound hands on the back of my head. I stopped and she wailed.

"No!"

"Keep your hands up," I ordered, more force in the command than before. Kylie's entire body shuddered. *Merde*, she loved it when I told her what to do. It was fucking stunning. My cock hurt so bad I actually started to hump the mattress.

Once her hands were where they belonged, I got back to work and ran the flat of my tongue up the length of her pussy. She tasted divine, sweet like honey. The knowledge that I was tainting all that sweetness made the act even hotter. I licked all around, slicking her pussy lips and flicking her clit on each pass. Kylie moaned and whimpered as she tried to break the grip I had on her hips so she could arch against my face, but I held tight.

Her quiet whimper of frustration was such a fucking turn on, I slid my tongue lower and thrust it into her pussy. That, combined with the slow circles I drew on her clit with my thumb, and minutes later, her body tensed and she screamed my name. I tongue-fucked her through her climax and watched her face. Kylie's jaw was clenched tight and the tendons of her neck taut as I wrung every last bit of pleasure from her body. When she collapsed, limbs loose and muscles limp, I climbed to my knees and grabbed the condom I snuck out of my pocket and stashed under the pillow while Kylie undressed.

I made quick work of rolling it down my rock-hard cock. I was so wound up, I jerked at the touch of my own hand. Fuck, if I wasn't careful, I'd blow the second I entered her tight little hole. Kylie stared up at me through hooded lids. What a fucking sight she made, hands bound, sweat at her collarbones, her entire body flushed pink with arousal. I grabbed her wrists with one hand and with the other, positioned my cock at her opening. I gave her one last questioning look, silently asking permission to proceed. When she sucked that swollen lip between her teeth and nodded, I wasted no time. In one hard thrust, I bottomed out inside her hot, wet channel.

"*Saint ciboire aux deux étages*, your pussy is fucking amazing," I said through clenched teeth. The Québécois came out instinctually, as it tended to do when my mind was busy being blown apart. Eyes closed, I held perfectly still, every muscle clenched, until the urge to explode passed.

"Fuck me, Sebastien, come on." Kylie jiggled her hips, making my balls pull tight.

Jesus fuck. Hearing my name on her lips almost tore the climax right from me.

"*Bout de crisse*." I shot Kylie a glare and in my deepest,

most threatening voice, said, "You don't give the orders around here, I do. Got it?"

Her pussy clenched around my dick and I let out a strangled shout. Clearly, I had her pegged. She fucking loved being bossed around.

Kylie was going to be the death of me. I'd be lucky if I lasted three minutes. I shoved one of her legs up and hooked her calf on my shoulder. One hand wrapped around her thigh, the other clamped around her wrists—probably hard enough to leave bruises and didn't that thought make me impossibly harder—I began to pump in and out, long, slow, agonizing strokes.

"Oh god," she moaned. "Yessss. So good."

Yeah, it *was* so good. Fucking fantastic, actually. Maybe the best I'd ever had, and I hadn't even climaxed yet. I fucked her harder and she took everything I had to give and more. Kylie's entire body jostled on the bed with each thrust, the smack of our skin adding to the erotic symphony of sounds. Her cries and pleading words, my grunts and groans, all it needed was...

I knew I was muttering in French, but the glazed look in Kylie's eyes let me know she didn't mind. In fact, it turned her on.

I released Kylie's wrists and warned her, "Don't move them." *Shit.* Another tight, rippling pulse of her pussy fisted my cock.

With one hand, I grabbed her face and squeezed Kylie's cheeks, hard enough to get her attention. Her eyes widened and I swear I felt her pulse around my cock as it kicked up a notch.

"I'm going to spank you. You want it?" I let go of her face and she licked her lips. Her pupils blew out and her eyes went dark. She nodded. "You don't like to admit what you like, do you?" I raised a brow and pulled my hips back, then plowed into her pussy, hard. "Don't like admitting what a deviant you are. Well, don't worry." I continued to punctuate each word with sharp jabs of my cock until I Kylie was wailing non-stop. When she neared the edge, I stopped and leaned over until my lips brushed her ear to whisper, first in French, then in English, "I'm a deviant, too. I won't tell anyone your secret, if you don't tell mine."

Not waiting for, or expecting, an answer, I straightened my spine and propped the backs of her thighs against my chest and held one of her calves on either side of my head. I knew I was close to the point of no return, so I had to make it count. I pistoned into her hard and fast, drilled her sweet pussy without mercy.

I raised one hand high and held it up so Kylie could see it coming and stop me if need be. She didn't. My palm landed on her flank with a resounding *smack*. I did it again, and fuck, Kylie screamed like she was dying from pleasure. *Fucking screamed*. Her pussy clenched so tight I was almost afraid my dick would get ripped clean off my body. I couldn't fight the urge to blow, so I didn't hold back. Two more shallow thrusts and I came on an ear-splitting cry, unleashing jet after jet of spunk into the condom.

Completely and utterly drained, I collapsed on top of Kylie and rolled to the side. As I lay there and caught my breath, after experiencing the best sex of my life, all I could think about was "did she like that" and "when can we do that again?"

And *that* was fucking scary.

6

Kylie

"Thanks for the help, Rita." I gave my new boss a small smile. Thankfully, my advisor at Georgetown called in a few favors and scored me the ultimate in journalism internships. I got to work—okay, for free, but still awesome—as a junior researcher at CNN.

"You're welcome, Kylie." Rita checked her platinum and diamond watch and frowned.

Rita Weissburg-Smith embodied everything I hoped to one day become. Strong, confident, and at ease in her own skin. Women in positions of power inevitably got slapped with labels like "bitch" or "emotional" or "harpy." When it happened to Rita, she let the hatred and insults slide right off her custom-tailored Valentino suit. The woman was brilliant, talented, and didn't care what anyone thought. She was amazing.

"It's late, so I'm heading out. You have a good weekend," Rita said as she tucked a lock of her shoulder-length dark hair behind her ear and effortlessly strode across the newsroom floor in three-inch heels that probably cost more than most people spent on clothes in an entire year. I sighed with envy. Rita looked every bit the role of powerful corporate executive.

"I will," I responded. The fib left a bad taste in my mouth. "You have a good one, too."

Rita disappeared and the click of her heels grew fainter with each step. I turned to gather my things from the drawer of my newly assigned cubicle on the huge newsroom floor. Piper Rigsby, one of a half-dozen interns who sat in the cluster of cubicles around mine, stopped typing to peer up at me.

"You could at least *try* to be convincing when you say that," Piper said.

Confused, I looked down at the pretty brunette who occupied cubical next to me. "Say what, exactly?"

Piper rolled her eyes and grinned. "If you're going to be a journalist, you need to sound confident and truthful. That..." She shook her head. "That was pathetic."

I scrunched my forehead. "I don't know what you're talking about."

"Exactly." Still smiling, Piper leaned back in her chair with an annoying smug look on her face. When I didn't respond, her smile slipped. Piper stood to meet me eye to eye, her expression sympathetic. "Hey, I know we're all journalists and everything," she waved around at the other interns, none of whom paid us any attention. "But I'm a good listener and I don't gossip. If you ever wanted to hang out, go get a drink or whatever, I'd be up for it."

It took me a few seconds to catch on. Wow. Piper was able to see right through my act. She knew everything I said was a front. Knew my smiles and attempts at making small talk were forced. In the weeks since I left DC, I realized the one thing I really missed was Nat. Having a best friend I could count on. Someone to talk to, spill my guts and know I would never be judged. Piper was offering to be that person.

Her background actually made her the perfect confidant, what little I knew, anyway. She graduated from Columbia and I remembered someone saying that when Piper lived in New York, she briefly dated one of the Yankees. It wasn't hard to believe. Piper was gorgeous, friendly, and perpetually happy. Easy to talk to and accepting of everyone, faults and all.

Maybe Piper was exactly what I needed. My moods had been all over the place since I spent the night—an amazing, thought consuming, life-changing night—with Sebastien St. Clair. I had been distracted and restless, like my skin shrank a size too small. Not unhappy, exactly, but not content either.

"You mean like tonight?" I shifted from one foot to the other, nervous.

Piper giggled. "Yes, like tonight. So what do you say?" She put on her coat and grabbed her bag. "Want to get out of here?"

I relaxed and gave her a small smile. Piper had a talent, an innate ability to make people comfortable, less tense. What made it special is that she didn't do it because she wanted something. It was simply Piper being herself.

"Desperately," I admitted.

"Come on, then." Piper jerked her head toward the exit. "I know just the place. We can walk."

For the first time in the seven or so days since I snuck out in the early hours of the morning and left Seb asleep in his hotel room, I laughed. The surprising part, is that it was genuine.

~

"So that's the gist of it."

I could tell Piper was trying not to let the shock show, not that I blamed her. It wasn't every day a coworker you hardly knew dropped a live grenade in your lap, then left you to fumble your way through putting the pin back in. But to Piper's credit, she remained calm and composed throughout my entire unbelievable story—Sebastien St. Clair, the bizarre gift, his proposition, and me ultimately agreeing to meet him at a hotel for sex with little to no hesitation.

Oh, believe me, I left out a ton of details. No one needed the skinny on exactly what went down in that hotel room. What Seb did to me. What I *let* him do. Those details would forever remain a secret between Seb and me. I still couldn't believe I shared my darkest desires with him, *out loud*. Not that I had any regrets. Seb turned my fantasies into the best night of my life.

"Well... That's, umm... Wow, Kylie. Just, uh, wow." Piper shook her head and slugged back the rest of her vodka tonic, then slammed the empty glass on the table.

I fidgeted and stared at my hands. Crap, I probably should have kept my big mouth shut. The prolonged silence that followed made me squirm until I glanced up at Piper only to find her lips pulled into a lopsided grin. She shook her head again, eyes sparkling.

"Girl, I don't know if I should high-five you for being amazingly awesome, or lecture you for being unthinkably stupid."

Relieved she wasn't judging me, I let out a huff. "I prefer the high-five, but I totally get why you think I'm stupid." Piper opened her mouth, but I held up a hand. "No, I get it. I don't know him, like, at all. Certainly not enough to meet him alone in a hotel room, especially since I didn't tell anyone where I was."

Piper gestured for the server and requested another round. After putting in our order, she turned to face me, giggled, and stretched her arm over the table, hand up, palm out. I stared at it until she cleared her throat.

"Seriously? You're going to leave me hanging?"

"Oh, umm. No." I touched my palm to Piper's in what would go down as the lamest high-five in the history of mankind. Piper laughed again and thanked our server when he deftly slid our drinks in front of us and cleared the empties. Piper lifted her full tumbler in the air and shook it, rattling the ice.

"I, for one, think this moment deserves a toast."

I squinted. "A toast? I thought you said what I did was stupid."

"Oh Kylie, believe me, what you did definitely fulfills the criteria for stupid." Despite the insult, Piper's wide grin was addictive, and I couldn't help but return it. "Just not for the reason you think."

Huh? I tilted my head and wrinkled my brow. "I don't get it. If it's not the obvious, what's the reason?"

With her free hand, Piper took hold of my wrist and raised my drink for me. "First, the toast." She clinked our glasses and leaned close. "You're stupid because..." Like a secret agent in an old spy film, Piper peeked to her left and right to check if anyone was listening before she continued. "If the sex was that great, you should have stayed long enough for round two." As I picked my chin up off the floor, Piper loudly announced, "To round two! It's always twice as nice."

If they weren't before, our neighbors were definitely

staring now. My face burned with humiliation, but I couldn't be mad. Piper had this way of disarming people, of turning an uncomfortable situation into a lighthearted one. Instead of dying of embarrassment and wanting to crawl under the table, I laughed along with her. Once the hysterics calmed down, I clinked to my glass to hers—willingly this time—and took a long swallow.

"I'll drink to that."

"Cheers," Piper proclaimed, lifting her vodka to her mouth.

We talked for hours, drinking and laughing until tears streamed from my eyes and my cheeks ached from smiling so much. Piper told me about her time in New York. What it was really like to date a famous athlete, all the way down to the dirty details and I ate up every last one.

"The scrutiny," she said with a wistful twist of her lips. "It sucked. One thing I learned is that people can be really mean."

My eyebrows rose. "Mean? Like how?"

Piper leveled a flat stare. "*Puh-lease*, Kiley. You must know what I'm talking about. Your brother plays for the freaking NHL."

I glanced around, hoping no one heard her mention Rocco. Everyone was absorbed in conversation. Satisfied, I shook my head. "Rocco doesn't date. I mean, I know he's not celibate or anything." The thought of my brother having sex made me shudder. "Never a serious girlfriend, though." I shrugged. "The press doesn't really write bad things about him."

Piper nodded. "Because he's one of the smart ones. Dating is hard enough for regular people. For those in the limelight, it's a freaking nightmare." She played with her drink, jabbing the half-melted ice cubes with the plastic stirring stick. "When I dated Brad, you know, the Yankee..." Piper's voice hitched and her eyes glistened. "The gossip columns and papers, and even people on the street, the things they said about me..." She blinked back tears and my heart ached for her.

"They trashed you?"

"Yeah, they did." Her voice was ragged and her cheeks flushed. A rush of sympathy welled up inside me for my friend. I reached across the table and took her hand.

"That sucks, Piper. I'm really sorry that happened."

She looked at me, her stare serious. "I hope you never experience it."

"I won't," I said a little too quickly. "I've been going to Rocco's games since I was fourteen. If anyone wanted to write about me, they would have by now. New York is different. It's like a fishbowl, all self-contained, and I've heard and seen how intense the fans are." I finished my drink and cupped the empty glass between my palms. "The... *thing*, whatever you want to call it, that I had with Sebastien," I waved my hand in the air to find the right words. "It was a one-off. He doesn't have my number and I don't have his. We didn't make plans to see each other again and I have no intention of doing so." I lowered my voice. "He can't ever know who I am. Like I said, Rocco would literally kill us both if he found out."

Elbow propped on the table, Piper rested her head on one hand and sighed. "You're so lucky. I always wanted a protective older brother." Her lips contorted into a puckered frown. "I'm an only child."

"Yeah, Rocco's great. Sometimes though, he can be smothering. Way too intense, you know? I guess I just wish he would give me the space to grow up and make my own mistakes."

Piper smirked. "Mistakes like Sebastien St. Clair?"

I winked. "Yeah. Mistakes like him. Totally worth it."

She threw her head back and laughed. "I know exactly what you mean." Her eyes sparkled with mischief. "Totally. Worth. It."

Seb

Try as he might to ruin my day, Rocco Calloway slammed into me over and over during practice, but not even Sasquatch could wipe the smile off my face. At the time, I felt like a jackass, but sending that note to Kylie ended up being one of the best decisions I'd ever made. I've had sex before, lots of it, in every way imaginable. But nothing compared to the utter rapture I felt when I thrust my cock into Kylie's tight pussy.

"Ow." I winced as my dick throbbed inside my cup. Hard-ons and protective gear don't mix well. The sharp pain in my groin made quick work of my swelling cock and I reached down and adjusted it.

Evvy's skates scraped ice as he came to a stop. "Problem?" He glanced at my junk and back up, grinning like an idiot. I yanked my hand away like it was on fire.

"Fuck off." I gave him a half-hearted shove. Bastard didn't move an inch. Evvy chuckled and shuffled close enough that none of the guys could overhear.

"Thinking about your Hot Blonde?"

I rolled my eyes. I knew telling Evvy about meeting up with Kylie was a mistake. Not that I gave him much. Just the basics—I propositioned her, she agreed, we fucked. Nothing else. Not even her name. For whatever reason, I wanted to keep her for myself, every last detail, the way she tasted, her scent, the sounds she made as she came. They were mine.

Only... they weren't, were they? For all I knew, she was fucking someone else this very minute.

"Dude. What the fuck is wrong with you?"

Evvy's voice snapped me out of my own head. I blinked and realized not only were we alone on the ice, everyone else having disappeared down the tunnel, but my jaw was clenched and I gripped my stick so hard with both hands, I was lucky it didn't snap in half. It took immense concentration, but I managed to relax my muscles as I shrugged off Evvy's concern.

"Nothing. I'm fine."

"Riiight. Okay, Sebby. Whatever." Ev pushed off and skated toward the tunnel.

"I told you not to call me that!" I shouted after him.

He held up a gloveless hand and flipped me the bird.

Asshole.

Coach instructed everyone to hang out after showering. He had an announcement to make. I already had a hunch as to what it might be, and if the lead cannonball in my stomach meant anything, I was right.

We gathered around our lockers, some of us sat, some didn't. I stood in front of mine, shoulder to shoulder with Ev. My job was awesome. I was a lucky bastard to get to play hockey for a living and I knew it, except for when shit like this went down.

"Shut the fuck up." The room fell silent at Coach's gruff bark. Frank Vernon commanded a room like no other. He was hands down the best coach I'd ever played for, even if he could be a total prick at times. His sharp gaze wandered, making eye contact with each of his men. "Management gave me the date for the annual team dinner." A chorus of groans and grumbles erupted. "I said, shut up!" Hands on hips, Coach shot everyone his death glare, perfected by years of dealing with young, stubborn hockey players. "I don't like it any more than you, but they're the ones that pay us and we hafta do what they say. Period." One of the veteran players mumbled under his breath. Coach's head whipped around and he literally snarled. "Franzie, got somethin' to say?"

Franzie shook his head, eyes wide. "No sir, Coach."

I hid a smirk behind my hand. Amazing. Coach V. could even make a bad ass future Hall of Famer like Dominic Francola tremble in his skates. While Coach gave out the details, my mind drifted back to Kylie. For the millionth time since that night, I wondered what would have happened if she stayed? Part of me wished she had, just so I could wake up, roll over, and take that pussy again. The other part of me was annoyed she beat me to the punch. *I* was the one who left someone in bed, not the one who *got* left. Hell, I probably only dozed off for a couple minutes, but when I woke, Kylie was gone. There hadn't been another home game since, so I didn't have a chance to see her, though I was undecided on what to do when I did.

Sending another note seemed desperate, and Sebastien St. Clair *wasn't* desperate. But I'd give my left nut to have her in my bed again. God, she was so damn responsive. Everything I did to her resulted in an amazing reaction, every slap, every thrust of my hips, fuck... I'd never made a woman come by playing with her tits before. That was the hottest thing I'd ever seen.

Evvy's sharp elbow dug into my side as Coach asked a question.

Oh shit.

"Sorry, Coach. I didn't hear you."

Coach frowned, jowls looking... well, jowl-ier than

usual. "I know, St. Clair. That's why I'm telling you to fucking pay attention!"

I straightened up and ignored Evvy's low chuckle. Bastard. Coach continued to explain that the dinner was mandatory, blah, blah, blah, same old bullshit as last year. And the year before. And the one before that.

He was almost done when the hairs on the back of my neck pricked. My gaze slid past Coach to land on Calloway. The look he was giving me was so dark, so menacing, so filled with loathing, I nearly flinched. Nearly. I would never give Bigfoot the satisfaction of thinking he got under my skin.

I glared back wondering what the fuck his problem was this time. I was the one who was black and blue from getting bashed into the boards over and over during practice. In fact, I was so caught up in everything Kylie, I didn't even bother to retaliate against the jerk. Not once.

When Coach turned his back to me, I mouthed, "Fuck you," to Calloway. Sasquatch didn't react, but I noticed his shoulders crank another notch higher. Dude was wound as tight as a nun's asshole. If he got any tighter, he'd shit fucking diamonds. Before Calloway had a chance to reply, Coach clapped his hands.

"Get out of here. Check your emails for directions to the restaurant, and for fuck's sake, look presentable." A quick exchange of glances with Evvy and we bolted for the door. As it closed behind us, I heard Coach tack on, "I'm talking to you, Lebedev, you goddamn slob."

Evvy and I cackled all the way to the parking lot. I might have been laughing, but inside I wondered what the hell was stuck up Calloway's ass this time. Knowing him, I was sure I'd find out soon enough.

~

"THEN WE TOOK the kids to the aquarium. Oh man, you should have seen them. It was so much fun to watch them press their cute little faces against the glass. I took a ton of pictures, see?"

My vision blurred around the edges as I zoned out in an attempt to protect my brain from the bombardment of three dozen identical photos of two small blonde children I couldn't tell apart, even if someone held a gun to my head. My idiot teammate went on and on about his rug rats, eagerly flipping through his phone to show me *all* the adorableness. Rude as it was, I couldn't gather enough energy to pretend to give a shit. Anyone who knew me should have a fucking clue, I'm not the type to give two shits about their kids. Or *any* kids. Or the aquarium for that matter.

The only thing that kept me from either dropkicking the guy's phone or dropping to the floor and convulsing, was the Jack and Coke in my hand.

Speaking of which...

I glanced behind me and noted the previously long line at the bar had dwindled.

"I gotta grab a new drink, Hallzy." I held up my empty glass and rattled the mostly melted ice.

"Oh sure. No problem." Second line center Jake Hall lowered his phone. His eyes glistened with disappointment.

Too bad all I could think as I turned on my heel was, *thank fuck, I'm free.*

The opportunity presented itself and I booked it, unable to get away fast enough. Another clutch of people I didn't want to talk to had gathered around the bar. Thankfully, most were immersed in their own discussions. Probably about more shit I was one hundred percent certain I didn't want to hear about. Aside from the impromptu family slide show, it was my lucky night, because I squeezed between two people unnoticed and had another Jack and Coke in my hand in less than three minutes.

Christ, my head ached. Pounded into submission by inane small talk. I despised small talk. Give me Evvy and a couple rowdy friends, a pitcher of beer, and a game on TV to argue over, and I was content. Ask me to stand in one place for more than five minutes and discuss traffic, gardening, or someone's mother-in-law's second bunion surgery, and I went catatonic.

I took a sip, turned, and leaned back, elbows propped on the bar. I made sure to tilt my body away from the crowd so no one would approach, but positioned myself so I could still check out the room. If I finished my drink fast enough, I could order another without having to move.

I did just that and it wasn't long until a pleasant warmth trickled through my veins and my muscles relaxed. A half-hour later I was thoroughly buzzed. Enough to think I might actually have a sporting chance to survive the next two hours without clawing my own eyes out. I didn't drink to excess often. Not only did it remind me of my useless parents, but it always seemed to lead to fists flying and blood spurting. A few Jack and Cokes wouldn't get me sloshed, but damn did I feel good.

Starting that very morning, we had an unheard of six days off in a row, so naturally, management went and fucked it up by deciding it was the perfect time to hold the team's annual dinner, or as I liked to call it, "A night of forced torture that happened to involve fancy clothing, inane chatter, and thank fuck, alcohol." The restaurant they booked was decent, run by the owner of a local brewery, which stood next door. It was a popular place, and I'd eaten there before. A lot of my teammates and most of the higher ups brought wives or dates.

Which reminded me... I scanned the room and exhaled. No Amanda, yet. If there was anyone looking out for me, she wouldn't show. I really didn't want to see her. Not after the ugly way I left things a month or so ago. Plus, no way did I want my personal life anywhere near my bosses. That was why I didn't ever bring a date to these things. I lifted my glass to my lips and snorted.

Date? I didn't even need a reason to not bring a date. Why the fuck would I want to bring a woman? Not only did I *not* date, I'd have to deal with her boring chitchat. It would be my job, and mine alone, to entertain her ass and introduce her to everyone. That meant more small talk.

No fucking thanks. Even the possibility of a quickie in the restaurant crapper wasn't temptation enough to make me endure the misery of bringing a date.

I spotted Evvy halfway across the crowded room, chewing the fat with one of our corporate managers. Per usual, Evvy's hands gesticulated wildly as he spoke. Even though I'd much rather sulk alone at the bar, I decided that joining Evvy was my best option if I wanted to keep people from approaching me and, at the same time, remain somewhat sane.

With a heavy sigh, I pushed off the bar. As I took my first step toward Evvy, out of the corner of my eye a cascade of gold hair caught my attention. I sucked in a breath and held it.

No fucking way.

I stopped dead in my tracks, my gaze glued to a blonde woman on the far side of the room. No, not *a* blonde. *The* blonde. Kylie. Hot Blonde. The very same Hot Blonde I sent the gift to. The one I'd propositioned. The one I had a near-religious experience with. A spark zapped my momentarily still heart and I exhaled.

Kylie was at the Comets' dinner. Stood only a few yards away. But why? Who did she come with? She wasn't an employee. I knew that for sure. I'd asked around in what hopefully came across as a non-creepy, non-stalkery manner. In retrospect, I should have realized Kylie's front row seat meant she knew someone in the organization. Seats that good didn't hand themselves out.

I twisted around to check out the rest of the room, not that I'd figure out who Kylie came with that way. I didn't see her arrive, therefore, had no way of knowing which bastard I'd have to maim in order to get her all to myself.

Again, just the thought of some slimy douchebag putting his hands on her flawless skin made my pulse thunder in my ears. The one important detail I *did* notice, was the lack of a ring on her finger. Any of her fingers, actually. If she came with a date, they weren't married. That meant I could, and would, do whatever necessary to ensure the mysterious Kylie didn't want anyone but me by the end of the evening.

I returned to my spot leaning on the bar and waited for the perfect moment to present itself. My gaze never left Kylie's stunning face. When she excused herself from a conversation with one of the wives to slip out a side door, a door I happened to know led to a sprawling stone patio, I made my move. A few people tried to stop me, pull me into some inane conversation. Good thing I didn't mind being rude. I refused to be deterred. I was a man on a mission and no one would get in my way, not unless they wanted a knuckle sandwich to the eye socket.

Without looking back, and disregarding a woman who

muttered unflattering comments about me under her breath when I wasn't wowed by her flirting, I pushed through the crowd and exited the same door as Kylie. Blood thrumming and stomach fluttering in anticipation, I stepped out into the crisp winter night to claim my prize.

Except... *shit!* I didn't see her. To my knowledge, there was only one way in and out of the patio area, so Kylie had to be somewhere. I stalked to the far end of the patio, turned the corner, and sucked in a lungful of icy winter air. *Saint cibore*, from far away Kylie was gorgeous, so how did I forget how beautiful she was up close, without a half-inch of scratched plexi between us?

She was positively stunning.

Kylie stood, alone, with one hip resting against the twisted metal railing, which meant that, thanks to her amazing dress, the exposed, bare expanse of her spine faced me. My breath hitched. That fucking low-slung dress would be the death of me.

She would be the death of me if I didn't stop obsessing.

I wondered what would it be like to have the liberty to walk over and press right up against Kylie's body. To feel the searing heat that came off her skin. To rub my stiffening cock against that fantastic ass. An ass that looked even better with my bright red handprint across it.

I approached casually, not hiding my presence, but not announcing it either. Kylie must have been deep in thought, because she didn't notice me until I put my hands on the railing next to her and even then, she didn't so much as twitch until I spoke.

"Nice evening, don't you think?"

"Oh my god!" Kylie jumped and her wine glass slipped from her hand. I winced when it shattered with a *pop* in the parking lot two stories below. Mouth forming a perfect 'o', she bent over the rail and gaped in horror. "Oh no."

"Whoops," I said with a grin. Kylie looked distraught, worried about breaking one little glass. I thought it was fucking adorable.

Adorable until Kylie straightened and aimed her intense stare directly at me. *Merde.* Her gaze was so heated, so focused, my brain stuttered and stalled. The electrical signals shorted out and the gray matter went offline, rendering it completely useless. My pulse raced and I felt the painful hammering of my heart against my ribcage. The wisecracking, smooth talking Sebastien St. Clair had up and left the building, and the inconsiderate bastard left behind a bumbling, speechless dumbass. I literally couldn't come up with a single intelligent thing to say in the face of such beauty. I was pretty sure "ummm" or "duh" didn't count.

Kylie's gaze narrowed as if annoyed, or secretly wishing she could burn me to a crisp by shooting laser beams from her eyes. As she studied me, Kylie's harsh expression softened and began to morph into something more familiar. Something I could definitely work with. I watched as the pupils in the center of familiar, rich golden-brown irises dilated. It didn't escape my notice when Kylie snuck a quick peek at my body. Maybe refreshing her memory?

My brain rebooted and came back online as her attention returned to my face. The winter night was so quiet, I could hear the slight hitch as Kylie inhaled. I put the pieces together one by one and when I had enough in the proper place, comprehension zapped me like a Taser to the balls.

My out of control desire wasn't one-sided. Kylie wanted me. I might be the only one with an unhealthy obsession, but the fact that she was still interested was good enough for now.

"You made me drop my drink." The way her lip pouted out, combined with the irritation in her voice, made me want to laugh out loud. Yeah, she definitely sounded annoyed, but I didn't miss the simmering hunger or blatant interest that betrayed her.

Pretending not to care, I shrugged, and tucked my hands in my pockets. "Yeah, sorry about that."

"Hmph." Her cheeks flushed and she looked away. Kylie shivered and wrapped her arms around herself.

"Where's your coat?"

Hell, she was practically naked, not that I was complaining, but it was cold out and the only thing she wore was a slinky, black cocktail dress. One with no back and a skirt that ended way above her knees to show off long, toned legs. Legs that had been wrapped around my waist as I pounded into her. I silently thanked whoever inspired her to wear that minuscule dress. I wasn't knocking it, believe me. It was fucking fantastic. And as much as I hated the thought of covering her up, she shouldn't be outside in January wearing a tiny scrap of fabric.

"I left it in the car." Kylie ducked her head and pulled that sexy, full, lower lip between her teeth, invoking a couple of smoking hot memories. Her high cheekbones blushed a shade darker, and the beautiful rosy color spread to her ears.

Holy sexual torture.

I needed to adjust the painful semi in my slacks, but figured that would be crude. Or hey, maybe she would be impressed by the size of my package? A nice reminder of how talented I was with it. Yeah, no. Bad idea. I kept my hands off my dick and suffered in silence. I couldn't manhandle my cock, but I *could* find out more about Kylie. In spite of my hatred of small talk, I dove in head first.

"So, I didn't expect to see you here. Who in the organization do you know?" I clenched every muscle in my body as I waited to hear the name of the guy I was going to pound into a bloody pulp.

Her eyes glittered and narrowed to slits. "Why do you want to know?" Kylie smirked and that was the moment I knew I was fucked. If I wasn't careful, she would absolutely own me. A simple snap of her fingers and I'd gladly do whatever she asked, up to and including rolling over and begging at her feet.

Like before, the sound of my name coming from those sinful lips, in that husky voice, made my balls tingle. Instead of grabbing Kylie and slamming my mouth down on hers like I wanted to, I laughed.

"You're a trip. You know that?" Two could play this little game. With a shameless grin, I leaned in until my mouth touched the curve of her ear. The falter in her breath made my cock swell against my zipper. "I want to know the name of the man I have to teach some manners to, since he didn't take proper care of you, and left me to lend you my clothes."

Kylie frowned when I retreated. "I'm not wear—"

I shrugged out of my suit jacket and draped it over her shoulders. Yeah, yeah, it was chivalrous and all that, but to be clear, I'm *not* a gentleman. Far from it. Case in point, I couldn't help but brush my fingertips across her creamy skin as I pulled my hands away. Sneak in a little grope. Light as the touch was, the heat of her flesh was like a third-degree burn. Kylie shivered again, only this time I was pretty sure it wasn't from the cold.

Hmm, she could try to hide it, but I knew she wanted me.

Kylie grinned, a wicked, sexy, fuck me grin that made all the blood in my body head south.

"I plead the fifth," she said.

Fucking hell, that voice. Undoubtedly feminine, with a hint of smoldering rasp woven through it. She may as well have been jerking me off.

I smiled, even though I wanted that goddamn name. Kylie was dangerous. I had to play it right or I risked pissing her off. Then I would have nothing. No name, no flirting, and no Kylie.

"Alright," I said reluctantly as I made sure the fake smile stayed pasted on my face. I held out my hand. "Nice to meet you. Again."

Kylie hesitated, but eventually slipped her small hand into mine. If I thought the tingle from the stroke of fingertips on her shoulder was amazing, full hand to hand contact nearly made me blow in my briefs. Somehow, the minimal touch sizzled almost as strong and scorching hot as full-blown sex, the sensation akin to a static shock, only more intense. Electricity hissed and popped at a cellular level, the sparks lighting up every last one of my erogenous zones— and with Kylie, I discovered there were a lot more than I previously thought.

With a layer of thick, potent desire that roiled just below the surface of my skin, I never wanted to let go. Somehow, I managed to keep the handshake brief, though I held on a little too long. Long enough to be awkward. Kylie frowned and when she tugged to free herself from my grip, I reluctantly released her.

She immediately used her reclaimed hand to clasp the front of my jacket closed, to shield her bare skin from the bitter wind. The air between us went from inferno to glacial, comfortable to cumbersome, like two total strangers who fucked once then bumped into each other unexpectedly.

No surprise since that was exactly what we were.

Kylie looked down, thick lashes fluttering against her

rosy cheeks, then glanced up to meet my gaze. The unintentional, yet undeniably seductive move made my mouth go dry and the static shocks returned with a startling jolt.

"So," she said, "I never asked. What's the deal? Why did you send me your jersey?"

Even wearing what looked to be fairly high heels, I stood a lot taller than Kylie. So much so, she had to tilt back her head to meet my eyes. I loved smaller women, but they couldn't be breakable. If they were too fragile, they couldn't take the rough manhandling I preferred. I had specific needs, most of which required a partner who wouldn't crack under stress. After putting her through the motions, Kylie passed the test with flying colors.

I had to smother a groan at the memory of pinning Kylie down, making her stay still as I pleasured her. I shook off the images and refocused on Kylie, who continued to peer up from under those impossibly long lashes. She had no idea how sexy she was, innocence and seduction in one irresistible package. The material covering my groin tightened and my gaze dropped to Kylie's amazing mouth, full and thick and painted an alluring shade of red. I thought about how those lips tasted, and how I would love to taste them again, currently painted the color of fresh strawberries. Then I pictured those same lips stretched wide around my dick.

We never did get around to that.

That would be... I practically shuddered. There were no words to describe Kylie's mouth. My cock strained for release, letting me know its demands.

Ignoring the hard prick poking at my slacks, I gave a casual shrug and hoped I acted as if I wasn't fighting a rock hard boner.

"First, it's called a sweater. Only Americans say jersey,

which is wrong." She narrowed her eyes as I continued. "Second, I figured you could use a few pointers, you know?"

"Jersey, sweater, whatever," Kylie said with a wave of her hand, and a bit of the boldness I first encountered on the patio returned. She met my stare, looking unamused. "You think I need pointers?" she asked, her tone flat. I grinned.

Feisty. I liked that.

"Yeah. Clearly you need help, you know, like making sure you don't embarrass yourself by wearing the sweater of a less than awesome player. Which, for your information, is anyone but me." I tossed her a wink.

Kylie's brow pinched adorably and she stammered. "Wait, what? Y-you... you... *ugh!*" Frustrated, she stomped her foot.

Luckily, I caught the subtle upward curve at the corner of her mouth. That one tiny gesture let me know I was golden. I wondered if it would be too much to pump my fists and let out a whoop. Probably. Kylie giggled, and the lightness in her voice sounded amazing. I was enthralled... until she finished her thought.

"You're kind of a pompous ass."

Right.

"So I've been told."

I couldn't tear my eyes away and didn't care Kylie called me out. I *am* a pompous ass. My easy acquiescence made her smile and the action lit up her face. She shone so bright it was as if the dark skies turned sunny, a beam cutting through the clouds to spotlight her smile. My dick gave another restless twitch, reminding me that Kylie was smoking hot and a wildcat in bed. On top of that, she proved she was fun to talk to, and most important, stood within reach. My fingers itched to touch again.

"Hmmm."

When she didn't elaborate, I frowned.

"What's *hmmm* supposed to mean?" I asked, then winced at my whiney tone. Yeah, that came out sounding kind of pathetic.

Kylie's smile grew wider and she shook her head.

"Nothing. It's nothing."

I crossed my arms over my chest and stared. "Fine. Don't tell me. Just remember, if you were wearing your new sweater right now, you wouldn't be freezing and therefore, wouldn't need me to rescue you from hypothermia." At least I didn't stomp my foot, though I might have thought about it.

Kylie raised a perfectly arched brow. "But if I was wearing the *jersey* you so kindly gifted me with, I wouldn't get the chance to experience such unexpected chivalry from the man they call *The Sinner*." She raised a hand and *oh fuck*, the little minx skimmed her hand down her chest, fingering the plackets of my coat while simultaneously biting that sexy lip. I had no doubt she knew *exactly* what she was doing, a reminder of when she bit that lip as I spanked her pert ass. "Thanks for the jacket, by the way... Seb."

Holy shit. I was ready to give her whatever the fuck she wanted as long as she kept talking. My mind already categorized Kylie's raspy voice as pure sex. Toss in her seductive flirting, and it only made it worse. I wanted to hear her shout my name again and again as I shoved my cock deep inside her. She was taunting me. Trying to get a reaction. And fuck, she got one all right, only I don't think yanking down my fly and pulling out my cock was the reaction Kylie was going for.

I should only be so lucky.

"Uhh," I cleared my throat. "You're welcome," I eventually choked out.

During the course of our conversation, we drifted closer. By the time I noticed, our hips were nearly touching, as were our arms.

I couldn't pass up the opportunity. Knowing how Kylie felt, meant I couldn't to keep my hands to myself. I lightly touched the sleeve of my jacket, wishing to god it was her bare skin.

"I'd like to see you again, but you left before I could get your number." At my admission, Kylie's eyes nearly bugged out of her head. I hated having to ask for her number, but her surprise amused me. "What? Why wouldn't I want to call you? I mean, I did give you a gift and all. After what we did last week, we're practically dating."

What the actual fuck? Why did I say that?

Kylie sputtered, then smothered a laugh. "We are *definitely* not dating."

"Once you give me your phone number, and I call you, we'll get together again. Then we'll be dating." I shot her a confident grin.

Date? I don't date. What the hell are you doing, St. Clair, you dumbshit? Fuck the date. Ask her to come home with you right now.

It was too late. I already started down an unknown path and there was no way I was pulling a U-turn and ruining my chances. More than anything, more than the Stanley Cup, I wanted Kylie naked and chained to my bed, properly this time, and was damn determined to get it, no matter the cost. If it meant pretending we were going to date, promising fucking flowers and dinner and all that romantic shit, then that's exactly what I'd do. Didn't matter, as long I got to be with her again. For whatever reason, my gut told me if I pressed for sex, even if she accepted, it would be the last time. After that, I'd never see her again. And god, did I want to see her again.

"Why on earth would I give you my number?"

I shifted until I pressed against Kylie from shoulder to hip. Still touching my jacket, I slid my hand up and down, the lapel between my thumb and fingers, and gave a gentle tug.

"You're already wearing my clothes. I've seen you naked. You've seen me naked. We both enjoyed it. Why not do it again?"

I bent down until our eyes were level, my mouth so close to those tempting lips I struggled not to close the distance, pin her hands behind her back, and devour every last one of her moans. I maintained eye contact, and caught the exact second the wary look in Kylie's eyes changed to something much more promising.

"Give me your phone," she instructed, her eyelids at half-mast and her sexy rasp even deeper than before.

The dichotomy between vixen and ingénue, naive girl and temptress, feisty and nervous, fascinated me. Yes, I wanted to have sex with her again, but more than that, I wanted to know what made Kylie tick. A first for me, I admit.

I pulled the brand-new device from my pocket and prayed it wouldn't spontaneously combust in my hand. Without pulling away from her eyes, I offered it to her. Our icy fingers grazed and this time *I* was the one to shiver and *fuck*, I one hundred percent knew it wasn't from the temperature. It was cold outside, but there wasn't a single part of my body that wasn't on fire—burning and smoldering as white-hot flames licked their way up and down my spine. My insides scorched to ash and my nerves pulsed with electrical charges, ready to detonate. The sensation was eerily similar to the pressure of the uncontrollable, heated rage that would push outward when my temper flared, only it was... different. Before I could overthink it, Kylie handed back the phone, thankfully unexploded.

"What did you put your number under?" I asked as I scrolled down the contact list. Messing with the device was risky. My tendency to ruin anything electronic meant there was a chance I could lose her number simply by screwing around with the damn thing. But curiosity won out. I wanted to know Kylie's last name and more than that, *needed* to know how to find her. With her teasing behavior, the way she easily tossed every one of my smartass remarks right back at me without missing a beat, the way she ducked out on me at the hotel, I figured whatever Kylie put her number under would be totally unexpected.

She didn't disappoint.

Kylie grinned and I just about incinerated from the flirtatious spark in her chestnut eyes. She was a study in contrasts—brave one moment, shy the next, then a screeching, clawing banshee as she came on my cock. I loved not knowing what to expect. Kylie took a confident step toward me and became the pursuer instead of the pursued. She crowded my space until my lower back pressed against the rail. My cock jerked again and I honestly feared I would bust a nut right then and there.

Oh god.

Bold as fuck, Kylie reached out and drew her index finger down the front of my dress shirt, stopping right above my belt buckle. I hissed and held my breath. No way could she miss the obscene tent formed as my cock pounded against my fly, all but begging to be released from its cloth prison. My eyes drifted shut and I concentrated on not shooting my load.

"I put it under N."

"N? Why? What for?" I felt giddy. Almost, drunk.

Kylie moved closer until we touched. I groaned, only half paying attention to the conversation. How could I with her spectacular body pressed against me, the soft curves of her breasts flattened against my pecs? I couldn't hold back the sounds of pleasure that rumbled out of me. Eyes still squeezed shut, I felt her hot breath gust across my ear and damn if I didn't shiver again. I vibrated with sexual tension while blistering heat shot straight to my groin. It gathered and grew in my tight, aching balls.

"For *Not A St. Clair Fan*, of course."

So damn sexy—*Wait? What?*

By the time my eyes flew open, Kylie was gone.

A slow grin spread across my face. The sexy little vixen was going to pay for that, but *fuck* it was so goddamn hot. I pressed the heel of my hand on my raging hard on and grimaced. I would have to do something about it, and soon.

I scrubbed my hands down my face. *Saint ciboire.* Kylie was sexier than I could ever imagine. Even more than both my memories and my fantasies, and I spent a *lot* of time fantasizing about her, in many, many dirty, nasty, filthy, and depraved ways.

What could I say? I was The Sinner after all.

Kylie threw down the gauntlet, one my darker side couldn't wait to scoop up. I hoped she had something to hold onto, because this ride was about to get real bumpy.

7

Kylie

"What the hell was with you tonight?"

Rocco's brusque tone, amplified times ten inside the confines of the SUV, hurt my ears. Already annoyed with him for the way he acted the week leading up to tonight's dinner, his booming accusation made my hackles rise. In fact, I nearly bit my tongue in half stifling the urge to yell back.

I should have expected his wrath. Rocco acted like a gigantic ass all evening. Truthfully, we'd been arguing on and off since the day they announced his annual team dinner, something they did in DC did every year as well. In the past, I accompanied Rocco as his date, and figured this year would be no different. Rocco, naturally, being the Neanderthal that he is, ordered me to stay home. He may as well have set fire to a dumpster, then tossed a container of gasoline on top. History proved, forbidding me to do something tended to have the opposite effect. That meant come hell or high water, I was going to get my way and go to the damn dinner whether he liked it or not.

Rocco spent a week arguing, manipulating, and pouting his way into unsuccessfully forcing me to change my mind. He'd never say it out loud, but I knew the one and only reason he didn't want me there was the inevitable presence of Sebastien St. Clair.

Which was exactly why I wanted to go.

After the I had an amazing time on the patio, absorbing the revelations brought by my conversation with a shockingly charming Seb, I didn't regret the decision. Yes, I tempted fate by willingly putting myself in the same room as both Rocco and Seb, but then again, Rocco had been a total jerk about it. Not that his worries were without merit. No, my brother's instincts about Seb being bad for me were right on the money. But he didn't know that. With Rocco completely in the dark about my clandestine hook up with Seb, his dictatorial stance was completely out of line.

Why should I miss out on an evening of fun simply because the mere thought of Seb and I sharing space sent Rocco's protective streak into hyperdrive?

Rocco was right, of course. I shouldn't have gone. If I had been thinking with my brain instead of my hormones, I'd have agreed to stay home. Rocco was a lot of things, but stupid wasn't one of them. There had been a fairly high chance he would catch Seb trying to talk to me, and if that had happened, Rocco would have noticed the familiarity between us, then all hell would have broken loose. Blind luck was the only reason Seb and I walked out of the restaurant intact.

I shivered at the thought of Rocco knowing I had literally been in bed with the enemy. Yet my desire to see Seb was worth the risk. Was it dangerous? Yes. Stupid? Definitely. Did I still do it? *Pfft*, please. Of course I did.

Rocco wasn't the only one to inherit the Calloway stubborn gene.

That didn't mean Rocco was happy about it. We fought before we left the condo, which ended up working in my favor. He held a grudge like no other and avoided me the duration of the dinner. That was fine by me. It meant Rocco didn't notice when I slipped outside, or when Seb followed.

The sound of Rocco blowing air out of his nostrils like a bull ready to charge, tore me from my thoughts. I glanced across the console to find him tense and stiff, hands gripping the poor steering wheel so hard it looked like he believed that if he were to relax even a single muscle, three tons of SUV would go flying off the road. Every last one of Rocco's knuckles was white as a sheet. Frankly, I was surprised the wheel hadn't bent under the pressure. Rocco had huge hands and the strength to match.

And he was still pissed.

Having nothing positive to say, I returned to staring blankly out the front window. A few minutes later, out of the corner of my eye, I saw Rocco glance in my direction. Still angry, I wanted to bask in my righteous fury a little while longer, but when I shifted to get a better look at his face, my heart tripped. He looked nothing like my loving brother. Instead, Rocco's handsome features were twisted into a disapproving scowl.

I knew that look. Something was bugging him. Something that had nothing to do with our current fight. I didn't bother to ask. There was no point. Years of experience taught me I had no chance of prying answers out of my pig-headed brother. Stuck in the SUV with nowhere to go, I couldn't get away with ignoring his earlier question, so before he lashed out and said something worse, something that would spark another huge fight, I came up with an excuse to get him to back off and leave me to contemplate my conversation with Seb.

"Nothing is 'with me' tonight," I said, complete with sarcastic air quotes. "I just don't feel well."

I stared out the windshield and made sure to keep my facial features blank and my eyes unfocused. Rocco is a freaking human lie detector. The guy can spot a fib like no one else. I always used to joke that if his hockey career didn't pan out, Rocco would be great as a CIA interrogator. To make my performance more believable, I threw in a moan and put a hand over my abdomen.

"I think I ate something that disagreed with me."

Just like that, Rocco's agitated expression vanished and his shoulders bunched up by his ears. He clenched his jaw and snarled, "Well, if that's the case we're never eating there again. Fucking assholes poisoning my sister."

Oh great. Here we go.

Rocco took my teeny, tiny little white lie, grabbed onto it with both hands, and took off. In less than a minute he had worked himself into a lather under the false belief I got food poisoning at the team dinner. If I hadn't stopped fake groaning long enough to beg Rocco to take me straight home, he would've already swung an illegal U-turn and double parked in front of the restaurant so he could storm through the door and beat the holy hell out of the poor chef. Which, considering I *didn't* have food poisoning, would be bad.

In fact, beating the hell out of *anyone* was bad. For Rocco, such an over-the-top reaction was pretty much par for the course. When confronted, his default setting hovered somewhere around maximum violence, on the ice, anyway. The NHL had strict rules with regard to fighting off the ice and players could receive punishment for doing so— anything from a financial penalty to the loss of their job. Rocco was good at managing his temper... most of the time. His weakness was me. Specifically, when someone either hurt me or he thought I was about to be hurt.

Thinking about what Rocco would do if he knew which body parts Sebastien St. Clair used to touch mine... I shuddered.

"Are you going to throw up?"

I swung my head around to stare at Rocco. "No, why?"

Rocco's response was to frown. Deep lines creased his face. He suddenly appeared much older than his twenty-six years.

"Because you're shaking like a leaf." Rocco reached over and pressed the back of his hand to my forehead. I made an irritated sound and smacked it away.

"Stop it."

He huffed. "I'm checking to see if you have a fever. C'mon, Ky, you could be really sick."

Oh, for fuck's sake!

"I'm fine. Honest. Please just focus on driving. I'd like to get home in one piece."

The night our parents drove away and never came back had turned me into a bit of a stickler when it came to driving safety. Not wanting to turn the black mood even darker, I willed the past away and sank down in my seat.

Feeling petulant, I crossed my arms. When my body began to ache, I realized I was so stressed out from both the reminder of the accident that changed our lives forever *and* from Rocco's non-stop nagging, that I was clenched tight. In an attempt to relax, I subtly ducked my chin and sniffed, seeing if I could detect a trace of Seb's cologne on my skin. Desperate for another hit of the fragrance that wrapped around me when he placed his jacket over my shoulders. The same jacket I handed back before I left. Seb tried to insist I keep it, reason being it was a cold night and I was wearing, quote, "next to nothing." It pained me to turn down the offer, but *ohmygod*. If Rocco caught me wearing— in his words—"that walking dickbag" Sebastien St. Clair's jacket, the apocalypse would be upon us.

When I couldn't find even the slightest hint of Seb's rich scent, I pouted and slumped deeper into the passenger's seat, using my teeth to worry at my bottom lip. The whole secret thing with Seb—the point of which was supposed to be fun and exciting—was in reality, pain in the butt. A really big, really complicated, really sexy pain in the butt. Potentially violence-inducing, if Rocco found out. At least he didn't catch us talking on the patio or know about the jersey crammed in the back my closet. *Sweater*, I quickly corrected myself, then rolled my eyes and smiled.

I must have been insane, to smile while Rocco stewed next to me. I was playing with fire and knew it, and struggled to decide whether or not Seb was worth the trouble. To be honest, the guy was kind of a jerk. Cocky, rude, violent, and hot under the collar, not unlike someone else I know.

I snuck a side-eye at Rocco, who continued to fume, then returned to staring at the road.

Despite the many negatives, when I spoke with Seb, I discovered he did indeed possess several redeeming qualities. He came across as sweet, thoughtful, and armed with a charming personality, not to mention that air of danger that had me hooked.

I thought about Seb way too often, pretty much all the

time. I could admit I wanted him again. But after spending time with him, talking, I wanted to get to know him, and that was bad. Sex, well, that was easy. Sort of. We could continue to meet up on the down low, have lots of mind blowing orgasms, and if I could successfully pull it off—keep Seb in the dark about my identity, and Rocco in the dark about everything.

But sex would be all we would ever have. No way we could ever manage any sort of relationship. Was great sex really worth it if in the end if all I ended up with were a few amazing orgasms and a broken heart? Maybe. But the entire scenario screamed hazardous to both of our healths if discovered by Rocco. Well, mostly Seb's health, but Rocco would be sure to save some wrath for me. Mostly for sneaking around with, again, quote, "a walking, talking asshole with an anus for a mouth."

"Hey."

I flailed, caught off guard by Rocco's volume as his voice once again ricocheted within the confines of the SUV. Pulse racing, I glowered in his direction. "What, Rocco?"

His dark eyes looked wounded. "I've been calling your name for the past minute, Ky. We're home."

I blinked and looked around. Mortified, I realized the SUV was not only parked in one of our designated spots in the underground garage of our high-rise condo, but the engine was off and he had his door open.

"Oh." I reached for my door and hopped down before Rocco started back up with his whole "are you okay" inter-rogation. My heels clicked as I strode toward the elevator bank and I heard the scuff of Rocco's shoes as he did a light jog to catch up. "Before you ask, I'm fine," I repeated the as he reached my side. Again, Rocco looked hurt. In the blink of an eye, the hurt twisted into a scowl.

"Christ, Kylie. You're acting like *I* did something wrong when *you* were the one who avoided me all night."

He honestly thought I avoided him? That was rich, since he was the one avoiding me.

Rocco shoved his hands in his pockets and stared at the ground, then lifted his gaze to mine. "Whatever." The cold dismissal hurt my heart. Rocco turned away as he spoke again. "I'm just worried about you."

His obvious concern squeezed my heart like a vise. I blew out a long breath and put a hand on his arm. It took way more concentration than I should've been able to scrounge up, what with my brain still recovering from flirting with Seb, but somehow, I managed a small smile.

"I know. But seriously, Rocco, I'm fine."

What I wanted to say was that I was a twenty-one-year-old woman and perfectly capable of taking care of myself. That I didn't need my brother to micromanage every aspect of my life. That I didn't need him to freak out every time I felt like taking a walk, or heaven forbid, going out on a date. I don't know if it was my conversation with Seb, or the idea of possibly seeing him again that made me want to backtalk Rocco, but a slew of harsh words sat on the tip of my tongue. When I opened my mouth to unleash my verbal fury, Rocco looked at me. I snapped my jaw shut. The sadness that clung to Rocco sent a wave of guilt so big it almost knocked me flat and the insults washed away.

"I'm sorry, Ky. I just... I don't know what I do if something were to happen to you." Rocco pulled me into a bear hug as the elevator dinged and the doors slid open.

Rocco's arms fell and he motioned I should go first. Great. Now I felt like double shit. When our parents died, times were tough. Really tough. I had been consumed by grief, but Rocco? He had it worse. Barely an adult, Rocco had to juggle the loss of our parents, *plus* a new career, a move across the country, and on top of all that, he had to suffer through a crash-course in figuring out how to be a father to his orphaned teenage sister. Everything thundered into Rocco's life in a massive avalanche of crap, the debris heaped on his doorstep without regard to how he felt.

My usual guilt pile tripled. It grew bigger and bigger until it seeped out of my pores. My annoyance at Rocco's meddling seemed petty in retrospect. Our fighting, pointless. My eyes burned and I slipped my hand into his, intertwined our fingers, and squeezed.

"Thanks for caring, bro."

Rocco smiled and my throat constricted, making it difficult to swallow. In that moment, screwing around with Seb didn't seem worth the hurt it would inevitably cause. And it *would* cause hurt, to both me and Rocco. How was I supposed to lie to my brother's face just so I could get laid? He'd done nothing but love me, take care of me, and give me everything I ever needed and then some. Nineteen-year-old Rocco Calloway didn't think twice about sacrificing years of bachelorhood, taking a pass on any opportunity to have a relationship, to spend all of his free time with his little sister. And he did it without complaint, at a time when he should have been focused on going out with guys his own age, being young and living the high life with his teammates.

And in turn, what had I done for Rocco? Nothing, except constantly whine that he cared too much.

Pain pressed at the back of my skull and I knew I had a whopper of a headache coming on. Emotionally tapped out, I said good night and we each went to our rooms, strategically placed on opposite sides of the condo. The set up was great for privacy, not that I ever did anything that required privacy. No way would I ever bring a guy here. Just the thought made my hands sweaty and set panic fluttering in my stomach.

Shaking off the guilt and nerves, I showered and changed into a sleep tank and shorts, resigned to the fact I needed to put family first. Pursuing anything with Seb, even if only for sex, was a fantasy and that's where it would remain. I winced and clutched at my shirt over my heart. The thought of not seeing Seb again, never touching him again or feeling his hands on my skin, made my lungs feel too small and my eyes began to burn. I blinked back hot tears.

What the heck was wrong with me? We hooked up *once*. One time. It really shouldn't be difficult to break things off. To accept that not only was it a bad time to get involved with someone, but also that out of the roughly seven billion people on Earth, Sebastien St. Clair had to be the worst possible someone I could choose.

The worst, at least, in Rocco's eyes. Me? I didn't have to think about it. Without a doubt, I would choose Seb again. I wanted him with every fiber of my being. Desperately.

Admitting the truth felt like twisting a knife in my gut. I didn't know the man, not really. Yet, I didn't want to give him up.

Like a zombie, I went through the motions of getting ready for bed. In the middle of brushing my teeth I heard my phone ping from the bedroom. I glanced at the tiny digital clock on the countertop. It was well after midnight. Odd.

I smiled around my toothbrush. It was probably Nat drunk texting again. She tended to do that, usually after she hooked up with a guy and regretted it the second she got home, or when she wanted to brag about how awesome he was in bed. I spat and rinsed and wandered to the night-stand to check.

Hmm, I didn't recognize the number and had no clue who it was... until I read the text.

Unknown: When can we get together again Not A St Clair Fan? I'd like the chance to persuade you to become one.

My breath hitched and my pulse stuttered. Seb. My hands shook so hard I almost dropped the phone. Luckily, I caught it before it clattered to the hardwood floor.

What the heck was wrong with me? Why did a stupid text, or even just thinking about Sebastien St. Clair freak me out in a good way? Something about the man called to me, sent my hormones into overdrive. Was it because I saw him as some kind of a kindred spirit? Did I think he might be the only person I could trust to further explore my desires?

I stared at the text. For the first time in my life I wanted to do something wholly selfish, and not to piss off Rocco, but rather, to fulfill my own needs. Trembling, I swiped the screen and my fingers hovered over the keypad.

Did I do what made Rocco happy? Or pursue my own happiness?

It took what felt like forever to decide, but was only a few seconds. Mind made up, I tapped out a response as fast as possible and hit Send before I backed out.

Me: I think I could be persuaded

I GRINNED when it pinged almost immediately.

Unknown: You didn't answer my question as to when I can see you again. And I would think after such spectacular sex, I wouldn't have to persuade you to be my fan, yet the contact info you entered says you're not.

I BIT my lip to suppress a laugh.

Me: Oh. I thought u were talking about persuading me to be a Remy fan. Wrong St Clair, sry

NOW I COULDN'T HELP but giggle. The man was so damn cocky. He deserved to suffer a little.

Unknown: I see how it is. Do you know why they call me the Sinner?

I INHALED SHARPLY. Yes, yes, I did know why. And from what I heard and experienced, the name most definitely fit. Plus, it was indescribably hot. Not wanting Seb to get a big head, I feigned ignorance.

Me: No. Why?

THE LITTLE BUBBLE POPPED UP, three gray dots that taunted me. I held my breath while I waited for a response.

Unknown: because I break ALL the rules

I READ the text and swore I almost climaxed.

Game. Over.

He won. After that, there was no way I would pass up a second chance to get down and dirty with Sebastien St. Clair. He was funny, sexy, and wickedly talented in bed. Plus, he had that edge of danger I so craved. So Rocco hates the guy. Whatever. Only an idiot would turn Seb down. Rocco just doesn't need to know. And Seb? Well, he doesn't need to know Rocco is my brother. Right? Good.

Kylie: Fine. When and where?

I YELPED when the phone in my hand rang. My finger

slipped on the screen a few times before I finally swiped the stupid thing to answer.

"Hello?"

"I knew you'd see things my way." Smooth as velvet, Seb's voice had me stifling a moan. Suddenly uncomfortable, I sat on the bed and shifted to maneuver my legs so I could rub my thighs together to try to relieve the needy ache. One that grew low in my belly and quickly spread everywhere, the hot, tingling sensation lighting every nerve ending on fire.

"Oh, you did, did you?" I teased. "Why would you think I'd cave?"

I could practically hear Seb's grin. "Because I'm a charming bastard."

This time, I couldn't suppress the laugh. "You forgot cocky."

"Trust me," he said. His low, rumbling tone sent erotic vibrations straight between my thighs. "Trust me. I never forget how *cocky* I am."

My jaw dropped at his unmistakable innuendo. I opened my mouth to say something, anything, when Seb burst out laughing. I joined in, the sound addictive. The two of us went on and on, cackling like a couple of kids.

"You're ridiculous," I said when I finally caught my breath.

"Yep."

"Hmmm."

"Oh no. I'm not letting you get away with *hmmm*, this time. Tell me what you're thinking, even if it's bad. I'm a big boy. I can take it."

"You sure are," I joked. My face burst into flames and I clapped a hand over my mouth. I could not believe I said that. It wasn't like me. At least, not the Kylie I knew. I wasn't bold and brave. But maybe it was who I was supposed to be, free and flirty and yes, a little bit naughty. It felt good so I decided to go with it.

"Oh sweetheart, you're tempting me to reacquaint you with exactly how *big* I am. In fact, when can I see you again?"

Unable to control myself, I giggled again, acting like a teenager with a crush. My flushed skin burned hot as a fresh wave of desire rushed from the top of my scalp to the bottom of my feet. If Seb's words were the kindling, then his deep voice was the match. One strike and my insides incinerated.

"Um, you want to see me again?"

"Well, yeah? That is why I asked for your phone number." There was an uncomfortable pause when I didn't answer right away. "Let me help you out. I'm free tomorrow and I don't have another game until Tuesday."

Which I already knew because of Rocco.

I covered the receiver so Seb wouldn't hear my snort. In no way did I want him to know my brother was Rocco Calloway. In fact, I couldn't imagine a worse scenario. It was highly likely there wasn't anything that would send Seb running faster in the opposite direction than knowing I was related to his sworn enemy.

"Okay. I think... I think that sounds good."

Seb chuckled. "You *think* it sounds good? Wow. That's a ringing endorsement if I ever heard one."

My cheeks ached from smiling so much. "No. I mean yes. I mean, I don't work tomorrow, so it works for me."

"Perfect, I'll text you to arrange a time to pick you up."

I think I stopped breathing. *Pick me up?* There would be no *picking me up*. We were having a clandestine affair. The kind with secret meet ups and stolen moments and awesome sex, not coming to my house and picking me up as if it were a... a date!

Sebastien St. Clair could not pick me up in front of the building. Knowing Rocco, he'd have his nose pressed to the glass the minute I stepped onto the sidewalk.

"Oh, that's not necessary. I'll just meet you wherever."

There was a brief pause before Seb replied. "It's really not a bother to pick you up."

The way Seb said it reminded me of Rocco, the "end of story" implied. From experience, I knew there was no point arguing. In Seb's mind, the decision was made.

"Fine." My stomach did a flip and a knot of butterflies exploded. I should have said no. This was such a bad idea. Yet I kept going. "Let me know what time you'll be here and I'll meet you downstairs. You don't need to park and come all the way up."

If Seb refused to compromise, it meant the end of our very brief tryst. Hell would freeze over before I chanced Seb knocking on my door, potentially ending up face to face with Rocco.

"That sounds good."

Thank you, lord.

I exhaled in relief and ignored my racing heart and jittery hands, the result of a burst of adrenaline at the thought Seb and Rocco fighting on our doorstep.

"G-great. Perfect."

"I'll talk to you tomorrow, and Kylie—?"

Damn, his voice was so freaking sexy, it just wasn't fair. It got my brain so scrambled I could hardly think. "Y-yes?"

"I'm confident that by the end of the night... well, let's just say you'll be shouting that you're my new number one fan."

By the time I thought up a witty response, the line

went dead.

Oh. My. God.

He was dangerous. And bad. This was a bad idea and Seb was most definitely a bad choice. Everything about it was bad. The worst.

I was never going to survive this affair intact.

8

Seb

Practice took for-fucking-ever. Then again, I never noticed before. Probably because I never had anything to look forward to. Hockey was it for me. I never paid attention to how long I shot pucks or switched out various lines and plays or speed drills.

Until Kylie.

I glanced at the clock, again, which pissed me off. Thanks to my amped-up state, it took an inordinate amount of concentration to ignore Sasquatch and his bevy of judgmental grunts and dark glowers. In my effort to be a good little team player, I clamped my big mouth shut, put my head down, and did what I was told. By some miracle, I finished practice without jamming my stick down Calloway's throat. Barely.

I counted it as a win.

Through the tunnel we trudged, and to my extreme annoyance, my inconsiderate teammates failed to use my catchy and, in my humble opinion, fitting nickname for

Calloway—Sasquatch. Nope. The dirty traitors called him
Rocky, which to my utter delight, Calloway despised, or the
vomit-inducing nickname Calloway brought with him. One
he earned—and yeah, I could begrudgingly admit he really
is that good—his first year in the NHL.

I remember during my brief time in the minors, I sat
perched on the edge of my seat in the apartment I shared
with three other guys, beer in hand, as we watched Rocco
Calloway, the unstoppable rookie defender, take down
forwards left and right. Hell, I'd actually *admired* the prick,
until the following year when I got called up and had to play
against him. I'd never admit it. Not even under threat of
castration. I figure I must've had some kind of brain damage
or been suffering from a concussion to think Calloway was
anyone worth looking up to.

Fast forward several years and in a moment I couldn't
have plucked from my wildest imagination, I found myself
in a supremely shitty position. I'd have bet money
Calloway's nickname would never pass my lips, let alone be
said directly to his ridiculous, snarling, Sasquatch face.

We'd always been on opposing teams, so what reason
would I have to use it?

Whenever I pulled up an image of Rocco Calloway, the
names that came to mind were simple—Sasquatch and/or
Asshat and/or Bastard. Oh, and a bunch of Québecois
obscenities that probably wouldn't go over real well with
management if I shouted them at their newest hire, especially since I'm not the only one on the team who speaks
French.

With Calloway officially a Comet, it was up to me give
him the same respect I showed my other teammates, which
kind of made me throw up in my mouth a little. What really
ticked me off was that not one of my backstabbing team-

mates gave a single fuck that the man was literally the devil on skates. Management patently expected I would fall in line and do what any player worthy of the NHL did—suck it up and treat your teammate like family.

I snorted. I'd rather be fucked up the ass with a broken beer bottle.

Speaking of *le diable*.

Calloway emerged from the showers, towel slung low over his hips, all his stupidly huge Sasquatch-like muscles on display. With an annoyed huff, I turned my back to him and jammed my feet into my favorite pair of lace-up boots. Behind me, I heard the loud smacks of backslapping and high-fives, while my supposed "family" praised Calloway. "Nice practice, *Assassin*," or "Way to go, *Assassin*," or "Great job, *Assassin*." I thought Calloway was way more *ass* than *ass*assin, but one thing I refused to hear Coach say was that I wasn't a team player.

Dammit, my team means *everything* to me. With the exception my little bro, they're all I've had since I strapped on a pair of beat up used blades for my very first peewee league. The family I always wished I had. My escape. My safe place.

Now, with the inevitable arrival of the token bastard relative—don't laugh, you know who I'm talking about. Everybody has one. The pervy uncle or drunk second cousin you prayed skipped out on holidays, and instead not only crashed the party, but never left, predictably taking up residence in your spare bedroom. Thank you Rocco fucking Calloway for being the relative who rounded out my fucked-up family.

I shouldered my bag and turned to leave. Unfortunately, I caught a perpetually scowling Rocco Calloway out of the corner of my eye. *Fuck me.* Where was that broken beer bottle when you needed it? I steeled my jaw and dipped my chin, swallowing several times to keep down the grilled chicken salad that threatened to make an unwelcome encore, and sucked up my pride.

I met Calloway's hostile glare and forced out, "Great practice, Assassin," when what I really wanted to say was, "*vas te crosser avec une poignée de clous*," which basically means "fuck off," or, if you want to be literal, "go jack off with a handful of rusty nails." Entirely appropriate for the situation.

Sasquatch's, I shuddered... I mean, *Assassin's* eyes widened under his Cro-Magnon ridge. I never hid the fact that I hated his guts, so he had no reason to think I'd be cordial to him in any way. Calloway stood there a second, looking too genetically related to a true Neanderthal to be considered human, as he came up with what I knew would be a rude, cutting response. One that would undoubtedly humiliate me and make me wish I hadn't bothered to put any effort into accepting him, especially since he regularly treated me like a scrap of toilet tissue stuck to his shoe. According to "experts," I was supposed to be satisfied by "being the bigger man" or something idiotic like that.

Which, we all know is a total load of horseshit. I can one hundred percent verify that being a dick feels way, way better.

When Calloway didn't respond—I wasn't sure he even blinked—I pushed my way out of the changing room and stomped down the hall. Instead of shouting or pummeling the wall with my fists, I forced my head down and checked to see if Kylie sent any texts (she didn't).

"Seb."

I winced and sped up.

Keep walking, St. Clair. Pretend you didn't hear.

Hurried footsteps grew closer. "Seb!"

Fils de pute!

I peered over my shoulder to glance at Amanda and ended up doing a double take worthy of a Three Stooges episode as I scrambled to a halt. *Whoa.* If there's one thing I can unequivocally, without a doubt, say is true about my ex-fuck buddy, it's that she never stepped out of the house looking anything less than perfect. From the top of her silky, thick head of hair, down to her sexy painted toenails.

I flicked my gaze up and down her body, and had to strain to not frown. She wore jeans. *Jeans!* With flat shoes, not a spiky stiletto in sight. Topped, not by her usual silk blouse, but a plain navy tee. Amanda pulled her shiny waves into a high, tangled knot I'd never seen on her before. The style took years off her face. To the point I felt a bit uncomfortable having screwed her senseless. Without the makeup and power suits, Amanda could pass as jailbait.

I couldn't help but gape.

"Mandy?"

I locked onto her lush lips, which normally looked ready to suck my dick. Except they were pinched into a thin, tense line. I glanced up and only then did I notice Amanda's eyes. They were all bloodshot and swollen, and around her nose was red and raw. It looked like she'd been... *oh fuck.* I cringed. Crying.

I took a giant step back. I don't do crying females. *Nuh uh.* To this day, thinking about it makes my skin crawl. I have no clue what to do or say around a weeping woman. It's like handling a live grenade. One wrong move and they'd explode, zero hesitation in taking you down with them.

"Do... do you have a minute?"

Câlasse. Amanda sounded different, almost vulnerable. Being an idiot with a Y chromosome, I blurted out, "Sure."

The second it came out of my mouth I wanted to kick my own ass.

"No one's in the lounge." She pointed to a nearby door.

Instead of saying, "no" and bolting for my truck, I nodded and followed Amanda into the media lounge, the one visitors and reporters use while they wait for press conferences and the like. She closed the door and I broke out in a cold sweat. Memories of the clink of the front gate at the detention center as it snicked shut, the finality of that sound and what it meant, sent ice trickling through my veins. Locked in for twelve months. Caged. Trapped. The day I got out of that shithole, I vowed I'd never let anyone trap me again.

I took a shuddering breath. The walls of the media room shrank and a burning pressure pinched my lungs. I shivered and broke out in chills as nausea pushed its way up my esophagus. I swallowed several times just so I wouldn't puke. My nerves jittered and the prickly sensation of ants under my skin returned tenfold.

"What do you want?" I barked. Amanda flinched, and I cursed under my breath.

It wasn't my fault, it was just, that *room*. The perception of being imprisoned. My rational mind knew nothing bad was going to happen. I could reach out and open the damn door whenever I felt like it, but tell that to the fucked up part of my brain. For a second, I swore I heard the *aaack, aaack* of Henri Allaire as he cleared his throat over the thundering of my own heart. The tingling of an oncoming panic attack took root, ready to seize my lungs and shut down all but the most basic of bodily functions.

What I really needed was to light a fucking Valium scented candle and huff that the fumes until pink elephants danced around me.

"I, um..." Amanda twisted her fingers together and ducked her head.

My jaw fell. I was beyond flabbergasted. Screw the panic attack. What was unfolding before me was shocking. I watched Amanda Brooker, a confident and powerful woman with a firm, no bullshit, take-no-prisoners attitude, nervously squirm and twitch. Awkward as fuck, she reached up and brushed a stray strand of hair out of her face, then took a deep breath.

"Look, I know I took things too far and you got upset."

I stared, wary, but decided to be honest. "Yeah, you did."

Amanda frowned, but didn't look away. "I'm so sorry. I just... I was hoping maybe we could, you know, forget about it and go back to the way things were. I thought maybe tonight..." She reached for me, but hesitated and dropped her hand.

My anxiety, fueled by the confrontation as well as Amanda's bizarre behavior, made my racing pulse stumble. I stared in disbelief.

"Let me get this straight. You... you're saying you want to keep fucking? Even after...?" The *I acted like a total bastard and treated you like a fuck toy* was inferred.

Amanda inhaled, held steady, and never broke eye contact. That was more like it. More like the assertive woman I met two years ago and found irresistible.

"Yes."

Years upon years of being trained to expect every argument to turn violent, usually with me ending up cornered and verbally abused, or more often, nursing injuries, had honed my instincts to expect every confrontation to result in pain. Between the walls that were steadily closing in, Amanda's tears, and her wanting to get back together, those were the instincts that took over. Unfortunately for Amanda, it meant I turned full-on defensive asshole.

"Fuck no!" Amanda's face fell and her wide, wounded eyes shimmered with fresh tears. Horrified by my complete absence of tact, I scrambled to fix Amanda before she broke. "I didn't... *fuck*. I didn't mean it like that."

See? That's why I hate this kind of shit. I dragged my hands down my face and tipped my head back to stare at the ceiling.

"I'm sorry, Mandy. It's not..."

I couldn't bring myself to resurrect the ol' *"it's not you, it's me,"* chestnut. She'd never believe it anyway. I needed something that didn't make it sound like my rejection was Amanda's fault, and also let me escape without plunging the knife further into her spine. If she cried, as in really started to sob and get all snotty and messy... I wasn't emotionally equipped to deal with that.

An image of Kylie flickered in my head and again, mouth before brain, I announced, "I'm seeing someone."

Amanda's jaw fell and her eyes flared. But hey, at least she was no longer on the verge of tears. I double checked to be sure. *Dieu merci*. Yep. Dry eyes. In fact, Amanda looked kind of... *oh fuck*, Amanda looked pissed.

"You bastard piece of shit," she hissed.

Shocked, I backed into the wall and held up my hands, which shook like I chugged six espresso shots in a row. Anxiety clawed up my throat and those damn ants skittered across every inch of my body.

It was my worst nightmares come to life. *Cornered. Trapped.*

Memories flashed hard and fast. I counted each breath to separate the present from my disturbing past. In, one... two...

Amanda shifted closer, her lips peeled back in an ugly sneer. "Were you seeing her while you were still screwing me, Seb?" Amanda's sweet, youthful face, a face I once enjoyed seeing in the throes of passion, twisted with rage.

"We were never exclusive!" I lashed out, furious with Amanda for literally backing me into a corner as she dredged up a subject we discussed to death and then some. She was only one of my many fuck buddies and she knew it.

My anger did nothing to displace the fiery glare she aimed at me, as she awaited further explanation. Forced to think on my feet, I yanked an excuse out of my ass, and put the final nail in my relationship with Amanda.

"The girl I'm seeing, it's a new thing. I don't... I can't... *shit*." I thrust my hands in my hair, then let my arms fall to my sides. "What do you want me to say?"

"You and me, *two years*! The sex, the laughs and good times, did all of that mean *nothing* to you, Seb? Two goddamn years! Was I so unimportant that a couple of weeks after you left my bed you found a *girlfriend*? Something you adamantly insisted you'd never have, by the way." Amanda's chest heaved and she bared her gleaming white teeth.

I was at a loss and my silence sent Amanda over the edge.

She got right up in my face and drilled a finger into my collarbone. "You're a real fucking son of a bitch, Sebastien St. Clair. You know what?" Her expression grew a little hysterical and her voice pitched up. "I hope you fall in love with her." Now it was my eyes that bulged. "That's right, *love*. That's exactly what I said. I hope you fall hopelessly, head over heels in love with this poor woman, and she dumps your pathetic ass. Then —" Amanda stabbed harder and I had to clench my jaw to keep from breaking her wrist, "—

then you'll know what it feels like to want something more than anything, only to have it ripped from your arms."

With that, Amanda spun on one of her non-stilettoed heels and flung the media room door open so hard it bounced off the wall and slammed shut after she stormed out. It felt like I got cross-checked by a runaway train. I closed my eyes and sagged against the wall as I attempted to process whatever the fuck just went down. Amanda had no right to be pissed at me for finding someone else. It's not like I *meant* to hurt her.

Deep down she isn't a bad person. Like I said, it wasn't her, it was me. I simply didn't want to be tied down. To anyone. In retrospect, thinking back on our lame excuse of a relationship reminded me how increasingly suffocating the air between us grew every time we hooked up. By the end, Amanda's bedroom felt like a prison.

Clammy with sweat, my NHL mandated tie tightened like a noose around my neck, and my dress shirt stuck to my skin, I escaped the media room and didn't look back. By the time I reached my truck, Sasquatch slash Assassin slash Asshat slash What-the-fuck-ever, was long forgotten. Amanda... well, she wasn't forgotten, but at least I was no longer on the verge of losing my shit, though I could really use a distraction.

I snorted. Irony is such a cunning bitch. Getting cornered and yelled at by my ex-fuck buddy left me itching to call up a convenient outlet...you know, like a fuck buddy.

I went to retrieve my phone to call one of my other, less fun but otherwise satisfactory, hookups. My cock throbbed and visions of Kylie flashed through my head. The phone slid back into my pocket, the mood for a random dial-a-fuck passed. What I wanted was to call Kylie to work out my aggressions. But we were too new, which sucked because it seemed, for the moment, my dick was fixated on her. I guess I would be going without. For now.

Twitch, twitch...

Son of a... I ignored my asshole eye and cranked the radio. My one-track mind kept drifting back to Kylie. Gorgeous and funny Kylie. Teasing, sexy, irresistible Kylie. The more I fantasized about getting her naked, the lighter my mood became. I spun a dozen different scenarios that were so damn hot even the sharp twinge in my side where Calloway hit me during practice couldn't wipe the smile off my face.

When I got home I texted Kylie to let her know I'd be there at seven. Since she had a roommate, we couldn't hang out at her place. Good thing I already had our date planned out. Against everything I'd learned, rules I'd strictly adhered to for years, I decided to bring Kylie back to my place. For one thing, it was private, plus my bed had all the necessary gadgets to make the evening perfect.

After spending five minutes glaring at my phone as if it personally offended me when Kylie didn't respond right away to my text—while simultaneously expecting smoke and sparks to fly out the stupid thing or for it to catch on fire —a message popped up with her address. I recognized it. Nice place.

With the arrangements taken care of, I spent the remaining agonizing hours putzing around. My stomach clenched now and then, and at one point, got so bad it felt like I swallowed a cannonball. I pressed a hand to my midsection and grimaced. I should probably snag a snack before I head out. Hopefully, food would take care of any nausea.

Since I can't cook for shit, unless people were clamoring for burned rice, I dumped the ingredients for a protein shake in my fancy blender and hit start. It whirred for about thirty-seconds, then made a strange gurgling sound. *Oh shit.* I didn't move fast enough. The top flew off the blender and its contents shot upward in a swirling funnel of brown. It blasted me right in the face and I ended up with chocolate in my ears, eyes, nose and mouth, and all over the ceiling and floors, as well as my clothes.

Maudit bâtard!

I wiped my face and glanced at the clock. One hour. I hurried through a second shower, mopped up the mess in the kitchen with the damp towel wound around my waist, then stalked into my closet. As I pulled out a fresh set of clothes, my still-empty stomach twisted into a knot. I froze, afraid I might have that panic attack I worried about. I stood perfectly still and waited. My pulse remained steady and my hands didn't shake. I frowned as I tried to suss out the reason for the churning sensation in my gut.

Not panic. *Nerves.*

I laughed, but it sounded off. Too high-pitched. I couldn't believe it. Me, Sebastien St. Clair, The Sinner, total player and ladies' man, was *nervous* for a date. I shook my head and shoved one leg into a pair of pants, then the other, and pulled a clean shirt over my head. I stopped and checked again. Nerves still going strong, though I would be the first to admit it had been a weird day.

Between giving Calloway an actual complement—not that the dickhead said thanks or anything, Amanda cornering me, and the words "I'm seeing someone" coming out of my mouth. Oh, not to mention the blender fiasco, which, truthfully, wasn't all that out of the ordinary. If anything, I should have been surprised it didn't fly apart sooner. Most shocking of all was that I was sincerely nervous to see Kylie, like a teenager about to get his dick wet for the first time.

I figured if I did anything else out of character before the clock struck midnight, the world would spin off its axis and fly right into the sun.

Better to play it safe than sorry and remember to be a selfish jackass.

You know, for the safety of the planet.

I'm considerate like that.

I CHECKED the time as I stood in front of the bathroom mirror to check my hair for the umpteenth time as I tried to rationalize away my nerves. Countdown: five minutes to date time. The phone rang while I was checking my teeth for stray food particles. I hoped it wasn't Kylie calling to cancel, because in some way, shape, or form, I was going to see her. One glance at the screen and I let out the breath I was holding.

"Rémy. *Ça roule ma poule?*"

Phone to my ear, I leaned over the sink and used my free hand to pick at random strands of hair and ensure each one lay just so. Ironically, it takes a hell of a lot of time to fix your hair so it looks like you *didn't* spend a lot of time fixing your hair.

"Seb?"

My hand froze over my head when I heard his voice waver. It was a sound I recognized immediately, and it gutted me. Despite trying to shield him from the worst of our childhood, something in my brother's world had gone sideways, and whatever it was sent Rémy into a spiral.

Fuck the hair. I turned from the mirror and leaned a hip

against the sink, as I ignored the sick feeling in my gut and the overwhelming urge to crush my phone to bits, while punching the mirror until my knuckles were torn and bloody. After several deep breaths, I pinched the bridge of my nose and did my best to keep it together. For Rémy. Not that long ago, he asked me to back off. I had to trust that if he needed my help, he would ask for it.

"Rém, what's going on? *Est-ce que ça va, mon frère?*"

"Yeah. I'm okay, bro. Just wanted to, uh, talk to you."

That did nothing to assuage my worry. In fact, it freaked me out. I seamlessly slid into rapid fire French. "Talk to me? About what?"

Oh shit, oh fuck, please no. Don't let it be another episode. Don't let it be the one and only thing I can't save him from. If it was, there was literally nothing I could do. Knowing that Rémy was suffering felt like a kick to the junk. For years he kept his issues hidden. Became adept at avoiding me and concealing the evidence of his anguish. When he slipped up and I found out what was going on, I was devastated. It should be me who hurt, not Rémy. I was the one who ended up in juvie and therefore, couldn't stop my brother's gentle soul from fracturing. In my absence, Rémy found a way to soothe his demons, a way that made me irrationally, blindingly outraged, yet sick to my stomach.

His prolonged silence sliced a gash across my abdomen and my insides spilled out onto the floor. The only way I knew Rémy hadn't hung up was the sound of his soft inhales and exhales.

For years, I accepted, even courted the physical abuse doled out by our father. The hatred and violence, the hitting, slapping, punching, kicking, burning with cigarettes... I've had so many sprains and hairline fractures, to this day I still can't believe the DYP (Department of Youth

Protection) didn't take us away from the old bastard. Not to mention the myriad of scars that crisscrossed my body as a reminder of my past. I shivered.

I have scars, but Rémy has plenty of his own.

The echo of silence sent chills down my arms. Rémy is the gentlest person I know. Well, gentle toward others. Toward himself? My hands shook and my mouth went dry. Unfortunately, like me, my brother was destined to forever be tormented by the past.

Twitch, twitch, twitch...

"Rém?" I gripped the edge of the sink and gnashed my teeth. The helplessness in the face of my brother's pain was pure torture.

Twitch...

"I'm okay." Rémy's deception sent another agonizing slash through my soft tissue and organs. I struggled to breathe and stuffed my knuckles in my mouth to hold back a sob.

"Don't do it. Please," I whispered. "Tell me you didn't, Rém."

After a beat, Rémy sighed. "I didn't. I won't. I told you, I don't... I don't do that anymore." Another lie, not that I could prove it. "Anyway. I gotta go, Seb. I just wanted to see what you were up to and say hi."

I let out an unamused chuckle. It was highly likely Rémy called as a distraction so he wouldn't give in to his compulsion. That didn't upset me. I was more than willing to be his distraction if that's what he needed. If he wanted a distraction...

"Hey," I said. "You probably won't believe me, but not only do I have a date, but I'm bringing her back here."

"Really? To your place?" Despite Rémy being caught in a tangled, bleak, web of darkness, a myriad of nightmares fought against invisible foes that existed only in my brother's mind, he sounded shocked. I laughed at his incredulity.

"Yeah. There's a first for everything."

"Umm, I guess so?"

I checked the time. If I didn't leave, I'd be late picking up Kylie. *Shit.* I didn't know what to do. Rémy made the decision for me.

"Go on your, *uh*, date, Seb. I'm fine, I promise." I hesitated, and he called me out on it. "Seriously. I'm gonna call Jankowski and see what he's up to."

Though I was reluctant to hang up, I didn't have a choice. We were separated by hundreds of miles, plus Rémy wanted to deal with his own issues, not to mention I promised to butt out. My hands were tied, and not in a good way. I huffed loudly to make it known I wasn't going down easy.

"All right. But you call me if anything happens. If you even *think* about it. You got that?"

"Yeah, yeah. I got it. And Seb?"

"*Ouais?*"

My eyes stung and an invisible band cinched around my chest. To this day, Rémy doesn't know to what lengths I would go—what lengths I had already gone—to shelter him from reality.

"I swear, I'm doing a lot better." Rémy tried to sound confident, but I know him too well to fall for it.

How was it I had zero remorse for doing what I did back then, but when my brother attempted to be brave so I wouldn't worry, I turned into a sloppy, emotional wreck?

"Good." My voice cracked.

"Talk to you later," Rémy said, effectively ending the conversation. I scrubbed a hand over the back of my neck.

"Okay. *Tu me manques, mon frère.*"

"Miss you, too. *Au revoir*."

The call ended. I snatched my keys out of the glass dish next to the door and hurried for the elevator before I changed my mind and booked a flight to Charlotte. I clutched the steering wheel, knuckles blanched, and body tense. It took the entire fifteen-minutes to calm down from my agitated state. Normally, I'd be wound up and pissed all night. It just so happened I was highly motivated. If I didn't rein it in, Kylie would bolt the second she laid eyes on me. I didn't need the rearview mirror to know I looked half-crazed, which pretty much summarized how I felt.

Dear old dad. No longer around and still shitting all over his sons' lives.

I stopped in front of Kylie's building, a sleek, modern skyscraper of luxury condos. Not cheap. And not the kind of place you lived if you needed a roommate. I briefly wondered what Kylie did for a living. She had to make decent cash if she could afford a place in the high-rise, even at half the rent. Maybe she came from money, not that I was about to ask. I might have the tact of a bulldog on meth, but questioning someone's financial status is pretty fucking rude, even for me. Plus, I just didn't give enough of a shit to bother.

After sending a quick text to let Kylie know I was outside, I dropped the phone into a cup holder and cranked up the beats. The loud thumping bass provided perfect cover for so I could shout at the top of my lungs and punch the steering wheel over and over until my hands were red and swollen and my throat was raw, without anyone hearing me lose my shit.

"Fuck, fuck, fuuuuuuuck!"

I struggled to breathe, and it felt like my head was going to explode like my blender. Instead of chocolate, brains would jet out and splatter the interior of my Ford. Mid-shout, I spotted Kylie trotting down the short flight of stairs to the street. I gulped down air and willed my body to relax so she wouldn't witness the remnants of my tantrum.

Once I got the fury strapped in, I turned down the music and hopped out, then circled the truck to open the passenger door. *Damn.* Her beauty breathed life into my stagnant lungs and a gentle wave of calm soothed the ends of my frazzled nerves.

"Hey," I said as I raked my greedy eyes up and down her body. Fucking gorgeous. Neither my memories nor my fantasies did her justice.

"Hi."

Kylie smiled and just like that, I was fucking putty in her hands. For the first time in my life, the perpetual distress I felt concerning my brother got shoved to the back burner. Pushed out of my head by the enticing sight of Kylie's full lips, white teeth, and glittering brown eyes. The light scent of citrus tickled my nose and all of my synapses fired at once, every cell in my body ultra-aware of Kylie's presence.

I held out a hand. She raised a brow, but accepted it. The minimal physical contact of our entwined fingers, that tiny bit of skin on skin, sent a shiver down my spine. I smothered the urge to grope her ass as I helped her into the tall cab.

"Thank you," she said once she was settled in.

The agitation, guilt, and utter frustration vanished. I don't know how she did it, but Kylie acted as a balm on my black and hollow soul. Somehow, she made me forget. Made me feel *human.* Silenced the constant screaming and the nagging doubt. Grateful for the distraction, I winked. Hope-fully, flirting would keep me from thinking too much, both about Rémy, and how different I felt around Kylie.

"You're welcome." I grinned and closed her door, then

shoved my hands in my pockets and rounded back to the driver's side, exhaling a long breath that puffed out a misty cloud in the frigid winter air. I could do this. I *needed* to do this. A hot tumble with a hot woman sounded like the perfect way to dig out from under the landslide of shit Rémy's phone call buried me under.

I pulled out onto the streets of Atlanta and, to my dismay, the stomach-cramping nerves returned, along with a nice fat dose of uncertainty. It started as an innocent, *"Maybe this was a mistake"* and quickly progressed to *"What the hell was I thinking?"*

The cab began to shrink around me, and it became difficult to concentrate on the road. *Shit.* I couldn't do this. Why did I think I could invite a woman into my home? It wasn't something I did.

I glanced at Kylie. Going by how happy she looked, she felt the complete opposite. Kylie really wanted this. Wanted *me.* Her cheeks were flushed and healthy and small smile played on her lips. Hell, her skin practically *glowed.*

"So, where are we going? Another hotel?"

I laughed and glanced over before I returned my attention to the slow-moving traffic. "Am I that predictable?"

Kylie paused, then said, "I'm not sure. I don't really know you."

I brought the truck to a stop at a red light and turned to face Kylie. *Was I that predictable?* I squirmed under Kylie's scrutiny and the verbal diarrhea began. "This is kinda, um, new territory for me. Bringing someone to, uh, my place. That's where we're going. I don't... I haven't... No one goes there." I tightened my grip on the steering wheel, not at all comfortable discussing my social proclivities.

For the first time in a long time, I felt ashamed. Ashamed at the way I treated women, as if they were disposable playthings. Ashamed that Kylie assumed I brought every woman I met to a hotel for a quick fuck, not that she was wrong, mind you. That was exactly what I did, unless the woman lived nearby, then I went to her place for, um... yeah, okay fine, for a quick fuck.

Kylie deserved better than that.

She looked like she was about to say something, but the light switched to green before she got the chance. I tore my gaze away and immersed myself in making sure I didn't drive off the road. Kylie remained silent for several minutes. When she finally spoke, she caught me by surprise.

"Why me?"

Huh?

"Why you?"

"Yes. Why are you bringing me to your place? You said you don't do that, so I want to know, why me?"

I repeated the question to myself and tried to come up with an excuse that wasn't shallow, *"because you're smoking hot and I can't wait for your roommate to leave so I can hold you down and slam into you from behind"* or utterly ridiculous, *"because for whatever reason, it seems that you're the only one who can tame my fury"* and came up blank. After a few more moments of awkward silence, I decided the only thing to do was answer as honestly as possible without pissing Kylie off.

"I have no idea."

I shrugged so she wouldn't think being invited to my place was a big deal. I didn't want to risk her reading into it and getting all attached like Amanda. *That*, I definitely didn't need. Kylie was either satisfied by my non-answer or annoyed, because there were no more questions after that.

I unclenched when we reached our destination. The ride was short, but it felt like I went three rounds with Georges St-Pierre. I shifted to slide out of the truck, beyond grateful to leave the close quarters of the truck's cab. The stifling closeness was driving me fucking insane. Intense stares, luscious lips, and that goddamned heavenly citrus scent, made me half-hard and wholly frustrated. I desperately needed some fresh air.

And because I'm an idiot, instead of opening the door and clearing my head, I turned to Kylie, who hadn't moved, and almost choked on my tongue. One of her slick lips, lips I envisioned wrapped around my cock, was caught between her teeth. I stared, jealous of those teeth. I wanted to be the one to bite on that soft, pink flesh.

"Uh," I shook off the image of those lips wrapped around my cock. "Are you okay?" I asked.

Please don't tell me you changed your mind. I need this. I need you.

I wanted to get her upstairs and would say whatever it took to make it happen.

Kylie stared out the window. "I know this is probably something you do a lot," she waved a hand around. "Except, like you said, the part about going to your place. But... um, you should know, this, it isn't something I do. I mean, I did do it, with you, that one time, at the hotel. But that's, um, it."

I stared at her, confused. "I'm not sure I know what you mean."

She let out an adorable huff and lifted her gaze to mine. "Having sex with strangers. It's not like me. I don't do that." She frowned and her nose crinkled. "Only, I guess it is like me, because I did it, but only with you."

I might have stopped breathing. "Wait. You're saying, I mean, what you're saying is, you don't do casual hookups and that I'm the exception to the rule? Me?"

Kylie nodded and tugged that ruby red lip back between her teeth. *Saint sicrisse.* I held back a groan. She was so fucking hot, if she didn't have guys tripping over her left and right I would eat my custom made Bauer Supreme, handle and all. Or maybe she did, and she wasn't interested. If that were true, it meant out of all the available men she had the opportunity to screw around with, she chose me. My semi continued to grow toward full hardness at the idea of being the only one to successfully seduce Kylie into shedding her inhibitions.

"I appreciate you telling me. Now," I gave her a lopsided grin and ignored my steadily thickening dick, "since you aren't fond of strangers, why don't we go upstairs and get to know each other a little better?"

Kylie's cheeks flushed and she glanced away, self-conscious. For that brief second, I swore she was hiding something from me.

Something big.

How intriguing. My naive little temptress had a secret.

The more time I spent with Kylie, the more addicted I became. I couldn't wait to peel back each new layer so I could slowly discover what made her tick.

Fuck.

I was in big trouble.

Kylie

I had no idea why I agreed to meet Seb. I mean, I did know, kind of. Obviously, I had a screw or two loose.

"Want something to drink?"

In the foyer of the luxury suite, high up in the W Hotel, Seb took my coat and hung it on an old-fashioned coat tree. Then he stalked—it's the only way I can describe it—toward me. His eyes sparked with mischief and his wicked grin made my stomach do flips.

The Sebastien St. Clair. With me. In his home. Yeah, screws loose or not, he *was* the reason I decided to step so far out of my comfort zone—a detrimental to my mental health, Rocco coronary-inducing, devastatingly sexy reason.

The entire situation—when one took into consideration the fact that Seb was hands down the absolute worst choice in bed partners, oh, and don't forget Rocco hated his guts and probably wanted to punch him whenever Seb was near —was a disaster in the making. Of course, all of that was why I couldn't bring myself to walk away. The danger of being discovered by Rocco, combined with the fact that Seb tying me up was the hottest thing to ever happen to me, had me hooked. Seb was heroin and I was the junkie who craved my next hit. I knew full well he was bad for me, yet I knew I would keep going back for more, until he either destroyed me or I OD'd.

"Well?"

I startled out of my thoughts. Right. Seb. Waiting. Drink.

"Um, a drink would be great. Thanks."

Seb's gaze fell to my mouth. He licked his lips and stared them as if he wanted to devour me. Tiny flickers of electricity crackled along my skin and my heart skipped a beat or two. Yeah, I could use a drink. Or four. A little alcohol would go a long way toward helping me relax, then, at the very least, I wouldn't make a complete fool of myself and jump Seb's bones in his foyer.

Without thinking, I mimicked his actions and moistened my lips. Seb's pupils expanded and his breath hitched. My muscles clenched with anticipation at the sound. Oh god. Jumping his bones in the foyer was sounding better and better. Thankfully, by the time I began to mentally peel off his clothes, Seb had wandered deeper into the condo and missed my needy expression.

"Coming right up." His husky tone shot straight to my groin. As Seb circled around a gorgeous granite-topped island, I squeezed my thighs together to relieve some of the aching need. It didn't work.

On the other side of the island, Seb reached up and removed two glasses from an overhead cabinet. In doing so, his T-shirt hiked up to expose a slice of hard, tan, deeply grooved abdominal muscles, and my mouth watered at the sight. Would Seb fuck me on the island? Stand between my splayed thighs and pound into me until I screamed?

"Here you go."

"Thanks." I tried to hide my face, cheeks burning from the impromptu fantasy. Seb gave me a look, but thankfully didn't ask.

Not willing to chance saying something dumb and make an even bigger fool of myself, I lifted the glass, tipped it back, and swallowed the contents in one go. Big mistake. My eyes watered as an unholy blast of hellfire ripped down my throat, and back up again. It felt like someone took a blow-torch to my esophagus. In between sputtering coughs, I heard Seb chuckle.

"You do realize Scotch is meant to be sipped."

I wiped the tears out of my eyes and glanced up from my fiery hacking fit in time to see Seb hold up his glass. Then, in complete contradiction to what he said, with a flick of his wrist, every last drop of the amber liquid disappeared down that gorgeous throat. My lusty gaze locked onto Seb's Adam's apple as he swallowed, and I stifled a moan. He caught me staring and smirked.

"I didn't want you to be lonely."

Lonely. How Seb made that word sound like an invitation for sex, I didn't know, but he did. A fresh burst of desire rippled down my spine and I my attention snapped to his bright blue gaze. Seb's hunger was obvious, his eyes dark and hooded as he stared at my mouth again. My fingers tightened around the glass.

Blistering heat—whether from the alcohol or the way Seb was undressing me with his eyes—spread through my veins. Every beat of my heart stoked the flames hotter and hotter until I was consumed by the passionate inferno. A sudden, desperate need to have Seb's hands on my sweltering skin pushed me into action.

I arranged my mouth into what I hoped looked like a sexy pout and, feigning confidence I didn't feel, I put down the empty tumbler and flattened my palms on the cool stone surface. I studied Seb's lips and, since it worked before, slowly licked mine.

"I'm not lonely," I purred, hardly recognizing my sultry tone. Seb held his breath, gaze locked on my mouth. I navigated around the island as I slid a single fingertip along the slick granite. "At least, I won't be once we get to the real reason you brought me here. Or did you think you'd have to talk me into it?"

The flush on Seb's throat and cheeks was satisfying in a way I'd never known. I felt powerful. *I* did that to him. I made Sebastien St. Clair blush, something I doubted happened that often. Eyes glazed, lips parted, Seb's mouth hung slack, but only for a second. One second was all it took for him to blink away the haze of lust. Without missing a beat, he put his glass on the counter behind him and closed the remaining distance between us in two large strides. His expression was feral and in looking at it, I chalked up my first attempt at seducing a man as a success.

Seb struck first. He crashed into me, his strong arms wrapping around my waist to keep me on my feet. Before I could gather my scattered wits, his lips descended. We came together in a desperate meeting of mouths. Teeth and tongues clashed. Seb dominated the kiss, owned it. It was messy and uncoordinated, slick and hot, and I loved every moment of it. In fact, I leaned into Seb and willingly gave up control. He sensed the moment I surrendered and growled as he reached down to palm my ass. Large hands splayed across my backside. He tugged sharply and our groins collided. The friction added fuel to the already roaring fire.

"Bedroom," Seb whispered when he released my mouth and shifted to nip his way down my jaw.

Seb didn't wait, and we were moving before I answered. He walked me backward through his suite and effortlessly maneuvered us around furniture and other obstacles without missing a beat. Too caught up in the way Seb sucked, licked, and bit my mouth and throat to pay attention, I handed over the reins, trusted Seb to get us to our destination in one piece, mostly because there was no way I was going to be the one to end the hottest kiss of my life, especially not for something as silly as tripping over furniture.

As with everything else about the man, Seb didn't disappoint. Faster than I thought, the backs of my knees hit the soft edge of a mattress. I shifted my weight to sit, but Seb wanted nothing of it and dug his fingers into my backside, effectively forcing me to remain upright. Satisfied I would stay put, Seb let go and took a step back.

"Clothes first." The words were barely out before Seb reached over his head. In one graceful motion, he grabbed his collar and yanked off his shirt to reveal a torso that was so perfect, it could have been chiseled out of stone and put on display in the Louvre. While I ogled every flawless dip and hard ridge, Seb got to work on me. His hands were surprisingly dexterous as he made quick work of the tiny buttons on my blouse. The silky fabric scarcely had time to flutter to the floor and Seb's mouth was on my skin.

"Oh god."

I moaned, arched my neck, and threw my head back as Seb licked a path from my shoulder to my clavicle. He worked his lips and teeth against hidden bundles of sensitive nerve endings while I clutched at his biceps and reveled in the feeling of hard muscle beneath my fingertips. He kissed his way further down and stopped between my breasts. Seb sucked at the thin, tender skin. Hard enough that it stung.

I flinched. "Hey!" I was supposed to sound annoyed, but it came out more like a wanton moan. I pushed ineffectively at Seb's head and pushed words out between heavy breaths. "You're going to leave a mark."

Seb smiled against my breastbone and sucked the spot one last time. He straightened to his full height and I gulped. *Ohmygod.* He is so, so much taller than me. So much bigger... all over. There's just so much of him. His eyes were wild and dark, face and throat ruddy, and lips red and swollen. He was the sexiest thing in the history of ever.

Seb grinned at my indignation. "That's the idea." He nuzzled my ear. "I want to mark you all over."

My dignified response was to shiver and practically hump his leg. The thought of Seb staking his claim appealed to my baser instincts.

Seb flicked open the button on my jeans. I did the same. We worked together to shed the rest of our clothes. Once we were naked, Seb hauled me against him like he did in the kitchen. Again, his hands went straight to my backside and he kneaded my ass in a sensual massage. It was the dead of winter and the room slightly cool, but Seb's body was a furnace. Heat radiated off his skin and kept the chill away.

He dipped his head and sucked my earlobe into his mouth. My cries bounced around the bedroom. I scrabbled for something to hold onto, and clung to his broad shoulders for support.

When Seb let go and stepped away, I whined at the loss. He leveled a look so stern, I pressed my lips together and squelched the urge to pitch a fit.

"I'll be right back. I have to get something."

I nodded and the tense lines around Seb's mouth disappeared and his eyelids went back to half-mast. He was clearly pleased by my easy capitulation. He stared at me, gaze filled with raw hunger and promises of things to come. It was so hot I wanted to reach between my legs and touch myself.

"By the time I get back, I expect you to be on the bed, hands over your head and legs spread." A shockwave blasted from my scalp down to my toes and the subsequent rush of blood made me lightheaded. Apparently, bossy and dominating really turned my crank. The second Seb left the room, I climbed onto the mattress, determined to do exactly as instructed.

Never had I felt so exposed, completely naked, splayed out and exposed on Seb's bed, amongst the buttery soft white sheets and fluffy duvet. My fingertips stretched to the headboard and my feet were positioned shoulder-width apart. Like that, Seb would be able to see *everything*. The thought both thrilled and embarrassed me. I had to close my eyes, as if not seeing meant I wasn't acting like a complete nympho, all but begging for Seb to do whatever he wanted to any part of my body.

I waited for what seemed like forever. Okay, maybe not that long, but long enough that I mentally took note of everything I felt with my four remaining senses. Eyes still squeezed shut, I focused on the wild hammering of my heart, the slight chill in the air that made goose bumps prick along my skin and hardened my nipples into peaks, and the slick, needy ache between my thighs. The air tasted faintly of woodsmoke, the sheets held the light scent of sandalwood. I exhaled shakily, mortified yet beyond excited.

Over my head, I fisted the sheets and relaxed. I needed to get it together before Seb returned. There was nothing as unsexy as finding a trembling, nervous wreck in your bed, and it significantly raised the odds that Seb would take one look, wrinkle his nose, say, *"ew,"* and send me packing.

"Sorry about that." My eyes flew open and I let out a startled squeak. Seb gave me an adorable crooked smile and a shiny glint caught my eye. I looked at Seb's hands, *er*, the items in his hands, to be specific. When I realized what he held, my face grew hot, but I vibrated with arousal. "Had to get these." He gestured to his collection of steel-linked chains and leather cuffs, taunting me by casually dangling one from a fingertip.

I swallowed thickly. "Okay."

Sebastien cocked his head and studied me. "You sure you want this?" He held up a pair of studded leather cuffs. They swung over the bed, and I couldn't tear my gaze away, hypnotized as they rocked back and forth.

"Yes."

More than anything.

Seb's lips slowly unfurled into a wide grin, one that held no amusement. No, it relayed every filthy intention he had in store for me. I shivered as my imagination went wild. One at a time, Seb wrapped a pliable leather cuff around each of my limbs. To those he attached a short chain between a D-ring on the cuffs and an identical one fixed onto the bedposts. A light went off in my head and, though I was still excited, my insides spasmed with anxiety. The reason Seb wanted me at his place had nothing to do with me being special. He bought me there so he could utilize his personal BDSM equipment.

My brief boost in confidence faltered and I clenched and unclenched my fingers as doubts assailed me. After he secured each arm and leg, Seb rounded the bed and stood back to admire his work.

Fuck it.

Any concerns over why I was there fell to the wayside, as I blushed and fidgeted under Seb's intense scrutiny. I no longer cared if I was special or why he chose me. The hormone-laden blood that flooded my system, along with the rapid thrumming of my pulse, demanded my attention. I wanted what Seb offered. Badly. His particular reasons no longer mattered. Only mine.

Seb winked. "Don't be embarrassed, Kylie. If you only knew how fucking hot you look right now."

I might not have been able to see everything, but based on Seb's expression and the very interested reaction of a certain part of his body—one he reached down and fisted so he could slowly stroke the stiff length—I knew he was pleased.

"You're not special" flicked through my mind again, but I pushed it out. I wanted Seb and was not about to ruin it, especially not because of something so pointless as feeling insecure.

Seb took a few minutes to stare and stroke himself. I stared back, watching his fist move as I tried not to fidget. When I thought I might burst if he didn't touch me, Seb finally released his impressive erection and climbed up on the bed. His significant weight jostled me, but because of the bindings, I only moved a bit and remained in the center of the island-sized mattress.

Okay, Kylie. Relax.

I took a deep breath and exhaled. Seb looked at me with the most carnal expression I'd ever seen.

Oh, boy.

Let the games begin.

Seb

I kneeled between Kylie's long, sinewy legs and took the time to memorize every last inch of her body. If I didn't think there was at least a fifty-fifty chance she'd disappear—for everything to have been a dream from the time she got into my truck up to that moment—I'd have pinched myself. Kylie was simply too good to be real. Too perfect.

Again, I dragged my gaze up and down her fit, curvy body, and with the exception of several mouthwatering freckles I would soon taste, there wasn't a single flaw to be found. Her pale skin flushed in various places as I gave her a thorough inspection. She squirmed for me and that stunning rosy hue spread. I took in the swell of her breasts, not too big and not too small, the taper of her slender, but not too skinny waist, the arc of her hips, and the glistening slit between her thighs. I licked my lips, not knowing where I wanted to start. So many things to do and try.

I zeroed in on her breasts and smirked. Kylie liked nipple play. I leaned forward and placed my hands on her outstretched arms, then ran my hands from her wrists, over her armpits, and down to the soft swells of her breasts. Kylie let out a little mewl when I circled her dusky nipples and lightly pinched them, rolled them just hard enough for her to feel. Kylie's lips fell open, but she stayed quiet and instead used her eyes to beg for more.

My cock kicked and I grinned. I pinched harder, but not quite as firm as she wanted. Still, her reaction was beautiful. Kylie panted as the anticipation built. Her chest heaved up and down and her ribs went in and out as I played her body like a finely tuned instrument. Once I got her nice and worked up, I gave her nipples an aggressive twist and squeezed... *hard.* She groaned and her bucked hips off the bed. It was so hot, when she shouted my name my dick ached from the rush of blood.

Oh fuuuuck.

"Seb! Oh god..."

"You like it rough," I said, mostly to myself, confirming what I already knew about her. I did it again.

Kylie moaned loudly and her back bowed. "God yes. H-harder."

Jesus. It felt like every drop of blood in my body rerouted to my cock. It pulsed and throbbed painfully. I wanted to plow that sweet pussy so badly my balls hung heavy and my dick spit up pre-come. But I wasn't done exploring. I wanted to take my time and enjoy my new playground. Instead of twisting her nipples, I licked my lips, bent over, and took one in my mouth, using my fingers to manipulate the other. I pinched the tight bud and simultaneously bit down.

Kylie screamed and my cock jerked angrily. An honest to god fucking *screamer.* One of my biggest kinks. Well, after the chains, and cuffs, and a tiny bit of pain... whatever. Hard no longer described the state of my dick. Tire iron was more appropriate.

In the hours that led up to that moment, ever since our rendezvous in the hotel attached to the arena, I had constructed a million different scenarios, various versions of foreplay. Most of them involved bringing Kylie to the edge of orgasm over and over as she writhed and bucked. Her skin would be covered in bite marks and bright red handprints and she eventually begged me to fuck her. Cried for it. Every last one of those fantasies went up in smoke as I watched Kylie lose her ever-loving mind from a bit of nipple stimulation.

She was fucking made for me.

"Oh god, oh god, oh god..." Her head thrashed from side to side and her body twisted what little it could within the confines of the chains. I couldn't look away, thoroughly entranced. Kylie's reactions went way beyond anything I'd experienced, and we hadn't even got to the good stuff yet.

"*Maudit calvare*," I muttered under my breath. Kylie was breathing so hard and fast she didn't hear me. In fact, the glazed-over look in her eyes said she was off in another universe. The fact that I did that to her, sent Kylie soaring, and with so little effort, blew my damn mind.

Moving faster than should be possible without a pair of blades on my feet, I unclasped the cuffs on Kylie's ankles and rolled on the condom I'd dropped on the bed. Fuck foreplay. My dick was going to snap off if I didn't get inside her. Without instruction, Kylie kept her legs spread. She panted heavily and waited to see what I did next.

"I'm sorry." I growled in desperation. "I planned to draw this out, but I can't wait any longer." With that, I shoved my cock in her tight pussy and kept going until my balls touched her skin.

Kylie groaned as I split her open. The silken walls of her pussy clenched and rippled around my dick and already, a familiar, tingling sensation rocketed down my spine. I squeezed my eyes shut and stayed perfectly still to keep from shooting my load. How fucking embarrassing would that be?

Once the urge to blow receded, I stared at Kylie. She looked up and with the force of a heavyweight's swing, the breath punched out of my lungs. Hands cuffed to the bed, hair mussed, lips puffy, and cheeks crimson, Kylie lifted her sinful legs, wound them around my waist, and clasped them at the ankles. The sight was beyond erotic, it was pure fantasy porn, not to mention it brought me *thatmuchcloser* to her, which pulled my cock *thatmuchdeeper*.

Physically, Kylie was a perfect ten, but it wasn't her body that had me captivated. I was riveted by her eyes, the reflection of desire, need, and overwhelming trust.

She made me feel like a god.

I began to move. Slowly at first. I studied her carefully and shifted positions based on Kylie's reactions. When I stabbed in deep at one particular angle, she yelped each time. Bingo. Keeping that position, I sped my thrusts, hammering her fast and hard, over and over until her body glistened with sweat, her muscles quaked, and her loud moans morphed into one long, unending wail.

I felt the first spasms of Kylie's pussy, and lifted her leg to drape it over my shoulder and expose the side of her luscious ass. I waited until her climax took hold, lifted my hand, and brought it down. It landed on her skin with a loud crack as she came.

Kylie arched her back tight as a bowstring, and *screamed* my name. Her entire body shook and the chains rattled as the pleasure overcame her. I smacked her ass a second time, using the pain to draw out the orgasm. Kylie's eyes took on a hazy, faraway look—she was flying.

That was my cue. I picked up the pace and pistoned in and out, the wet heat gripping my cock like a slick glove.

Sweat dripped down my cheeks and I struggled to hold onto Kylie's hips as my fingers slid across her skin. It only took a few thrusts for my rhythm to stutter. I came so hard I thought I might black out. Lights sparked and my vision went fuzzy. I gripped her hard enough to leave bruises and emptied my balls deep in her pussy, spurt after spurt of glorious ecstasy. It wasn't until I pumped every last drop from my balls that I groaned, collapsed on top of a panting, wrecked Kylie, and closed my eyes to catch my breath.

I wasn't sure how long we stayed like that, me slumped over Kylie, except that it felt... weird. Not bad, weird. In fact, it felt the opposite. Good, weird. Except I don't cuddle. Ever. I fuck, I get up, I get dressed, and I leave. The mere fact that my first instinct wasn't to spring from the bed and hustle Kylie out the door, had me worried.

"Can you...?" The rattle of chains drew my attention.

Shit. I was so out of it, so relaxed and content, I forgot to release Kylie.

"Yeah."

I shuffled to my knees, ignored the fact that my legs felt like jelly, reached up, and slid open the buckles. Then I massaged Kylie's arms and shoulders to get the blood flowing. She'd be sore tomorrow, but hopefully it would be a feeling she enjoyed. Maybe think of me every time a muscle twinged.

"You okay?"

From the blissed out look on Kylie's face, the question was redundant. Even so, I shouldn't have cared how she was doing. Never did about any of the other women.

Again, until Kylie.

I climbed off the bed, pulled on my jeans, and fled to the safety of the bathroom. Behind the closed door, I ran the faucet to make it sound like I was actually doing something useful rather than hiding. I propped my hands on the sink and stared into the mirror.

Instead of the moody, glaring, angry man I was familiar with, the guy in the reflection looked... happy. He smiled and his eyes sparkled with satisfaction. I wasn't sure who the fuck the asshole thought he was, but his stupid grin unnerved me.

I splashed cold water on my face and haphazardly dried off, chucking the towel on the floor. There would be plenty of time to have an existential crisis later. After all the shit I'd been though, I deserved a break. Five fucking minutes of happiness.

Satisfied I could play it cool and not start drawing little hearts with our names inside, I took a deep breath, ignored the unfamiliar, fluttery sensation in my belly, and exited the bathroom. My ability to play it cool sucked, because my gaze went directly to the bed.

And my stomach promptly did a triple lindy and splattered all over the floor.

Good things didn't happen to me. Happiness didn't happen to me. I was forever destined to be bitter and angry.

Karma, you vicious little bitch.

The bed was empty.

9

Seb

Fully dressed, down to her shoes, Kylie was standing in the main living area, her spine as stiff as a board. Her posture blinked like a glaring neon sign that all but shouted *"Danger, danger! You've got a runner on your hands!"*

Seeing Kylie so desperate to leave sent my good mood into a nosedive. I went from the top of the world to the pits of hell in one second flat.

"Leaving already?" The words were out of my mouth before I could stop them, and I regretted it immediately.

St. Clair, you fuckwad. Could you sound any needier?

Kylie didn't look in my direction. "Um, yeah. I need to, uh, get going. My....uh, my roommate is expecting me."

Good thing she wasn't looking at me, because I think I actually mouthed the word, "*wow.*" She had me so fucking turned around, I didn't know what to think. Not only did I *not* introduce her to my front door a heartbeat after I came, but Kylie just gave me what might actually qualify as the flimsiest excuse since, *"I have to wash my hair tomorrow,"* or, *"I have an early meeting,"* both of which I may have used at one time or another.

Like I said, Karma.

I clamped down the urge to be snarky and replied with a cold, "That's fine," instead. Kylie flinched, not that I blamed her. My tone was glacial enough to put icicles on the ceiling fan.

She turned to me and my pulse stumbled when I looked in her eyes. Gone was the sexy, smoldering heat, the enthusiastic passion, the woman who, not five minutes ago, trusted me enough to let go of her inhibitions and follow me down the rabbit hole. In Kylie's place sat someone else, a stranger, and, from the closed-off expression and guilt-ridden eyes, she held more secrets than Jimmy Hoffa. You didn't need to study kinesics to read Kylie's body language. The unspoken, *"get me the fuck out of here,"* may as well have been scrawled across her forehead in black Sharpie.

Stranger-Kylie glanced in the direction of the door.

Fists at my sides, I had to force out, "I'll get dressed and take you home."

The words sounded foreign, like someone else spoke them. Hell, I *felt* like someone else. Self-doubt wasn't familiar to me. Neither was the overwhelming desire to drop to my knees and beg Kylie to stay. To strip her clothes off, pull her into bed, wrap her up in my arms, and never let go.

So what did I do? Did I speak up? Did I confess my desires to the woman who banged a hand on the plexi and into my life, only to flip my world upside down? Did I ask her to stay, or try to talk to her about what she was thinking?

Of course not. I'm an asshole. At least I'm consistent.

The drive passed in complete silence and, despite wanting to grimace, I maintained a detached, unaffected facade, as if I weren't fucking *dying* inside. When I stopped in front of Kylie's building and put the truck in park, she glanced up at me from under her lashes. She got a look at my emotionless features and winced. I almost felt bad. Almost. The ache in my chest along with my unwavering assholiness, kept my mouth shut and my ass in the seat.

Kylie mumbled so low I strained to hear. "I guess I'll, um, talk to you later?"

Seriously?

I wanted to yell. To shake her senseless. To insist she tell me what was wrong. But I refused to let her see how much the knife to the gut hurt. I didn't respond with words. I couldn't, afraid my voice or my willpower would snap like a twig. Instead, I answered with a sharp nod.

Kylie's eyes shimmered with tears, but to her credit, not a single one fell. She scrabbled for the latch and flung open the door. I wish I could say didn't watch her walk into the building and continue to stare until long after she disappeared from sight, but when it came to Kylie, I was weak. I didn't know why, but she was the chink in my armor. My Achilles heel. My soft spot.

I scrubbed my jaw and cursed myself out; not just for indulging in stupid fantasies about a relationship I would never have and certainly didn't deserve, allowing them to invade my thoughts, but for not taking that leap of faith. Grabbing on to what could very well have been my one and only chance at true happiness.

It was probably for the best. A guy like me didn't end up with a woman like Kylie. There was no doubt in my mind, if I pursued her, I would break her heart and ruin her life.

That's what I was good at. Ruining things.

It didn't stop me from spending the rest of the day plotting a way to see Kylie again. Because deep down, I was a selfish prick. I'd go after her, despite the risk to her well-being and with total disregard for how it might affect her.

That was how I lived. With the exception of Rémy, everything I touched turned into a shitshow. Despite my best efforts, even my own brother ended up with a heaping load of issues that rivaled mine.

There was no reason to expect anything with Kylie to turn out different.

I was a wrecking ball and, unfortunately, someone was going to end up smashed. Whether it was Kylie or me, I didn't know.

I plugged my phone into my sound system and swiped until I found the playlist I wanted. Loud, thumping music reverberated throughout the condo as I made myself a late-night snack. Immersed in my thoughts, I ate, cleaned up the kitchen, and made sure the door was locked.

Was there a chance Kylie and me could somehow work out?

My personal experience shouted a resounding, "*fuck no,*" but hell, I wanted to cling to that sliver of hope, no matter how unlikely. I mean, how much shit did one person have to go through before he was due to catch a goddamn break?

That was my last thought right before I went over to the stereo and reached out to turn off the music.

"Son of a—"

I managed to yank my phone free as a power surge fried my very expensive, state-of-the-art sound system. Sparks shot out of the receiver and it let out a blast of whiny, high-pitched, ear-splitting feedback. Tiny flames erupted from the receiver. I stuck a finger in each of my ears to make they weren't bleeding.

"Motherfucker!"

I ran and grabbed the fire extinguisher from under the sink and sprayed the flames before the sprinkler system came on. Disheartened, but wholly unsurprised by the sequence of events, I sagged in resignation and stared at the charred remains of ten thousand dollars with of equipment as the sharp scent of melted plastic and electronics singed my nostrils.

Me? Catch a break? Yeah, right. I had a better chance of becoming the Prime Minister of Canada.

Peoplekind. What a douchbag.

Kylie

The following week was rough, minutes felt like hours and hours felt like an eternity. I spent ninety-nine percent of the slow-moving time thinking about Seb. It was so bad, it got to the point where not only did my work suffer, but I kept catching Rocco shooting me confused looks. Once, he even asked point-blank what my problem was. I got so sick of his constant pestering that I finally blurted out I had a raging case of PMS.

Rocco's eyes went wide and he fled the room. I might have taken a little pleasure in that. Nothing scared men like the threat of discussing your menstrual cycle.

Friday had rolled around, again, and even though I loved my internship, I couldn't wait for five o'clock so I could go home. Why? Not a clue. It wasn't as if I had plans, except to sit around and mope, wishing I was with Seb. Maybe it would happen... in an alternate universe. A universe where Seb wasn't an emotionally stunted man-whore and my brother wasn't a hot-tempered, bullheaded, meddling idiot.

"Hot date?"

Piper approached my desk and I attempted to smile, but it was a weak effort. With anyone else, I wouldn't have bothered. Piper, however, isn't *"anyone else."* I had to show her everything was okay. If I didn't, she would pry. Piper was the only person who knew about Seb, and she had taken to drilling me about him at the most random of times. The woman was relentless. Good for a journalist, bad when you wanted to forget.

At least I didn't tell her I hooked up with him *last* Friday. To Piper's frustration, over the last week, each and every time she cornered me, I talked my way out of giving her an explanation for my weirdness. Eventually, she would call me out on my bullshit. I just hoped my time wasn't up.

"Nah, just tired," I said as I filed a few papers, mostly to avoid making eye contact. As observant as she was, Piper was even more so when she looked you in the eye.

"Riiiight." She perched on the edge of my tiny cubicle desk, clearly not about to go anywhere until she got what she wanted. "So, you're saying your mopey attitude all week was because you were tired." Piper rolled her eyes and shook her head. "Nuh-uh. Try again."

"Come on, Piper," I whined. "Can we not talk about this?"

"Talk about what? The fact that you're really into this guy, the fact that you're trying to hide it from me, or the fact that you don't want to admit any of it?"

I huffed and crossed my arms. "It was just a bit of fun. Remember? You and I already talked about this. And, um, you were right, by the way." I took a sudden, acute interest in my stapler, and flipped it over in my hands. "It was a mistake to get involved with him." Of course she heard me, despite my mumbling.

"But totally worth it, right?" I glanced up at Piper and, to my surprise, she was grinning.

As usual, her smile was contagious and tugged at the

corners of my mouth. I chuckled, but it was accompanied by a painful ache in my chest.

"Totally. Yep," I agreed.

"See, I told you—" Piper read my wounded expression and her face fell. "Oh my god, Ky. I was just kidding when I said you were into him."

I ducked my head so she wouldn't see me cry. Piper's hand curled around my arm. I pushed my hair out of my face, tried to keep it together, and failed.

"I swear I didn't know," Piper said. "It's more than that, isn't it?" She stared at me and realization flitted across her features. "Oh my god. You don't just like him... you're falling for him."

I wiped my eyes and waved her off. "Not really. I don't even know him. So no, I'm not falling for him. I just wish—"

"You wish it wasn't so complicated," Piper said when I got too choked up to finish.

"Yeah."

It didn't matter whether or not I liked Seb, we could never be together, not for real. First, Rocco would never accept it, and second, Seb would never accept *me* if he found out Rocco was my brother. Besides, it really was just sex. At least, for Seb.

Another jolt of pain squeezed my heart and I winced.

"I'm so sorry, Kylie. It sucks. I know exactly how you feel when you want to be with someone, but extenuating circumstances make it impossible."

"It does suck," I agreed. With a final sniff, I stood and smoothed my hands down my clothes. Chin up, trying to maintain some sense of dignity, I asked Piper, "What do you say we go out and forget about men and their extenuating circumstances?"

Piper's eyes glittered and that wide grin returned. "Let's go."

~

"I DON'T GET YOU, Kylie. What is it? Suddenly you don't like hockey anymore?"

Exhausted by the subject, I sat on the couch and watched Rocco pace back and forth, his perma-scowl front and center, v-shaped wrinkle front and center.

"I told you, I've been busy with work and when I'm not there I'm catching up on sleep."

More lies. God, Rocco deserved so much better. But it wasn't as if I could tell him why I couldn't go to his games. The possibility of Seb trying to, or worse, successfully making contact where Rocco would see, scared me to death. No way would Rocco miss his arch-nemesis chatting up his little sister. Nothing good would happen if I went to the Comets games, both in terms of Rocco, and my fragile, melancholy heart.

Rocco shot me a glare. He didn't buy my pathetic excuse and, in his defense, it was pretty crappy. Plus, I let him down and that sucked.

"Then they're working you too hard. You shouldn't be so worn out that you can't spend a couple hours watching hockey on your own free time." He resumed his pacing. The long legs on his six-foot-six frame devoured the room in a couple of strides before he turned and went the opposite direction. "And what about weekends?" Rocco stopped and threw his hands in the air. "Why all of a sudden do you have to work on weekends?"

Of course, he was right. I was Sunday, and I *didn't* work weekends. That was what I said to avoid the exact argument we were having. I actually spent the day before hiding at Piper's, not at work.

It had been a little over a week since I saw Seb and, to my frustration, my intense desire for him hadn't dulled over time. Instead, it only seemed to grow bigger, the chasm wider, emptier, and needier.

Piper told me to suck it up and call him, but I couldn't do it. For one thing, Sebastien St. Clair is a love 'em and leave 'em type of guy. And second, spending time with him was way too complicated. If I had been thinking with my head instead of my hormones the night he asked me to meet him at the hotel bar, I would have said no. Especially if I knew saying yes meant I would never watch my brother play hockey in person again.

I frowned and the more I thought about it, the dumber the logic sounded. I mean, was I serious? I wasn't going to any of Rocco's games as long as he played on the same team as Seb? The whole thing was stupid. So stupid, in fact, I was beyond over it, over Seb and Rocco and their macho ridiculousness.

"Fine," I said. Rocco froze mid-pace. Since Saturday's was a matinee, the Sunday game would be at night. "I'll go tonight. Does that make you happy?"

Instead of answering, Rocco grabbed my hand and hauled me off the couch, straight into one of his patented, bone-crushing, bear hugs. "It makes me ecstatic, Ky. You being there means everything to me."

I winced. *Way to plunge the knife in further.*

"I know it does." I held back a snuffle. "I'm sorry I haven't been there for you, Rocco."

"Well, you'll be there tonight and that's all that matters."

You won't be saying that if everything goes to hell.

Good thing I had a plan. A stupid one, but hey, every-thing I did lately turned out to be stupid.

Why change things up?

~

THE COMETS easily defeated Chicago 4-2 and Rocco played one of the best games of his career. At first he didn't under-stand why I insisted on switching seats. When I explained I'd rather sit a few rows back than have the penalty box block my view of the ice, he understood. Sort of. The divot between his brows said no, but he didn't argue. Good enough for me.

Because I'm an idiot, I kept stealing glances at Seb from under the rim of the baseball cap I wore low on my head. Seb glanced toward my old seat several times throughout the game, searching for me. At first, it made my heart hurt. Then, once I had time to mull it over—and maybe two or three beers. Okay, fine. Four beers—it made me mad. Seb knew how to reach me. If he missed me so damn much, which I doubted was the case, he had no one to blame but himself.

And yeah, it stung that he hadn't bothered to reach out —no calls, no texts, nothing. I kept reminding myself Seb's behavior wasn't anything unexpected. We weren't dating. We weren't even friends. We had sex, period. That was what he did, right?

So why did it hurt so much?

I slunk out of the game early and passed out on my bed fully clothed.

All right, fine. I had *five* beers. Don't judge.

~

NEARLY TWO WEEKS to the day since Sebastien chained me to his bed, my desk drawer vibrated. I was almost done typing up a report on gang violence in Chicago and didn't want to break my concentration, so I finished the last sentence and hit send before I checked my phone. When I slid the drawer open and caught sight of the screen, I might have stopped breathing.

A text. From Seb.

My pulse kicked into high gear and I chewed on the inside of my cheek. The arctic temperature of the open newsroom shot up a good twenty degrees. *Celsius.* I picked the phone up carefully, as if it might bite my hand, and swiped the screen. I fumbled once or twice and had to read the message several times before it sank in.

Seb: Plans tonight?

HOLY. Crap.

I blinked. Then blinked again before rereading the text two more times and looking up at the high ceiling as if it might collapse on my head.

I figured the sky must be falling because Seb actually reached out.

"Oops!" The phone slipped and I flailed. I probably looked demented as I juggled the thing over my desk to keep it from clanking back into the open metal drawer.

My hands and feet felt numb. I couldn't believe he did it. Seb texted, *and* he wanted to see me again. I was simultaneously thrilled and terrified. Everything about Seb was a terrible idea. Getting more involved would only make it worse for my mental well-being when the inevitable happened and everything went sideways. Yet a tiny, traitorous part of my brain, the part that hoped that against all odds we could end up together for real, did a victory dance.

That itty-bitty part of my brain hip-checked common sense aside, and made the idiotic decision to jump without a net. I typed a response before I wimped out.

Me: No, why?

I DRUMMED my fingers on the desk and waited for a reply.

Seb: Pick u up @ 7?

MY OUT OF CONTROL, horny, hormonal half lit up. It knew precisely what Seb had in mind. My romantic, foolishly hopeful half, well, it wilted under the crushing weight of disappointment.

I knew better than to expect romance from a man like Sebastien St. Clair. To call him emotionally stunted would be a compliment. He couldn't find romance if he had two extra hands and six sets of eyes.

Sex, Kylie. It's just sex.

My fingers flew across the tiny screen.

Me: I know where you live. I'll come to you

THE LONG PAUSE made me smile. I pictured the frustrated look on Seb's face as he wrestled between the desire to control everything by insisting he pick me up, and pure logic that said I was perfectly capable of making the fifteen-minute drive to the W. Those three bubbles popped up and stayed there for way too long, taunting me, until *finally* the swish of an incoming text broke the silence.

Seb: Fine. Code for garage 3637# Park in spot 28

I IMAGINED his disgruntled expression and laughed out loud. A few of my colleagues popped up from neighboring cubicles like prairie dogs to shoot me questioning looks.

Me: C U then.

I PLANNED to call Nat when I got home. Hopefully, my best friend would hammer some freaking common sense into my thick skull. Historically speaking, my judgment when it came to men was questionable at best. I needed Nat to stop me from thinking of Seb as relationship material. He wasn't, and even if he was, Rocco was a very obvious, tatted and muscled six-foot-six barrier to any happiness I might find with Seb. No doubt she would call me a bonehead. Nat would keep my expectations reasonable. Wrestle them down to the level they belonged when it came to a future with Seb... subterranean.

Still, that stupid little voice in the dark recesses of my mind persisted. Had me thinking—no, had me *fantasizing*—that someday Seb and I could actually be a couple. That we would fall madly in love, Rocco would wake up one day, get over himself and his annoying—if somewhat justified—hatred of Seb, and the two of us would have his blessing to make adorable little hockey babies and live happily ever after.

I sighed and thumped my head on my desk.

Like I said, stupid.

Seb

Of course I was irked that Kylie insisted on driving. Her being one hundred percent correct didn't make me feel any better. It absolutely made more sense for her to come to me, instead of me going to her only to turn around and drive right back to the W. Logical or not, it aggravated me, but it wasn't worth arguing over, especially since I had big plans for Kylie. Specifically, my cock getting to know her pussy a lot better. And maybe I wanted to know a little more about Kylie as well.

After making a few calls and grabbing a quick shower, I glanced at the clock and frowned. I started getting ready way too early and was faced with an excessive amount of time on my hands and nothing interesting to occupy my bouncy-ball brain. Over the years, I came to discover bad things happened when I had loads of free time.

I stood next to the windows and watched it rain. The wind blew fiercely and people darted around, covering their heads with their jackets or papers, or whatever they could find. In the more entertaining instances, they had umbrellas, which ultimately turned inside out, to my great delight.

I stepped away from the windows, and the second I did, unhelpful thoughts whirled around inside my head like an F-5 tornado.

There were too many questions and not enough answers. Why did Kylie stop coming to Comets games? Why was she there to begin with? Were those her seats or did she borrow tickets from a friend? And the one that bothered me most, that dangled like a carrot in front of the spinning hamster wheel in my skull every minute of every day... Why was Kylie so eager to get the fuck out of dodge forever ago?

Forever ago?

I pinched the bridge of my nose. It had only been two weeks, yet it felt like I hadn't seen her in months and *that* was fucking scary.

Unbeknownst to me, I have deeply buried masochistic tendencies. It had to be, because I spent the next hour and a half agonizing over those questions, chucking handfuls of spaghetti at the wall to see what stuck and what ended up in a cold heap on the floor.

Pointless.

If I wanted the truth I had to suck it up and go to the source for answers, hence, me asking Kylie to come over.

I wasted so much time spiraling down a bottomless black hole of "*Why did Kylie do/say/think xyz,*" I was startled by an incoming text.

Not a St. Clair Fan: *in the elevator*

Ah, fuck. I glanced at the time. Seven-thirty, and what was I doing? Getting myself nice and worked up so I would be a complete mental basket case when Kylie showed up.

Dammit. I cracked my neck and shook out my hands as I tried to clear my mind. I didn't want Kylie to think I was distracted, not that I wasn't always distracted, but still. She deserved, and would receive, my full attention. Everything else could wait.

A soft knock on the door announced Kylie's arrival. I took a few deep breaths to calm down. Satisfied I wouldn't come across as a crazy, wild-eyed, psycho, I opened the door, and with a silent *whoosh*, all of the air sucked out of the room.

Kylie looked up at me and blinked those big brown eyes. Eyes I got lost in every time I stared at them. Slowly, a frown began to form at the corners of her mouth with a matching, tiny indent between her brows, in a cute little V-shape.

Aaaand, she was waiting for me to stop fucking slobbering all over her...

"Sorry." I stepped aside to let Kylie enter. "I forgot how beautiful you are," I blurted out.

Fucking-A. It was not my night.

"Hi," she said, gaze flicking around the foyer, alighting on anything and everything except where I wanted it. On me. I made the most of the opportunity and studied Kylie. She fascinated me. Before we met, I never knew anyone who could shift from confident seductress to shy ingénue so quickly and seamlessly, and not even know she was doing it. Her naiveté was natural and charming. I found her so intriguing, I pretty much waited on tenterhooks to see what Kylie would do or say next.

"Traffic bad?" I asked as I circled around and reached for her coat. Greedy as I am, I couldn't stop from brushing my fingers across the back of her neck. The tiny hairs stood on end and Kylie shivered. It was barely noticeable, but her reaction sent all the blood in my body rushing south.

Great. Now I had a cramped boner to contend with.

"A little." Kylie shrugged out of the coat and watched as I hung it on the rack.

With pleasantries taken care of, there was nothing to stop me from moving things along. Even if the biggest, most-badassed defender in the NHL dropped out of the sky and stood between me and Kylie, I was going to get some answers out of her. I went right into her personal space and then stepped closer, going until the blistering heat radiating from her body hit me like a shot of testosterone to the family jewels.

When she realized I wasn't going to stop, Kylie's eyes grew wide. Aggressive and determined, I got so close, she had to tilt her head back to look at me. I stared down and she swallowed nervously. Like a magnet, my eyes were drawn to the slender lines of her throat, then back up when Kylie licked her lips. Watching her tongue slide across her mouth, all shiny and slick, was torture. My balls hung heavy and my cock grew hard.

It was too much. *She* was too much.

I was done.

Questions? What questions? And more important, who gave a shit?

I reached out, wanting to be tender and sweet for a change, entirely different from my typical snatch and grab. I moved slow enough to be classified under the Geneva Convention as cruel and inhuman punishment, cupped the sides of Kylie's face, and lowered my mouth to hers. She didn't miss a beat.

Kylie parted her lips, welcomed me in, and turned what was supposed to be a gentle kiss into something deeper and so much fucking hotter. The last shreds of my willpower disintegrated. I shoved my tongue into that inviting mouth, and one taste was all it took. A desperate sound rumbled from my chest and I wound my arms around Kylie's back to pull her flush against my body.

It hadn't been my intention to jump her the second she walked in the door. I had planned for us to talk a bit before we got to the naked stuff, but she offered and I'd be damned if I was going to say no. If someone told me to close my eyes and imagine heaven, Kylie would be front and center, yet at some point she also became my personal hell. When it came to Kylie, I was weak. She made me break my rules. Bust down the carefully constructed walls that surrounded my heart.

Kylie moaned and rubbed against me. That was all it took for me to no longer give a flying rip about rules or questions or anything but getting skin to skin. I had to get inside her. *As soon as physically possible.*

"Bedroom," I growled.

In a moment of déjà vu, we re-created the exact scene from the last time Kylie was there. Same as then, I'd only give up her mouth when I was dead, so we continued to swap spit as I walked her backward through the condo until we reached the master bedroom. Instead of shoving Kylie onto the bed and stuffing my cock between those thick lips, which, frankly, wasn't that bad an idea, I continued to kiss her. For whatever reason, I didn't want to stop. Not yet, anyway.

I located the hem of Kylie's shirt and slid my hands under the material and up the satiny skin of her back. At the same time, Kylie's fingers flirted with my waistband, then came to rest on my hips. She dug her thumbs in on either side and my hips jerked.

"Fucking, hell," I muttered as I thrust a thigh between her legs and pushed up, practically lifting her off the ground. Kylie's whole body trembled and her head fell back.

"Don't stop," she pleaded. With her mouth out of reach I went for the nearest available surface and dove in to lick and bite the tantalizing skin of her exposed throat.

"I have no intention of stopping," I growled. God she tasted so fucking good. If hedonism had a flavor, she was it.

We ground against each other for minutes, hours, days... I wasn't counting and didn't give a shit. It got to the point that if I didn't get something hot and wet clamped around my dick, I had the very real fear it might really start to hurt.

The bed was too far away, so I grabbed Kylie by the shoulders and propelled her toward the nearest surface, which happened to be the wall next to the door. She smacked against it. The breath left her lungs and I wasted no time. I plastered the front of my body to hers and rubbed my erection against her abdomen. It still wasn't enough. I was so hard I could have used my dick as a crowbar. Kylie, moaned and groaned as she clung to my arms and humped my thigh.

Equally frustrated, we came to a conclusion at the same time—there were too many layers separating us. Desperate hands scrambled and fingers fumbled, our mouths came together again and again as we tore each other's clothes off.

"Hurry," Kylie gasped.

Her frantic, pleading tone made my balls pull up, primed to blow my load before I got inside her. I clenched my teeth and focused on keeping it together. Fuck, Kylie was going be the death of me. With an impatient grunt, I grabbed her ass with both hands and hoisted her up the wall to claim my spoils like a conquering marauder. Kylie wrapped her legs around my waist and hooked her ankles at the base of my spine. Out of patience, I held Kylie up with one hand and aimed my cock with the other, then dropped her down and thrust my hips up, burying myself so deep I think my dick touched China.

Stars shot off behind my eyes. It felt so good, I went momentarily blind with pleasure. The tight, wet heat of her pussy was fucking rapture. Angels sang and fireworks exploded.

"Je veux te lécher des hanches jusqu'aux pieds. Je bande por toi," I groaned, the French coming out of me in a torrent. My head grew heavy and I struggled to breathe. I had to press my forehead against Kylie's in order to maintain what little fragments of control I had left. "You feel so fucking good," I managed to say in English.

When my vision cleared, I looked at Kylie. Her expression was one of absolute bliss and the sight made my dick throb. Spurred into action by a non-stop litany of tiny mewls and groans of pleasure that came from her mouth and the way she squirmed on my cock, I shifted my weight to use the wall as leverage, and fucking went for it. Bending my knees, I pounded up into Kylie at an unforgiving pace. Jackhammered in and out like a man possessed. She didn't say a word and I wondered if it might be too much. All at once, the dam broke and a flood of nonsense and half-sentences tumbled from her lips and I knew she didn't want me stop.

"Oh... oh.... God, yes. Seb, more... harder... like that, yes!"

"Fucking hell, Kylie. *Tu me rends folle.*"

"Don't... stop. I-I... o*hmygod.*"

I stared into her eyes and she stared into mine as I rolled my hips and fucked her against that wall. Out of nowhere, my chest constricted and my throat grew tight. *Oh shit.* I felt it happening, emotions creeping in, and it was scary as fuck. I was unable to do anything to stop from tumbling head-first into a bottomless abyss. The connection between us grew so strong, it became a palpable entity in the room. My only consolation was that I knew Kylie was right there with me, falling hard and fast. She hung on for dear life, her fingernails biting into my shoulders added another layer to the absolute frenzy I was in. The mind-bending pleasure built, and so did the invisible ties that bound us together.

I moved faster, but never tore my gaze from Kylie's dark eyes. Her pupils grew so large I no longer saw the beautiful golden brown. Sweat dripped down my back and rivulets trickled down my chest. I braced my feet as liquid heat coiled at the base of my spine. No way could I last much longer, but I'd be damned if Kylie didn't come first.

Snarling, I pressed closer and flattened Kylie against the wall, using my pecs to pin her in place. The added support allowed me to hold most of her weight in one-hand. I slid my other hand up and lightly wrapped my fingers around Kylie's delicate throat. She cried out and her eyes misted over.

Oh, shit. Shit, shit, shit...

I gasped and my sack scrunched up tight. Kylie fucking *liked* my hand around her throat. I squeezed, not a lot, just enough for her to get a taste of my strength. A small bite of pain and an intoxicating rush of fear. Enough to let her know how easily I could cut off her air supply.

Kylie's mouth fell open and her eyes glazed over with lust. She made no move to stop me or tell me to move my hand. I applied a little more pressure and those gorgeous eyes rolled back in her head. *Sweet baby Jesus.* She didn't like it, she fucking *loved* it. Every last depraved thing I did to her, she loved. Kylie shook and trembled and let out a long wail,

the perfect accompaniment to the slapping of our skin as I
continued to take her apart.

Kylie let out a loud, erratic gasp that ended when every
muscle in her body clenched tight. Her pussy clamped
down, a scorching hot vice around my cock. She shuddered
violently, threw her head back, and screamed.

"*Ohmygod*, Seb... Seb, oh god. *Yes, yes!*"

"Oh, fuck!" Her pussy gripped my cock like an iron fist,
squeezing so hard it ripped the orgasm right from my balls. I
came so forcefully I struggled to stay upright as I shot jet
after jet after jet, the pleasure unyielding. Legs quaking, I
pumped in and out a few more times to drag out the ecstasy.
One final thrust, and the shout that burst from me was loud
enough to shake the light fixtures.

I buckled against Kylie and let the buzz from the high of
great sex hum through my veins. She didn't complain. Probably couldn't. I figured she screamed herself hoarse. We
stayed that way for several minutes, me holding her against
the wall—or the wall holding both of us—my softening
cock still buried inside her. I was too sweaty and exhausted
to attempt to move, and more than a little worried my legs
would give out and we'd both end up on the floor with his
and hers bruised tailbones. Seemingly content while she
caught her breath, Kylie went limp in my arms.

Like everything else, all good things eventually came to
an end. My dick slipped out, and Kylie hissed. She unwound
her legs to gingerly place her feet on the floor. I didn't
remove my hands right away, afraid she might be unsteady.

See? I can be a gentleman.

"I'm good." Kylie's voice had a rough, sexy rasp, and she
licked her lips. She looked at me and grinned. "Really good."

Really good?

Taken aback, I took a minute and gaped like an utter

asshole. Kylie never ceased to amaze me. Don't get me wrong, I wasn't insulted, in fact, it was the opposite. I just had what I can definitively say was the best sex of my life and, unlike most women—scratch that, *every* woman—I'd been with, Kylie wasn't acting all clingy or demanding or whiny. She wasn't insisting we snuggle or make plans for the following day.

No, Kylie smiled and laughed; effectively shattering the stereotype that women believed fucking equals commitment.

"Me, too." Going by the ache in my cheeks I knew the width of my grin matched hers. In the pile of discarded clothes, I located my jeans and slipped them on. "Why don't you get cleaned up? I'll meet you in the kitchen."

Her eyes shone and she had a rosy flush to her skin. It was a good look on her, fucked out and relaxed, and not leaving a dust trail to the door.

Kylie nodded. "Okay."

It wasn't until I realized she wasn't bolting that I truly relaxed. Shit, I sounded like a chick, but I was relieved. Part of me worried Kylie would do a repeat and run the second we both came. What was worse, the presence of Kylie's car meant I had no control over when or if she left.

Not that I'd keep her locked up and chained to my bed, or anything like that. Probably. Maybe. Fine, I totally would. But she stayed, so no need to resort to extreme measures.

Feeling uncharacteristically optimistic, I whistled a random tune as I grabbed a container from the fridge and stuck it in the microwave. I set the time as written on the attached note. By the time Kylie joined me in the kitchen, the food was done and I had two place settings out on the island.

"What is this?" She eyed the plates suspiciously, which —*dammit*—made me nervous.

Contrary to the near crippling anxiety that reached out and seized my insides, I gave her a casual shrug. "It's nothing. I have a chef who makes meals for the week and labels them so I can reheat them. I figured, you know, you might be hungry."

"Oh."

Oh? What the fuck did that mean?

"Oh good I'm hungry?" or, *"Oh, why did you bother since I'm taking off now? Bye, thanks for the fuck?"*

"Here." I ignored my nagging thoughts and handed Kylie a glass of ice water. She took the tiniest of sips before putting it down. "Are you hungry?" Without taking my eyes off her in case she tried to disappear, I gestured toward the barstools tucked under the granite slab. Hoping to encourage Kylie to stay, I pulled one out and sat, feigning indifference, even though, on the inside, I was on my knees, begging her not to go.

"Okay." Kylie sounded uncertain, but she joined me and that was what mattered.

We ate in relative silence, then, with no other activities planned, it was time. I spent days preparing and plotting, grappling over the best way to get some answers without coming across as nosy, and came up with a pathetic, but simple solution—use food to keep her busy while I asked the approximately ten thousand questions I've saved up since the first day I saw her in DC, all stunning and furious behind a sheet of scratched up acrylic.

I put down my fork and wiped my mouth, then angled my body in Kylie's direction. After steadying my nerves, I took a deep breath and went for it.

"So, how come I haven't seen you at any games recently?"

Kylie froze with her fork halfway to her mouth. She set it down slowly, deliberately, but not before I noticed how her hand shook.

"I-I've been busy."

Disappointment socked me in the solar plexus, though I wasn't surprised. I pretty much expected her to give a vague response. That was why I started with an easy one.

"Busy with work? What do you do?"

"Um, I don't. I mean, I'm doing an internship. Not exactly working. I'm still... I'm still in school. After the internship I'll get my degree."

I gaped. Not only because Kylie actually answered the question, but because it never occurred to me that she might be a student. Which brought to mind an uncomfortable follow up.

"School? Um, how old are you?"

Kylie snorted, then she blushed furiously and covered her mouth and nose with both hands. It was fucking adorable.

"Don't worry, I'm twenty-one. Totally legal."

I exhaled. Thank fuck for small miracles. I should have asked before taking her to a hotel. I knew better than to mess around with a chick without making sure she wasn't a one-way ticket to registered sex offender status.

Yet another blaring alarm warning me that Kylie totally knocks me off my game.

Her giggle tore me from the overwhelming relief in finding out she isn't jailbait.

"What?"

"The look on your face," she said as she stifled another laugh. "Like you missed stepping on a land mine and getting blown to bits."

Her light, ringing laughter penetrated the hard shell

around my black, empty soul and filled me up with warmth. Seeing her smile, I don't know. Something about it did wonders for my state of mind and I found myself smiling and laughing along with her.

What was her secret? I mean, how in the hell did she do it? How did she manage to completely disarm me each and every time we were together? When she wasn't being mysterious and frustrating, that is.

"Actually, that's a pretty accurate description of how it felt," I admitted. Heart done having an attack, I got back to the interrogation. Kylie's guard was somewhat lowered, and I wanted to get as many answers as I could before she shut me down. "Who do you know in the Comets organization?" She frowned like I just asked her how much she weighed. I hastened to clarify. "It's just that I know those seats of yours are owned by management."

The question went over like a high stick to the head. Kylie's frown deepened, and I watched those thick walls of hers crash down. Anxiety crept back in as I waited to see what she did. Eventually, Kylie shrugged.

"I don't know anyone. My boss gave them to me."

I squinted and tried to decide if she was being honest, and if not, what reason she had to lie about it. I didn't accuse her of being untruthful. I know I'm an insensitive jackhole, but even I wouldn't do that.

"Well, who's your boss? Maybe I know him or her."

The words no sooner passed my lips and Kylie was shaking her head. "You don't." She pushed back the stool. I cringed as the metal feet scraped against the floor. Kylie stood and carried her dish to the sink. "I should get going."

Years of practice schooling my expression were the only reason I kept my distress from showing.

What. The actual. Fuck.

I was positive she was hiding something and, goddammit, I wanted to know why.

Doing my best to squelch the rising panic and failing, I darted around the island and toward the sink, which was wedged in a far corner of the kitchen. Kylie was busy freaking out about whatever shit she felt she needed to keep from me and didn't see me coming until I was practically on top of her. When Kylie turned around, I darted in and pinned her against the sink with my hips, then braced my hands on the countertop on either side of her body, effectively caging her in. Kylie's face crumpled. She looked like she was on the verge of a meltdown.

Could whatever Kylie didn't want me to know really be that bad?

I had a difficult time imagining what she could possibly say that would scare me off. To be honest, the fact that she *couldn't* scare me off should be precisely what *did* scare me off.

After the intense moments we shared, staring into each other's eyes, watching our emotional bond deepen as we soared toward ecstasy—*Me! Fucking emotional bonds!*—I should be the one melting down. Not Kylie. *I* should be the one to send her on her merry way, not the other way around. I'm the guy who hides things, who doesn't discuss his personal life, who remains emotionally out of reach.

The role reversal didn't sit well with me. I fucking hated how it made me feel, and then I *despised* the fact that I was feeling anything at all.

"You're lying and I want to know why."

Okay, so maybe I am a big enough jackhole to accuse her of lying.

I shifted closer, using my size to intimidate her. Of course, I forgot who I was dealing with. Kylie never did what a normal person would do, and, as a result, she was completely baffling, which made me want her that much more. Kylie didn't shrink or back down and tell me what I wanted to know. She didn't get all teary on me, either.

Kylie, my little firecracker, crossed her arms and glared. It was so harsh, it would reduce most people to a weeping puddle on the hand-scraped hardwood floor. Her lips curled back and she just about snarled.

"I don't have to listen to your bullshit accusations, Seb. Get out of my way."

I had to hand it to her, Kylie was no shrinking violet. In fact, seeing her stand up to me was a huge fucking turn on. My idiot dick, which should be plenty satisfied, started to grow stiff. Fantasies of wrestling a furious Kylie into submission filled my head and it got even harder.

"I said *move*."

I blinked and gazed down. Even fuming mad Kylie was gorgeous, though I found her level of anger confusing. I didn't ask anything that warranted that much hostility.

"*Sacrement. Calmez vous belle.*" I held my hands up to show I wasn't a threat. Kylie's forehead crinkled and I shook my head. "I'm sorry. Let's try that again, in English." I took a deep breath. "Calm down. You don't need to be angry. All I want is to get to know you."

Her chin quivered and regret flashed across her face.

"This?" Kylie's voice cracked and she gestured between us. "Is just sex. I don't owe you anything and I refuse to stand here and be interrogated like a criminal." She cleared her throat and spoke forcefully. "Now, if you don't mind, I have to go."

Dumbfounded, and admittedly, more than a little hurt, I reeled as if she hauled off and slapped me. My retreat left just enough room for Kylie to slip by. I followed, but by the time I got with the program, Kylie had her coat on and her keys in her hand.

I was certain I wouldn't survive another round of cut and run.

"*S'il vous plâit*, Kylie, don't do this." She hesitated, and my hopes went up, then her steely resolve returned, and crushed those hopes under her heel.

"I can't do this. I-I want to, Seb. I do. I-I just—"

I clung to her admission like a life preserver in a tumultuous sea. "You want to do what? Be here? Be with me? But you think you can't? Why not? Whatever it is, you can tell me. I'll understand."

She shook her head and mashed her lips. "You can't, and you won't. I'm sorry." Kylie looked at me. Her eyes were damp and glistening. "I-I'm really sorry."

I opened my mouth to respond, but nothing came out.

It didn't matter. She was already gone.

10

Kylie

Over the next few weeks I did anything and everything possible to keep my mind off of Seb. Being busy helped, but nothing could erase the fingerprints he left on my soul. We hadn't spent much time together, and yes, I didn't know Seb very well, but the few moments we shared altered the way I viewed the world, changed a vital part of me. A part I didn't know I possessed until Sebastien St. Clair reached inside and yanked it to the surface.

"Kylie?" Few things could pull my attention away from my computer. My boss was one of them. I stopped typing and glanced at Rita as she stood next to my chair, perfectly coiffed from head to toe, as usual. "You do realize you're not getting paid to be here," Rita pointed out, her sculpted brows squished together. "These long hours aren't healthy, believe me, I know."

"I'm aware of that."

Ignoring my reply, Rita continued to stare until I

squirmed like a little kid. With the exception of Rocco, she was the only person I'd met who could send you on a guilt trip with a single look. I had to hand it to them, Rocco and Rita had the *"frown and make you feel like a disappointment"* face down pat.

Rita's forehead smoothed and her eyes expressed genuine concern. She rested a hip on the corner of the desk and crossed her arms. "Then go home. Or did you not notice your shift ended three hours ago?"

Three hours?

I leaned back to stretch my stiff neck and casually glanced around the cavernous workspace. The bustle of activity appeared par for the course, but then, CNN is a twenty-four-hour news network. The graveyard shift was as busy as during the day. There aren't any windows in the main newsroom, so I couldn't look outside to see if it was dark out. But the fact that I didn't recognize a single face in the crowd, well, that in itself said plenty. Plus, the *um*, roughly million or so clocks that hung on the walls and represented cities in every time zone across the globe, including Atlanta. Those were pretty telling, too.

"Are you in trouble?" Rita asked, her voice low. "If there's a reason you don't want to go home, HR has people you can talk to."

"What?" My eyes just about bugged out of my skull. The last thing I needed was for my boss to think I had an abusive home life. "No! I mean, no thank you. I'm fine. It's nothing like that, I promise."

I tapped my fingers on the arm of the chair as I tried to explain my situation without disclosing any actual facts or details. My personal life was... well, personal. Rita didn't get where she was by backing down easily. Like Piper, she wouldn't be satisfied until I gave her more.

I sighed and rubbed my temples. "I guess... I guess you can say I'm, uh, going through a breakup of sorts. Kind of." I winced at how lame it sounded.

Shockingly, it worked. Understanding crossed Rita's face and she looked relieved. "Ah, those can be tough. Sorry about that." She leaned closer and tipped her chin toward my computer. "I've dealt with my share of breakups by burying myself in work." I nodded, glad she could sympathize. "But... to be honest?" Rita continued. My optimism shriveled. "In the long run, the only thing that heals you is time." She patted my shoulder. "Go home and get some sleep."

Rita turned and walked away. I knew her parting words weren't a suggestion. They were an order. Wonderful. I powered down and cleaned up my area. Satisfied everything else could wait, I grabbed my bag, shrugged on my coat, and headed out. The closer I got to my car, the worse I felt. My insides twisted and I thought my heart might flop out of my chest and land on the oil-stained concrete of the parking garage.

"Go home and get some sleep," I muttered. "Fat chance."

Between the stress of avoiding Seb, and somehow still making Rocco happy by attending home games, sleep had become a precious commodity. On top of that, ignoring the constant flurry of texts and phone calls from Seb was draining. Worse? The total silence that followed a couple days later when I didn't respond to a single one.

I should have been happy Seb gave up and moved on. That was my intention. So why did it feel like my sternum cracked open? Not that it mattered. What I *should* have been asking myself was, how on earth did I *ever* think I could get involved with Seb and walk away in one piece?

Because I'm an idiot. An idiot who went and fell in love with the unattainable Sebastien St. Clair.

"ARE you sure you don't want me to ask if there are any seats closer to the ice?"

I ground my molars and gouged my nails into my palms to keep from shouting at my overly helpful, highly irritating, tirelessly helicoptering brother.

"No. Thank you. I'm good where I am." As though he didn't know that already, considering he asked the exact same question before every single game and in turn, got the exact same response. Every. Single. Time.

Rocco shot me the stink-eye as he headed for the door. "So sue me for wanting to make you happy."

Exasperated, I threw myself onto the couch, face first. "I'm happy," I said, muffled by the cushion. "Now please, stop asking about the stupid seat."

I didn't need to see him to know Rocco had a scowl plastered on his mug. Whatever. He needed to get over it. Okay, fine. Some of the blame for my current mess was on me. Over the last few weeks my moods had been all over the place—from depressed and on the verge of tears, to furious and boiling over with rage. Poor Rocco ended up on the receiving end of most of my erratic emotional swings. That didn't excuse him from being a jerk, though, and his constant nagging had finally wormed its way onto my last remaining nerve.

"You know you can talk to me, Ky." *Oh my god.* I groaned and thumped my head into the cushion. He's so damn persistent and, from the sound of it, Rocco wasn't near the door anymore. He was standing next to the couch. "About anything."

You say that now...

I sat up and shoved my hair out of my face. "I know that, Rocco. And I know you mean it, but there are some things you're better off not knowing. Trust me."

Rocco scoffed and went to take another step closer. When I leveled a serious stare, he hesitated. I watched as Rocco consciously adjusted his posture, relaxing each limb, almost de-puffing his considerable bulk to appear smaller, less frightening, as if he were getting ready to approach a timid animal. A venomous one that might lash out at any second.

He wasn't that far off.

"We don't need to have any secrets between us," he insisted.

You asked for it, bud.

I tilted my head and innocently fluttered my lashes. "Oh, because you've told me everything, hmm? Like about the time you hooked up with those two women from—"

Rocco jerked back like I electrocuted him, and thrust out a hand. "Stop! Just... *ugh!* I don't even want to know how you found out about that."

Normally, I would have found it amusing to see my big, tattooed, bad-ass brother all flustered and flailing, cheeks red with embarrassment. But all his reaction did was hammer home my point.

"See? Sometimes we're better off not knowing. Ignorance is bliss and all." I waved him away. "Go. You're going to be late. This is something I have to work out on my own and you're going to have to accept that."

Rocco might be forced to accept my decision, but that didn't mean he had to like it. His huge hands fisted at his sides and his face flushed an even deeper shade of red, if that were even possible, only from anger, not humiliation over his sister knowing details about his sex life.

"Christ, Kylie," he spat. "You're really something, you know that? You've become this, I don't know, like a complete stranger lately. I don't even know who you are anymore. I don't know how to act around you or what to say. This... it isn't like you. It isn't like *us*." He snatched his keys from the hook next to the door and, because I didn't feel bad enough, gave me a final, parting blow before he slammed the door behind him. "I miss my sister."

The tears didn't fall until Rocco was gone. He was right, I was a mess. But I also knew shutting him out was the right thing to do. The ordeal with Seb wasn't something I could confide in him. Rocco couldn't be the one to pick me up from that particular fall. I needed something, no *someone* else, to cheer me up and help me get out of my funk.

I sat up so fast the room spun.

I knew exactly who to call.

"Just like old times, right?" Nat grinned from ear to ear. I glanced around the arena. It was early and the place was still pretty empty. The majority of the crowd trickled in as we waited for the game to start.

"Just like old times," I agreed.

Calling my best friend and asking, no *begging*, her to visit was the least dumb thing I'd done in a while. Having Nat around reminded me of all the fun we used to have back in DC. Pre-Seb.

Going to a Comets game, on the other hand? Probably the dumbest thing I'd done in a while.

Because I had a guest, and because Rocco can't keep his big fat nose out of my business, he snuck behind my back and asked Nat if she preferred to sit right on the ice. Since I didn't explain my new seating arrangement, Nat accepted Rocco's generous offer. The result was two seats front and center, smack dab in the first row next to the Comets bench. After Rocco told someone in management his sister's best friend was visiting from out of town, prime seats were arranged for their defensive star.

Rocco's meddling meant there was approximately zero chance of me going unnoticed by Seb. What, with us fifteen feet away from where he'll be sitting and all. Nat kept telling me to relax. That Seb would be too busy playing hockey to have time to search though every face in the crowd. If that's what she thought, Nat didn't know Seb. There wasn't much the man failed to notice. I mean, he spotted me in a sold-out crowd the night of Rocco's very first game as a Comet. He actually remembered me from the *one* time he saw me in DC, where he only got a brief glimpse at my face, and that was in between exchanging blows with Rocco.

I would say Seb qualified as not only being very astute, but that he possessed some sort of supernatural GPS ability or something.

I got lost in my thoughts as I hid under my Comets ball cap. So much so, I didn't notice Nat flagging down a beer vendor until she thrust a foamy cup under my nose. The strong scent of yeast and hops assaulted my nostrils.

"Here. This should help you unclench." Nat laughed at my subsequent scowl, but that didn't stop me from tossing back half the beer in one go. I smacked my lips loudly and made and exaggerated *"ahhh"* sound.

"Happy?" I asked, grinning around a thick, foamy mustache.

"No, no I'm not, actually. I don't like seeing you like this, Ky." Nat leaned in. "He's not worth it." She handed me a napkin and I wiped my lip. "Honestly, he's not. You're a mess, and over what? A hot guy you slept with a couple times?" I appreciated her concern, even if it didn't help.

"You're right." I relaxed some and pulled out of my slouch to sit up straight. "You're totally right." With a dramatic flourish, I finished my beer and crumpled the empty cup, one-handed. "Screw him. He's no one to me." A sharp, hot blade pierced me between two ribs, but I pushed past the pain in the hope I could will it to be true.

Nat lit up. "That's the spirit." She threw an arm around me and hugged me to her side, while I held up a twenty and searched for the nearest beer vendor. It was going to be a long night.

Because I'm a little bit sneaky and a lot spineless, I made sure I happened to be in the bathroom the exact moment the Comets took the ice for their warm up. A little while later, during player announcements and the national anthem, I was conveniently waiting in line for a snack, even though the tight ball in my stomach rejected the idea of food.

Unfortunately, after three trips to the ladies' room and two for snacks I didn't want, I ran out of excuses to leave my seat. Plus, the evil eye Nat perfected—complete with single arched brow—over the years kind of scared me.

She was lucky I'm not an *"I told you so"* kind of friend, because two minutes into the second period, during a line change, it happened. Seb flew toward the bench so his replacement could take his place. He curled the fingers of his bulky gloves around the edge of the low wall in order to propel his body over it, and his piercing blue gaze landed directly on me. It was as if Seb somehow knew I was there.

Was drawn to me. He couldn't have known, obviously, and the way his eyes widened with surprise, he didn't expect to see me.

Mid-leap, Seb tripped and almost fell flat on his face, or he would have if his teammate hadn't been there to break his fall. Seb landed on top of the guy. His forward momentum sent them both crashing to the ground in a jumbled heap of equipment and skates.

After untangling their limbs and sticks, Seb took a seat on the bench, but he never stopped staring at me. Not once. I watched as his face quickly went through a dozen different emotions. They changed so fast it made it difficult to pick them out. The ones I *did* recognize? Confusion, anger, and astonishingly, a deep sense of sadness. The first two were for obvious reasons. I didn't know what to make of the third. I knew Sebastien didn't want me to leave the other night. In fact, he protested vehemently. I figured his objection was due to interest in having another round of sex. But maybe I was wrong.

Had Seb been serious about trying to get to know me, or was he faking interest because I was an easy lay? I assumed it was the latter. Could I have been wrong?

The bright lights of the arena stung my eyes and I everything blurred as a sudden and intense surge of doubt made my head hurt. I clutched the armrest until the pain passed.

"Are you okay?" Nat asked as she stuck her face in front of me until her nose almost touched mine. Worry creased her brow.

Only then did I realize I was rubbing my head. I dropped my hand. "He saw me, Nat. You didn't see the look on his face... It was... I-I don't know what to think... I thought he didn't..." I stumbled as I tried to explain Seb's distraught expression only to discover I couldn't. Nothing I said would accurately capture the complex workings of Seb's mind or what he may or may not feel.

While I worried my lip, Nat contemplated what I said, or tried to say, anyway. Being a woman of action, when she reached a conclusion, she stood and tugged on my hand. "Come on. Let's go."

Thank god. Now that he'd spotted me, there was no way Seb would let me leave without attempting to reach out and arrange a meet up. Either so he could wheedle an explanation out of me for taking off or, at the very least, to talk. Both would result in a sweaty usher bringing his request to my seat or, god forbid, Seb leaping over the boards and stomping into the stands in full hockey gear to deliver the message himself.

I shuddered in horror. Seb might very well be frustrated enough to do just that.

Maybe sneaking out was cowardly, but then, I never claimed to be brave. If I had to look into Seb's devastated eyes, I would crumple like a used napkin and give him whatever he wanted and then some. I'd give him everything. I'd give him me.

Unfamiliar with Atlanta and its weird one-way streets, Nat used the map on her phone to get us home safely. She correctly surmised I was too distracted to be behind the wheel.

Neither of us said a word. Not in the car. Not in the elevator. Not as we walked down the hall to the door. Inside, I didn't bother to take off my coat and shoes. Instead, I went for the sofa and dropped like a stone.

Nat took her time, hanging her coat and putting her shoes by the door. She passed my pathetic self and headed to the kitchen. Dishes clanged and the fridge opened and closed several times. When Nat finally joined me, she had a bowl of chips and a container of salsa in her hands, and two cans of soda tucked under one arm. She put everything on the coffee table and immediately dug in. I ignored the food. The brick of guilt I swallowed still occupied most of the room in my stomach. Nat had no such issues and demolished more than half the bowl in mere minutes.

"So," Nat said as she used her jeans to brush the salt off her hands. "Are you thinking this guy might have genuine feelings for you after all?"

Straight to the point. How very Nat. With my gray matter flapping in the wind and complex thinking impossible at the moment, I appreciated the direct approach.

I stared at my hands, finding my fingernails fascinating all of a sudden. "I don't know. Maybe?" Frustrated and twitchy, I pushed the hat off my head and ran my hands through my hair. When that did nothing to lessen the anxiety, I heaved my feet up onto the couch and sprawled out on my back. "From what I know about Seb, it's not really his style. He's like, the perpetual party boy bachelor. Never one to settle down or form attachments."

"Everyone grows up eventually, Kylie."

What? I sat back up and goggled, unable to believe those words came out of the mouth of Natasha Westwood, a woman who warned me time and again that I needed to be cautious around men. A woman who went off on long rants about men and their inability to commit at least once every four to six months since the day we met.

And she had the gall to sit there and look offended by my reaction. "What? It's true," she said.

"I know. You're right, it is true." I nodded in agreement. "Just... coming from, you know... *you.*" I gestured toward her.

The hint of a smirk tugged at the corner of Nat's mouth

and, *oh my god*, she started to blush! I didn't know my unflappable, hard as nails friend *could* blush. I always figured the embarrassment gene passed her by.

"Yeah, I know. Totally out of character. And I still think men are immature, emotionally stunted toddlers," she added. I rolled my eyes at that. "But, I don't want to stop you from going after something you want. Something that, despite my personal beliefs, could end up being real."

The finality with which Nat spoke caused my stomach to detach, heavy weight still tucked inside, and sent the whole thing into a free fall.

"I... we... I can't be with him, Nat. You know this."

She got up and sat next to me on the sofa, close enough our shoulders brushed. Her expression was as serious as I'd ever seen it. Nat looked me in the eye and said, "You can."

I snorted. "Yeah, if I want to risk death by Rocco."

Nat took my hands in hers. The grounding touch soothed the bouncy nerves that pinged around my stomach —which currently lay splattered at my feet—and a warm, calming sensation spread through my body.

"Don't be silly. Rocco would never kill you. He'd just kill Seb." She said it with a straight face, but couldn't keep the mischief out of her eyes.

We both burst out laughing.

Thank god for Nat.

Regardless, I had no idea if I could a) trust Seb to recip-rocate my desire to take things further, b) trust my hot-headed brother to not murder Seb, or c) trust my own feelings.

It took Nat's levelheaded approach to allow me to think about it rationally. Without her, I'd have been in my bedroom with the lights out, curled up in a ball in the corner, drool running down my chin as I rocked back and forth and muttered a bunch of nonsense.

Even with Nat's guiding presence, and despite the fact I wasn't curled in said ball, I couldn't be positive there wouldn't be a straight-jacket, a padded room, and a huge orderly named Lars, at some point in my future.

It was so unfair. Cupid and his stupid, defective arrow. I wanted to throttle the conniving, diaper-clad, pudgy-cheeked baby. Screw him and his sick sense of humor, using his power to strike the heart of the most inconvenient man to walk the earth and make me fall for him.

Cupid. What a brat.

FIVE DAYS LATER, three since Nat flew back to DC—*but hey, who's counting?*—my phone blew up. Of course, because all things unfortunate tend to find me like a heat-seeking missile, I was at work when it happened. In a meeting. With the entire department. And two corporate bigwigs.

I entered the conference room, took my seat, and set notifications to vibrate. Generally, vibrate did the trick. When you get a single random text or call. When it buzzes eight times in a row and keeps going and going, again, and again, and again, well, that's another story.

Unfortunately, vibrate didn't stop everyone seated in a five-foot radius from turning their heads in sync to stare at me. It gave me the creeps, like my coworkers were a bunch of cyborgs with identical programming. I bit the inside of my cheek to squelch my nervous laugh.

My cheeks burned as I fumbled to silence the phone, and, because on a scale of one to ten, my luck is negative six, when I finally pulled it from my messenger bag, it began to vibrate again. Surprised, I squealed and the phone bounced off the table and onto my lap.

Kill. Me. Now.

My embarrassment was short-lived. I looked down and saw the screen and the oxygen got sucked out of the room. Heat scurried up my spine, and turned into a hot, prickling awareness that began at my scalp and trickled all the way down to my toes.

Aware that I wasn't alone, and everyone was probably looking at me, I pretended nothing was wrong. Then I glanced at the flurry of text and missed call notifications covering the locked screen, every last one sent by the same person, and grew concerned. They were all from Seb.

Despite the subarctic climate of the conference room and the gale force winds that blew from the vent directly above my head, sweat beaded along my upper lip and my blouse stuck to my lower back. When I bent down to slide the phone back into my bag, my hands visibly trembled.

"Kylie?" I jerked upright and nearly knocked myself unconscious on the edge of the table.

"Whoa." *Headrush.*

I squeezed my eyes shut, counted to three, then opened them up slowly. The room continued to list to one side, then the other. Faces were indistinct blobs of color and the lights in the ceiling shone brighter than usual.

"Kylie? You don't look so good. Are... are you okay?"

Piper.

"I think..." Nausea burned my throat and I panicked as it crawled toward my mouth. Terrified I might get sick all over the conference table—or worse, one of the executives *(don't forget, bad luck magnet)*—I pushed up from my chair and rose onto shaky legs. "Excuse me," I muttered, already halfway to the door.

Misfortune must have taken a coffee break, because I made it to the ladies' room in time to duck into a stall before I upchucked the croissant I stuffed down on the drive to work. To my surprise, I felt instantaneously better after ejecting the offending pastry.

I flushed and stumbled to the faucets, wet a paper towel, and leaned heavily on the sink to dab at my pale, sweaty face. Relieved I only made half an ass of myself instead of full-ass had I barfed on someone, I tossed the crumpled paper in the wastebasket and got busy washing my hands. While I lathered, I made the mistake of glancing at the mirror. I froze.

Ohmygod, Rocco wasn't kidding. I *had* changed.

To the point I didn't recognize my own reflection. Bright eyes looked dull and tired. Two huge, dark circles curved beneath them to further emphasize how exhausted I felt. If I subtracted my vomit-induced flushed cheeks from the equation, the rest of my complexion was waxy and washed out. I turned sideways and studied my profile as I ran a hand down my abdomen. My hip bones stuck out and my face appeared gaunt. Almost sunken.

Somewhere along the way, I lost several pounds and hadn't noticed.

I lifted a hand to touch a too-prominent cheekbone and whispered, "What is happening to me?"

The bathroom door opened and I stumbled back from the sink. As I lost my footing, my hands slapped the flow of water and it sprayed all over my front. Two women entered, chatting and laughing, oblivious to my nightmare. I snatched a handful of paper towels and blotted uselessly at the ruined silk of my blouse. Tears stung my eyes, but I'd be damned if I broke down in the bathroom at CNN. I patted some more, which did absolutely nothing to mask the large, semi-transparent, splotch that stretched across my left breast.

I inhaled through my nose. *Do not cry.*

With my lace bra showing through the wet spot and paper towels clutched in my fist, I bolted from the bathroom and went straight to my car. I needed a moment to get it together. By the time I returned to the conference room, mostly certain I wouldn't lose my shit, the meeting had ended. Of course. I peeked under the table. No bag.

Could it get any worse?

I sighed and awkwardly held an arm across my boob. Hopefully, Piper brought the bag to my cubicle, though I had to admit, if a less savory coworker decided to go on a spending spree with my credit cards, I couldn't have cared less. There were other, more pressing matters that required my attention.

I swiped at my shirt one last time and gave up with a resigned huff. The only way it would dry was to give it time. I locked down every last one of the weepy emotions that sat on my chest and pressed down with the weight of a six-ton elephant, went to Rita's office, and knocked on the doorframe. Rita glanced up from her computer and did a double take, eyes wide.

My fingers curled into the sides of my wool trousers. I was sick and tired of everyone giving me *that* look. Fine. I get it. I can't take care of myself and look like something the cat yakked up. That doesn't mean I wanted or needed a pity reminder from everyone in my life.

"Kylie. Do you need to go home?"

Normally, I would brush Rita off and insist upon staying. Work was good at keeping me from thinking about, well... *him.* But I could practically see the unread texts and voicemails that hung over my head. There was no way I was getting anything done until I dealt with them.

I nodded and rested a hand on my stomach, which had started to act up again. It seemed throwing up a lung, and maybe a spleen, was a temporary fix.

"Yeah, I think maybe I caught a bug or something."

Rita hummed in agreement. "Then go home and get some rest. And, Kylie..." I paused at the door and peered over my shoulder. Rita smiled, but it was tinged with sadness. "Don't come back until you're feeling better."

I swallowed, my throat tight, and said, "Thanks," then hurried to collect my things while placating a few coworkers who asked if I was okay. They also gave me the *look*. The same one as Rocco, Nat, Rita, and every other person I came in contact with. Not quite pity, not quite concern, but rather, something in between, some nebulous emotional offering that did nothing but make me feel like a giant loser.

I went straight home, sat on my bed, and stared at my phone for over an hour before I deleted every last text and voicemail without reading or listening to a single one. I ignored the sharp ache in my heart and began the painstaking process of changing my phone number.

By the end, tears and snot were sliding down my face and hitched sobs kept breaking free until I eventually gave up and let it take its course. I cried until I was a sloppy, emotionally wrung-out, disaster. I hated to excise Seb from my life, but in the end, reality and self-preservation won out over hopes and dreams.

Because I knew if I didn't cut and run, I'd fall in pathetically unrequited love with Seb. And if that happened, he'd destroy me, because I knew he'd never, ever love me back.

Better to make a clean break while I still retained a scrap

of dignity. I sniffed and used the back of my hand to wipe the thick trail of mucous that dripped from my nose.

Dignity. Right.

What a joke.

Seb

I shoved my phone back in my pocket. Nothing. *Rien. Zéro.* Not a single response. No matter what I did, Kylie refused to talk to me. Refused to explain why she left me high and dry, both at my condo and again at the arena. Refused to explain anything.

I figured not knowing was the reason I ended up obsessed and desperate, to the point I'd gladly give my right arm just to speak with Kylie. I was floundering, needing to understand why she ditched me, ditched *us*—after we shared what was, for me, anyway, a life-altering moment.

Kylie took off and I became insecure and pathetic, left to grasp at straws to figure out what the fuck happened to turn her from relaxed and basking in the afterglow of amazing sex, to basically telling me to drop dead.

Or maybe that was all a bunch of bullshit I concocted to avoid the harsh truth. Excuses because I was too fucking scared to admit how I felt. To admit I cared about Kylie way more than I wanted to. That for the first time in my life, I wanted a woman for something other than an easy—though admittedly mind-blowing—lay.

And wasn't the universe one big fucking hilarious assclown.

After nearly a decade of screwing chicks whose names I didn't remember and didn't give two shits about before, during, or after I fucked each one of them senseless, Mr. Funny Fucking Universe decided to deliver a woman who was perfect for me in every way—a woman who, for the first time in my life, didn't make me want to slap duct tape over her mouth and kick her out the door—only to flip that shit on its head and send her running from *me*.

That cunning bitch karma bit me right in the ass. Not that I didn't deserve every last shitty thing that happened to me over the years, considering what I did to my father, wasn't there for my brother, and a lifetime of unapologetic, unrelenting selfishness. No one in his or her right mind would call me a saint. Nope. I'll always be a bastard. The NHL's High Priest of Assholiness. *The Sinner.*

"Dude, maybe you've had enough."

Evvy's grating voice pulled me from my pity party.

"Fuck off, Ev." I swung my arm over my head and to the side to keep my drink out of Evvy's reach, and cursed when the cheap as fuck whiskey slopped over the edge and splashed all over my hand and sleeve. After the crap-tastic month I'd suffered through, I more than earned the right to get thoroughly and unequivocally shit-faced, and that was exactly what I was doing. No one was taking anything from me, not unless they wanted a broken wrist. Or two.

"Sebby," Ev hissed in my ear and threw a heavy arm around my shoulders to keep me from swaying. "We're in public. On the road, you fuckstick. If Coach catches wind of you being drunk and disorderly, he'll bench your fucking ass."

Huh. We were on the road?

I shoved Evvy off and wobbled back and forth until I had the presence of mind to grab the edge of the nearest table. Once there was a fifty-fifty shot I wouldn't immediately faceplant onto the empty plates and glasses on the table, I glanced around the bar. *Hmph.* Not a motherfucking clue where we were. Looked like every other goddamn hotel bar in every other goddamn city.

Must've forgot we were on a road trip. I snickered. That was fucking hilarious.

"Where are we again?" I asked, knowing it would make Evvy throw a clot.

"Jesus Christ," Ev muttered.

Hazey lumbered out of nowhere and thrust a fat finger in my face. "Idiot drunk need go to room to sleep." The huge goalie turned to Evvy. "You need help getting stupid upstairs?"

I huffed, irritated at that nosy bastard Hazey, getting all up in my busizzz, buiszz, bizzee, bizzou... *Fuck!* Bizz-ness, *dammit!* Up in my bizz-ness.

I spun around, and surprise, surprise, tripped over my feet and accidentally elbowed some random dude in the back of the head.

"Watch what you're doing, asshole," the dipshit growled from his seat at the nearby table.

Our eyes locked and a slow, evil grin spread across my face. The night just kept getting better and better. Fuck Hazey. I found a bigger, stupider, and way more satisfying target to unload on.

"Well, well, well," I slurred, drunk as hell and without a single shit to spare. "Sasquatch. How very not nice to see you." I pretended to look around, then returned my gaze to Calloway and smirked. "Did Mrs. Sasquatch tag along? Or is she spending the week waxing her furry pussy?" Calloway grimaced, looking beyond offended, and I doubled over and laughed until my abs burned and my cheeks ached.

He pushed to his feet and I had to tilt my head back to look at the oversized fucker. "You're a disgrace, St. Clair."

I continued to grin as I poked Calloway in the chest with

the hand that held my drink. On an extra-exuberant poke, amber liquid sloshed all over his crisp white dress shirt.

"Oops." I snorted and quickly downed the rest. "Ta-da! No more spills."

"What the fuck is your problem?"

I put the glass on his table and made a talking hand puppet. "Blah, blah, blah. You need to ask Doc about arranging to have that huge stick surgically removed from your ass. It's probably starting to fossilize up there."

Calloway's face turned crimson and the tendons in his neck popped. It was fucking fascinating, like watching a rabid animal in its natural environment. He opened his mouth to say whatever the hell it is that Sasquatches said, when the music blared from his pocket.

"This isn't over," Calloway snarled as he yanked his phone out. He stomped off, but didn't go far enough, because I heard him ask, "Is everything okay?" to the person on the other end.

That was all I caught because Sasquatch had left the building. Er, bar. What*(hiccup)*ever.

"C'mon, Seb." Ev grabbed me by the biceps and hauled me toward the elevators.

"Hey. I'm not done. I wanted another." He ignored my pleas and continued to shove and pull. I tripped several times, twice on my feet, once on someone else's feet, and once on the carpet, staying upright only because Evvy held tight. "Oh fucking great," I groaned.

Rocco Calloway stood by the elevators, looking all pissed and Sasquatchy as he waited, phone pressed to his ear. I scowled at the *fils bâtard géante d'une putain*, then giggled at my own wit.

"That means, giant bastard son of a whore," I said to Ev, who had no clue what I was talking about.

Calloway's annoying voice kept interrupting my buzz. "It's fine. I'll be home tomorrow and we can talk about it... Okay, good... Love you, too." He disconnected the call and stuffed the device back in his pocket.

I leered and shuffled closer. "Mrs. Sasquatch?" I asked with a suggestive waggle of my brows. "Did you ask her about that alpaca pussy of hers?"

Calloway's dark eyes flashed and he gave me that *look* of his. The one that made me feel like a shitstain on his XXXL briefs. "None of your goddamn business. That's who it was."

"Sorry, man," Ev said.

I waved Ev off. "No worries, Evvy."

Calloway and Ev stared at me like I sprouted a second head.

"He was talking to me, you fucking dipshit," Calloway said with no shortage of disgust. "Apologizing for your idiot ass acting like a moron."

I glanced back at Ev, who was shaking his head and staring at the ceiling. *Fucking Judas bastard.* The elevator dinged and the three of us stepped in. I started to crack a joke about there not being enough room, but as the doors closed a hotel employee with ruddy cheeks and a suitcase in his hand stuck his hand in the way and wedged inside when they popped back open, effectively ruining my plan to both insult Calloway and deck him in the eye socket the second the shiny chrome panels slid shut.

We, minus the sweaty bellhop, got off on the same floor. Calloway jostled us so he could be at the front of the tiny metal box. He stalked down the hall, reached his room, and slid his card in the lock while I was still stumbling off the elevator under Evvy's power.

Perfect.

We would walk by right as Calloway got that door open.

Then I would make my move. I was thinking donkey punch to the back of his ridiculously large head.

"Oh no you don't, buddy. I don't think so." Ev correctly interpreted my intentions and dug his fingers into the meat of my arm.

"Ow! Fuck, Ev."

Unbothered by my pain, Ev hustled me down the hall and once we got to my room, he thrust a hand in my pocket to dig out the key.

"Not so fast!" I said. Ev's fingers squirmed and searched and I couldn't stop giggling. "You hafta buy me a drink if you wanna get to third base there, Casanova."

Evvy rolled his eyes and unlocked the door with one hand, keeping a tight grip on me with the other. He cursed until the light went green, and shouldered it open. With an unceremonious thrust, Evvy shoved me into the room.

"Hey!" I shouted as I tripped and sprawled face first on the hideous hotel carpet.

"Go to bed and sober up," Evvy said. He chucked the key overhand. It bounced off my forehead and landed between my legs.

"I don't know what your problem is lately, and to be honest, at this point I can't say I give a fuck. But when you do stupid shit that affects the team, stuff that..." Evvy sighed and rubbed a hand down his tired face. "Just grow the fuck up, Seb."

I slumped, feeling like a toddler caught with my hand in the cookie jar. Evvy spun on his heel and stormed out, leaving me to wonder if there was any truth to what he said. I mean, what *was* I trying to do, getting drunk in public? I knew better. Did I want to self-destruct? Wallow in misery until I fucked up my career beyond salvaging and got drop-kicked out of the NHL?

I sat on the bed, propped my elbows on my knees, and bent over to rest my face in my hands. It didn't take a whole lot of self-reflection to figure it out. Even drunk I could easily pinpoint my problem. Three guesses? If you said blonde, sexy, and frustrating as hell, you win a prize!

None of this would have been happening if I never met Kylie. Everything was fine until she showed me everything I didn't know I was missing and never really wanted until then.

Okay, that was total bullshit. *Fine* was stretching it. I wasn't *fine*. It was more that life was *tolerable*. Before Kylie, I didn't have an all-consuming emptiness that devoured my heart piece by piece. My bursts of rage were a million times easier to deal with than feeling pathetic, and lonely, and depressed all the damn time.

Unfortunately, I had no idea how to get Kylie out of my head and move on. No idea how to live without her smiles and touches and her sweet laughter.

Arms spread wide, I flopped back on the bed and went over every little detail about Kylie I could dredge up, every second we spent together, every touch, every sigh, every whisper, until the edges of my vision went black and I passed out cold.

11

Kylie

"Ky? You home?"

I flushed the toilet and struggled to get off the floor before Rocco found me and freaked out.

"Ugh," I muttered under my breath as I trudged to the sink to brush my teeth and get the nasty taste out of my mouth.

After being out of town for eight long, never-ending days, Rocco was back home. I literally counted down the hours up until his return. Seriously, nothing made you appreciate having someone until you were sick and alone.

"Kylie?"

I glanced in the mirror to make sure I looked presentable and almost fell down. *Oh my god*, I looked awful. Like... like *total crap!* My complexion was sallow and my skin dull. I quickly ran my fingers through my tangled nest of hair and pinched my cheeks to give them color.

Yeah, no. Still looked like someone ran me over with a

truck, then backed up and did it a couple more times for good measure.

I sighed. Total crap would have to do because... makeup? I didn't have the energy. After a brief wobble and a pause to wait for the headrush to pass, I went hunting for Rocco.

Perfectly tailored in head to toe black, I found Rocco in the living room, looking like a movie star. He spun around and gaped at me. The "v" between his brows itself known and with a sinking feeling, I realized I hadn't done enough to hide my impression of an extra on the set of The Walking Dead.

"Hey. You're here," I said lamely.

Rocco wasted no time confirming my thoughts.

"Jesus Christ, Ky. What the fuck happened to you? You look like hell."

Beyond relieved to have him home, I laughed off his observation. "You're too kind."

In two long strides, Rocco crossed the room and pulled me into an embrace, except it didn't feel right. He didn't wrap his arms around me or crush me against his chest. In fact, it was the opposite of one of his patented, bone-crushing hugs. Rocco held back, almost afraid if he squeezed to hard I would crack like an eggshell.

"You know what I mean," he whispered in my ear. "God, Kylie. You said you were sick, but—"

"You didn't expect me to look sick."

Rocco stepped back to look at my face. "Yeah. I guess so." He reached up and ran his thumb across my cheekbone, eyes filled with worry. "You've lost weight and I can tell you haven't been getting enough sleep." He traced the dark circles, so stark against my pale skin they looked like matching shiners.

Not in the mood to discuss the reason for my insomnia

—i.e. Rocco's gorgeous, unattainable teammate—I pulled back and wrapped my arms around my waist, as if I could physically hold the pieces of my heart together.

"I've been sick," I snapped, annoyed Rocco was giving me grief when I'd spent the majority of the last eight days hunched over a toilet, yarking my guts out. "I'm sorry if I'm not the picture of health."

"Don't do that," Rocco said, seeing right through my attempt to push him away. He gestured toward the couch and sat. Reluctantly, I curled up on the other end and hugged my knees to my chest. Rocco turned sideways and draped an arm along the back of the sofa. "I feel like a shitty brother for not being here for you." His eyes glistened aaaand here comes the guilt for putting that look on his face. "But I'm here now. Maybe..." He cocked his head and narrowed his gaze. "I think I should take you to the doctor."

Oh hell no. The last thing I wanted was to wear half a sheet, sit my naked butt on an ice cold metal table, and let someone poke and prod my body to his or her heart's content. I gave Rocco what I hoped was a casual shrug.

"Let's give it another day or so. I've been able to hold down small meals. I really don't think it's anything worth worrying over."

"I always worry about you," Rocco stated plainly. "I always will. You're my sister."

I reached out and gave Rocco's hand a light squeeze. "I know. And I'm grateful to have you."

It was the truth. Without Rocco I didn't know how I would have made it that far, let alone the previous few challenging weeks. Nat's visit was great, but it was a cute little Care Bear Band-Aid slapped on top of a massive, gaping wound. After Nat flew home, I spent too much time thinking about what I'd never have, while wishing circumstances were different. Time spent remembering the way Seb stared into my eyes as he brought me to new heights of pleasure, the way his hands moved across my skin, his touch almost reverent.

The myriad of emotions was so big and so overwhelming, every time my mind turned down that road, I expected them to burst from my chest. To stop the downward spiral, I would conjure up the image of Seb's hurt and confusion, written plainly on his handsome face, as I walked out his door for the last time.

Seb probably hated me. Thought I played him. Used him for sex. Which had been my intention... initially. When I realized I was falling for him, everything changed. I had to end it before I got in too deep. Only, Seb didn't know any of that, because I didn't tell him. Instead of confessing how I felt and facing rejection like a big girl, I shut him out, then ignored his repeated attempts to reach out.

If I were him, I'd hate me too. I *did* hate me. Hated what I did. Seb didn't deserve it. And it didn't matter that he was a shameless man-whore who probably treated every woman he hooked up with the same way I treated him. That didn't give me the right to discard him like yesterday's garbage in a bid protect my heart.

"Why don't I heat up some soup and you pick out a movie," Rocco said, his smile plastic, oblivious to my turmoil as he freaked out over my illness. "Like old times."

I managed to return the smile. Like Rocco's, it felt fake. "If you want it to be like old times, we need to have popcorn not soup."

"Meh. I figured your stomach would do better with something that doesn't have a gallon of fake butter dumped on it."

Rocco stood and patted me on the head before he

wandered into the kitchen. I listened to him bang around as he prepared dinner. Cabinets opened and closed and the microwave hummed as he heated up the soup. I scored the nearest throw pillow and held it to my midsection so I could curl around it. Maybe a movie would help keep my mind off Seb.

I snatched the remote off the end table and turned on the gigantic, hyper-masculine, eighty-thousand and some-thing pixel, flat screen TV, and scrolled through the movie menu. Of course, my one-track mind refused to be derailed. I wondered what kind of movies Seb liked and chuckled when I read one of the titles, *Die Hard*. Based on the way he behaved on the ice, I'd bet Seb favored hard-core action.

Rocco handed me a steaming bowl of chicken noodle soup and sat down. I pushed start and heard the familiar opening music of the Bruce Willis flick.

What? So it reminded me of Seb? I guess I'm a martyr, because I seem to enjoy suffering. Grumpy and achy, I slurped my dinner and settled in for two hours of classic Hollywood shoot 'em up entertainment.

Midway through, my thoughts drifted. Was that what it would it be like if Seb and I were a real couple? Would we cuddle on his couch, me in his arms so I could use his firm pecs as a backrest?

A barefoot, bloody, and battered Bruce Willis soared through the air with a fire hose tied around his waist and I almost burst into tears.

It was hopeless.

I was never going to get over Sebastien St. Clair.

Seb

I shouted a long string of obscenities in French and whipped my gloves across the changing room. Spitting curses left and right, I paced in front of the bench and fought to rein the urge to pummel something. My hands clenched and unclenched at my sides.

"Fucking blind-ass referee," I growled.

The rest of the team filed in and, for once, they did the smart thing and gave me a wide berth. Except that idiot, Evvy, who plopped his ass down on the nearest bench.

"Rough game, eh?"

I stopped short to squint at him. "Rough game?" I asked, incredulous as I took a step closer. "Rough game?" I repeated, bending over until I was up in Ev's face. "A rough fucking game is getting tripped up or missing a shot," I shouted. My nostrils flared as the familiar, comforting blanket of rage curled around my shoulders and my vision went red. "Getting four bullshit penalties and having Coach pull me from the game, a game we lost spectacularly by the way, isn't a rough game, Ev. It's a fucking nightmare! *Colice de marde. Putain d'idiot arbitre.*" Evvy knew enough French to get the gist. His eyes narrowed and his mouth pulled tight.

"Listen, I understand you're pissed." Ev spoke slow, enunciating each word. "But you need to stop yelling and you really need to get the fuck out of my face." His voice dropped an octave and got all growly. If Ev weren't my best friend, I would have taken a swing at him. Instead, I blinked in surprise, because Evvy never gets angry.

I took too long and Ev had to repeat himself. "Step. The fuck. Back." He looked at my hands and I copied him, surprised to find them balled up, my knuckles were white. I stood in a defensive stance I didn't remember taking.

Thanks, *mon pére,* for programming me so that when I'm nice and pissed, I get ready to attack.

God, it would be so easy, such a *relief,* to lash out violently. And fuck, I wanted it. Craved the release. It had been weeks since I'd gotten laid. Since Kylie. Easily the longest I'd gone without sex since I discovered the joys of pussy behind the middle school with Gabriella LeBlanc.

Without a way to let out the intensifying fury—a result of my shitty game play due the undeserved and unexplained silent treatment from Kylie combined with mounting sexual frustration—I played one of the shittiest games of my career. Just thinking about it sent a hot flush racing up my neck and face, and my fists rose independently from my brain.

Ev's eyes widened and I crowded closer. As a result, he didn't have enough room to stand. I watched his muscles tense as he braced for the blow. Ev was no pussy. If I hit him, he'd fight back, and it would hurt.

"St. Clair, you useless sack of shit! Get your ass in my goddamn office!"

Few things could have stopped me from taking that swing. Frank Vernon's vicious bark was one of them. The release valve opened, and the intense pressure rushed out, taking my anger along with it. I lowered my fists and gave Evvy a sheepish grin.

"Sorry man. It's just..." I gestured toward my head and spun a finger in circles next to my ear. "I'm all fucked up, and an asshole for taking it out on you."

Ev nodded sharply, but didn't say a word.

"Now, St. Clair!" I flinched and hurried into Coach's office, gear and all, including my skates. "Shut the door and sit the fuck down."

I did as ordered and wedged my body into a chair that was

way too small to fit a hockey player in full game pads. No way would I bitch about it. Not with Coach glaring at me like he wished he could set me on fire and dance around my ashes. After my horrifying performance, I knew I was in for one hell of a chewing out and waited for the verbal lashing to begin.

Coach didn't disappoint. He sat, silent, and let me sweat. His rough, scarred hands folded on his desk amongst dozens of piles of paper and an assortment of dirty coffee mugs. I flushed and squirmed in my seat, or would have if I weren't jammed in so tight it would take an industrial sized shoehorn to get me out. No one in my life made me feel like a disappointment the way Coach did. Fuck, not even my own father made me feel so small, but maybe that was because I was too busy getting the innocence beat out of me to worry about anything other than overwhelming, piss your pants terror.

"All right, St. Clair, I've had enough of your bullshit." Coach's jowls shook as he spoke. "You've been acting off for weeks." Fuck, I thought I did a good job not letting my personal shit show. I started to say something, but Coach held up a hand and gave me a look that made me snap my mouth shut without further comment. "I didn't say anything because whatever you're dealing with is, well, frankly, it's none of my goddamn business." Coach's bushy caterpillar brows squinched in the middle and he glared at me. "Until it affects my team." He stood and placed his palms flat on his desk, leaning toward me until his face was almost directly above mine. "Tonight, it affected my team. *You* affected my team!"

My cheeks blazed. I stared at a bloodstain on my left thigh and wondered if it was mine or one of the two guys I pummeled in the first period or the guy I pummeled in the third period. Or was it one in the second and two in the third?

"Now," Coach sat back down and lowered his voice a few hundred decibels or so. "I don't care what you got jammed up your lily-white Canadian ass that has you so screwed up, but you better take care of it, St. Clair. I won't have a liability on the ice. You might be one of the highest scoring forwards in the league, but you keep acting like a goddamn monkey fucking a football and I'll scratch you from the lineup and let you ride the bench until your nuts freeze solid!"

Ouch!

When it seemed like Coach might be done whipping rocks at my head, I took a chance and glanced up. He raised his brows, suggesting it was my turn. Fuck. What was I supposed to say?

Sorry Coach, I can't concentrate because I'm hung up on a chick?

I pictured Coach's reaction and stifled a snort. No doubt that would go down about as well as a whore with busted knees. The only thing I could scrounge up was a pathetic, "I'm sorry."

Coach V's furry brows inched further up his broad expanse of forehead. *"I'm sorry?"* He repeated. "I'm fucking sorry? That's all you got for me?" Coach scoffed and leaned back in his chair, which—due to the daily torture of supporting two hundred forty or so pounds of hollering, angry, ex-hockey player—squeaked like he sat on a mouse, and folded his arms across his chest.

"I-I don't know what you want me to say," I admitted. "Um, it won't happen again... uh, Coach?"

Jesus. The office was stifling. Were the walls closing in?

Coach stared as if trying to decide whether he should hit

me or if I should ride the short bus. Eventually, he sighed and pinched the bridge of his nose.

"Get the fuck out of here, St. Clair."

I couldn't stand fast enough. No really, with my pads on, when I stood, the chair came with me, fused to my ass. I shoved the arms. It popped free of my backside and clattered loudly when it hit the floor. I had one hand on the doorknob when Coach tossed out his parting words of wisdom.

"If you don't get your act together, not only will I bench you, I'll make you see the team therapist."

I shuddered. Damn if the cranky old bastard didn't know exactly what to say to keep my ass in line. *Therapy?* Um, fuck no. I cleared my throat a couple times and replied without turning to look at Coach V. "That won't be necessary. I'll make sure of it."

I took off, knowing I'd keep my word. During my time in lockup, I spent hours in therapy, talking out my "problems" until I was hoarse and my brain had liquefied to one step up from vegetable. None of it helped. All that time spent "reflecting" and I left juvie just as angry and fucked up as the day I went in.

By the time I got back to the changing room, everyone was gone. Except Ev. Dressed and showered, my best friend leaned against the wall near my space. Great. One more person to add to the shame pile.

"I already apologized, Evvy. Not sure what else you want from me."

Ev stared at me like I was the biggest fuckstick on the planet. And maybe I was. What the hell did I know anymore?

"I don't want anything from you, Seb. I wanted to make sure you were okay."

I cursed. More guilt. Seemed I brought a lot of that upon myself lately.

I didn't want to argue, so I started to strip, eager to put some space between my long-suffering olfactory nerves and my rank, swampy hockey gear. "I'm good," I said as I dropped the last pad, wrapped a towel around my waist, and headed for the showers.

"Wait." Ev grabbed my arm as I walked by. "Dude, I know something's up with you. Not to get all Dr. Phil, but you haven't been yourself." He shook his head. "That's not entirely true. It's like you were better for a while. Kinda like a happier version of you." Evvy grimaced. "But now you're back to being an angry son of a bitch. Angrier if that's even possible. Just...if I can do anything to help—"

He didn't mean to, but Ev's little speech dredged up memories of Kylie and it pissed me off. I tore out of Cal's grasp, ready to bite his head off, and caught myself. I was too fucking exhausted, being angry all the time, skin like an overinflated balloon, all tight and itchy, ready to pop at any second. It was time to pull the plug, let out the extra air, and stop being a miserable bastard all the damn time.

I gave Ev a wan smile and patted his arm. "Thanks, man. I appreciate the offer but there's not much you can do."

He pushed off the wall and nodded. "I get it. Just... take care of yourself." Ev lightly punched me in the shoulder and left.

I cranked the water to peel your skin off hot and stood under the spray as I wondered what to do next. When it came down to it, there was really only one viable option, because constantly pining over Kylie, fucking up my game and my head, sucked. I either had to confront her and get some answers or forget she ever existed and go back to burying myself in detached, meaningless sex with easy women.

I winced. The second option kind of made my stomach hurt.

It made the decision easy.

Kylie

"Kylie?"

Oh god. No, no, no.

Between the desperate ache in my heart for Seb, the need to hide my mental anguish from Rocco, and my stupid stomach, fine one minute, making me do the fifty-yard dash to the bathroom the next, the last thing I needed was to be around someone with a freaky, superhuman ability to suss out emotional issues.

"I'm okay, Piper," I said from where I hunched over the toilet in one of the stalls at work.

"You don't sound okay. Besides, don't think I haven't noticed you've been getting sick a lot lately."

I rolled my eyes. *See?* Like Rocco, Piper was too darn observant. I was convinced they were both X-Men and half expected Patrick Stewart to roll in from stage right whenever one of them entered a room.

I flushed, exited the stall, and washed my hands. A quick glance in the mirror and some of the tension left my body. For once I didn't look like I went fifty rounds with the porcelain god. A little pale, maybe a bit of sweat at my temples. I could live with that. I dried off my hands and headed for the door.

"Kylie..." Piper shifted to block the exit. "What's going on?"

"Nothing."

Piper glared, her way of letting me know she thought my answer sucked. I huffed and threw my arms out.

"Fine," I said. "I've been dealing with a bit of a nervous stomach. It's no big deal. No fevers, no body aches, no chills, just my stomach." The look Piper leveled reminded me yet again of Rocco, over-concerned and hovery, but all-knowing, like a mother hen-helicopter hybrid.

Piper frowned. "Kylie," she leaned close and whispered, "have you thought that maybe you're, you know..." Piper gestured toward my stomach, "*pregnant*."

The word landed on the top of my head like an atomic bomb and exploded, wiping out everything familiar, everything I thought I knew, and replacing it with the horrific, stark truth. I bit my lip and dredged up memories of the times Seb and I were intimate.

Reality hit, and it hit hard and fast, dropping a ten-ton bomb on my head and leaving behind the desolate, frigid remains of a nuclear winter.

"Oh my god." I bent over and placed a hand on my stomach. "There was one time..." The night Seb held me against the wall and fucked me until my eyes rolled back in my head. The time I felt an emotional connection. The one that sent me into a panic and I ran.

"I think... I'm not sure. Oh, Jesus. There might have been once..." I frowned. "It's possible... maybe we didn't use protection."

There was no *might*. No *maybe*. We didn't, and I couldn't believe it didn't occur to me until that moment. We were so caught up, the passion so fierce, stopping for a condom slipped both of our minds, and after... well, I can attest to the fact that when you're busy sobbing a river out of your eyes, the last thing on your mind is whether or not you used a condom during sex.

Piper gathered my shaky hands in hers and waited until the shellshock passed. "After work, together, we'll go to the store and get a test. You shouldn't be alone, and I know you said you can't tell your brother."

Oh my god! The room spun and I grew faint.

"Oh shit, Kylie!" Piper flung an arm around my waist and hauled me out of the bathroom. She dropped me on the couch in the employee lounge and hurried back with a cup of water. "Here, drink this." I mechanically obeyed.

What would Rocco do when I told him? Me getting knocked up, unmarried and still in school would give him a coronary. Pull the pin and toss the grenade in his lap that Sebastien St. Clair is the father? Seb spending a month in the ICU at Grady was the best-case scenario.

A hysterical laugh burst free as I pictured Rocco's face when he found out his "sweet, innocent" little sister carried the spawn of Satan in her womb. The image of a baby with Seb's face and a tiny pair of red horns poking out from a full head of dark hair, waving a little pitchfork in his pudgy fist, popped into my head, and I laughed even harder. Tears trickled down my face and my abdominal muscles strained. Ten minutes later, the truth sank in and gradually, tears of laughter turned genuine, and hysterics morphed into hiccupping sobs.

"I can't be pregnant," I whispered. "I just can't." I sniffed and rubbed my midsection.

Piper squatted next to the sofa. "And you might not be."

A spark of hope flashed and I clung to it with both hands. Then I looked at Piper and the spark fizzled out. Even Piper didn't believe what she was attempting to sell. That brought on a fresh round of tears.

"Oh, Kylie," she said, "I'm so sorry." Piper smoothed a

hand over my hair as I wept. "I can't promise the perfect outcome, but everything will work out in the end."

I was pretty sure I didn't agree.

THE SOUND of my heartbeat whooshing behind my ears drowned out Piper, who was calling out my name and pounding hard on the bathroom door. The moisture in my mouth evaporated. As a result, my tongue got stuck to the back of my teeth. I'm not sure if I tried to move, but it didn't matter. I couldn't, rooted to the cold marble tiles beneath my feet. All because of the innocuous looking stick in my hands, white with a bright pink plus sign staring at me from its pee-stained window.

Time passed.

I have no idea how long I stood there, unblinking, but it must've been a while, because Piper picked the lock with a nail file. She tumbled in, file in hand, frazzled and wide-eyed.

Piper shuffled up next to me and peeked over my shoulder. I didn't look at her. I didn't have to. Seeing her pity would only shove me over the edge. It wouldn't take much considering I was already clinging to the cliff above Crazytown by my fingertips, body dangling precariously, dangerously close to loosing my grip on sanity and going on a long, painful drop to the bottom.

"Oh, Kylie." She gently pried the test from my hand and set it on the countertop, then guided me out of the bathroom and maneuvered me to sit on the bed. Piper joined me and wrapped an arm around my shoulders. "I know this isn't what you wanted, but I stand by what I said. Everything will work out. It always does, even when it seems like it's impossible for things to turn around and there's no light to show you the way."

I took a deep breath and lifted my wobbly chin.

"You're right." My voice shook, betraying my attempt to pretend I was fine. I plowed on, not that I had a choice. Hiding under my comforter for the next nine months would probably freak Rocco out. "I can do this."

Piper smiled. "You can. And I'll help you anyway I can."

I glanced away, feeling sheepish for asking. But she did offer. "Do you think, if I need you to, you might be able to be there when I tell Rocco?"

Piper giggled and gave me a light squeeze. "Of course I can."

The road was going to be bumpy to downright rocky at times, but Piper made me believe I could get through it in one piece. That maybe the pregnancy wasn't worst thing in the world to happen, as unexpected as it was. People had babies all the time, right? People with way fewer resources and money.

Then I remembered not only did I have to inform Rocco of his impending unclehood, I had to tell Sebastien he was going to be a father, and my blood went ice cold.

I dashed for the bathroom, dropping to my knees in front of the toilet just in time to lose the cup of tea I forced down at Piper's insistence. I used the back of my hand to wipe my mouth, then closed my eyes and rested my forehead on the edge of the toilet as fear gripped my lungs.

If the mere *thought* of telling Seb had me kneeling at the porcelain throne, what would happen when I had to stand in front of him, look him in the eye, and tell him I was pregnant? My empty stomach heaved again, working in vain as sore muscles clenched over and over until my vision blurred and I was gasping for breath.

When the misery ended, I tucked my body against the wall, arms wrapped around my legs, laid my cheek on my knees, and sniffed. Piper came in and sat next to me in silence, her intuition spot on. We both knew there was nothing she could say that would make a difference. Even if Piper—and Rocco if he didn't toss me out in the street first —stayed by my side every step of the way, I essentially had to do it alone.

"I'm not ready to tell anyone yet," I said.

"Understandable."

Mentally drained, I dug the heels of my hands into my eyes. "You don't think it's selfish? I mean, not telling Rocco or..." My heart stuttered. I couldn't bring myself to say his name. "*Him* right away?"

Piper drew up her own legs to mimic my pose. "I don't think there's a right or wrong way to handle this. It's difficult and emotional and you have a lot to work through and think about." I forced myself to meet Piper's gaze, and this time, instead of pity I saw sympathy and support and friendship. "You have to trust that when the time is right to say some-thing, you'll know."

My eyes began to leak. "I don't deserve a friend like you."

Piper pulled a face. "That's ridiculous. Everyone deserves a friend. Especially when times are tough and we're too weak to carry on. We need a friend to pick us up and carry us to the other side." She lifted her chin from her knees and took a deep breath. "I always thought that if I hadn't isolated myself from everyone, if I could talk to someone I trusted when I went through my breakup and everything, maybe I would be in a better place. You know, mentally. Maybe I wouldn't doubt my judgment when it comes to men. Maybe I would finally be able to get over what happened and put myself out there to meet someone."

I sniffed and let out a humorless laugh. "I'm so screwed."

Piper tilted her head. "What do you mean?"

I laughed again. "You're way stronger than me, Piper. You had me fooled, because I thought you were past all that. If you don't have your shit together, I don't stand a chance in hell."

She shook her head. "That's what makes the difficult times in our life beautiful, and what makes humans so resilient." My gaze narrowed. Piper patted my knee. "Adversity, Ky. It forces people to do things they never thought possible. Overcome obstacles they believed were too big to conquer. Some people, like me, get crushed when the pressure turns up, but you..." Piper studied me with her intelligent, all-seeing eyes. "You're different. You're a fighter. Right now you probably think I'm crazy. Right now, you feel weak and helpless and trapped with no way out. But if there's one thing I'm good at, it's reading people," Piper gave me a serious look. "And you won't go down without a fight."

She was right about one thing. I did feel weak and helpless and trapped. I tried to take her words to heart, even if I didn't quite trust them. Piper was no dummy, though. If she believed in me, I had to think positive.

A wave of fatigue crashed over me. Suddenly, all I wanted to do was curl up in my bed, go to sleep, and turn off my brain for a little while.

After all, I had nine... er, eight, whole months to freak out.

Seb

"This is the dumbest idea I've ever had," I muttered as I walked back and forth on the busy sidewalk, dodging a constant flow of pedestrians. When I almost crashed into an old lady and sent her sprawling, she gave me a suspicious side-eye. Probably thought I was nuts. Maybe I was.

An arctic blast slapped me upside the head. The sting and burn from the glacial current was so strong it felt like a sandblaster ground off my top layer skin. The temperature was cold enough that my breath puffed out in front of me in little clouds of mist. Even under my thick knit cap my ears were steadily going numb. I huffed in disgust.

Some Canadian I am.

I glanced up at the gleaming tower of luxury condos, then checked the time on my phone. *Two hours*. I'd been stalking Kylie in twenty-something-degree weather for two hours. Creepy? Definitely. But she wouldn't return my texts or calls and I couldn't stop obsessing. I guess what I needed was closure, at least, I think that's the bullshit term they use. I needed to know what I did to make her cut me completely out of her life.

The front door of the building opened and, just like every other time since I arrived, it swung ajar. Unlike those times, instead of someone other than Kylie stepping into view, I glimpsed a flash of blonde hair and my breath caught in my throat.

Kylie.

She exchanged a few quick words with the doorman and trotted down the short flight of stairs without noticing me yet. At the bottom, Kylie paused and her expression grew confused. Slowly, as if she knew I was there, Kylie turned her head in my direction. Her shocked gaze locked onto me and my body ached with longing, lust and loss and need and a bunch of other shit I didn't want to think too hard about. The flash bang of desire crackled and popped. It flickered and burned, consuming me from the inside out until I was on fire. A myriad of unfamiliar feelings swelled until they crowded my lungs and made it difficult to get enough air.

Kylie glanced around and I held my breath. The soft skin of her throat flickered as her pulse leapt and she tensed up, like she was about to do a repeat of that awful night and pull a runner.

Too fucking bad I had no intention of letting her get away. I hurried to close the distance between us until we stood almost nose-to-nose, er, nose-to-chin. Less than a minute exposed to the cold air and Kylie's cheeks and nose turned a rosy shade of pink. Her eyes sparkled and the sun backlit her hair so it shone like a golden halo around her head. She was breathtaking. An angel.

Kylie shifted from foot to foot and I realized she probably wanted to know why I ambushed her.

"Hi."

I wanted to smack myself. *Jesus. Fucking smooth, St. Clair.*

Kylie blinked. "Hi. Umm, w-what are you doing here?"

Again, her eyes darted around, as if she were avoiding looking at me. She seemed nervous, reminiscent of the moment before she took off and left me high and dry. Kylie twitched and fidgeted, and my internal alarm blared. Something was wrong, as if she felt guilty. Maybe for leaving. Or avoiding my calls. Or not answering my texts. Hell, maybe she should feel guilty.

"I, uh, I know you don't want to talk to me," I stammered. "But, uh..." Fuck. I couldn't form a sentence out to save my life. I rubbed the back of my neck just to have something to do. "Shit, this is awkward." My arm fell back to my side and I gave Kylie my biggest, saddest puppy dog eyes. "Can you, I mean, can we talk? I only need a minute." Kylie frowned, and I knew she was about to say no, so I pulled out something I never say to *anyone*. "Please?"

I saw the exact moment Kylie gave in. Her shoulders crumpled and she kind of shrank into herself. She appeared, I don't know, weary. I hated that I did that to her. I wanted to make Kylie laugh and smile and shout my name in ecstasy, not hunch over and get sad.

"There's a coffee shop at the end of the block." Kylie jerked her head to the left.

I nodded. "Let's go."

Neither of us spoke during the three-minutes it took to walk to the café. The silence was suffocating, like a heavy wool blanket tossed on my head, its weight smothering my mouth and nose. We stepped into the café, greeted by a much appreciated blast of warm air. My nose and ears burned as they thawed out.

"Why don't you sit and I'll get the drinks," I suggested. "What do you like?"

See? More proof I was halfway off my damn rocker. Nothing made a lick of sense anymore. I didn't know Kylie well enough to know how she took her coffee. Or if she even liked coffee. But I stood outside her home and pounced when she came out.

Fuck, I'm such a self-centered prick.

"Okay. A small coffee, please. Cream no sugar."

A few minutes later I sat across from Kylie at a tiny two-seater table. Our knees kept accidentally bumping and I dug my fingers into my thigh to hold back a moan as my leg tingled and burned where we touched.

Kylie took a perfunctory sip of her drink and pushed it away.

"Does it not taste good?"

Kylie blushed and got flustered. "No. I mean, yes. It's good. I-I just forgot, I'm trying to lay off caffeine."

"Oh." I gave her a smile I hoped came across as a charming. I might be an asshole, but I could be a fucking charismatic bastard when I wanted to. "I could never do that. I'm so dependent, if I could, I'd walk around with a caffeine IV hooked up 24/7."

She didn't laugh, but the corners of her lips twitched. The tiny, sort-of smile only lasted a fraction of a second. Still, I took it as a win. Once the moment passed, the uncomfortable silence stampeded back in and barreled into us, like that big fuck Calloway in a ballet class. It was this tangible thing that sat on the table and shoved us further apart.

Well screw that. I was sick and tired of being driven away.

"Listen," I said. "If I did anything to hurt or offend you, I wanted to say I'm sorry."

As she thought about what I said, Kylie tugged her bottom lip between her teeth, and chewed on it. A host of conflicting emotions slammed into me head on. Lust sent a rush of concentrated heat to my groin while intense longing flopped around inside my heart like a fish out of water.

I coughed and forced myself to stay on topic. "Um, I figured, you know, with the way you ran out of my place, I must've done something wrong."

Kylie dropped her gaze to the table. The urge to keep talking, to fill the silence with chatter, was so strong I had to concentrate on keeping my mouth shut. After weeks of failed attempts, I had Kylie in close physical proximity. I wasn't about to ruin it because she needed a little time to work out what she wanted to say. It was the most excruciating moment of my life. Like waiting for an axe to fall and chop off a chunk of my soul.

Finally, she looked up, eyes glistening with tears.

Fuck. Whatever I did was that bad?

"You didn't do anything, Seb." Kylie sniffed and shook her head back and forth, lips pressed together. "It sounds like such a cliché." She glanced back up at me. "But I swear, you did nothing wrong. It's all me."

It's not you, it's me. Really.

My pulse stuttered, skipped a beat, then took off at a sprint, as if I topped it off with a shot of high-octane fuel. I figured I would get Kylie to talk to me, she'd explain what happened, tell me I acted like a jerk, that when I did XYZ it made her upset. I'd apologize, she'd forgive me, and everything would go back to how it was before.

"I don't understand," I admitted.

"And I-I'm sorry... I can't tell you any more." The moisture in her eyes overflowed in two damp trails that trickled down her cheeks. Without thinking, I reached out and used my thumb to wiped one away. Kylie's breath hitched and her pupils dilated.

She still wanted me. The knowledge sent my heart soaring, yet only made me more confused. Her mixed messages were killing me.

"I know we can work something out," I pushed. "I want to see you again." With my arm still stretched across the table, I opened my hand and pressed my palm against the side of her face. Whether she knew it or not, Kylie leaned in to my touch and rubbed against my hand as if seeking comfort. "You said you wanted to stay with me, at my place that night," I explained. "That's what you said before you left. If you wanted to stay, then why leave? I don't understand. I didn't want you to go if that's what you thought."

Kylie pulled back and left my arm hanging stupidly in midair. I tucked it into my lap. Her bottom lip trembled. "It's complicated, Seb. Just... trust me. We can't keep seeing each other." With no further explanation, Kylie stood and I fucking panicked.

I jumped out of the chair and grabbed her arm. "Why are you doing this? What is so bad that you're willing to throw away something we both know is amazing?" She continued to shake her head. I crowded close to whisper in her ear and Kylie's scent filled my nose. My eyelids drooped and my cock took interest. God I missed her. "Kylie, this isn't like me. I don't beg, and I swear, I've never been interested enough in a woman to do it, but I'm doing it now. For you. Please. I'm begging you not to leave. You're the first, the only, woman I've wanted this way. You're special and I don't know why because I hardly know you. That's what I'm asking for, the chance to know you."

Kylie's voice was low and cracked periodically, like she was about to break down for real. "You're a good man, Sebastien St. Clair." She stepped away and I let her go. "Goodbye."

Once again, I watched Kylie walk out on me.

This time for good.

12

Seb

I t took a good three minutes of standing in the hall, going back and forth in my mind, trying to figure out if I was making the right decision, before I finally said, "fuck it" and knocked. Loud footsteps approached from inside and I snorted. Evvy isn't exactly light on his feet. On the ice maybe, but on land, the guy's about as graceful as a charging rhino. I was wound so tight, I flinched at the slide of the deadbolt, then cursed myself for being such a pussy. The door opened to reveal my best friend—distant best friend as of late, but still my best friend. I hoped so anyway. Hell, after the way I'd acted the last couple months, I wouldn't blame Ev for kicking my ass to Vancouver and back.

We must've drifted farther apart than I thought, because from the way Ev's eyes narrowed and he crossed his arms over his chest, he wasn't thrilled to see me.

I scuffed my foot on the doormat and ignored the prickly heat in my face. "Hey, Ev. You got a minute?"

Ev blinked and his posture relaxed somewhat. He held the door open and stepped back. "C'mon in." Ev closed the door and I stood in the center of the room, feeling like the king of all shitheads. "Want a beer?"

Thank fuck for Evvy and his ability to be laid back in a tense situation.

I exhaled. "God yes."

He laughed and grabbed two from the fridge, popping the caps. Ev returned to the living room and extended one to me. "Have a seat." I took the beer and sat on one of the leather sofas, while Evvy flopped onto his favorite recliner. The ancient thing creaked under his weight. Held together by duct tape and a prayer, the battered cushion was probably permanently dented in the shape of his asscheeks. "So, what's up?"

Using blunt fingernails, I picked at the pale ale label , not sure where to start. Let's just say discussing feelings and shit isn't in my wheelhouse.

"I guess... I mean, honestly? I don't know." Ev frowned and scratched his stubbled chin as he gave me a blank look. Fuck, I was going to have to say it. *Out loud.* "I'm sorry," I blurted. "For acting like such a dick." Evvy sat back and snapped his mouth shut with an audible *click.* I didn't blame him for being shocked as hell. I don't apologize to anyone, and he knew it. "No, it's true. And I don't want you to say everything is okay or give me an easy out." I took a sip of beer, placed the bottle on the coffee table, and rested my elbows on my knees, hands laced between them. "I know sometimes I act like a bastard—"

Ev barked out a laugh and shook his head. "Understatement of the year, my friend."

My lips tugged up and a chuckle rumbled from my chest. "Right? But seriously, these past weeks..." My fingers twitched, needing something to do. I snagged the beer and threw back a long swig. After wiping my mouth on my sleeve, I stared at a random spot on the carpet. A beat later, I took a deep breath and looked back up at Ev. "There's no excuse for my behavior. I just don't want you to think it has anything to do with you, man, because it doesn't."

The amused expression slid from Evvy's face and he shifted to sit on the edge of the cushion. The poor recliner creaked loudly. "Is everything okay? Is it your brother?"

No one knows the ugly truth about the St. Clair brothers. Not Rémy's dark secret, and definitely not mine. Not even Ev. But Ev's been around long enough to overhear plenty of conversations I had with Rémy and he knew damn well how protective I got.

I tightened my grip around the beer and shook my head. "No. Rémy's fine."

Evvy frowned, tilted his head to the side, and stared. I started to sweat under the scrutiny. Nervous, I took another long swallow. Eventually, Ev put me out of my misery. "Is it...? Does this have anything to do with that chick? You know, the hot blonde?"

My heart stuttered along with my ability to speak. "You... I don't... I mean..." *Fuck it.* I slumped back on the sofa. "Shit."

Fucking Ev. Too goddamn observant. I didn't know whether to throw the bottle at his head and run, or snatch him out of that hideous fucking chair and hug the guy for forcing me to man up and admit what had me twisted tighter than a virgin's panties at a bukkake. I put the beer back on the table and dragged both hands down my face.

"I have no clue how you do that shit, Evvy. You must be a fucking mind reader. Yeah, it has to do with her." I expected Ev to proceed by drilling me about Kylie, but he didn't. He just drank his beer and waited for me to elaborate. "Jesus." I grunted. "You're gonna make me say it, aren't you?"

Evvy grinned. "Yep."

"Bastard," I said with zero heat behind it. I sighed and cracked my neck, then proceeded to spill my guts all over Calvin Everette's living room floor. By the time I finished, Ev was speechless. In fact, he gaped in obvious disbelief. Waiting for Ev to spew a bunch of judgmental shit and rude jokes about me acting like a chick sent my anxiety through the roof. The silence between us grew heavier and thicker by the second until I was so fucking tense, I lashed out. "What, don't have anything to say?"

Ev exhaled loudly and scratched his whiskers again. The battered chair screeched in protest when he leaned all of his weight on one rickety arm and a tuft of fluff popped out of a tiny tear. "Honestly? You're an unpredictable guy. I'm used to dealing with it. I didn't think there was anything you could say or do that could shock me. But this? I'm trying to take it all in. It's just, I don't know, kind of hard to believe."

I scowled and fought the urge to jump to my feet and start swinging. "What's so hard to believe?" I was pissed. I just bared my goddamn soul and Ev was being an asshole about it. My fingers dug into the cushions as I reined in my temper. An unpleasant realization smacked me upside the head and I bolted upright, bristling with anger. "Oh, I get it. You think it's funny I got dumped, right? That it, Evvy? It's fucking hilarious, right? You think I got what I had coming to me after treating women like shit all these years?" Ev wasn't wrong about that, but I didn't come here for my best friend to dump all over me.

I shifted to get up and leave, because I didn't need to hear anymore, but stupid Ev—who apparently doesn't appreciate the joy of having four working fingers and an opposable thumb—put a hand on my arm to stop me. I glared down at the offending digits curled around my wrist. At least Evvy was smart enough to remove his hand.

"No, Seb. It's not like that." Jaw clenched, I shot him a look that could melt a goddamn diamond. Ev smirked. "Okay. Maybe it's a little like that," he admitted. "But that's not what I was talking about."

I was still fuming mad, struggling not to knock Evvy on his idiot ass. While I desperately wanted to hear the satisfying crunch of my knuckles as they impacted with his face, I *really* wanted to hear what he had to say. Expending a great deal of willpower, I unclenched and settled back down. Evvy was undaunted. The fucker stared right at me. In that moment, Ev looked more serious than I'd seen him in the five plus years we'd known each other. The intensity of his gaze was so overwhelming my palms grew damp.

"I'm not shocked that she dumped you," he said without prelude. "And I don't mean because you deserved it or any stupid shit like that. No matter what you did, she owed you a reason. I'm shocked because never in a million years did I think I'd live to see the day Sebastien St. Clair fell in love."

What the fuck was Ev talking about? In love? I wasn't in love.

I started to tell Ev exactly that, but the second I opened my mouth my throat seized up and my chest felt tight. A buzzing noise vibrated in my ears and I sat on his couch, jaw slack, unable to come up with a response.

"Hey." A hand appeared in front of my face, fingers snapping. I blinked and sucked in a huge gulp of air. "Jesus, Seb. Don't do that, it's fucking disturbing."

It took a minute to catch my breath and a couple more for Evvy's comment to sink in. *Love?* "I-I don't think..." I cleared my throat and started over. "I don't think... I mean, I'm not sure I know what love feels like."

I glanced up at Ev, fully expecting him to have a teasing smirk on his face. I wasn't sure what was worse, the fact that he wasn't smirking, or the fact that Ev was completely unfazed by his announcement while my insides were pulverized by a pinball that bounced around haphazardly, the metal sphere slamming into a tender organ only to ricochet and take out another. Any more hits and the "Tilt" light would come on as I hyperventilated and passed out.

Ev shrugged and finished his beer. The entire universe as I knew it just got sucked into a black hole, and Evvy was sitting there all casual and shit, like it was a regular fucking Tuesday night event.

"How does anyone know what it feels like?" he asked. "I don't know, dude. Never been in love, either. From what I've heard, I think you're supposed to, you know, like *feel* it."

"That makes no sense." I squinted at Evvy. "I'm just supposed to *know*, but I have no way of actually knowing because I've never been in love, unless I have and didn't know it at the time, which I obviously didn't know, because I don't fucking know what love feels like! That's what you're saying." My head spun from the catch-22 of the motherfucking millennium.

Evvy threw back his head and laughed. "You got it, my friend. And that's why men will never figure out women. We're too slow on the uptake when it comes to feelings and pretty much walk around with our heads jammed up our asses ninety-nine percent of the time."

"Christ," I grumbled. "I'm not saying I agree with you, but let's pretend I'm in love with her." I held out a hand and used my fingers to tick off the points. "She refuses to see me, won't tell me why she won't see me, and systematically rebuffed every single attempt I've made to get her to see me. So what the fuck am I supposed to do?"

"If you figure that out, let me know, because you, my friend, will have solved the mystery that has stumped men for centuries."

I huffed and threw my hands in the air. "What mystery is that, oh great swami?"

"Women."

"Women." I sighed, then looked at Ev, surprised when I smiled. "You got another beer?"

He stood and ruffled my hair. "Why don't I grab a six pack or two?"

I patted my hair down and nodded. "Sure. Why not?"

I was going to need them.

I snorted.

Love.

What. The. Fuck.

Kylie

"Oh god, oh god, oh god..." I shook out my hands, paced in a circle, and returned to stare out the window. The view from our condo wasn't great, just a bunch of random buildings and the highway, but I didn't care. Taking in the beauty of the Atlanta skyline isn't my thing. I prefer to people watch . I looked at the street, but my eyes were unfocused, seeing nothing.

I moved away from the window, too wired and too distracted to concentrate. It felt like my stomach lining unzipped and was in the process of turning inside out. The tightly coiled ball of nervous energy overwhelmed my ability to stand still. By the amount of pacing I'd done over the last month or so, I'd turn into Rocco if I didn't stop.

A couple weeks ago I had my first doctor's appointment. Piper, being the amazing and supportive friend she is, went with me at my request. I shoved a sweaty hand in the pocket of my slouchy cardigan to retrieve a crumpled ultrasound picture. I'd spent countless hours staring at the blurry black and white image, mesmerized by a single, tiny, dark circle in the middle with an arrow labeled 'baby' singling it out. Proof of an *actual* baby. My hands trembled and I shoved the picture back in my pocket.

I closed my eyes and placed a hand over my flat abdomen. There wasn't a single external sign to indicate I had a baby growing inside me. Without the morning sickness, I probably still wouldn't know. The entire concept blew my frazzled mind to bits.

God help me, I was waiting for Rocco to come home so I could tell him. At three months, it was only a matter of time until I began to show. The longer I waited, the more furious Rocco would be that I hid it from him. Not that he wasn't going to be furious either way. He was. *Big time.* But I was tired of secrets, and, after everything Rocco sacrificed to raise me, he didn't deserve to be lied to.

I physically winced from the shock of pain that gripped my heart. *I was such a hypocrite.* Here I was thinking Rocco deserved to know I was pregnant, when I couldn't bring myself to tell the father, who *actually* needed to know. Seb gave me the perfect opportunity to tell him when he approached me on the sidewalk a week or two back. As I sat across from Seb at that little café, and I tried to keep him from seeing my hands shake and myself from, god forbid, projectile vomiting, I'd gone back and forth a dozen times, waffling on whether or not to just blurt it out.

Doing it in public, with witnesses, wasn't really fair to Seb. Plus, in the end, I couldn't do it. I rationalized it as needing to be one hundred percent certain of the pregnancy first, and made a promise to myself that after the first doctor's appointment, I would ask Seb to meet again. That was two weeks ago. Piper supported my decision to not tell him about the pregnancy, but I knew she thought it was a mistake. She wasn't wrong. If Rocco got a woman pregnant, and the woman didn't tell him, I would be furious. I would rant and rail, and curse the woman from Atlanta to DC and back, insisting Rocco deserved the opportunity to know he had a child.

Like I said, hypocrite.

The deadbolt clicked and my heart leapt into my throat. I hurried to sit before Rocco entered. If I didn't, I was afraid I might pass out from nerves, and if I hit the deck, Rocco would take me to the nearest hospital. If that happened, an emergency room doctor would be the one who told Rocco about the baby while I lay blissfully unconscious. Then my brother would apply a beat down to an innocent doctor and probably end up in jail. That particular sequence of events wasn't on my bucket list, so best to avoid it altogether.

"Hey, Ky," Rocco said as he shrugged out of his wool overcoat and loosened his tie. The Comets just ended a five-game road trip that kept my brother out of town for ten days. An entire week and a half without Rocco gave me plenty of time to decide how to break the news. I had the whole speech planned out. Face to face with Rocco, I forgot every last word. "Kylie?" Rocco's brow crinkled. "Are you okay?"

"Umm, oh, yeah." I couldn't look my brother in the eye.

"What's wrong?" The couch sank as Rocco sat next to me and placed a heavy hand on my knee. My chest constricted and my eyes stung. I forced myself to look at Rocco. His expression was so worried I wanted to cry from guilt. Stupid hormones. "Kylie? You're scaring me."

It was time. The moment arrived to let my brother down. To fall from the pedestal he put me on and bounce off of every single sharp-edged step on the way down. And I was seriously regretting telling Piper I could do it alone.

"I, umm..." I licked my lips and refrained from plucking at my sweaty tee. "I-I have something to tell you and you're, uh, not gonna like it."

Rocco frowned but gave my knee a gentle squeeze. "I love you, Ky. It can't be that bad." When I didn't speak, his voice pitched up. "Spit it out. I'm kind of freaking out here."

I took a deep breath. "Okay. Okay. I, uh, so I need to tell you... I found out..."

"Kylie, I'm getting really fucking scared. Just tell me."

Oh Jesus. I can't do it.

The whites of Rocco's eyes showed and his complexion drained of blood. All I was doing was screwing up and making everything worse. Better to just rip it off quick. Like Rocco used to do when I had a Band-Aid. He'd hold my hand, look at me, and say, "On the count of three. One..." Then he'd yank it off before three, before I tensed and made it hurt more than necessary. It was my turn to return the favor.

"I'm pregnant." Once I got the words out, I cringed and squeezed my eyes shut, waiting for Rocco to explode.

I waited. And waited. And... nothing. I cracked one eye open and chanced a peek. Rocco hadn't moved. Not an inch. In fact, I wasn't sure if he was breathing. He looked like a statute. If I didn't see him blink, I'd wonder if he had turned to stone.

"Rocco?"

I stuck out a finger to poke his side when he exhaled

loudly. His mouth worked for a moment, opening and closing a few times before he came up with a response, and even that wasn't much.

"Pregnant?" His voice cracked on a high note.

Heat flooded my face and I glanced away. "Yeah, pregnant."

I couldn't see it, but he shifted as little bit more life flowed back into my brother. "You're... *pregnant*?"

Oh my god! How many times was he going to make me say it?

"That's what I said, Rocco."

The ache in my chest grew more painful and I fought back tears. I had expected a fight. Expected there to be yelling and screaming and for accusations to be slung recklessly back and forth. What I didn't expect was for my brother to turn into some detached, empty shell who wore Rocco's skin like a costume. "Aren't you going to say something?" This time, it was my voice that cracked, and it felt like my heart was going to crack too. For letting Rocco down so spectacularly.

"You're pregnant. My little sister is pregnant." Any emotion was gone, his tone as dry as the Sahara at high noon.

I watched as gears the turned and Rocco processed the flaming dumpster I dragged into the room. As he worked through each step, the Rocco-costume receded and my brother became more and more recognizable. When his neck flushed and the muscles of his jaw began to tick, I knew my initial prediction of Rocco's fury was indeed correct. I scooted over on the couch and put a bit of space between us.

Mount Saint Rocco was going to erupt.

"Someone got my little sister pregnant," he muttered.

"Some bastard stuck his filthy dick in my sister and knocked her up." Rocco spoke to himself as if I wasn't there, his way of dealing with a bevy of conflicting emotions. Once he picked one—and from the increasing venom in his voice I was pretty sure I knew which emotion the roulette wheel would land on—well, that's when the fun would begin.

The red flush spread to Rocco's ears and scalp and he ground his molars together so hard his cheeks bulged and the tendons in his neck pulled as taut as guitar strings. Slowly, silently, Rocco rose to his feet and stalked over to the very same window I was staring out earlier.

With his back to me, Rocco spoke. The volume steadily increased until it reached eardrum-busting. "Kylie, tell me who this motherfucker is, right now! I'm going to hunt him down and skin his ass alive." He mumbled under his breath and his eyes flashed with rage.

I'd seen Rocco angry before. I'd heard him yell and rant. He'd shouted at me, I'd shouted back. He'd punished me whenever teenage rebellion took hold and I pushed too hard. We'd argued dozens of times over the years. But I'd never, ever, heard Rocco sound so... cold and detached. I shuddered from the arctic undercurrent, then steeled myself and responded.

"No."

Rocco spun to face me, nostrils flaring and brows at his hairline. *"No?"* He crossed back to the couch and towered over me, hands on hips, the picture of glacial fury. "No, as in you're not going to tell me who this prick is?"

I shrank into the cushions but held my ground. "No. I'm not going to tell you who he is. It's not his fault—"

"Of course it's his goddamn fault!" Rocco roared. He paced back and forth in front of the sofa, hands and arms gesticulating wildly. "Some irresponsible piece of shit gets you pregnant and you don't think it's his fault?" He scoffed so loud it hurt my ears. "You weren't knocked up by the motherfucking stork!"

I scowled. The scales tipped, and my courage returned as quickly as Rocco's temper hit its peak. Angry Rocco was present and accounted for, and while I might fold under the scrutiny of Disappointed Rocco, Angry Rocco I could deal with. I stood and stormed up to him.

"Yeah, well, he wasn't the only one participating in the fucking!" Rocco winced at the reference to me having an actual sex life, god forbid.

Rocco crossed his arms over his enormous chest, his glare so furious it wouldn't have surprised me if the sofa spontaneously combusted. "So this asshole has nothing to do with the fact that you're pregnant? Has no responsibility whatsoever?"

I rolled my eyes. "Don't be obtuse, Rocco. It was both of our faults. I wanted it, he wanted it, and we forgot to use protection. End of story."

Rocco gaped, staring at me as if I sprouted whiskers, a tail, and pink bunny ears. "Forgot protection?" He breathed in and out through clenched teeth and resumed pacing, hands flying all over the place. "Who the fuck forgets protection? Have I not drilled that into you over and over again?" He had. Both of us hated every awkward, uncomfortable minute of the discussion, but Rocco did in fact lecture me about safe sex. He stopped in front of me again and threw his arms in the air. "What the actual fuck, Kylie!"

My lower lip quivered and I wiped a tear with the back of my sleeve. "I'm sorry," I whispered.

Through blurry vision I watched as my brother struggled between his need to rant and rage, and his instinct to comfort his sister. It took a few minutes, but instinct won out. Rocco pulled me into his arms. After a long sigh, he kissed the top of my head. "We'll figure it out. Everything will be okay."

"Y-you don't h-hate me?"

"What the hell, Ky? I could never hate you." Rocco hugged me tighter. Swallowing around a lump, I shoved a hand between us and fished out the ultrasound picture, blindly thrusting it at him. Rocco let go so he could take it. I stepped back and bit my lip as I watched his face. A half-dozen different emotions played across it in the span of seconds; confusion, curiosity, wonder, and yep, fury. Then he smiled and ran a finger across the tiny circle. "I'm going to be an uncle."

"Yeah," I sniffed.

God love him, underneath the anger and disappointment, Rocco was proud. "An uncle. Uncle Rocco." He turned to look at me, and his smile grew wider. "I think I like the sound of that."

I choked out a laugh and threw my arms around his neck. "I love you, so much."

Strong arms surrounded me. Arms that caught me every time I fell, no matter how far or how hard. "I love you, too, sis."

After we hugged it out and the cloud of rage cleared the room, Rocco handed the picture back, held my gaze, and said, "I'm still going to kill the bastard who did it."

Of course you are.

Some things never change.

Seb

"You got to pick last time."

"Fuck you, Jonesy. Hajek picked last time, remember?"

"Shit, who could forget that weird Russian music?"

For fuck's sake.

I rubbed my temples as my idiot teammates fought for control of the sound system in the changing room. Everyone worked out an unofficial rotation of sorts, and when it was your turn you could plug in your phone and play whatever song list you wanted. I gave zero fucks what we listened to. It was the constant bitching that plucked my last nerve.

"My music not weird. Russian music good."

Jesus, now Hajek was adding his two cents, and since the goalie had more than a few screws loose, putting in his two cents was more like someone throwing a handful of pesos into the change bucket.

"The fuck it isn't."

The bickering continued until it felt like my head was going to explode. Practice hadn't even started yet and I felt like I went three rounds in a cage fight with an angry bear.

"Maybe your American guitar music is weird, *da*? All those... those song about sad love."

"Shut up, Hazey. Country music is the bomb."

I ignored the ice pick that stabbed holes in my skull, shot to my feet, and crossed to where four of my dumbass teammates wrestled over control of the dock. Too busy slinging insults to pay attention, I shoved my way between them and plucked it right out of Yates's hands.

"Hey! Give it back," Yates, a rookie center, whined.

"Over my dead body," I snarled. "You're screeching like a bunch of howler monkeys with gonorrhea and now I have a fucking migraine."

"So what?" Yates replied, a little too snidely for a newbie. I didn't appreciate his attitude.

"*So*, what that means is I don't want to listen to you bags of dicks bitching over music."

Yates tried to snatch the device out of my hand, but just like he did on the ice, the dumbass telegraphed every move. I held it over my head. Since I was not only taller, but already wearing my skates, I kept it out of reach easy. Out of the corner of my eye I saw Hajek circle around behind me. Sneaky fucker thought he could steal it while Yates kept me occupied. I dodged Hazey's attempt to grab the dock and nearly face planted when I tripped over Jonesy's fat foot. Lucky for him, my blade didn't slice off a toe. I caught myself and managed to stay upright.

In retrospect, it might've been better if I just gave up the damn thing, because the speakers chose that moment to blast the cringiest high-pitched feedback I'd heard in my life. Even worse than when my stereo... *oh fuck.*

Everyone in the room shouted and covered their ears, including myself, which meant I had to let go of the portable sound system. It hit the floor and cracked. Plastic components splintered and flew in every direction. *Typical.* But at least the feedback stopped.

"Son of a bitch, St. Clair. You know not to touch our electronic shit," Yates complained.

"Da. Agree. You are bad luck for all the device," Hazzy added.

Yeah, I was.

I stared at the now deceased dock. If Paul Bunyan weren't splitting my head with his eight-foot axe, I probably would have laughed. As it stood, between my crappy mood, last night's revelation about Kylie over beers with Ev, and three hours of practice to get through, when all I wanted to do was to find a couple aspirin and wash them down with a Jack and Coke, the assholes were lucky I wasn't already throwing punches.

"Oops," I said, smirking. "At least now you won't argue over music." With that, I turned and headed for the tunnel.

The barrage of curses flung at my back bounced right off. Dealing with angry teammates was way easier than dealing with that god-awful Russian music. Jonesy was right, it was weird and it sucked.

"St. Clair!" Coach's bark sent a rusty iron spike through my eye. "You're fucking late!" Scowling, he glanced around. "Where's the rest of your slacker teammates? Everyone else is already on the goddamn ice." Coach gestured in the general direction of where most of the team was doing warm-up drills.

I winced, wishing to god I wasn't wearing gloves so I could rub my aching head. "They're coming, Coach."

He grunted and turned back to the ice. "Speed drills, four at a time, sixty-seconds each! Get your lazy asses in gear!"

The shouting, combined with my ear's close proximity to Coach's air horn of a mouth, sent an ice pick into my eye socket.

Twitch, twitch, twitch.

Ugh. It was going to be a long, painful practice.

THE ELEVATOR DOORS slid open on the fourth floor of the arena, home to the Comets business offices. I could count on one hand how many times I'd there. Locker room, rink, and sometimes the media room—those were more my speed, for the most part. Surrounded by slick, expensively dressed professionals, made me feel like an elephant swing-dancing with a herd of gazelles.

"Can I help you?"

Startled, I jerked my head up. A middle-aged woman seated behind reception smiled politely, but her eyes questioned my presence.

"Um, yeah. Sorry," *twitch, twitch,* "I'm looking for Amanda Brooker. She's, um," *twitch,* "one of the corporate sales managers."

Smooth, Seb. Real fucking smooth.

The woman smiled, for real this time, and pointed to her right. "Just down the hall, third office on the left. Do you want me to let her know you're coming?" She reached for the phone.

I shook my head. "Nah. I'll just pop in."

They must get big, doofy, hockey players up here all the time, because the receptionist continued to smile at me like I was a not too bright toddler. But it didn't look as if she was thinking about calling security to have the inarticulate jock removed, so I guessed I was okay. I hadn't been sure if I'd be allowed to see Amanda without an appointment. What the fuck do I know about how corporate works?

When I reached Amanda's door, I took a deep breath before lightly knocking.

"Come in."

It was my first time in Amanda's office and to be honest, I wasn't sure what to expect. I pushed open the heavy door to reveal an impressive, tastefully decorated space with several windows along the back wall. Amanda sat perched behind a contemporary glass and chrome desk, polished and proficient, every bit the executive. I found it a little jarring. I was so used to Amanda sweaty, naked, and writhing, waiting for me to abuse her hot body, it was easy to forget she was a smart and successful woman.

"Are you just going to stand there and stare, or did you need something?"

Amanda didn't sound angry, but she wasn't rolling out the welcome mat. Considering I'd prepared for her to immediately toss me out on my ass and call me a shithead, I'd take irritated any day of the week.

"Sorry. Um, I'm just a little, uh, thrown off by, you know..." *twitch*. I gestured at the sleek surroundings.

Amanda smirked and moved her laptop to the side so she could rest her manicured hands on the desk. "What?" She said with a smirk. "Not used to seeing me with my clothes on?"

I chuckled. "Something like that."

"Have a seat." I lowered myself into one of the gray leather chairs that faced her desk and took everything in, from the pricey looking art on the walls to the stunning view of Atlanta over Amanda's shoulder. "Why are you here, Sebastien? I'm guessing it's not for interior design ideas."

"Oh." My cheeks burned and I flicked my gaze back to her familiar green eyes. "No, umm, not for that."

She smiled. "I didn't think so."

"Yeah, so, I came to say I'm sorry."

The unflappable Amanda Brooker's jaw came unhinged, and I squirmed in the leather chair. It was a rare occurrence, mostly because I don't like how apologizing makes me feel —vulnerable. Something I learned at an early age to avoid at all cost.

"Y-you came to apologize... to me?"

I didn't blame Amanda for being suspicious. I'm an asshole through and through and treated her like shit. An apology was probably the last thing she thought she'd hear come out of my mouth.

That made two of us.

"Mandy," I leaned forward and propped my elbows on my knees, while making sure to maintain eye contact so she knew I wasn't kidding. "I acted like a total shitstick. I see that now. I just..." I rubbed a hand over my chin and sighed. "Let's just say that lately I've been seeing my past behavior in a different light, and I'm sorry for what I did."

Amanda continued to gape, staring at me as though an alien had abducted my body and was pulling my strings like a human puppet. Clearly, she needed a moment—the silence went on—or two.

"I-I don't know what to say." She twisted her fingers. Amanda didn't fidget, so I must have knocked her for a loop. She looked as uncomfortable as I felt. "This is, um, wow, unexpected."

The strangled laugh that burbled up from my chest probably wasn't the best response. Amanda frowned. Yep. Not good. I cleared my throat and tried again.

"Some... *things* have, uh, happened. Things that forced me to reevaluate what kind of man I want to be."

Twitch.

The whole thing was so awkward, talking about feelings and shit with a woman I used to tie down and spank. Amanda sucked in a breath and her eyes flared, lashes fluttering as she tried to blink away the shock.

"What?" I asked, defensive.

"It...it happened. I can't...I mean, I don't believe it." She was muttering to herself so I could barely hear.

"*What* happened? What don't you believe? Jesus, Mandy, you're freaking me out." And she was. My pulse raced and by that point my shirt had stuck to my back. I sat on my hands so I wouldn't slap one over my tap-dancing eye.

"You."

I huffed, despising her cryptic bullshit. "Me what? Fuck, just spit it out."

"You fell in love." Mandy looked at me, astonished. "You actually fell in love."

My body temperature plummeted to absolute zero. It was as if someone injected a syringe of glacial runoff directly into my carotid. I clenched my teeth to hold back a shiver. "No. No I didn't." The protest sounded pathetic, even to my own ears.

"You did," Amanda repeated. Her voice got louder and her confidence grew. She gave me a wicked smile, and chill bumps pricked their way down my arms. I could almost feel the weight of the guillotine that hung over my head. See the gleaming edge of the razor-sharp blade. "You fell in love with someone and... Oh my god! She doesn't love you back." Amanda pointed at me and I squirmed. *I fucking squirmed!* "That's why you feel so bad about how you treated me. You finally know what it feels like."

I waved her off and chuckled weakly. "You don't know what you're talking about. I'm not in love."

Amanda damn near cackled with glee. "Stubborn as always. It's not your fault, Seb. You wouldn't know love if it ran you over, broke every bone in your body, and parked on your chest."

I scowled, crossed my arms, and stuck my chin out. "I would too."

Amanda only laughed harder. "See? Stubborn, just like a man."

I continue to frown, but I couldn't shake the idea she planted it in my head.

What did love feel like? Was I in love with Kylie?

"You're right," I admitted and sagged into the chair. "I don't know what love feels like. I didn't exactly grow up in the most loving environment, so my role models are slim pickings." I shrugged. "I mean, I love my brother, but I'm guessing that isn't the same thing."

Amanda looked at me. Like *really* looked at me. And not with pity. It was more like sympathy, maybe? Or maybe I was full of shit and she was actually comparing me to an emotionally stunted goat.

"No, Seb. It's not the same thing. Loving a family member is one thing, loving another human being with your whole heart and soul, essentially finding your other half, is much bigger. I can't really explain it," she said. "I do know that if all you think about, day and night, is that person, and when you're not with them there's this..." Amanda put a hand to her chest. "This huge hole, like an ache, and the only time it goes away when you're with them."

Jesus. That sounded exactly like how I felt. I swallowed and glanced away. It was better to stare at the fancy artwork than let Amanda and her super-human perception dig any further into my psyche. When a few moments passed in silence, I sacked up and bit the bullet. What the fuck did I have to lose anyway? Kylie didn't want me and I nuked any relationship I had with Amanda. Nothing I said could possibly make it any worse.

"Maybe," I licked my lips and ignored the way my fingers trembled. "Maybe I am in love."

"Maybe you are. You're the only one who knows for sure."

The conversation was getting way too deep for a knucklehead hockey player with a chip on his shoulder the size of Newfoundland. I rubbed my hands together and tried to wrap things up before I suffocated.

"Anyway, I uh, didn't come here to talk about love or to rub anything in your face. I just, um, wanted to apologize.

Apparently, I have a fuck ton of unresolved shit going on." I twirled a finger next to my ear. "Remember the time we first met?" I blurted it out before I could stop. Instead of making an excuse to leave, for whatever reason, I smiled and kept going. "You were so energetic."

Amanda giggled, the sound so sweet I could've kissed her for yanking the shroud off of the somber mood. "That's a nice way of putting it."

I grinned widely. "You were. You still are." My smile faded. "We were friends once. I know I'm not the man you want me to be, and I won't be able to return your feelings, but I shouldn't have been such an asshole." Tears shimmered in Amanda's eyes. "I'd like it if we could be friends again. If maybe you could find a way to forgive me, not that I'd blame you if you hated me."

Amanda stood and circled around her desk, arms spread. I rose to meet her just as she closed her arms around me. I returned the embrace and we stood there for a moment, two people who both needed someone to hold. Eventually, Amanda sniffed and pulled away.

"Sorry." She snagged a tissue from a nearby box and dabbed beneath her petite nose. "I don't want to drip snot on you."

I gave her a playful shove. "After everything we've been through I think I'd be okay if you used me as a human Kleenex. It's the least I could do."

Amanda rolled her eyes and wrinkled her nose. "That's disgusting."

I winked. "Yes, yes it is." Amanda laughed, then gave me a shy grin. "So, friends?"

"Yeah, that would be great."

～

"WHAT ARE YOU TALKING ABOUT, RÉM?"

I tilted my head and used my shoulder to hold the phone to my ear while I fetched a snack from the fridge. I would kill for a protein shake, but I never got around to replacing my blender after it went FUBAR. Mostly out of fear that the new one would become self-aware and attack me in my sleep or something.

"My season is essentially over," I said. "The Comets have no chance at making the playoffs. Your team on the other hand, has a good chance of claiming the Cup."

"It is pretty exciting," Rémy agreed, his voice echoing his obvious enthusiasm. "The Rush hasn't made the playoffs since way before I joined, and this is their... *our* best season on record. We still have to win against Chicago, since they already clinched their division."

I scoffed as I stacked a precarious mound of turkey and cheese on a slice of bread and slathered mustard on the other slice. "No problem. Chicago's first line is shit compared to yours. It's not even close. Just because they won a lot in the past and they're Original Six doesn't make them unbeatable."

"True."

Rémy sounded so much better. He freaked me out the last time we spoke. It had been a while since I'd been that worried about him. When he hit a dark period during the hockey season, the stress ate at me. Too many games and not enough time off means I can't go to Charlotte to be there for him, which I take as a personal failure.

"So, why did you really call, Seb? Because I know it's not to talk about work."

I put the sandwich fixings back in the fridge and, with my hands freed up, untucked the phone and stared at it.

How the hell did Rémy know that? I returned the device to my ear.

"You suck." The little shit laughed, which only made me slap the on the other slice of bread on top of the sandwich and press down hard enough to poke a hole in it. I sucked the mustard off my ring finger. "Fine. I called to check on you. Happy?"

"Seb, I promised I'd call if anything happened, and I meant it. You know I'm fine. So... try again. Why are you calling me?"

I sneered. *Perceptive bastard.*

I cut the sandwich in half and tossed the knife in the sink with a loud clatter. "There's this girl," I began.

Rémy whooped and cackled. "I knew it! I knew it had to be about a chick."

I rolled my eyes. "Yeah, yeah, make fun of your brother. Go on, get it all out." And boy did he ever. Rémy laughed and wheezed for five minutes straight. Then he goaded me relentlessly, English *and* French. I ate my sandwich while I waited for him to get over himself. "Are you done?"

In between breaths, Rémy said, *"Whew!* All done. I swear."

"Whatever, *imbécile.* Anyway, I have a question for you. It sounds, umm, kind of stupid, but, uh, do you know... I mean, how do you know if you, you know, are in love with someone?"

Twitch, twitch.

"Wait. You...you're in love with this girl?" Rémy sounded as stunned as I felt. Just weeks ago, I would've bet money I'd go to my grave without ever having a conversation about love.

"I don't know. That's why I'm asking, you. *Maudit bâtard,*" I snapped, frustrated.

The traitorous shithead started to laugh again. I growled, and Rém forced out a hurried apology. "I'm sorry! I just never expected this, not from you."

"Yeah, well that makes two of us."

"Well, uh, if you're serious about knowing—"

"I am."

"Okay, well, I'd say just the fact that you're calling me to ask makes me think the chances are pretty high that yes, you're in love with this girl."

I bent over like I took a slap shot to the groin, and *dammit*, that stupid empty, too familiar ache returned. The hole in the heart sensation. I noticed it at least thirty times since Amanda pointed it out a few days earlier.

Que je sois damné.

Rémy and Amanda were right. I was in love. And for the first time in my life I was faced with something I couldn't fight or fuck out of my system.

Without being able to turn to my tried and true outlets, I had no idea what to do next.

Shit. I'm an emotionally stunted goat.

CLAD IN HEAD TO toe hockey gear, I stomped out of Coach V's office in a dark thundercloud. If the changing room hadn't been packed to the gills with players in various states of undress, along with the clamoring horde of media vultures, I'd have chucked my Bauer clear across the room. Coach chewed my ass for so long I wouldn't sit properly for a week. His words screeched at me full blast, again and again, like a myna bird stuck on a loop. *What the hell was that? Your head isn't in the game. Straighten your shit out. God dammit, St. Clair!* And my personal favorite, *You fucking*

numb-nuts! By the time he finished reaming me out my left eye was spastic.

Twitch, twitch, twitch.

Stupid, bastard, shitstick, eye!

Unfortunately, I had no one to blame but myself. Everything Coach said was true. I played like I belonged on the fourth line of a peewee hockey team. My head *wasn't* in the game. I fucked up and it cost us.

Not in the mood to deal with what would, undoubtedly, be a metric shit-ton of harping about my crappy playing, I hid around the corner until the last of the journalists left—good because the buzzards couldn't pick at my desiccated carcass, bad because without the media's presence to keep the guys in line, my teammates had no problem firing dirty looks across the room and mumbling slurs under their breath.

Didn't matter. Anything insult they came up with, I already attributed to myself. The loss weighed heavily on my shoulders and probably would for a while.

A swell of anger surged and rapidly expanded. Because I'm fucked in the head, I found the sensation comforting. I hadn't felt it in a while, only once or twice since I met Kylie. If it returned, I could take it as a sign I was over her, right? That I could get on with my pathetic life and fill my days and nights with meaningless bullshit—fighting, fucking, and hockey. Then I would remember something about Kylie, some small detail—her smile, her laugh, her smoldering expression when she checked me out and thought I wasn't looking—and I knew damn well that if given the chance, I would go through the pain all over again.

By the time I got around to buttoning my cuffs, most of the locker room had emptied out. No one spoke to me. They were either pissed I fucked up or had been around long enough to know when I was dangerously close to losing my shit. Didn't make a damn bit of difference to me. Not when there was a six-pack with my name on it waiting for me at home.

Naturally, nothing in my craptastic life ever went to plan.

I draped my tie around my neck and began a half Windsor, right as Evvy, the only one on the team with big enough nads to approach me when I was in a mood, walked over. In the mirror, I watch Ev trip over a glove in the middle of the floor. He stumbled and, trying to regain his footing, two hundred plus pounds of defenseman did a face plant.

I frowned and peeked sideways at him as I pulled the knot tight and flipped down my lapels. Aw shit. Ev scrambled to his feet, visibly excited despite the crash landing.

Whatever had Ev near bursting, I didn't want to hear it. I shoved at his shoulder and said, "Go away."

Evvy laughed and his eyes shone. The dude was bursting to spill, and whatever it was, was huge. Before he said a word, Hajek's loud mouth boomed, "You be uncle. It is good, da?"

I rolled my eyes. Sounded like someone's sibling successfully reproduced. Big fucking deal.

I glanced at Hazey, then back at Ev, and tipped my head toward the goalie. Hazey stood a few feet away with a bunch of other guys.

"What's going on over there?" I didn't care, but hoped to distract Evvy so I could make my escape without getting sucked into his gaiety and general mischief making. Six pack. Remember?

Evvy leaned in close, lips unfurled into an evil grin. He whispered so low it was difficult to hear over Jonesy practically shouting his congratulations.

"It's Calloway," Ev announced gleefully. "Apparently his very *unmarried* little sister went and got herself knocked up."

"And I care because...?" I gave less than zero fucks about Calloway's slut sister.

"You need to go over there and bust his balls. Go look at his phone," Evvy muffled a laugh. "He's got a picture the fucking ultrasound."

I lifted a brow. "What? Fuck no. Dude's always got his dick in a know about something I said or did." I shoved my arms into my suit jacket and fastened the first button. "Calloway's sister issues are none of my business." With that, I turned to leave. The six-pack was calling me.

Evvy stopped my by grabbing my wrist. "C'mon, Seb," he whined. "It's been months and the guy still looks at you like he's waiting for you to stop breathing... preferably while he strangles you. He's sensitive about the sister being 'unmarried' and 'too young,'" Evvy did air quotes with his fingers. "His words, not mine. Now's your best chance for payback. Go. I'll wait here." Ev grinned and leaned back against the row of fancy wood lockers.

"*Tabernak! Ça fait chier!* You're such a prick, you know that?" I spat.

Evvy's response was to jerk his chin Calloway's direction. Our teammates were huddled around his towering Yeti head. Everyone was smiling, clapping Calloway on the back, and congratulating him. You'd think with everyone cheering him on, the moody prick could scrounge up a smile. Nope. Guy looked constipated, as usual.

With a sigh, I shoved my hands in my pockets and walked around the Comets' logo to join the small gathering.

"So, what's up?" I asked. "Calloway win the lottery?"

Hazey's massive mitt smacked between my shoulder

blades so hard I almost stumbled into Jonesy. "Rocco to be uncle. Is good news."

I pretended to perk up. "Oh?" Calloway shot me a scowl and I couldn't help it. Evvy was right. I was having fun. I smirked. "What? You got a brother or sister we don't know about?" Which, thanks to Ev, I already knew, but it was oh so much fun to twist the guy's panties.

Calloway snarled. His lip peeled back and his knuckles blanched around the phone in his hand. "Sister," he ground out between clenched teeth.

I smiled wider. Fuck, it was too easy. Calloway's sister got knocked up, and he didn't exactly look like he wanted to break out the cigars any time soon. So what if she wasn't married? Dude had a stick up his ass the size of the Washington Monument.

"You got pictures?" I pointed at his phone. "What kind? The sonogram or some shit?"

Going by Calloway's glare, I swore, if he could, he would've doused me in gasoline and cheerfully lit the match, then celebrated around my burning pyre.

"Yeah."

I had to see, if only to rub salt in the wounds. I plucked the device from Calloway's Sasquatch paw before he could stop me.

I looked down and squinted. "Uh, I have no idea what I'm looking at," I admitted. The picture was black and white and fuzzy all over, kinda like the TV from Poltergeist when it sucked the little girl into it.

"Dude," Franzie, a second line defensemen, squished in next to me. "You can't see the baby? It's right *there*." His finger thrust into my field of vision and tapped on the screen. "Right. There."

Squinting further, I tried to see what Franzie saw and came up empty. "All I see is static. You got a better picture?"

Calloway reached for the phone, but I was faster. I dodged his attempt to snatch it and, just to be an asshole, flicked to the next photo. The grin fell off my face so fast I was surprised it didn't land on my shoes. A picture of a familiar blonde haired, brown-eyed woman, smiling from ear to ear, filled the screen.

My cackle cut short and every last drop of blood in my body drained from my face. My eye began its Riverdance and everything went out of focus. Calloway grabbed his phone with a snarl. Good thing, too, because my hands shook as hard as an eight point five earthquake, and with my disastrous history regarding all things electronic, I would've dropped it. I didn't even care when Calloway proceeded to curse me up one side and down the other for having the gall to steal his phone and invade his privacy and *blah, blah, blah*.

No. I was too busy going down in a fiery explosion. I was Alderaan, and that picture was the Death Star, its laser beam obliterating everything I thought I knew, turning it into an asteroid field.

"Sebby. Hey, what's going on?" When I didn't respond, Ev grabbed my shoulders and gave me a shake. I snapped out of the daze and glanced around to discover everyone in the room staring at me. Including Calloway.

He didn't know. He didn't know about me and Kylie.

If he did, no doubt I would have been kissing Calloway's knuckles weeks ago. He would've swung first and asked questions later, beating me to a pulp while shouting words from George Carlin's list.

I staggered back and clutched my chest. *Maudit!* Calloway's... *sister!* Kylie was Sasquatch's sister? Kylie...

Calloway? The enormity of the revelation made my knees buckle and a choking panic crept up my throat.

"I-I have to get out of here." I shrugged Evvy's hands off and ran.

Twitch, twitch, twitch.

Yeah, my eye was probably going to twitch for the rest of my life, up to and including the moment they lowered the coffin six feet under.

"Seb!"

I ignored Ev and kept going until I stood next to my truck, feet spread, torso bent in half, and hands braced on my thighs as I sucked in the cold winter air. Not because I was winded. Because I didn't want to pass out from shock.

"Seb?"

Christ on a motherfucking cracker! Why can't everyone mind their own fucking business?

Literally, nobody gave two shits about me, ever, until the minute I wanted to fuck off and be alone. Then a bunch of over concerned busybodies popped out of the woodwork to go all Dr. Phil on my ass.

Twitch, twitch, twitch.

Amanda called my name again. I stood up straight and pressed both thumbs against my spasming eye.

"Mandy, not now," I growled.

God, I was such a miserable twat.

"Well, don't get all overexcited on my behalf," she snapped.

I dug for my keys so I could get the hell out of there and process the cargo jet full of shit that decided to use my brain as a runway. Amanda walked over, heels clicking on the pavement, and my anxiety shot higher than a junkie with a needle hanging from his arm. I wrapped my fingers around the key ring and exhaled. *Talk to Amanda and get it over with as fast as possible.*

After that, I had no fucking clue.

Alcohol? Leap off a tall bridge? Alcohol then leap off a tall bridge?

"You know," Amanda huffed. "You're the one who came to me to ask if we could be friends, and against my better judgment I decided to give you a chance." I clenched my fist and the sharp bite of the keys dug into the meat of my palm. The pain kept me focused on Amanda instead of what I just learned. "Do you treat all your friends this way, Seb? Because if so, scratch me off what has to be the shortest list in the history of ever."

A few months ago, I would have ignored Amanda's bitching, jumped in my truck, and burned rubber without a fuck to give. In fact, I gave serious thought to doing just that, but sadly, I didn't want to be that guy. I *wasn't* that guy. Not anymore. I changed, and found it mighty damn inconvenient to actually care about Amanda's feelings.

Being a dick really was way easier.

I met Amanda's ticked off glare and sighed. "Sorry, Mandy. I'm not trying to be an asshole. I just have..." I waved a hand in the general vicinity of my head, something I'd been doing a lot lately. "A lot of crap to process."

The judgmental expression slid off Amanda's face. She took another step closer and touched my arm. Sincere as hell, despite all the shit I put the poor woman through, she felt fucking bad for me, which didn't make me feel any better. Just hand me the Heel of the Year award and call it a day.

"What's wrong, Seb? You're white as a ghost." Amanda blinked her big green eyes as she looked up at me. "Do you need to talk about it?" I shook my head, but Amanda, tenacious as ever, checked her platinum watch and pushed on. "Seriously, I have time. If you want, we can go get a cup of coffee or something." She smiled, nothing sexy or seductive about it. "That's what friends do, right?"

My shoulders slumped. On the one hand, I wanted to take Amanda up on her offer. Half of me wanted to dump the entire unholy nightmare into someone else's lap to deal with. If anything, Evvy should be the one I called to confess that Calloway's pregnant sister was Hot Blonde from the games. I couldn't wrap my head around it and an outside opinion would be a blessing, but the idea of discussing the swirling toilet bowl that was my personal life with Ev made me nauseous. I trusted the guy and all, I just didn't feel like getting all Steel Magnolias in front of my best friend and teammate.

My other half, the more rational half in my undeniably useless opinion, wanted to jump in the truck and drive until I either ran out of gas or flew off the edge of the earth. Didn't care which so long as I ended up as far as possible from the entire fucked up situation.

Because I'm an idiot, as proven time and time again, I chose to do neither.

"Your offer is really sweet, Mandy. And yeah, that's what friends do." I shuffled my feet and stared at my shoes. "I won't make for good company right now. Don't be mad. It's nothing personal. I just don't want to fuck things up with you again."

The hand on my arm gave a light squeeze and I tore my gaze from my shiny wingtips long enough to catch Amanda's sympathetic smile. "Okay, but if you need to talk you can always call me."

Twitch, twitch, twitch.

I slapped a hand over my eye and bit back a scream. I

had no fucking clue what to do. Did I find Kylie? Run? Pretend I never saw Calloway's picture? On top of the crushing indecision, I had a million and a half questions for Kylie. Such as, why didn't she tell me her brother was Satan? Why did she dump my ass? Besides the obvious—that I'm a raging asshole.

I was losing it, the reactors in my gray matter destabilizing as I cruised toward a nuclear meltdown. My lower lip quivered and I swore to fucking god, if I ended up crying in front of Amanda, I was going to find the nearest overpass and plow my truck into a concrete support.

"Oh, Seb."

Amanda's voice cracked. I made the mistake of looking at her. Tears welled in her eyes and I nearly lost my shit. Without hesitation, she wrapped her arms around my waist, an offer comfort in my time of need. Something I never did for her because it never occurred to me to do so. Not once.

With my face buried in the neck of my ex-fuck buddy, I, Sebastien St. Clair, a.k.a. The Sinner, cried like a baby.

13

Kylie

For all the women out there who didn't already know, it's revelation time! Everything anyone's told you about pregnancy is an outright *lie.*

I couldn't get the advice from my most recent doctor's appointment, out of my head. It was like one of those annoying Justin Bieber songs. You don't want to like it, but can't stop thinking about it. I kept repeating the words, and for whatever reason, always did it using the same placating "doctor knows best" voice. *"You're only four months along, Kylie, don't worry so much. You've hit the second trimester, so it'll be smooth sailing for at least another two to three months. Relax and enjoy the break. After that, well,"* he chuckled, and I remember wanting to kick him in the nuts. *"That's when the baby will really start to sap your energy."*

I hustled toward the arena, looking ridiculous. Gasping for breath, I sucked in air as if the short distance from the car to the door were a marathon instead of across a parking lot. Stupid male doctor. He didn't know what the heck he was talking about... *smooth sailing*. What a joke! A man does not, and never will, have a single freaking clue what it feels like to be pregnant.

Ugh! My chest ached and with each inhale, the cold air felt like a billion knives in my lungs. Luckily, the staff entrance was in sight, less than fifty yards away. I had no problem getting in. Not only did I know all of the guards by name, I was also the proud owner of my very own official laminated Comets badge, which I kept tucked safely in my pocket. Most family members didn't get one, only staff. Per his usual MO, Rocco went above and beyond with his heli-coptering, and threw a massive hissy fit until Comets' management folded and gave him whatever he wanted, probably to make him shut up and go away.

Just a little further and I'd be inside, out of the below freezing temperatures. My lungs were on fire from both the exertion and bitter cold. I was seriously regretting having slacked off on cardio in the last few weeks in favor of moping.

Daniel, the guard on duty, saw me coming and smiled. I opened my mouth to say hello but animated voices caught my attention. Glancing to my right I saw the outline of two people having an intense exchange of words. Hands made sweeping gestures and the volume of their voices steadily rose. *None of my business.* I turned toward Daniel and the beckoning warmth, when the man just about shouted. I stopped so abruptly, my foot slipped on a patch of ice and I almost landed face first on the pavement.

"Miss Calloway?" Daniel asked. He reached for me, brow furrowed in concern.

"Shhh." I flapped a hand so he would be quiet. I wanted hear what the couple was saying, or more specifically, I *needed* to hear one of them, because I recognized the voice.

When it came to everything Sebastien St. Clair, my response was on par with that of Pavlov's dogs. Seb sent my hormones —and my ability to make smart decisions—spinning out of control. I pressed a hand to my midsection and swallowed.

The only reason I was at the arena was to find Seb and tell him about the pregnancy, but hearing his voice, knowing he was close by, made my resolve falter and my stomach queasy. It felt like my internal organs fell into a blender set to liquefy. I tried to identify who was with Seb, but it was dark and they were several rows away.

Dan said my name again and, without tearing my gaze from the couple, I told him, "I'll be right back."

Seb spoke and the sound made my heart flap wildly. It knocked against my ribs, determined to break free of its cage and fly away. Despite driving to the arena with every intention of coming face to face with Seb, hoping to catch him after the game, in hindsight I should have chosen a different venue. Someplace other than where Seb—and Rocco—worked to break the news that in a few short months, like it or not, Seb would be a father.

But I didn't. I didn't call or text him first, either, even though the topic would be better handled in private, with advance notice Seb's place would have been marginally less idiotic, though I knew exactly what would happen the second the door closed behind us. We'd end up naked and sweaty and no words, other than "yes, oh god, more," would be exchanged. As much as I wanted that—like really, really wanted that—it was time. Seb deserved to know about the baby and that Rocco, a man he despised like no other and vice versa, was my brother.

As I walked toward the couple, the person with Seb spoke, and froze. My feet turned into blocks of lead, too heavy to lift. I couldn't see who was with Seb, but her voice was unmistakably female. Shaking off the concrete shoes, I took a few more steps. I wanted to hear what they said.

Too little, too late.

As I inched within earshot, conversation wrapped up. I watched horrorstruck, as they slid their arms around each other and embraced. I gasped, the sudden pain in my heart so sharp I struggled to breathe. I knew I shouldn't watch, yet continued to stare, in spite of the nightmares that would likely plague me for weeks on end. They interacted with a familiarity typically shared by lovers. Whoever she was, he knew her intimately.

I shivered and wrapped my arms around my waist, blinking back hot tears. I thought my situation couldn't get any worse, what with expecting an unplanned baby with a man my brother hoped would drop dead. Turns out I had no idea what I was talking about, because what happened next sliced me open from stem to stern. Seb reached out and the hands he used to worship my body cupped the woman's face. He leaned down and pressed his lips, which once mapped out every one of my erogenous zones, against the woman's in a gentle kiss. Even in the darkness, I could see it was quick and perfunctory, like a kiss you gave a family member, but my battered heart felt the impact all the same.

The ground heaved beneath my feet and I held back a surge of nausea. *I shouldn't be here.*

Humiliated, I backpedaled. Of course—because, why not?—I tripped over my feet and stumbled. Dan asked if I was okay. I ignored him. My mouth was so dry I couldn't speak if I wanted to, which I didn't. An enormous lump clogged my throat and the thick band around my chest pulled several notches tighter.

One careful step at a time, I backed up until I stood under one of the tall halogen lights. The sudden brightness dilated my eyes, ruining my night vision so I could no longer see the couple. A sob choked me, but I swallowed it back. I didn't want to break down where Seb, and his lady friend, could witness my destruction. After two or three raspy inhales, I collected my proverbial shit and swiped at my damp cheeks, which proved futile. As quickly as I dashed the tears away, more sprung up to take their place. I heard Dan's footsteps and, not wanting him to catch me crying lest he report was he saw back to Rocco, I spun and fled to the protective bubble of my car. Adrenaline pumped through my veins and my entire body started to tremble. Throw an unplanned pregnancy on top of the flaming heap, and my mental state went into a free-fall.

Between the shuddering, full-body sobs, and endless stream of tears, I have no idea how I managed to drive home without crashing. Engine off, I sat in my car and glanced at Rocco's empty spot. Prayer isn't really my thing, but I closed my eyes sent up a quick thank you to whoever saw fit to give me a brief reprieve before I had to deal with Rocco, though he would be home any minute.

Listless and depressed, I didn't want to move. Maybe if I cried hard enough, I'd pass out. Then when I woke the nightmare would end and my life would be normal again, sans unattainable men and the stupid desire for danger and cheap thrills. It was Rocco, and the thought of him finding his pregnant sister a snotty, weeping mess in her car, that got my ass moving. I dragged my carcass to the elevator, rode it to the correct floor, unlocked the deadbolt, trudged down the hall to my room, and shed my clothes, and it only took seven minutes. I ended my unsuccessful excursion under my rainfall showerhead, hoping the loud pounding of water would drown out the pitiful cries that tore from my chest. I got three whole minutes of solitude before Rocco knocked on the bathroom door.

So much for taking a little time to process what happened.

"Kylie? I thought you said you weren't going to be here when I got home."

I did say that, because I thought I'd be with Seb.

Crap, crap, crap.

I rinsed the soap from my face before answering. "Plans fell through." I cringed. My voice sounded like I gargled with straight up gravel. I closed my eyes and prayed for the second time that night.

Please don't let Rocco have heard that.

"Okay."

I tracked Rocco's heavy footfalls as they exited my bedroom. Once I was sure he was gone, I let out the breath I had been holding. What had my life had come to? Hiding in the shower for a few minutes of privacy? I needed to find my own apartment, because thought of Rocco hearing me sob sent a bolt of fear down my spine. Rocco hated to see me cry. It made him beyond upset and he always overreacted.

I wiped the water out of my eyes and glanced down at the small swell of my belly. *No moving out for me any time soon.* Not with a baby on the way and no one to help. That depressing little nugget brought on a fresh wave of despair. I wanted to hate Seb, but I couldn't. Besides, I had no one to blame but myself. I accepted his invitation to meet in the hotel bar, knowing exactly who he was and his reputation with women. I chased the high of being with a man like Seb. The thrill that came from sneaking around behind Rocco's back.

I was such a mess, I cried until my fingers pruned and thick steam filled the shower stall. Then I turned off the water and towel dried. I sighed. Rocco would be waiting for me. I pulled on some comfy sweats, braided my damp hair and let it hang down my back, and went looking for Rocco before he came looking for me. Easy enough. I opened the bathroom door to find him sitting on my bed, handsome face creased with stress, mouth distorted into a frown.

I took a deep breath and plastered on what had to be the fakest smile ever.

"Umm, hey."

How lame. If Rocco didn't think something was wrong before, he definitely did after that.

Right on cue, Rocco's dark brows knitted, and the familiar wrinkle above his nose made its first of what would likely be many appearances of the evening.

"Sit," he demanded as he pointed at the bed. "We need to talk."

"Can we maybe do this tomorrow?" I made my way into the walk-in closet. "I'm exhausted."

After dumping my dirty clothes in the laundry basket, I whirled around, completely unprepared to find my brother practically up my ass. I ended up face to chest with a wall of muscle and squealed in surprise. Rocco stood just inside the closet, all huge and menacing with his big body towering over me and blocking the only exit.

Rocco's harsh expression faltered and he deflated a bit. Then he let out a long sigh, one that made me want to roll my eyes so hard they'd get stuck up inside my head.

"Fine," he snapped. "Tomorrow. But I mean it, Ky, no backing out." Rocco thrust a finger at me. "Get some sleep and we'll talk in the morning."

Without waiting for me to respond, Rocco stomped off like a caveman, lumbering out of my bedroom, footsteps loud as he disappeared down the hall. Well, at least one good thing came out of Rocco's pissy attitude. With our impending "talk" hanging over my head, I was so good and wound up I managed to spend least ten whole minutes not obsessing over Seb.

Tomorrow, I had to tell Rocco about Seb. A blot of fear shot through me. Rocco really would kill Seb. I was in a lose-lose situation, stuck between a rock and two prehistoric-minded, testosterone-fueled, hockey players.

By the time I finished sobbing under the duvet, feeling pathetic and sorry for myself, I had squeezed out every last tear I could possibly produce and then some. Despite the fear, despite seeing Seb with another woman and chickening out, despite how Rocco was going to react, I knew what I had to do. A round of confessions and brutal honesty, for Rocco, Seb, and myself.

Eventually, pregnancy exhaustion took over and I fell asleep, not that I got any rest. I tossed and turned all night, images of Seb and his mystery woman haunting my dreams.

Seb

FUCK. My. Life.

I drained the last of the whisky from the tumbler and slammed the glass on the countertop. Everything was so fucked up. Kylie—*my* Kylie—is that bastard Calloway's sister. Hot Blonde is related to Sasquatch. I barked a sarcastic laugh and shook my head. God has one hell of a sick sense of humor.

A quarter of the bottle of single malt was gone. I had a decent enough buzz going to find the fact somewhat hilarious. How the fuck did an asshat like Rocco Calloway end up the brother of such a stunning, kind woman? It boggled the mind. Then again, look at my piece of shit sperm donor of a father, the undisputed King of all asshats. Dear old Dad made Calloway look like Mother Theresa. My gaze flicked to the whisky and I frowned. *Mon père* loved to drown himself in alcohol. So much so, it permeated from his pores all hours of the day. I tensed at the similarities and clenched my fingers as I fought with my conscience.

Did needing a drink to process the shitstorm mean I was turning into my father? No one would blame me for getting blitzed considering what I'd found out.

I returned my gaze to the bottle and sneered at it. Knowing I might be more like my old man than I wanted to believe pissed me off. My lips curled back from my teeth and I snarled.

I am not my father!

Anger, shame, humiliation, and a shocking amount of self-loathing erupted to the surface. I whipped out an arm, snatched the bottle and glass, and threw them both at the sink on the other side of the kitchen. The glass exploded and the shards went flying. Whiskey splattered on the floor, the counters, and across the front of my shirt. Alternating between fury and despair, I slid down the cabinets until my ass hit the ground.

The outburst helped clear the fog of alcohol. I pinched the bridge of my nose to lessen the pounding headache that hammered inside my head. It didn't help.

Twitch, twitch, twitch.

Christ on a bike! Motherfucking eye. Frustrated, I slammed my head against the cabinet. Lucky for me, it's mandatory that hockey players have skulls made of titanium, or it probably would've hurt.

Kylie was pregnant with *my* kid and I had to wonder, if I

hadn't snatched Calloway's phone, would I have gone my entire life without knowing I had a son or daughter? I leapt to my feet and began to pace. Hands laced behind my head, I went back and forth, retracing my steps as I struggled to process how fucked up everything was.

A thought hit me and I stopped dead in my tracks. My jaw unhinged and my hands fell to my sides. Holy fuck. All this time, Kylie... she knew who I was. No way did she not know about the animosity between me and her asshole brother. Kylie *knew* when Calloway or me figured out what was going down, it would turn into a complete shitshow, and she screwed around with me regardless.

That was it. Decision made, I went to grab a shower and get some sleep. I needed a clear head for tomorrow, when I had what would likely be the most important conversation of my life.

Kylie

IT WAS late morning by the time I rolled out of bed. Pleasantly numb inside, I calmly and methodically showered, brushed my teeth, got dressed, and even put on makeup. The panic didn't hit until I left the safety of my room, then I had to force my feet to take me down the hall. I sniffed at the air and my stomach growled. Food.

"Here." Rocco pulled out a chair when I stepped into the kitchen. A bowl of soup sat on the table, silverware, a napkin, and a glass of water at its side. "You sit and eat," he ordered. "When you're done, you and I are going to have a little chat."

My stomach did a somersault. I was pretty sure I knew

exactly what kind of chat Rocco wanted to have. One with him hurling a ton of questions at my aching head. Questions I had, so far, refused to answer. The thought should have made me nauseous enough to put me off breakfast, but I was out of the dreadful, pukey, first trimester, and food was no longer something to avoid. It was necessary, to the point I ate all the time. I even started to crave strange combinations with sriracha sauce. I put it on everything, including a glazed donut once—don't be a hater, it was *amazing*. I polished off the pile of eggs and bacon in record time, and did it *without* sriracha.

It wasn't until I sat back in my chair that I realized I should have drawn out the meal to avoid "the talk." Rocco drilled holes in the side of my head, his way of letting me know not only was he done waiting, but "the talk" was happening right then and there and would be downright unpleasant.

I glanced up. Just as I thought, Rocco was indeed glaring, gaze steady and determined. Despite the shower sweat dripped down my back. He relaxed his tense expression— even though it was too late. I knew Rocco wanted to preach hellfire and brimstone—he folded his hands on the table and took a deep breath.

"Who is the father, Kylie?" Before I could answer, the bastard lifted a hand and gave me the face-palm, *the face-palm!* and continued. "And don't give me that song and dance bullshit about you being afraid to tell me because I'm going to beat up whoever it is that stuck his dick in my baby sister." His jaw ticked, and I snorted.

Yeah right, he so would.

Rocco gave me a withering look and I hunched down in my chair. Naturally, the nausea I thought would come earlier chose that moment to make its appearance, *after* I filled my stomach to the brim. In retrospect, I was glad I skipped the sriracha. Nothing was worse than fiery sriracha reflux.

"Kylie," Rocco persisted, trying—and failing—to keep his tone from sounding threatening. He laced our fingers and those stupid pregnancy tears flooded my eyes. "You need to tell me who it is, Ky. I promise I won't be mad. You're having a baby. Not only is it not fair to *you* because, at the very least, this disgusting asshole should pay for his kid, but it's not fair to him to not know he's going to be a father. It's also not fair to the baby to not give the other parent a chance to be in his or her life."

My lips trembled and tears poured down my cheeks. Rocco can say he won't be angry, promise he won't attack the father, but the second I Seb's name leaves my lips, Rocco would lose his ever-loving mind. Any scraps of sanity he possessed would burn to ash and disappear faster than my dignity.

It took me a bit to calm down enough to speak. When I finally did, my voice was choked up. I was truly scared to tell him. "Y-you're going to be s-so m-mad at me."

The feet of Rocco's chair scraped on the floor as he turned to face me. He reached out and clasped both of my hands and brought them to his chest. "You're family, Ky. I love you. Just tell me who it is. Whatever happens, we can work it out."

"I—"

The doorbell rang, followed immediately by loud pounding that rattled the front door. I exhaled.

Saved by the bell. Literally.

Perma-scowl in place, Rocco pushed to his feet and huffed. "I'll be right back."

I nodded. While Rocco answered the door, I took the

opportunity to duck into the nearby half-bath to attempt to clean up and blow my nose. Naturally, because everything in my life seemed to turn to shit lately, I was splashing water on my face when the shouting began.

Towel partially blocking my vision as I dried my face, I hurried toward the commotion. There was a loud crash followed by a dull thud that sounded suspiciously like a body hitting the floor. I dropped the towel and sprinted for the foyer. The sight that greeted me was so shocking, when I skidded to a stop I slipped on the hardwoods. My arms pinwheeled to keep my balance and my fingers scrabbled for purchase. By sheer luck I grabbed hold of a bookcase and kept from wiping out. *Barely.*

The teeny, tiny amount of energy I expended to get to the foyer in no way accounted for the galloping of my heart. No, that was entirely the fault of Sebastien St. Clair, in the flesh, standing in my home. Scratch the standing part. Seb was on the floor, his limbs sprawled every which way. Blood gushed from a split lip and one of Seb's eyes was well on its way to swelling shut. Rocco towered over Seb like an avenging angel, arm pulled back, fist balled up, about to land another blow.

"Rocco, no!" Without thinking, I ran and slid between Rocco and the father of my child. Jerk or not, I didn't want Seb to get hurt. A ham-sized fist flew at my head. Fortunately, Rocco had time to pull his punch. He snarled and gnashed his teeth.

"Kylie, get out of my goddamn way."

I shivered. Rocco sounded so cruel my pulse skittered. I steeled my nerves and held my ground.

"No." I hid my trembling hands behind my back.

"Kylie," Seb said from the floor behind me. "Don't put yourself in danger. Especially not in your... uh, condition."

I whipped around to face Seb, whose eyes immediately landed on my midsection. My face and neck burned with shame. I crossed my arms to cover the tiny baby bump and sniffed back a sob.

"What?" I croaked.

"Fuck you, St. Clair!" Rocco bellowed so loud I startled, yet I couldn't tear my gaze from Seb. "She's not the one in danger. I would *never* hurt my sister! Not like you, you sick son of a bitch!"

The tension grew so thick, I could taste it on my tongue. Rocco was a lit stick of dynamite, fuse shrinking, time to detonation counting down.

Seb growled and used the back of his hand to wipe the blood from his lip, which only served to smear it around. He climbed to his feet and flicked his bright blue eyes over my shoulder to stare daggers at Rocco.

"Fuck you, Sasquatch." Seb's lips curled back. Blood filled his mouth, and his sneer looked positively gruesome. "I would never fucking hurt her."

"You already did, you motherfucker! I'm going to *kill* you for screwing my sister and leaving her like this." Rocco let out a dark laugh that sent chills down my arms. I turned to my brother. He was literally shaking with rage. "I should've fucking known it was you, St. Clair. You're the only one I know who would do *anything* to get under my skin, even sinking so low as to pull my sister into your twisted mind-fuck games."

There was a fraction of a second's warning when Rocco's muscles tensed, then he lunged. Caught in the middle, I cried out. The rest went down so fast everything blurred together. Seb grabbed my arm and shoved me behind his body. That precious moment he used to get me out of the way cost him dearly. I regained my bearings just in time to see Rocco's huge fist connect with Seb's jaw. Seb's head snapped back forefully.

"Rocco! Stop." I tried to get between the two men. They glowered at each other, nostrils flaring like two bulls ready to charge. Seb threw out an arm to block me.

"Kylie, don't. I'm not going to let you get hurt. *Enfant de chienne.* If this *trou de cul*," Seb growled what I thought were insults in French as he gestured at Rocco, who responded by raising his fists. Rocco's knuckles were bruised and bloodied. "If he would stop acting like *un Néandertal* for two fucking seconds so I can explain, instead of attacking me."

Rocco's gaze went black and, for the first time in my life, I was afraid of my brother. He looked positively murderous.

"It doesn't matter what you have to say, St. Clair. I'm still going to beat the living shit out of you. You'll be lucky if you can walk out of here when I'm done, because I have every intention of breaking both of your legs." Rocco's deliberate and chilling delivery didn't shore up my confidence that he wouldn't do exactly that.

The amount of testosterone that swirled in the air grew thick so I almost gagged. Their macho posturing and tendency to resolve things with savagery had me stressed out beyond belief. It was overwhelming. I wouldn't stand there and watch my brother, who I loved, fight Seb, who I also loved. Plus, I was furious. With Rocco for acting like I was some frail maiden whose virtue required defending, and with Seb for being kissing that woman in the parking lot. Add in the yelling, the blood, and my whacked-out pregnancy hormones, and I was done. Finished. They could kill each other for all I cared, I just knew I had to get out of there, as far as possible from their hyper-masculine fog. Of course, it was the dead of winter and I wasn't currently wearing shoes or a coat. My initial plan of storming out the front door wouldn't work. I turned to my only other available option and took off down the hall, locked myself in my room, flung myself on the bed, and burst into tears. Mature, I know, but like I said... pregnancy hormones.

Over my hitched sobs I heard raised voices as the men continued to go back and forth. Idiots. At least there were no sounds of fists landing on bodies or grunts of blows absorbed. The shouts grew louder and louder until I realized those morons were headed for my bedroom, still arguing. I wanted to scream into my pillow. I wasn't fragile, but I was in no shape to deal with two stubborn alpha males as they butt heads and fought over me like rabid dogs over a lamb shank.

I flipped to my back and winced. My whole body ached, the exhaustion so all-consuming even my toes hurt. Right outside the bedroom door, their squabbling increased in volume and a scuffle broke out. Someone or some*thing* slammed into the door hard enough to make the frame shake. More yelling, more scuffling, more thumping against the door, and I snapped. I had reached my limit with them and their tendency to resort to playground rules to resolve their issues. The shroud of misery and despair receded like the outgoing tide, replaced by a tsunami of white-hot anger.

Molars grinding, I launched off the bed and stomped over to the door. My timing couldn't have been worse. I twisted the lock and flung open the door as Rocco threw Sebastien against it. Instead of coming in contact with the slab of wood as expected, Seb met empty space where the door used to be. His eyes bugged out and his arms whirled as he soared through the air and crash-landed in a heap on my bedroom floor. I gaped at Seb. He was bloodied and bruised, but his arms and legs appeared functional.

Yes, I was still mad at him for being an ass, but seeing

him injured while Rocco—who sported several scrapes and bruises of his own—seethed and his enormous body filled the doorway, the object of my fury changed. Rocco better batten down the hatches. He was about to be on the receiving end of Hurricane Kylie.

"What the hell do you think you're doing?" I shouted as I got in Rocco's face. Rocco jerked back, surprised by my outburst, and his enraged expression faltered for a brief moment before the furious scowl returned.

"I'm showing fuck-nuts here what happens when you disrespect my sister." Rocco pointed at Seb.

A demon must've possessed me or something, because size differential be damned. I slapped my palms against Rocco's massive pecs and gave him a mighty shove. Okay, so he didn't budge, but I like to think I got my point across. Rocco looked at me as if he had no idea who I was.

That made two of us.

"It's none of your damn business what Seb did or didn't do *to* me, *with* me, or *for* me!" Without laying a finger on him, Rocco staggered back as if I ninja-kicked him in the gonads. His mouth opened, but I didn't want to hear whatever bullshit was about to spew forth. "No," I said as I slashed my hand through the air. "You're not a part of this." I gestured between Seb—who sat on the floor, as stunned as Rocco—and myself. "If the two of us have something *we* need to resolve, it won't include you." I had steadily pushed on his chest, maneuvering Rocco into the hall without him noticing.

"He only did this to you to get back at me, Ky. Can't you see that?"

"Fuck you, Calloway!" Seb shouted from my room. "I didn't even know who she was until I saw your phone last night, you fucking Yeti."

I twisted around and glared at Seb, who looked appro-
priately chagrined. He slammed his mouth shut so hard his
teeth clacked. Satisfied Seb would behave while I took care
of my brother, I turned back to Rocco.

"Whatever he did or didn't do," I continued, "is between
the two of us. Now, I get that you don't respect him, and
that's your choice. You don't have to. But so help me Rocco,
you will damn well respect *me*. That means leaving us alone
while we talk."

Stubborn as always, Rocco started to open his pie hole,
again. My response was to slam the door in his stupid face
and twist the lock. The doorknob rattled and Rocco
thumped on the door. My hackles were so high they could
probably see them from the International Space Station.

"If you don't go away right now, Rocco, I swear on our
parents' grave I will pack my shit and leave."

Those were the magic words that took the wind right out
of my brother's sails. I knew I won. "Fine," Rocco growled
through the slab of wood. "But you yell if you need me and
I'll be right here."

Once he left, I exhaled and thumped my forehead
against the door.

"So, umm, do you have anything I can use to clean up?"

I yelped and spun around, clutching my chest. I was so
busy fighting with Rocco I forgot about Seb. Put one more
mark in the "things pregnancy does to you" column. It was
the only excuse I had, because something was wrong with
me. If I weren't pregnant, nothing could ever make me forget
about Sebastien St. Clair.

Seb pointed at his bloody lip. *Oops*. Right, he asked to
clean up.

"Oh, um, yeah. Hold on."

Flustered, I dashed into the bathroom and ran a washcloth under the faucet, careful to avoid peeking at the mirror. I knew how I must look, after all the crying and shouting and mentally draining caveman crap. I would bet week-old roadkill was easier on the eyes. I squeezed out the washcloth and took a deep breath.

"Thanks."

Seb took the washcloth and wiped his face, getting most of the blood off. The rest smeared until it looked like he lost the battle with a tube of MAC Russian Red lipstick. I knew I lost my mind when a completely inappropriate giggle burst out. Seb frowned and his brows squinched over his gorgeous blue eyes, which made me laugh harder. The adorable, puzzled look on Seb's face set off a fit of hysterics, one that likely left him wondering if I was entirely sane.

"Sorry," I wheezed between giggles. "I don't know what's wrong with me."

Seb, having his own moment of acting completely unlike himself, took my elbow and gently led me to sit on the bed. "Are you okay?" he asked as he sat so close our thighs touched.

God. I missed him so much. Being so near, the physical contact, him acting all concerned—the switch on my emotions flipped yet again and my laughter morphed into hitched sobs. I was so damn sick of crying, but couldn't stop. When Seb wrapped a comforting arm around my shoulders and dropped a kiss on the top of my head, holding me while I wept, I lost it.

"I-I'm s-sorry I didn't t-tell you." Snot and tears soaked into Seb's shirt as I clung to it, the material fisted in my hands. "I-I didn't know w-what to say."

Seb gently pried my fingers apart, then gathered my hands in his and kissed my knuckles, one at a time, the endeavor so sweet my breath caught. Pulse racing, I stared at

Seb, and a bevy of emotions bubbled up and over. I didn't know what to do or think.

"I know we need to talk," Seb said carefully. "About a lot of things." His breath caressed the back of my hand and his gaze dropped to my midsection. I felt him tense at the visual reminder of his impending fatherhood.

We *had* to talk about the baby, and I knew that. I just didn't want the rare, tender moment to end. Didn't want to argue, see Seb's gaze turn cold, or watch him stalk out of my room. He had to be furious that I kept a secret he should have been in on.

"But now isn't the time." The lines around Seb's eyes relaxed a fraction, as did his rigid posture. "You look exhausted, and you're upset. No need to add to the stress." He let go of my hands to squeeze my knee. "We'll talk later. After you've gotten some rest."

Seb went to stand and a burst of adrenaline sent me into a panic. I scrabbled for a hold and caught the hem of his shirt. I held it in a death grip, as I vibrated with the very real fear Seb might walk out of my bedroom and decide he never wanted to see again.

"Don't leave!"

With me clinging to his clothes, Seb sat back on the bed. He turned to look at me, his forehead creased with indecision. I watched Seb shuffle through a half-dozen emotions. Should he run? Stay? Talk? Shout? Cry? Pull out all his hair? As I stared into his eyes, I noticed one of them twitched. The tiny muscles spasmed every second or two, over and over.

"Please, don't go," I begged, officially shedding my last bit of pride. "We don't have to talk. I... Will you..." My heart thundered, nearly drowning out my voice. "Will you stay?" Seb glanced at the door. It didn't take a genius to guess why he hesitated. "Rocco knows better than to bother us," I explained. "I don't make false threats, and he knows it. The last thing Rocco wants is for me to move out. He'll be good."

Of that, I was confident. Hey, at least I was confident about *something*, because lord knows I had no flipping idea what I was doing when it came to Seb or anything else in my messed up life.

In a tender gesture, Seb reached out and tucked a wayward strand of hair behind my ear. I melted under the heat of his stare. Not heat, *warmth*. Like he cared. And in his own way, he had to. Seb wouldn't put up with Rocco's crap to get to me, wouldn't *bleed* for me, if he didn't care.

In the hopes I could persuade Seb not to go, I pulled up my feet and lay back. "Please. Will you lay down with me?"

I swallowed and patted the spot next to me. Seb squirmed and his eye continued to twitch. Then, decision made, he toed off his shoes and joined me on the bed. After positioning his tall body next to me, he grabbed me by the waist and proceeded to push and pull and maneuver me how he wanted, until he was spooning me from behind. Seb's long fingers fanned out across my hip, fingertips pressing into the flesh. The possessive gesture put a lump in my throat.

"I know we have to talk about the baby," he whispered, his breath on the back of my neck. Goose bumps pricked my skin and I shivered. "And we will. Later. Turn off your brain and get some sleep. I can practically hear the gears spinning."

I huffed out a laugh and closed my eyes, surprised to find I was able to relax, even with the odds that Rocco was lurking on the other side of my bedroom door somewhere around eighty-twenty. He could go pound sand for all I cared. I was warm and safe and *happy*.

As I drifted off, a smile tugged at my lips. When it came

to Seb, I still had my doubts, but they no longer seemed all that important.

Sleep came almost instantly.

Seb

Kylie's breathing grew slow and even, and I felt the anxiety leech from her body with every rise and fall of her chest. I was glad she was getting some sleep, because I wasn't. No way was I going to close my eyes. I'd run for president of the Justin Bieber fan club before I let my guard down with Rocco Calloway skulking around nearby. Bastard probably had his ear pressed against the door. If I had any idea Kylie lived with him... her, ugh, *brother*, I wouldn't have come.

Fuck it. That was a lie.

Even if I knew about Calloway, I wouldn't have done anything different. Except maybe been prepared for Sasquatch to attack me the second he answered the door. Sucker punched me right in the damn mouth.

My blood pressure rose. I clenched my jaw and shoved Calloway out of my head. I didn't want to think about him. Instead, I propped an elbow so I could watch Kylie sleep, a first for me, mostly because I was gone the second I busted my nut. I would have made an exception for Kylie, but she took off before sleeping arrangements were discussed.

I blinked away the gut-clenching memory and soaked in everything Kylie. She looked even more breathtaking in her sleep, her features relaxed, body pliant, and those thick lips slightly parted. More beautiful than at that idiotic team dinner, the one I'd been arm twisted into attending. The fact that in her sleep, she outshone the ball-tingling, backless black dress she wore that night, spoke volumes as to how stunning Kylie truly was. I studied the thick fan of dark lashes splayed across her cheek and the freckles sprinkled across the bridge of her nose.

My mind was blown. It wasn't possible that the angelic vision in my arms came from the same gene pool as the growling six-and-a-half-foot Yeti who lived to antagonize me at any and every given opportunity.

Based on the shadows under Kylie's eyes, she needed to sleep, but I couldn't stop from reaching out to lightly skim my fingers down her bare arm. Chill bumps pricked and I smiled. I waited for the chance to see her again, and had no intention of wasting the opportunity. I raked my greedy gaze up and down her body, intent on studying each and every square inch, to memorize every detail.

My leisurely, somewhat erotic, inspection came to a screeching halt when I reached her waist. I sucked in a sharp breath and slowly slid my hand toward the small but noticeable bump. My fingers flexed. For whatever reason, I had to touch it. To make sure it was real and not some fucked up dream I pulled out of my ass. My hand trembled, hovering an inch or so above *it*. The temperature in the room rose and my skin grew clammy. I swallowed.

As much as I wanted to pretend none of it was happening, I couldn't deny the truth. It literally stared me in the face. Under that subtle swell was a baby. An actual human being, growing as my hand hung in midair. My nerves unraveled faster than Colorado's first line defense whenever the puck crossed the blue line. I yanked my hand away and used it to swipe at the sweat beaded on my upper lip. Reality sank in and I started to freak out.

Careful not to disturb Kylie, I scooted off the bed and paced the room. Negative thoughts pelted my head like a sleet storm in Québec.

I scrubbed my hands down my face. I shouldn't be there.

I didn't know anything about babies or parenting. The kid would end up just like me, FUBAR. I read that shit's genetic or something. *Christ*. My mother died of alcoholism and a broken heart. After she was gone, every night Dad drank enough to tranquilize a fucking rhinoceros.

I tugged at the collar of my shirt. When did it get so fucking stifling in here? I gagged, suffocating on the thick heat, and sprinted for the door, focused on getting the hell out of there so I could breathe. Anything to release the pressure that clamped down on my lungs and stop my legs from giving out.

Hand wrapped around the doorknob, I glanced over my shoulder and gave Kylie one last, longing, look. A pang of despair hit as I took in her peaceful form. It felt like I was tearing apart, my soul ripping in half. Just *thinking* about Kylie made me bat shit crazy. Made the need to be near her or with her or anywhere in her general vicinity almost unbearable.

To willingly leave when I finally had her within reach? Virtually impossible.

The only thing to keep me from climbing back into bed and handcuffing her to me, was knowing she was way better off without me in her life. If I had anything to say about it, my kid wouldn't be subjected to a childhood like mine— barely existing, in a constant state of fear, inundated with pain that never completely disappeared, regularly cornered and beaten like an animal until he snapped and was forced to take a life, all before puberty.

Scarcely a man and capable of committing an act of unimaginable violence.

No one wanted their child raised by a murderer, and that's what I am. A murderer.

Kylie deserved better. Her kid deserved better. I closed

my eyes, ignored the motherfucking *twitch, twitch, twitch*, and snuck out, leaving my heart behind.

The hall was creepy quiet. I tipped my head to listen. Nothing. I glanced around, convinced Calloway lay in wait, ready to pounce and finish what he started. Bring it on. Whatever Sasquatch dished out, I most certainly deserved. I thought of it as penance for ruining Kylie's life. Hell, I welcomed the pain. Anything was better than the wrenching agony in my chest that left a hole in my cold, black heart.

I worked my jaw back and forth and winced. Calloway had landed a direct hit and it hurt like a bitch. I palpated the swollen area. A blinding streak of pain exploded behind my eye. *Jesus*. I couldn't deny the man knew how to fight. It hurt like a bitch. It was enough to stop me from turning around, going to Kylie, waking her up, and vowing never to let her out of my sight.

Every light was off except a low wattage bulb above the stove. Did Sasquatch go to bed? He went to sleep with me, in his home, unsupervised, and in bed with his sister? I shook my head and hissed at the way my face throbbed. Slipping out the front door was so easy, I was disappointed Calloway wasn't hiding, waiting for another shot. I wouldn't have even fought back. The guy might be a massive touchhole, but he deserved his pound of flesh. Fuck, if anyone shat all over Rémy the way I did Kylie, I'd probably end up in jail for murder. *Real* jail, not juvie.

Down in the parking garage, I fired up the Raptor and made my way to street level. The four hundred and fifty horsepower engine snarled. Feeling rather masochistic I pulled into traffic without looking. Horns blared and breaks squealed in my wake. I didn't look back. My driving bordered on aggressive on a good day. After the night I had, my vision blurred with what I refused to admit were tears. I shouldn't have been behind the wheel considering my mood verged on suicidal.

I had never felt so vulnerable. I didn't break. Not when my father's fists rained down on me, or when his ancient, steel-toed boots collided with my ribs, or when Rémy called in the middle of an episode and I was the only one who could talk him down.

I was the strong one. I was the one who took care of the people... or *person* in my life. I protected Rémy. Shielded him from the very worst, frequently lying to spare him the gruesome truth. How did I end up weak and defeated, wishing Rémy would call so I had someone to lean on, yet at the same time glad he didn't, the need to protect him so deeply ingrained I didn't want to dump my problems on him.

I drove in a fugue-state back to my place, unable to remember how I ended up parked in my assigned spot in the garage. I rode the elevator to my floor. Once the front door was locked behind me, I headed directly for the kitchen. I took in the wreckage of broken glass in and around the sink and caught the strong scent of whiskey in the air. A reminder I lost my temper. Snapped because I refused to believe I was in any way like my father, despite the mountain of evidence to the contrary.

I huffed out a somber laugh. What a fucking joke. I was more like him than I ever wanted to admit. A frequently drunk, exceptionally angry, and violent asshole who used and discarded anyone who dared to get too close, not giving a shit how much I hurt them as long as I got what I needed. And let's not forget, when fucking or fighting wasn't an option to calm the thrashing storm inside my head, I burned through whiskey like water.

Not like him, my ass. *I was him.* I was just too hung up on my own bullshit to realize it.

I tried to remain calm so I wouldn't fall back into Dad's habits and do a repeat of the night before. But fuck, I would kill for a drink. *Twitch, twitch, twitch...* I breathed in slowly through my nose and out through my mouth, counting up from one as I cleared my mind. I stood in my kitchen, breathing and counting until my fighting stance relaxed and my eye's Riverdance performance came to an end.

Determination, raw and pure—reminiscent of how I threw myself into hockey as a kid, used it as a way to get out of that shitty house I grew up in—surged. If I didn't want to become my Dad, a miserable, drunk, piece of shit, something had to change. *I* had to change. I crouched in front of the sink, opened the cabinet, fished out gloves and a sponge, and got to work.

Sebastien St. Clair, a.k.a. The Sinner, wasn't good enough for Kylie Calloway. It was time to clean up my act. Prove I was worthy of her love. Until then, I would stay away, but I wouldn't forget. I would wait until the moment was right.

Then? Game on. I take what was rightfully mine. My woman, my child, my family.

I checked the time and groaned. An unpleasant reminder morning skate began in a few hours. Ugh. The last thing I needed was a hot-headed Sasquatch up in my face. But if I had to make nice with that fuckstick Calloway took to deserve Kylie's love, I'd do it.

That didn't mean I had to like it.

14

Kylie

"I fucking knew it! I told you that bastard was a piece of shit."

I sat on the sofa, wrapped my arms around my knees, and curled up in a ball, while Rocco had his fifth nuclear meltdown of the morning, and the sun wasn't even up yet. I felt crappy enough without his help. I didn't need Rocco to pour salt on the raw, gaping wounds.

When I woke, refreshed and happy, Seb was gone. Despite Rocco harping on and on about how Sebastien was a womanizing asshole who was in no way good enough for me, as well a user, plus every other expletive you could think of and a few more tacked on that I'd never heard before, I was devastated, but unsurprised. Rocco thought I was a victim, innocent in what happened, but when I hooked up with Seb, I did in fact know exactly what I was getting into. The thrill of Seb's love 'em and leave 'em reputation was precisely why I pursued him, hence my sad acceptance that Seb took off in the middle of the night.

"I'm going to make that jackhole sorry he ever took his first breath," Rocco snarled as he swung around and thrust a finger in my face. "He'll regret fucking you over, Ky. I promise." Rocco dropped his hand and continued to stalk around the condo like a caged jungle cat. "The next time I see that shithead he's going to need an ambulance."

The tattered remains of my heart began to crack under the strain, but breaking down in front of Rocco, again, wouldn't help. It would only make Rocco even more furious, if that was possible. So I steadied my trembling lip and held in a sob.

"Let it go, Rocco. It's none of your business." I sounded like a broken record, lecturing the same thing over and over, but Rocco was the most stubborn person I'd ever met. He wouldn't be deterred. Rocco was going to clamp his frothing jaws around Seb's 'betrayal' and wouldn't let go until Seb suffered enough to quench Rocco's thirst for revenge. I was pretty sure there wasn't enough suffering in the world to make Rocco happy.

"What happens between the two of you might not be my business," Rocco growled. His eyes flashed with rage. "But you have to see it from my perspective. *My* teammate, a guy who's supposed to have my back unconditionally, seduced my little sister, stuck his dick where it didn't belong, knocked her up, and left her like she was a two-dollar whore."

My eyes filled with tears at the insult and I struggled to speak without losing my tenuous composure. "Thanks for making me feel worse than I already do by slut-shaming me." I shook with abject misery. But I wasn't done yet. I shot Rocco a glare and pointed at the opposite end of the sofa. "Sit down and shut the hell up."

The look on Rocco's face would have been comical had I

not been on the verge of kicking the crap out of him. He continued to gape, shocked. I tried to pull my brows into Rocco's 'v' and just about shouted, "Sit down, *now!*"

Rocco blinked and his shocked expression fell. I watched as his jaw clenched, cheek muscles ticking. Not an unfamiliar sight. At his sides, his fingers clenched and unclenched and I knew my brother was trying to decide if he was going to 'give in' to his baby sister's demand or stand his ground and fight. Eventually, he stomped over and dropped onto the sofa with a huff, loud enough to make sure I knew that even though he complied, he wasn't happy about it. I wanted to roll my eyes. As if I couldn't guess.

"You have quite a few uneducated assumptions stuffed inside that thick skull of yours that need adjusting."

I felt like death, the skin around my eyes swollen from crying and my nose all stuffy, but come hell or high water, I was fixing Rocco's messed up ideas.

"You need to realize, I'm this perfect person you've made me out to be. No, let me finish," I said when Rocco tried to interject. "I don't have a pedestal. I'm human, just like everyone else. I make mistakes. I have flaws. I do stupid things I wish I could take back." I exhaled a shuddering breath. "Seb wasn't lying when he said he didn't know me. But... I-I knew who Seb was... when we met. Knew his reputation. I knew he would probably break my heart. But Rocco, that's why I wanted him, *because* he was bad for me."

Rocco shook his head. "No. You didn't really know what he's like," he insisted. "You didn't know what a raging asshole he is."

I stared at the sofa cushion. "You're wrong. I knew exactly what he was like. I have this... need, Rocco. I like things that are..." I picked at an invisible thread. "Dangerous." I gathered my courage and met Rocco's confused gaze.

My cheeks burned as I explained my bizarre fetish. "I get off on the thrill of doing things I know I shouldn't do. If Seb hadn't approached me first, I was going to find a way to approach him."

They must have been having a fabulous time skiing in hell, because for the first time in my memory, Rocco was speechless. He stared at me as the awkwardness dragged on and on and on. When the silence became too much I cracked.

"Well? Aren't you going to yell? Aren't you mad at me for being stupid and careless?" Tears dripped down my face and I couldn't blame it on pregnancy hormones. I disgusted Rocco. From then on he would look at me and see a reckless, hot mess, not the sweet, perfect little sister he wanted. Ruining his image of me—his *faith* in me—tore me open like a paper bag and exposed all the ugly truths inside. "Rocco?" I croaked.

After an excruciatingly long time, Rocco scrubbed his hands up and down his face and sighed, then hung his head dejectedly. "No," Rocco said, his voice small and sad. "I'm not mad at... at you. I'm mad at me."

I jerked back. "What? Why would you feel that way? You have nothing to do with me being a total wreck."

Rocco lifted his head and looked at me. It looked like he'd aged a decade overnight. His eyes shone with unshed tears. "Don't you get it, Ky? I raised you. If you're a wreck, it's because I did something wrong."

I shook my head. "No. That's not true. It wasn't you." I unfolded my legs and scooted closer. "We lost our parents when we were more or less teenagers. Honestly, I'd be shocked if we *weren't* screwed up a little. That's not something you just get over." Hesitant, I reached out and, when he didn't protest, I put my hand on his knee. "I owe you everything, Rocco. *Everything.* I wouldn't lie to you. My strange, um, interests aren't the result of anything you did or didn't do. I pushed the boundaries long before mom and dad were gone."

Rocco put his huge hand over mine and threaded our fingers together. "I believe you." Some of the tension left the room and I managed a small smile. "But Ky, it doesn't change the fact that you're still pregnant, St. Clair still bailed on you, and I still want to kill him. So now what?"

My smile disappeared.

Now what, indeed.

Seb

"You look like shit, man," Evvy said as he slid to a stop next to me. The fucker dug in his blades and aimed a spray of ice so it arced right in my face.

I used my sleeve to wipe it off, cracked my neck, and exhaled, unwilling to fight back. My eye twitched all night long, and as a result, I was fucking exhausted. After cleaning the kitchen, I pretty much sat on the couch and zoned as my eye spazzed out to its heart's content. The last thing I wanted was for the damn thing to start up again right as finally I got it to stop.

I raised a questioning brow at Evvy and smirked. "Thanks, honey. You look lovely today, too, honey, all bright-eyed and bushy-tailed."

Ev snorted and jabbed me with his stick. "No, seriously, dude. You seem, I dunno, weird."

I rolled my eyes so hard I think I broke something. "We haven't even started practice and already you're nagging me." Gesturing toward the tunnel where the rest of our teammates slowly trickled onto the ice, I said, "If you're going to act like a clingy bitch, go find yourself a different hockey husband."

Evvy threw his head back and roared, and, sleep or no sleep, I found myself grinning, something I rarely did when I had to be at practice on less than two hours sleep. On top of the fatigue, both mental and physical, I made sure to arrive a good half an hour before everyone else. I was changed and on the ice before Calloway showed up and made a scene. And I had no doubt that's exactly what he would do. Without Kylie to intervene, I figured there was at least a ninety-three and a half percent chance blood would be shed by the time all was said and done.

"You don't do puck bunnies, remember?" Ev asked as he playfully shoved me.

"Are you saying you're a puck bunny, Evvy?" His response was to thump me in the chest with his knuckles. "Ow! You bastard."

"That's what you get for calling me a puck bunny," he grumbled.

"You started it."

The noise around us grew louder as the guys trickled onto the ice, their shouts and laughter echoing throughout the empty arena. I kept watch on the opening from the tunnel, expecting a rabid Calloway to shoot out onto the ice, face crimson and foaming at the mouth, out for revenge. Imagine how surprised I was when the man in question finally made his entrance, only to ignore me. He joined the Comets' defensive coach and the rest of the squad on the far end of the ice without so much as a glance in my direction.

I wasn't sure if it was good he didn't start shit, or not, but the uncertainty made me paranoid. I spent the whole night getting geared up for a knock-down, drag-out fistfight with the huge enforcer. Fuck, I was vibrating with anticipation, ready to draw blood. When Calloway snubbed me and skated off, the adrenaline that buzzed through my veins had nowhere to go and left me feeling twitchy and anxious.

Coach's loud whistle yanked me back to the present. I shook my head to clear out the cobwebs and joined the offensive squad. Practice was brutal. No sleep plus being too keyed up to eat breakfast equaled an unbelievably shitty performance. Coach rode my ass so hard I swore I'd find crop marks all over when I peeled off my pads. My timing was off, my dekes and passes disjointed and uneven. I couldn't get in the proper headspace, too wrapped up in worrying over what I would say to Kylie once I got my act together, and how she would respond.

"Okay!" Coach shouted. "Were gonna start with first and third line versus second and fourth line. Three on two scrimmage. Change out every sixty-seconds. So move your lazy asses!" He blew the whistle again. Not paying attention, I had skated too close. My ears rang for a good five minutes.

Roger Roussell, center on my line and team captain, got in place for the face-off. Second line center Alexi Ovechkin waited opposite Roger, grinning wickedly as he chewed on his mouth guard. Both Alexi and Roger are hypercompetitive to a fault. The match up would be interesting. I saw movement out of the corner of my eye and my attention strayed from the center line to further down the ice. Unfortunately, I found a pair of familiar dark, hooded eyes, shooting an equally familiar glare my way. Calloway sneered and returned his focus to the face-off. Regrettably, I couldn't say the same. The puck dropped and Rouzy snagged it. He spun and flipped it to me. I wasn't ready. The disc bounced off my thigh and rolled across the ice. One of the second line defensemen scooped it up and passed it to his forward.

"What in the name of god's hairy nut sack was that shit, St. Clair?" Coach V. roared.

I forced my head back in the game, eyes on the puck, and skated backward as I answered. "Sorry, Coach. Won't happen again." *Crisse*, I had to get a grip, and fast. After my spectacularly awful sprints and drills, it wouldn't take much for Coach to yank me off the first line.

I managed to keep it together for almost the entire scrimmage and even scored a goal off Hazey, not an easy feat considering the guy is one of the best tendies in the league. As a general rule, offensive and defensive lines don't switch out at the same time. Because they don't skate as hard and fast, defense stays on the ice a little longer before needing a break. After several shifts and line changes, Coach wanted to mix things up. Calloway ended up defending me and I figured Coach must be damn determined to see me carted off the ice in a straitjacket.

Not more than ten seconds after the whistle, the scrimmage turned into *un tas de marde*, as we say in Québec—pile of shit if you're American. Rouzy did a nice little deke and was able to pass the puck to me. Waiting in the crease, I caught it on my tape and whirled around, ready to score. Out of nowhere, Calloway blindsided me. His behemoth body slammed into my left side and I went down. I hit the ice so hard my helmet made a loud *crack* as it bounced off the ice... with my head still inside it.

The world went black for a second or two as I lay on my back and stared at the rafters. Lights popped in my field of vision and I half expected to see little fucking tweety birds circling my head. Sounds faded in and out, but I caught a few words said by my teammates.

"Jesus Christ, St. Clair. You okay?"

"He take hit. Get, how you say, bell rung hard, *da*?"

"What the fuck, Calloway?"

"Sebby, how many fingers am I holding up?"

The last question came from Evvy. Slowly regaining semi-consciousness, I swatted his hand out of my face and snarled, *"Vas te faire chier!"* Ev looked confused. I parroted his expression back at him.

"You're speaking in French, St. Clair," Coach said from behind me.

I staggered to my feet and frowned. The world spun in lazy loop-de-loops. "I told Evvy to piss off... I think." I scrunched my forehead and glanced around as I wobbled on my skates.

After a minute, my bearings returned. Able to focus more than a few feet in front of me, I scanned the faces on the ice. When I found the one I wanted, I launched at him, gracelessly knocking down several players in the process. Calloway had his fists raised, ready for me. But Calloway didn't expect me to keep going. His eyes went wide when he realized I wasn't going to stop. I barreled into him, so I could knock him on his ass like he did to me. Or, that was my intention. It didn't quite work out as I planned. Oh, Sasquatch fell all right, but the big bastard grabbed hold of my sweater and held tight, taking me down with him. Together, we crashed to the ice and without missing a beat started swinging. We rolled to our feet, trading jabs and cross hooks until the others got involved. It took three guys to hold me still, four for Sasquatch, the one-upper.

"You two shit stains, in my office. Now!"

Despite Coach's shout, Calloway and I continued to exchange murderous glares. Coach V. shoved me toward the tunnel and the defensive coach did the same to Calloway, who actually freaking growled when touched. *Come on!* How did no one see it? The guy had to be at least half, maybe three-quarters Sasquatch. Nothing else made sense.

Coach had enough sense to send a couple guys to accompany us so we didn't kill each other along the way. I was sure Frank Vernon wanted that particular pleasure all to himself.

I didn't trust Calloway to turn my back on him, so I faced the middle of the changing room as I undressed. I chucked my sweaty shit on the floor and yanked on a shirt and jogging pants. Onlookers waited, arms crossed, ready to intervene.

Calloway did the same. He discarded his pads, tore the tape off his ankles, and still managed to throw enough shade to block the sun for a week. I was almost done shoving my feet into a pair of sneakers, when Coach stormed past us, a thick cloud of fury following close behind. I knew from experience he wouldn't wait long. If you kept Coach V. waiting, it was at the very real risk of life and limb. Not me. Foregoing the rest of my clothes in favor of speed, I went into Coach's office and took a seat. Thirty seconds later, spine stiff as a board and a jaw you could use to cut glass, Sasquatch entered and lowered his behemoth body into the chair next to mine.

Coach slammed the door shut with a loud bang. It latched shut I wished he let us grab a shower first. Two men, fresh off the ice, who reeked of sweat and funky hockey equipment, crammed into a tiny room, made it damn near impossible to breathe without burning my nose hairs off.

"What in fresh hell is wrong with the two of you?" *Uh oh.* It was bad. It had been a while since I'd seen Coach so upset, and I didn't miss it one bit. His face flushed so red it looked puce. Or was it cerise? I always got those colors mixed up. "You with us, St. Clair? Or you wanna continue to

fucking daydream?" Coach shouted in my face. I flinched
and shook my head.

"No. I'm with you. Um, sir." The urge to gut punch
Calloway when he made a rude noise was strong. But I
wasn't stupid enough to start something with a furious
Frank Vernon standing within arm's reach. "Good." He
crossed his arms and stared, eyes flicking back and forth
between us.

The room tilted a little and I blinked until it stopped. I
lifted a hand to the side of my head and felt for a lump. *Ow.*
I must have hit the ice really hard considering I had been
wearing my helmet at the time.

Coach continued to grimace, jowls hanging, not uttering
a word. Bastard was trying to intimidate us. I hated that it
worked. Even more, I hated that it only worked on me, not
Calloway, who sat next to me, unflinching, cool as a fucking
cucumber. Coach opened his mouth to read us our last rites.
The shrill ring of the phone on his desk cut him short. The
three of us stared at it. I was pretty sure I'd never heard that
phone make a single sound. With the advent of cellphones,
landlines had gone the way of the dinosaurs.

"Son of a bitch," Coach muttered. He glared at the
clunky black desktop phone as he fished around in one of
his jacket pockets. Coach yanked his cell free and promptly
frowned. "Accidentally turned the damn thing to silent," he
mumbled, then twisted his upper body to snatch the trilling
receiver off its cradle and barked, "What?"

Whatever the person on the other end said made the
color drain from Coach's face. His knuckles blanched as he
gripped the phone. When Coach's worried gaze flicked to
Calloway, my stomach sank.

"I see... Yeah," Coach continued. "Uh huh... Got
it... Right."

Goosebumps pricked the back of my neck and icy tendrils of dread trickled down into my chest to slither around my heart. The look in Frank Vernon's eyes wasn't one was used to seeing from the gruff man. Sympathy.

Sasquatch, not being nearly as stupid as he looked, shot to his feet as Coach hung up the phone. My pulse thundered and I licked my lips. My gaze bounced back and forth between Coach and Calloway and loud alarms went off in my head.

I don't know how I knew, but whatever was going down wasn't good.

"What? What is it?" Calloway asked, his voice tinged with fear.

I didn't blame him for being freaked out, hell, I was freaked out. Didn't stop my mouth from falling open. I couldn't help but gawk at the man. Calloway had one setting and one setting only—irritated bastard. I never thought I'd see him on the verge of freaking out. To be honest, I didn't think anything in this world could put that stricken look on Calloway's face and seeing it ratcheted my anxiety up another notch.

Coach looked tired. He rubbed a hand over his bristly chin and let out a slow breath. Realization hit me like a Shea Weber slap shot to the liver.

Ohgod. The room tilted and went out of focus, and it had nothing to do with the earlier blow to my cranium. A sense of impending doom settled on my shoulders like a blanket made of chainmail and I swallowed back a rush of nausea.

I knew damn well there was one thing in this world that could send Rocco Calloway into this kind of a panic.

His sister.

"Fuck, Coach," Calloway said. He rose, towering over me as I sat frozen in my chair. I could feel the waves of tension radiating off of him. Not that I was doing much better. Between Calloway, Coach, and me the air grew thick with nervous anticipation, unease, and a healthy dose of fear. "Tell me... tell me what's going on." Coach V. hesitated, causing Calloway to grimace. "Coach?"

Shit, Calloway was scared shitless.

Cue the loosening of my bowels.

"That was the main switchboard," Coach finally said. "When no one could reach you or me on our cell phones, they went through the front office."

Anticipation killing me, I had begun to come completely unhinged, trembling from head to toe. I gripped the armrests, and my fingers dug painfully into the metal. I couldn't take it anymore and snapped.

"Come on, Coach!" I shouted in desperation. Frantic, I slid effortlessly into Québecois. My hands flew all over the place as I unleashed a tirade. "*Arrêter de caler. Je ne peux pas le prendre! Dis-le jus.*" Their puzzled stares had me out of my chair and ready to tear Coach a new one. "I said, stop dicking around and just fucking tell us what's going on!"

Calloway let out a low growl, which I promptly ignored. Too fucking bad if he didn't like me butting in. I had no fucks left to give, especially in regard to what he thought.

A wave of dread washed over me and the frigid fingers around my heart tightened. After all the shit I'd been through, dozens of broken bones, protecting my brother, pushed and beaten like a dog until I fucking snapped and bludgeoned my own father to death with my favorite stick... all that and never in my life had I been so close to losing my grip on sanity as I was in that godforsaken office. I was point two seconds from wrapping my hands around Coach's throat and squeezing the shit out of him when he finally spoke.

"It's your sister, Calloway. I don't know what happened, but she's been taken by ambulance to Piedmont Hospital."

My mouth went dry and the room slanted again. I swayed on my feet and put a hand on the corner of Coach's desk to stay upright. Thankfully, Calloway was better at keeping his shit together.

"I gotta go," he said right before he bolted from the room.

Coach turned to say something to me, but fuck it, I was out the door before he got the chance. I snatched my keys and wallet from my cubby and vaguely registered Coach shouting from his office. "Where the fuck are you going, St. Clair?"

I didn't respond. Calloway had already banged through the locker room door and disappeared. Determined not to be left holding my dick, I followed, hot on his heels. So many gruesome images assaulted me as I wondered what happened to Kylie, that I had to switch my brain to autopilot or I'd have a breakdown.

Calloway stopped next to his SUV and I was so out of it, I crashed into him, bounced off the wall of muscle, and landed ass first on the dirty pavement. To my complete and utter shock, Rocco Calloway reached down and offered his hand. I blinked, questioning if maybe the hit to my head did more damage than I thought.

"Come on," Calloway said, voice laced with impatience. He waved his hand for me to take. "You can't drive. You probably have a concussion and will end up blacking out behind the wheel." I put my hand in Calloway's and allowed my evil arch-nemesis to haul me to my feet. Calloway unlocked the door, climbed into his Range Rover, and explained, "You're a stubborn motherfucker, St. Clair. I know full well you're going to the hospital whether I want you there or not, and if you plow your car into a van full of kids because I gave you a concussion, I'll feel like shit. So get the fuck in." With that, he slammed the door and cranked the engine.

Alrighty then.

I scrambled around to the other side and closed the door. Calloway put the Rover in reverse and, tires squealing, tore out of his spot.

"Seatbelt," Calloway barked. A sharp retort sat the tip of my tongue, but I glanced over, saw the state the guy was in, and bit it back. Calloway was losing his shit too. He was just better at hiding it. I wasn't sure how close he was to Kylie, but from what little I gleaned, they were probably as tight as Rémy and me. If Calloway was even half as scared as I was, he needed to concentrate on driving, not listen to me shoot off at the mouth.

In under ten minutes, Calloway steered the Rover down Collier Drive. He banked the wheel and took the corner onto the drive that led to the emergency room *hard*. The back of the SUV fishtailed and Calloway stomped on the brakes. The wheels locked and we came to an abrupt stop in front of the entrance. I jerked forward. His insistence that I wear the seatbelt was the only thing that kept me from smashing clean through the windshield.

"*Câlice!*" I yelled as my hands reflexively shot out to brace against the dashboard. Heart pounding, I patted myself down to make sure I was in once piece. Satisfied, I turned to glare at Calloway only to find an empty seat, keys still in the ignition, door open. I tore off the seatbelt, threw open the passenger door, and searched for Calloway. "Son of a bitch," I muttered when I caught a glimpse of his red T-shirt as the automatic doors closed behind him.

I found Calloway at reception, a dark look on his face.

He towered over a wide-eyed woman who sat behind the desk.

"Where the fuck is my sister?"

Oh shit. I never thought of myself as reasonable, but if I didn't get Calloway under some sort of control, they would dispatch security, and if Calloway got arrested, I wouldn't get inn to see Kylie. Family only and all that bullshit. The hospital wouldn't tell me a goddamn thing.

"I'm sorry," I said to the woman whose name tag read Lisa M. I sidled up to Calloway and subtly nudged him out of the way. "We're looking for someone brought in a little while ago. Can you help us?"

"What the fuck are you doing, St. Clair?" Calloway growled under his breath.

I shifted to block Lisa M's line of sight and fisted the front of his shirt, then yanked him down so I didn't have to shout. "I'm keeping your ass out of jail," I hissed. "You're no good to your sister if you're locked up."

His rage-filled gaze burned into me. I peeked over my shoulder. *Shit.* I gave Lisa M. a fake smile. She looked scared, and why wouldn't she? It wasn't everyday you had two enormous, wild-eyed, panicky hockey players all up in your face. Add Calloway's menacing glower and we were lucky Lisa M. hadn't already screamed for help. Maybe she hit a silent alarm and the cops were on their way.

Lisa M. took a deep breath, and nodded. "W-what's the n-name?"

"Kylie Calloway," Sasquatch barked. I elbowed him in the ribs. That earned me a snarl, which I promptly ignored. Hands trembling, Lisa M. typed on her computer.

"Um, y-yes. R-room two oh f-four. M-maternity ward." She pointed toward a nearby set of elevators. "S-second f-floor."

Calloway sprinted for the elevators and smashed his palm on the button six or seven times. I empathized. I wanted to smash things too, but one of us had to stay level-headed. He did his part driving. It was his turn to fall apart. Instead of smacking his hand away and dropping him with a haymaker, I shoved my hands in my pockets in studiously ignored my eye.

Twitch, twitch, twitch...

The doors no sooner opened and Sasquatch moved. He practically barreled over an elderly couple and a middle-aged nurse who tried to step off and offered no apologies as he forced his way inside. Calloway turned and glared at me impatiently. Once the people were out of the way, I joined him. Calloway pushed the two over and over, as if abusing the button would get us there faster. If I weren't so damn terrified I would've laughed. Six and half feet of solid muscle versus a tiny plastic button, and the button was winning.

The chime dinged and the doors slid open, allowing the overwhelming sense of doom to return. Calloway tore past the nurse's station, instead choosing to follow the small, wall-mounted signs labeled with room numbers and tiny arrows. I trailed behind mindlessly. Calloway stopped without warning, and once again, I flailed and slammed into him. Calloway didn't react or seem to notice. He was too busy staring inside the open door of room two oh four. I stepped around him, but vacillated, torn between needing to see what was in the room and dreading what I might find.

Calloway stepped over the threshold. I held my breath and did the same.

It was a typical hospital room. The walls were painted a hideous toothpaste green and the few pieces of furniture were upholstered in shiny pleather a coordinating darker shade. It may as well have been painted to look like a three-ring circus for as much as I cared. All I saw was the tiny figure on the oversized hospital bed in the center of the room. Tubes and wires snaked from a plethora of machines and IV bags, attached to various parts of her body. I swore, my heart skipped a few beats. Seeing Kylie like that, eyes closed— either sleeping or unconscious—made it difficult to breathe.

Calloway stood at the bedside and held her hand, despite the tubes taped over the pale skin. Suddenly, I felt extraneous, like an unwelcome intruder. I lingered in the doorway and watched Calloway lean over to whisper muffled words in Kylie's ear. She responded and my knees almost gave out as relief rushed through me. Kylie sounded wrecked, but it didn't matter. She was awake and able to speak.

Calloway took a step back and turned toward me, lips pressed tight. He was irritated, but I could live with that. I was just grateful he wasn't tearing all my limbs off and beating the ever-loving shit out of me with them. I returned my attention to Kylie. She looked paler than the last time I saw her. Had that really been last night? It felt like a lifetime since I held her in my arms.

"St. Clair." I tore my gaze from Kylie's red-rimmed eyes to look at Calloway. His expression was pinched, but he pressed on. "C'mon." Calloway waved me forward.

One slow step at a time, I picked up my feet, one after the other. Everything in the room blurred as I approached Kylie. Tears dripped down my face and I could the rhythmic whooshing of my pulse joined the beeping symphony of machines. By the time I reached for Kylie's hand, my lips tasted of salt.

I swiped at my face with my free hand and sniffed. "Sorry."

A choked cough came from the periphery. I glanced at Calloway, whose eyes were damp as well. He caught me looking and shrugged, not giving a single shit I caught him tearing up. Fine. I admit it. I was shocked to discover the Tin Man had a heart. Then I touched my fingertips to my face. Calloway probably thought I was a heartless bastard, too, incapable of feeling any emotions that wasn't fury, indigence, or cutting sarcasm.

Guess we were both wrong.

"Seb."

My gaze snapped back to Kylie, and *fuck*, but she looked so damn fragile. I wanted to yank out all the tubes and wires, scoop her up, and take her out of there, but I didn't. Instead, I held my breath and waited for the worst, to find out if Kylie's... if *our* baby was gone.

"I'm here," I rasped, and gave her fingers a gentle squeeze.

Calloway walked around the bed to stand on the opposite side. "Ky, what happened?" Thank fuck he had the balls to ask, because there was no way I could. Not in my current state of mind.

I met Calloway's gaze and, we came to a silent understanding. All of our bullshit, the fighting, the animosity, the hatred, none of it meant jack shit anymore. I nodded in agreement. Calloway's nostrils flared, and we both returned our attention to Kylie.

Kylie's chin trembled and tears overflowed. She tugged her hands back to cover her face. She began to sob, and with each one her slender shoulders shook. Calloway and I exchanged glances. It was almost comical, if not for the whole "Kylie pregnant with my kid and in the hospital" thing. It was obvious neither of us knew what to do. We both looked to the other to do something and make it all better. Basically, we were typical men, completely useless when faced with a weeping woman.

"I—" Calloway began.

"Oh good, you're here." I spun around. A petite woman in a lab coat breezed into the room, her head down, focused on the tablet in her hand. "Which one of you is the father?" The woman lifted her head, and her dark eyes flicked back and forth between Calloway and me.

I licked my lips. "I..." My voice cracked. I cleared my throat and tried again. "Me. It's, uh, me."

She nodded and nudged me out of the way to get to Kylie, placing the tablet on the bed. "How are you feeling, dear?"

The doctor's lab coat said Dr. L. Patel, embroidered on the right breast in navy blue thread. Efficient as one would expect, she checked the machines, somehow making sense of the information when all I saw were squiggly lines and a bunch of numbers. Kylie sniffed and accepted the tissue offered by her brother.

"Fine. I'm tired, but fine."

"No pain?" Dr. Patel asked.

"No."

The doctor nodded and gently palpated Kylie's abdomen. My eye spasmed hard and my anxiety shot through the roof. The desperate need to know what the fuck was happening overrode any common courtesy.

"Excuse me? Can you tell us what the hell is going on?" I blurted. "Why is she here? Is the..." I faltered, took a deep breath, and pushed on. "Is the baby okay?" Out of the corner of my eye, I saw Calloway lean toward the doctor. He wanted answers as well.

Dr. Patel picked up the tablet to make notes or what the fuck it was that doctors did. "The baby is fine. Ms. Calloway experienced cramps and bleeding and called 911. An ultrasound diagnosed marginal placental previa." I stared at her. She smiled and explained. "It means the placenta is a little too close to the cervix."

"What does that mean?" Calloway asked, his gaze darting back and forth between the doctor and his sister.

"It means we will have to monitor Ms. Calloway carefully for the duration of her pregnancy. The condition usually resolves as the uterus grows, but sometimes it persists, in which case she will have to schedule a cesarean section for the birth."

I reached for Kylie and took her hand again, needing to touch her. Fear like I'd never known, greater than when I used to grab Rémy and hide in a closet, tuck my brother behind me, and listen as our father drunkenly tore the house apart searching for us.

Kylie glanced up at me through damp lashes. Her expression was pleading, begging me to make everything better. Knowing Kylie suffered and there wasn't a thing I could do, sucked. But the fact that I was the one to cause that suffering, damn near killed me.

"Thank you doctor," Calloway said. He came around the bed and shook the doctor's hand. I think I did, too, my memory started to get fuzzy around the time I entered the room. The next thing I knew, Dr. Patel was gone and Calloway was talking to me.

"I need a moment alone with my sister." I stood there, numb, but... not. Every inch of my body hurt, though the pain didn't quite register. "St. Clair!"

I flinched. "Huh? What?"

"Can you...? I'm asking if you'll give me a few minutes

alone with Ky." He was asking? Not simply shoving me out the door and locking it behind me? I checked with Kylie, who nodded.

"All right. I'll just, um, be outside." I glanced at Kylie again.

"Can you get me something to drink?" she asked. "Maybe a sweet tea?"

"Okay."

She rolled her eyes. "You know what? Make it unsweet."

"Sure, no problem," I hurriedly agreed. I'd bring her anything she asked for. Tea, change of clothes, Ferrari... whatever. "Uh, Calloway?" Calloway tore his attention from his sister to glower at me. "Um, did you want something? Coffee?"

Stunned, Calloway's irritation melted and he nodded. "Yeah. Sounds good. Coffee. Black, thanks."

I left the room and found the elevators. Alone inside the small metal box, I slumped against the wall and fisted my hair. If anything were to happen to Kylie... to my... to *our* kid. I wasn't certain I could ever claw my way out of the destruction.

I had been led to believe I was strong. That because of everything I'd been through in my tumultuous twenty-six years on this mostly miserable planet, I was tough, impervious to something as insignificant as heartache.

I was wrong. No one was immune to life's cruel twists and turns. Even Superman has a weakness.

Kylie Calloway is my own brand of kryptonite. The worst part was the overwhelming helplessness. The inability to erase all the negative shit. The only thing I could do was hope and pray that not only would Kylie and the baby be okay, but that I would come out the other side, not as the beaten and destroyed man I'd become, but someone better. Someone worthy of Kylie and the baby, worthy of their love and deserving of a place in their lives and hearts.

Kryptonite or not, I can't live without her. I'd be there for her, do my best to get through the pregnancy a painlessly as possible, even if it led to my complete and utter annihilation.

For a chance at having Kylie and a family, it was a price well worth paying.

Kylie

ROCCO PICKED UP A CHAIR, placed it next to the bed, and sat. It creaked when he lowered his weight into it, but surprisingly, the thing held up. I chewed on my lip as I sorted through the myriad of emotions I still had to process through. Seeing the blood and feeling faint, calling 911... everything happened too fast for me to do anything but react. Now that I had time to think, I was a bit overwhelmed. I turned off my brain and listened as the monitors beeped and whirred. The sounds were kind of soothing. The steady rhythm meant the baby was alive and well.

"How are you feeling?" Rocco asked.

I stared at my lap. After everything we'd been through, I was nervous. Rocco knew my secret. Knew about Seb. Rocco sounded calm, but I knew him well enough to detect an underlying current of tension. What I didn't know was whether that tension was caused by my health scare, by finding out about Seb, or a combination of both. But Rocco was there when I needed him, and for now, that was good enough.

"Okay," I said. "Tired, but not bad."

Rocco reached out and touched the shadowed skin under my eyes. "You look exhausted, Ky."

I shrugged. "Nothing new since..." I didn't finish. The *"since I got pregnant"* unnecessary.

Rocco exhaled and scrubbed his hands over his face and up through his hair, which stood every which way. "I'm glad the baby is okay."

My response was to giggle. Rocco looked at me as if I lost my mind. He grunted.

"What's funny?"

"You," I said. Maybe it was the drugs messing with my head, or my lack of sleep had made me delirious. Either way, inappropriate or not, I couldn't stop. "You look like don't know how to feel," I continued. "Happy the baby is healthy and I'm okay, or disgusted because of who I slept with."

"Ugh!" Rocco winced and covered his ears. "God, Ky! Don't. Just don't. I can't unhear that kind of shit." His reaction only fueled the laughter. Rocco scowled and waited patiently until I got control of myself. When I finally stopped, reality sobered me up quick.

"I'm sorry," I whispered. Rocco didn't ask why. He knew exactly what I was sorry for.

"Why'd you do it, Ky? I mean, not why you did what you did, you know, the, uh..." He pointed at my belly and turned green. "I don't want to hear the gory details. Just, I don't get it. Of all the guys out there, why him?"

I twisted the sheet into a tight ball, then let go, watched it unwind, and did it again. "Because he's dangerous," I mumbled. Rocco didn't interrupt, so I kept going. "Because I'm messed in the head, Rocco. I uh, like that Seb is for all intents and purposes, off limits. That...the fact that you didn't like it...it made it more exciting, or something. I just didn't think... Then, I realized I kind of like him, and..." I got choked up and Rocco ran his hand in circles on my back.

"It's okay, Ky. I'm not mad."

I shot up straight and met my brother's gaze. "You're not?"

He shook his head. "No. I'm so fucking glad you're okay, I don't give a shit about St. Clair." My mouth fell open and I stared at Rocco in disbelief. His lips twisted and after a minute, he said, "Fine," and jammed both hands in his hair. "Fine. Yeah, I care, but not enough to make it a thing. Not while you're sitting in the hospital after almost losing the baby."

"He's not as bad as you think." I said it so quietly I wasn't sure Rocco heard over the monitors.

His snort let me know that he did. "Yeah, he's that bad, Ky." He sighed. "It's not about me anymore." Rocco put his hand over mine, putting an end to my sheet-twisting. "Ugh, I can't believe I'm going to ask this?" He pulled a face. "Does St. Clair make you happy?"

Did he? Sometimes.

"I think he could," I said, going for honesty instead of deluding not only Rocco, but also myself. "We have a lot to talk about before I can think about that."

A quick rap on the door and Seb entered the room.

"Here." Seb handed Rocco a steaming Styrofoam cup and placed the other on the table next to the bed. Then he manhandled the wheeled tray and cursed under his breath when it wouldn't cooperate with his efforts to reposition it over my lap. After he muttered what I assumed were a few French-Canadian obscenities, the wheels rolled under the bed. Seb put the big cup of iced tea on the tray, then shoved his hands in his pockets.

"I'm going to take a walk." Rocco bent over and kissed

my forehead. He turned to Seb. "I'll call Coach and explain the situation." Seb's looked at Rocco, eyes wide. "Don't worry, St. Clair. I'll spare him the details. See you guys in a little while."

And then it was just us.

Seb slid into the newly vacated chair and took a sip from his cup, which smelled like coffee. He was a mess—slumped down in the seat, face haggard, right leg bouncing up and down. How someone could be totally exhausted and tense at the same time was beyond me, but that's exactly what Seb was.

We needed to talk, but I didn't know where to start. Seb left, disappeared in the middle of the night. I thought we were done. But he came to the hospital, and as much as I didn't want to give myself false hope, Seb didn't act like a man who didn't care.

"How did you know I was here? And why were you with Rocco?"

Seb put his coffee on the bedside table and shifted to the edge of the seat. With Seb so close, I could finally see what I failed to notice earlier. He was afraid. It was written all over his face, from the tiny wrinkles that creased his brow to the twitching muscles around his left eye. He reached for my hand and I felt a slight tremble in his fingers before they wrapped around mine. He nervously licked his lips. When our gazes finally met, tears shone in Seb's eyes and my throat burned as my own welled up in response.

"We were in Coach V's office when the hospital called." Seb rubbed the back of his neck, looked up at the ceiling, and inhaled. "Coach didn't even have to say anything. I just... knew. I don't know how, but I knew something was wrong, and the way he looked at Calloway, er, uh, Rocco, I knew it was about you."

"And Rocco let you tag along?"

"He didn't say I couldn't. I think we were both so intent on getting here, everything else was secondary." Seb shifted from the chair and sat on the edge of the bed and scooped up my hands in both of his and held them to his chest. "It wasn't about us, Ky. Nothing was as important as you."

I exhaled a shaky breath and felt a single tear slide down my cheek. "I thought..." I swallowed thickly. "I thought you didn't want me." I glanced at my belly and amended my statement. "Us." Seb jerked back like he'd been slapped. "You left."

"I did." He squeezed my hands. "I'm sorry. I should have said something. I needed time to work through everything, but I swear to you, Ky. I was coming back. I just needed to wrap my head around stuff, and get a plan in place."

"A plan? Since when do you plan anything? I thought you were Mr. Spontaneous."

Seb smirked. "You mean like sending gifts to beautiful women at hockey games?"

"Yeah," I said, fighting back a smile.

The smirk fell off Seb's face. "There's a lot you don't know about me," he said, sounding wrecked. "I'm not a good person. You deserve so much better."

I tugged my hands back and lifted them to his unshaven cheeks. Seb wouldn't look at me, so I did the only thing I could think of, and kissed him. When he didn't respond, I did it again. And again. Seb breathed through his nose and shuddered. Finally, he got with the program. Seb palmed the back of my head and slid his other hand around my waist, deepening the kiss with a moan, which I swallowed greedily. I happily let him take charge, and when Seb slid his tongue across my lips in silent demand, I complied. He tasted like coffee and longing and *home*. We made-out until my lips were swollen and my chin burned from his stubble. Seb pulled back and shifted from the bed to the chair and tunneled his fingers in his hair.

"Seb?"

He peeked over his shoulder at the door. Satisfied no one would interrupt, he turned back to me, his posture different, straighter, rigid. His body thrummed with nervous tension and he licked his lips.

"There's no good way to say this, so I'm just gonna lay it out there." The hairs at the back of my neck stood on end and a chill pricked down my arms. "When I was fourteen, I-I killed my father."

I held perfectly still and tried my best not to react. I didn't want Seb to think *he* frightened me. Was I confused? Yes. Shocked? Definitely. Frightened? Never. It was that moment I realized I trusted him—with my child, my life, my very soul.

"What happened?" I asked, urging Seb to continue. I didn't want him to relive what was clearly a painful moment in his life, but I had to know, and not out of some sick curiosity. I wanted to know everything about Seb. All of it, the good, the bad, and yes, even the truly awful.

Seb's eyes glistened and his neck flushed pink. The rosy color contrasted against his pale skin and, under the fluorescent lighting, his face appeared a sickly shade of green. Or maybe it wasn't the light, because when Seb described his childhood, I felt sick too.

"Mom died young. Cirrhosis. Dad drank too, but the tough bastard didn't do us a favor by croaking along with her. When Mom drank, she cried a lot." Seb blinked, a far away in his eyes. "When Dad drank, he got violent, and Rémy... shit, he was just a little kid. I..." Seb brushed away a tear that slipped out. "I couldn't let him hurt Rémy. I-I would hide Rémy, stash him somewhere in the house, then provoke the old bastard into coming after me."

A wave of overwhelming love and sorrow came over me. I knew Seb might not appreciate the gesture, or interpret it as me thinking he was weak, but I couldn't just watch as he ripped the bandages off of decade old wounds. I had to try and comfort him, even though it was too little, too late.

I scooted to the edge of the bed and grabbed Seb's hand, threading our fingers. "Go on," I said as I swallowed back a sob.

My heart broke for this man, for the boy he once was. Seb's brash arrogance suddenly made sense. He used the abrasive persona to hide his broken childhood, his lost innocence. Created a shield to keep people from getting too close, that way they wouldn't get a glimpse of the shattered man behind the curtain. I ignored the tears that dripped down my face. They didn't matter. None of it mattered—not Rocco, not my fears, not Seb leaving. Not when it was so obvious that Seb was scared to death he would turn into his father. I squeezed his hand and he took a deep breath.

"I remember one day, hockey practice went unusually long. Rem wasn't with me because I aged up to the next league. By the time I got home, Papa was shitfaced and had Rémy cornered. He was terrified. Blood dripped from Rémy's nose and... fuck, he was only seven years old." Seb pulled his hand free to cover his eyes. "I had my stick in my hands and saw red."

Seb's hand trembled and his shoulders shook. I touched his arm in support, but remained silent. It was Seb's story, and he needed to tell me at his own pace. Most likely, it was the first time he'd ever told anyone.

"I think I blacked out, or something, because the next thing I knew," Seb said, his voice thick with emotion, "I was covered in blood. The police were there, putting me in the back of their car, and Rémy was... I heard him screaming my name. He was in some woman's arms. She was trying to calm him down, but he was crying, fighting her to get to me. I-I tried, but... They handcuffed me. I couldn't do anything. And after that... I wasn't there for him."

Seb buried his face in his hands and sobbed. Screw the bed. I climbed down, wires and all, and curled in his lap. Seb wrapped his arms around me and I did the same. Then I pressed my cheek to his chest. My heart ached for Seb as he let it all out, years of holding in his sorrow, his pain. Nothing I said or did would erase the memories or what they did to him. My hands were as bound as his that day in Québec, even if I wasn't handcuffed. It didn't mean I couldn't share the burden.

"But you were there for him, Seb. You stopped a horrible man from hurting a child. You know he would have eventually killed one or both of you."

Seb sniffed and stood with me in his arms. He deposited me on the bed as if I weighed no more than a feather, and went into the attached bathroom. The water ran, and a moment later, Seb returned, his face red and damp. He stood awkwardly next to the bed.

"Sorry for unloading all that on you."

"Don't apologize to me," I snapped, furious that Seb's father not only abused him, but made him feel bad for sharing his pain with me. "I know you don't believe me, Seb, but what you did doesn't change the way I see you, or how I feel about you."

Seb features pinched. "How can it not?"

"Because, I promise you, Rocco would have done the exact same thing for me, and if I had to, I would have too." Seb was speechless, mouth working open and closed. Eventually, he shook his head and dropped back into the creaky chair.

"I don't understand," he admitted. "I'm an asshole, I've been nothing *but* an asshole since we met. I treated you like shit, and now you know I killed my *own father* with my hockey stick. How..." His voice cracked. "How are you not telling me to leave?"

The distance was too much. I climbed back in his lap and held his face in my hands. "You've got it all wrong, Seb. I'm the one who treated you badly. I agreed to meet you in that hotel, specifically because I knew it would piss Rocco off. Well, that and because you're smoking hot." I grinned and he huffed out a laugh. "You forgot that I'm the one who left you, because I knew I was falling for you. The idea of Rocco finding out no longer thrilled me, it scared me to death. I hid you, when I should have been proud to tell him I cared about you." I stared at Seb as I continued. "I do care about you, Seb."

Seb studied my face, checking for my sincerity. Whatever he was looking for, he must have found, because the corners of his mouth pulled up. "We're pretty fucked up, huh?"

I laughed. "Yeah. We are."

While he continued to look in my eyes, Seb placed a hand on my belly. "I can live with that."

My heart soared and I couldn't stop smiling. I was going to spend the rest of my life with the most complicated man I'd ever met, have his child. Seb made me happy. I knew he would protect our family, with his life if he had to. Seb might think he's a terrible person who did terrible things. That he's a *sinner*. But I know better. Sebastien St. Clair is a good man, a survivor. And he's mine.

With his palm still pressed against my abdomen, Seb

leaned close and gave me a feather-light kiss. I put my hand on top of his and felt a tiny nudge from the inside. Seb's eyes grew wide and he stared down.

"Did you... did you feel that?" he asked, awe-struck.

Right on cue, there was another tiny bump, directly beneath our stacked hands. I didn't want to cry anymore, but tears of joy burst free and I laughed. "I think it's the baby. It moved."

Seb stared at me like I hung the sun in the sky. No, more than that. He stared at me as if I invented hockey.

"*Il a bougé, le bébé.* It moved," he whispered. Seb's handsome face broke out in a huge grin and he kissed me again. "*Je t'aime.*"

I don't speak French, but recognized what Seb said. I swallowed past the lump in my throat and said, "I love you, too."

15

Seb

I sat on the edge of the bench, coiled tighter than a slinky. Sweat dripped down the back of my neck and I chomped anxiously on my mouthguard. I glanced at the scoreboard that hung above center ice. Less than two minutes left in the third period and the score was tied 1-1. Every single one of my teammates looked as antsy as I felt. If we won against Edmonton, we'd be in the Stanley Cup play-offs. I wanted it so bad I could taste the metallic tang of the Cup, picture it raised in the air as I kissed the hell out of it.

Coach called for a line change and I stood. When the right wing swung his leg over the board, I leapt onto the ice, heart racing. I hadn't been this nervous since I played in my first NHL game.

The puck was at the far end of the ice. Hajek had his hawk-like gaze locked on the small black disc, and Calloway fought against the Oiler's center to move it out of the crease. Over the last eighteen months or so I'd come to better appreciate Calloway's aggressive style, especially since I was no longer on the receiving end. The announcer declared one-minute left in the game. Calloway wasted no time and doled out a bone-crunching shoulder check that sent the Oiler ass-over-skates. The guy landed in a heap of pads, face first. One lightning quick turn by Calloway, followed by a perfectly executed flip, and the puck hit my tape dead center. I spun and charged down the ice, acutely aware of the players in my vicinity, tracking them in my peripheral vision. A streak of orange alerted me to the imminent arrival of a veteran Oiler—who happened to be a future hall of fame defenseman. He raced toward me, approaching fast.

"St. Clair!"

How I heard Roussell over the thunderous roar of the sold-out Edmonton crowd, to this day, I don't know. Roussell deked the other defenseman, and dashed toward the crease. I faked right, rotated the opposite direction, and quickly calculated where Roussell would end up when the puck reached his stick. I aimed the puck and slapped it away. I successfully confused the Hall of Famer, who spun around, looking down in a desperate search for the puck. I saw Roussell successfully snag my pass right before I was hit by a brutal body blow. The fucker slammed into me and aimed an illegally elbow up and under my pads. Bastard landed a sharp jab to my solar plexus. Stars burst behind my eyes and my vision went black around the edges. The cheap shot left me hunched over and gasping for air, but didn't knock me out. Thankfully, I was conscious when the horn sounded and the raucous noise of the home crowd cut off abruptly.

Roussell must have scored.

The next thing I knew, the announcer called my name for the assist and I was swept up in a boisterous celebration. The team crowded around me and Roussell grabbed me in a bear hug and lifted me off the ice. They cheered and shouted and I gave me so many slaps to the helmet I lost count. Even Hazey left his precious net to squeeze me with his Hulk-like strength. An icy glove slapped the back of my neck and I jerked around. Calloway's dark eyes crinkled in the corners, his smile visible even as he chewed on his mouthguard.

"Coach wants you out," he said, sounding amused. I started to argue, only to snap my mouth shut when Coach barked from the bench.

"St. Clair! Get your goddamn ass over here!"

I scowled and Calloway laughed. "There's only five-seconds left and you got sucker punched. Go sit." He steered me toward the bench. I didn't like it, but went without complaint. To be honest, my abs were killing me and I couldn't really breathe deeply enough to argue even if I wanted to. I hopped over the boards and Coach slapped my helmet.

"Great job, St. Clair." I blinked, confused by the strange, foreign way Coach V's mouth contorted up in the corners.

"Are you... *smiling*?" I asked, stunned. "Who are you?" Behind me, Ovechkin chuckled. The smile slid from Coach's face.

"Sit your ass down, St. Clair," he snarled, then returned his attention to the ice.

"Better," I mumbled under my breath, though I caught the slight twitch of Coach's lips. The man was beyond over-joyed and I had to admit, it was good—if not rare as hell—to see for a change. Ovechkin shifted down the bench to make room.

"Nice play," Ovechkin said, reaching up to slap my helmet.

"Thanks."

The sides lined up, and everyone on the bench moved to

the edge of their seats, holding our collective breath. *Five-seconds*. Provided nothing major went wrong, in five-seconds we would win the Eastern Conference title. The puck dropped and Roussell, the lightning-quick bastard, snagged the puck like a fucking champ. One expert fake out, followed by a smooth pass, and the final buzzer went off. The players on the ice threw their hands in the air, sticks held high. The rest of us tumbled over the boards to join them in a boisterous celebration.

After giving out and accepting congrats, I broke from the pack and skated up to the plexi to the left of the bench. Just like it always did—and hopefully always would—my pulse stuttered at the sight. Kiley stood in the front row, cheering, her friends Piper and Nat next to her. Rocco's girlfriend of almost a year, Mila, who worked wonders for Calloway's bristly personality, was on Kiley's other side. I winked and Kiley's eyes sparkled. God, how I love that woman. But my attention was quickly diverted to my heart, my reason for living, who wiggled in Kiley's arms. Pudgy arms reached for me and I got a toothless grin.

"Hey, champ," I said as I knocked on the plexi and looked at a pair of bright blue eyes, so similar to my own it was freaky. My son babbled and smiled as he strained harder to get to me. At nine months, Jamie—or James, after Kylie's dad—was not only fascinating, he was my whole world. Watching as Jamie started to recognize people, recognize *me* as his dad, simultaneously made me proud and put a lump in my throat at the same time. His little face literally fucking lit up when I entered a room. Talk about stroking your ego. Road trips were all but unbearable, but knowing Jamie and Kylie were waiting for me when I got home made everything worth it.

They *were* my home.

"Hi, daddy!" Kylie said in the high-pitched voice she does for Jamie as she waved his cubby hand for him.

I ignored the ear-piercing screeching of the female fans that tried to get my attention. Nothing and no one could pull my attention from the loves of my life. I blew Kylie and Jamie a kiss each, and rolled my eyes at the collective *"awwww"* from Piper, Nat, and Mila. Kylie helped Jamie blow a kiss back, and pressed his tiny hand to the plexi. I put mine on the other side, and even though we weren't touching, the love that flowed between us was more than enough for me. A shower of ice rained down on me. I wiped my face and neck and playfully elbowed my brother-in-law.

"Jerk."

Calloway shrugged, a grin plastered across his face, not one bit sorry for snowing me. He bent over, cooed at Jamie and, to Jamie's delight, knocked on the plexi with his huge hand. Mila waved at Rocco and I swear, the big dork had fucking hearts floating in his eyes, not that I was one to talk. I could fully admit that both Kylie and Jamie frequently reduced me to a love-struck idiot, armed only with their beautiful smiles.

"C'mon," Rocco said. "Cameras are waiting."

I glanced over my shoulder and concentrated on not frowning. Since the news broke a little over a year ago that I was going to be a dad, along with the subsequent engagement and quickie wedding to Kylie, my reputation had done a one-eighty. Don't get me wrong, the media remains the bane of my existence. They harass and cajole me and my family, sometimes stalking us around Atlanta to get pictures for their tabloid rags. When I was single, it was annoying, but the more unethical journalists started to target Kylie and Jamie, and I refused to take that kind of bullshit sitting down. More than once I'd gotten into a scuffle with an aggressive paparazzo. They sued, I won. Thankfully, the American justice system didn't allow depraved idiots to use their freedom of the press as justification to be allowed to terrorize a pregnant woman or a new mother and her baby.

I mouthed, "Love you," to Kylie and Jamie, and skated backwards from the plexi, toward the knot of players, team management, and journalists who gathered at center ice. The latter two stood on a carpet someone rolled out to prevent feet from going out from under unsuspecting people. I wish they hadn't. Fuck, I'd give a month's salary to watch a select few of my least favorite reporters faceplant.

"Let's get this shit over with," Rocco mumbled.

"A-fucking-men... *brother.*"

He threw his head back and laughed until tears streaked his face. When Calloway found out Kylie was pregnant with my kid, he beat the shit out of me, mostly because I wouldn't hit him back, not after I found out he was Kylie's brother. At the time, I didn't want to do anything to damage my fragile relationship with Kylie, or, oddly enough, with Rocco. A year and a half later, and we were almost as close as Rémy and me. Shocking, I know. Took *a lot* of getting used to, what, with a Sasquatch in the family and all. For the first few months, I wouldn't relax around him. I kept waiting for the inevitable punch to the back of my head when I wasn't looking. But if nothing else, Rocco loved his sister and nephew, and if that meant he had to accept me, that's what he did.

Turns out Sasquatch is a pretty stand-up guy. Who knew?

"Shut up," I said when Calloway kept cackling at me calling him brother.

My grin ruined the pout I was going for.

"Does Mila hate that as much as Kylie?" I reached up

and yanked on Rocco's playoff beard. He swatted my hand away.

"Ow, you fuck. And yeah, she despises it."

I chuckled. "Kylie told me it looks like I glued a ferret to my face."

Rocco's eyes went wide and, once again, he burst out in hysterics. "Oh my god! Sounds just like my sister. Mila, she just begs me to shave." Grinning, Rocco wiped his eyes and shrugged. "Nothing I can do about it. I'm not going to be the one to jinx the team by shaving."

"Me either," I agreed.

We were close enough that the media swarmed. Rocco threw an arm around my neck and turned his wide smile on the reporters. "Chin up, *brother*," he said from between his clenched teeth. "We're gonna get that Cup and then, this suffering will be totally worth it."

I glanced over my shoulder, needing to see my family. Kylie was happily chatting with Nat while Jamie chewed on a lock of her hair. A feeling of warmth, of comfort, of finally accepting myself and the love of another, spread through me.

I turned to Rocco and said, "It's already is, brother. It already is."

Now... How do I break it to him that I knocked his sister up again?

QUEBECOIS

Translation of some of Seb's favorite French-Canadian obscenities. *not to be confused with curses used in France*

Bâtard – Bastard

CÂLICE – For Fuck's sake!, Jesus fucking christ! (Strong)

Ciboire – Shit!, Piss!, Damn it!, God damn it!

Crisse – Get the Fuck out!, Don't give a Fuck!, Fucking angry!, Shit!

Enfant de chienne – Son of a bitch!, Shit!, Fuck!

Marde – Shit!, Damn it!, Crap!

Maudit – Shit!, Damn it!, Crap!, God damn it!, Piss!

Maudit bâtard – Damned bastard / Fucking bastard!

Merde – Shit!

Sacré – Shit!, Damn it!, God damn it!, Piss!

SACREMENT – Fuck!, Jesus fucking Christ! (Strong)

Saint ciboire– Christ almighty!, Christ!, Jesus Christ!

Saint ciboire aux deux étages– Christ almighty!, Christ!, Jesus Christ!

Saint sicrisse– Christ almighty!, Christ!, Jesus Christ!

TABARNAK – The King of all swear words, worse than Fuck. (Very Strong)

Tabarnak aux deux étages – Fuck it all to hell!

Trou de cul – Asshole.

Vas te crosser avec une poignée de clous rouillés – Fuck off! (literally: Go jack off with a handful of rusty nails)

Vas te faire chier – Screw off!

16

ALSO BY HEATHER C LEIGH

D ark Romances
      Junkie- Broken Doll 1
      Jagger- Broken Doll 2
Killer

ROCKSTAR ROMANCE (SPHERE of Irony)
    Incite — Adam
    Strike — Dax
    Resist — Gavin (M/M)
    Wreck — Hawke

THE FAMOUS SERIES
    Relatively Famous
    Absolutely Famous
    Extremely Famous
    Already Famous (Drew's POV)
    Suddenly Famous (a novella)
    Reluctantly Famous (a novella)

RICOCHET— Military Romantic Suspense
   Locked & Loaded
   Friendly Fire
   Extraction Point

AS LEIGH CARMAN- M/M Romance
   Players of LA -by Dreamspinner Press
   Match Point- Volleyball (Summer)
   Fair Catch- Football (Fall)
   Power Play- Hockey (Winter)
   Full Count- Baseball (Spring) coming soon

CLICK **below to get updates on new releases by Leigh Carman**

❧

THANKS

I'd like to thank everyone who helped this book come to life. Especially the Atlanta Gladiators for their hospitality in granting me a "backstage" tour of the world of professional hockey.

ABOUT THE AUTHOR

Heather C. Leigh is the author of the Amazon best selling Famous series. She likes to write about the 'dark' side of fame. The part that the public doesn't get to see, how difficult it is to live in a fishbowl and how that affects relationships.

Heather was born and raised in New England and after living outside Atlanta, GA for 15 years, currently lives in Houston, TX with her husband, 2 kids, French Bulldog, and a Hedgehog named Nina.

She loves the Red Sox, the Patriots, and anything chocolate (but not white chocolate, everyone knows it's not real chocolate so it doesn't count) and has left explicit instructions in her will to have her ashes snuck into Fenway Park and sneakily sprinkled all over while her family enjoys beer, hot dogs, and a wicked good time.

For more information
heathercleighauthor.com
heathercleigh@heathercleighauthor.com